TO Catch
A TEXAS
Star

LINDA BRODAY

sourcebooks
casablanca

Copyright © 2018 by Linda Broday
Cover and internal design © 2018 by Sourcebooks, Inc.
Cover art by Gregg Gulbronson

Sourcebooks and the colophon are registered trademarks of
Sourcebooks, Inc.

Published by Sourcebooks Casablanca, an imprint of Sourcebooks,
Inc.
P.O. Box 4410, Naperville, Illinois 60567-4410
(630) 961-3900
Fax: (630) 961-2168
sourcebooks.com

Printed and bound in Canada.
MBP 10 9 8 7 6 5 4 3 2 1

To Marley Rose Leal, the firstborn daughter of GiGi and Lee. Thank you for letting me borrow your name. The minute I heard it after you were born, my imagination started crafting a story—two in fact. Also thanks to your sisters—LeAnna, Angelina, and Natalie. The Leals are a very talented bunch and I'm proud to be related. And of course, I can't leave out Marley's baby, Arlo. Protect and love him always. Bless you all.

One

THE COOL NIGHT AIR BIT INTO HIS FACE AS NIGHT CREATURES scurried through the brush, perhaps looking for something to appease their hunger. Roan Penny's weary eyes narrowed into hard slits. He leaned against the side of the shack—his temporary home—and stared up at the huge, star-dotted expanse. Those stars put a million periods at the end of a long list of untruths and treachery.

How long he had to wander this lonely path seemed anyone's guess.

The words his father had spoken in a drunken haze filled his head: *You were cursed at birth when you came into this world under a waning moon. It's bad luck you'll be having, boy, and bad luck will follow you to your grave.*

That summed up his life perfectly.

Roan shifted his stance against Mose Mozeke's cabin. He glanced up at the waning moon, holding back the sense of foreboding. Something bad was going to happen—he could feel it in his bones. He only hoped that whatever trouble came calling was looking for him and not the kind man who'd become his only friend. Mose had taken Roan in about a year ago, saying he needed the company. Roan knew better. After taking one look at him, the kindly farmer had seen he'd had nowhere else to go.

Mozeke worked a small parcel of red dirt he took special pride in owning, only he was locked in a fight to keep it. Greedy men wanted that land, and the good folks of San Saba, Texas, were accusing him of being a squatter, trying to run him out. They'd have to go through Roan to do it.

Another skyward glance knotted Roan's stomach. A shiver raced through him, and he wished for his jacket that hung on a peg inside the door. The night breeze held an icy bite to it and the promise of a hard freeze, but it was the omen that froze his blood. He couldn't run, couldn't hide, couldn't abandon Mose.

Then he heard the pounding hooves of many riders. The ground trembled slightly beneath his feet, matching the quake inside. It appeared the trouble he'd been sensing had come.

"What's all that racket, son?" Mose stood in the doorway. His thin frame barely cast a shadow, his graying red hair gleaming in the flickering lamplight.

"Either we're having a bunch of callers or a herd of longhorns have stampeded, sir." Judging by the hair standing on the back of his neck, Roan would put his money on the first. "Get your rifle, Mose," he said quietly.

"'Tain't loaded. Meant to do that when I came back from hunting jackrabbits, but clean forgot. Doubt I'll need it."

Roan prayed Mose was right but his knotted gut told him otherwise. He recalled something Mose had said days ago. *Boy,* he'd said, *I've lived a long life, and this I know— fortune doesn't come in pairs or trouble in ones.*

Please let his gut be wrong.

He'd left his gun belt inside with his jacket, but thank goodness, he had one weapon on him—his Bowie knife. As riders emerged from a thick cluster of scrub cedar like a swarm of locusts, he took some tiny comfort in the sheath tucked under his shirt between his shoulder blades.

Each rider had his head covered. Holes cut in burlap

sacks revealed the glint of eyes in the reflection of the light of their torches. The eerie sight brought an extra icy feel to the late-October night air. They reminded him of hollow skulls unearthed from burial grounds.

The raiders stopped within several feet of Mose. The horses' snorts created clouds of vapor in the cool air. Small pockets of his own fogging breath kissed Roan's face.

The leader of the pack leaned forward in the stirrups. "Mozeke, we're here to take back what you stole. Leave or you die."

"I done told you before. Do what you feel you hafta do, 'cause my paper says this piece of dirt is legally mine." Mose's voice was firm but Roan knew he was scared. "Ain't no one gonna take me off my own property, not ever. You just run along now, and I'll be forgettin' you took it on yourself to rid me of my land."

"No one can claim we didn't give you fair choice."

"I can and I do." Roan strolled into the light, his movement fluid.

"Stay outta this. 'Tain't no concern of yours," the leader barked.

"That's where you're wrong, gentlemen. Now, slink back to where you came from, and I'll overlook your inhospitable nature." Roan flexed his hand, ready to act.

A flash spat from the man's rifle in answer.

Roan had been watching the marauders, anticipating the response, and dropped to his knees. The bullet missed him by an inch. Before the man could fire again, he quickly reached backward for the weapon hanging between his shoulder blades. The knife slid into his grip, and he sailed it with expertise into the flesh of the nearest assailant.

"Oh God, I'm hit!" The bushwhacker yanked the knife from his shoulder, holding it in disbelief.

To Roan's horror, a second shot rang out, and Mose crumpled. Roan could only watch the scene unfold as if time were held suspended. Overwhelming grief strangled him.

Other rifles fired, the blasts deafening.

When they stopped, his friend was no more.

Mose Mozeke sprawled faceup in the dirt, clutching his chest. Blood spurted between the man's hands—hands blackened from trying to make something from nothing.

"Damn you!" Most of all, Roan damned himself for leaving his Colt inside. He cursed the assassins for executing a man whose only crime was fighting to keep what was his.

"Throw your torches. Set the shanty afire." The gravelly rumble was wrapped in cold contempt. "Save the drifter. I got plans for him."

Air left Roan's lungs with great force. To burn Mose's house would complete wiping his existence off the earth. A huge beast inside yearned to give voice to the bloodcurdling yell that bubbled in his chest. Six men leaped from their horses on him, silencing the roar. Fists pummeled his face and body, the pain so intense he couldn't breathe. He lost count of time and might've lost consciousness for a spell. When he opened his eyes, the small, wooden structure was ablaze against the midnight sky. The few possessions he'd acquired, the most prized of which was the friendship of a lonely man, had vanished in the blink of an eye. He freed himself of his assailants' grips and stumbled toward his fallen friend.

Flames illuminated Mose. Eyes that had seen only the best in everyone now stared unseeing at the heavens. Roan jumped to his feet, his arms outstretched in an attempt to grab the nearest rider.

A rope whirred and tightened about him before he could, settling under his armpits. He grabbed hold of the rough hemp, his gaze on the man on horseback who'd snared him.

"We're gonna teach you what happens to meddlers, drifter." The rider's spurs dug into his horse's flanks. The animal launched into a full gallop and pitched Roan forward.

The hard fall knocked the wind from his lungs. He fought to breathe as he hurdled through a bramble patch.

His teeth bit into the soft flesh of his curled bottom lip. The taste of blood strengthened the fight in him. He clenched his jaw and grabbed the rope. Pulling himself forward just a few inches made sure he wouldn't lose more than the second layer of skin and kept him out from under the trampling feet of the whooping followers. His arm sockets paid a heavy price for the effort. Pain blinded him, stealing the air from his lungs.

It was nothing short of a miracle that he managed to hold on through the wild nightmare. Liquid fire had burned a path through every inch of him by the time the pack's bloodlust faded and they halted.

"Had enough, drifter?"

"Go to hell, you murdering bastards." Blood and dirt slurred Roan's strong words.

"Reckon it's time for more teaching, then."

"Yeah, we ain't near done yet." The hood-muffled second rider moved near—a mistake on his part.

Roan leaped for the masked man, yanking him from his horse. The hard ground knocked off the burlap bag, and Roan stared into the features of a young man who had yet to see his first shave.

That face burned into Roan's memory. One day they'd meet again.

Before Roan could land a punch, men grabbed him, and fists pounded his midsection. Others stomped him with their boot heels to satisfy their madness. Leaving him more dead than alive, they bound his hands and hoisted him across a horse's rump, then rode for miles over every rock, gully, and cattle trail. Each jolt gave his pain added meaning. At last they stopped, but he didn't take it as a good sign. They'd probably arrived at his grave.

He dragged in a breath, the icy air a shock to his lungs.

They dismounted and shoved him onto what appeared to be a road.

"Step foot back in San Saba, and we'll kill you," snarled the gravelly voiced leader.

Gasping for air, Roan curled on the rocky ground and stared up at the dreaded omen high above. The waning moon winked down from its perch in the heavens.

It had never brought anything but trouble. The crescent had appeared after midnight as his mother died and the night his father had given him away. Then again, a few years later, when the old woman who cared for him had passed on to her reward and not one person on earth had given a damn about the welfare of a twelve-year-old boy.

He cursed through the blood in his mouth as the vigilantes thundered off into the distance.

An unforgiving, unseasonable north wind pelted him, freezing his tears before they fell. He tried to struggle to his feet but sank back to the ground, fighting spasms that made everything whirl. If he didn't find shelter soon, he wouldn't have to worry about taking up breathing space any longer. His badly swollen eyes narrowed to mere slits, Roan scanned the area. No barn, outhouse, or chicken coop in sight. Hell, he'd settle for a fresh dung heap. At least the smelly stuff would offer a bit of warmth.

He hugged his tattered shirt against him and crawled forward off the road into some dead brush. Sharp stones poked into him and scraped off more skin. Although he grimaced, he savored the aches that proved he still had life in his body.

As long as he lived, so, too, did his chance for justice.

Two

MARLEY ROSE MCCLAIN'S BREATH FOGGED IN THE FROSTY morning as she headed to the nearby town of Tranquility, Texas. She loved this time of day because of the peace it brought. Nothing except the jangle of the harnesses and the horses' soft snorts broke the quiet.

Lord knew there was little silence to be had at her parents' ranch these days. Too many kids underfoot. Her mama had this peculiar habit of picking up stray kids like others took in animals. Jessie McClain had a heart as big as Texas and arms that appeared to be made for holding babies, and at last count, with this batch, her mama and papa had acquired a baker's dozen.

Thankfully, the children grew up, married, and left, only for new ones to take their places. The rotation reminded her of a plow turning over new sod at planting season.

When her parents' home had begun to bulge at the seams, Marley's father had built her a small dwelling next door. She loved living independently. A twenty-year-old woman needed her own things and the chance to make her own decisions. She often worried that life had passed her by, that she'd never get to do the things she yearned for. It often felt as though she were shriveling inside a little more each day.

Helping her mother with the children took so much from Marley that she often wanted to scream with frustration.

When would it be her time? Her dreams were withering away.

This trip to town provided an escape of sorts. Not that she minded hard work. She just longed for a break from time to time, and the need for staples for both houses gave her an opportunity for woolgathering and planning her future.

A sudden shift in the wind scattered her thoughts and she sat up straighter. The chilly breeze brushed ghostly fingers against her face, whispered in her ear, warning her of danger. Marley gripped the reins tighter and glanced around but saw nothing. She forced a nervous laugh and chided herself for her jumpy nerves. There was nothing lurking around waiting to do her harm.

Marley forced herself to relax yet couldn't quite block the unease that twisted and turned inside like a bucking bronc. Before she'd gone a dozen horses' lengths, she spied a flutter near the road. A piece of cloth that seemed to be stuck on a prickly pear. Curious, she set the brake and climbed from the buckboard, ignoring the brisk air that nipped at her ankles.

Inching closer, Marley scolded herself for not letting her oldest brother come along. He'd asked to come so he could visit with a friend in town, only he'd gotten caught up in chores and she hadn't wanted to wait.

Setting aside her thoughts, she focused on the scrap of fabric fluttering in the breeze. It appeared to be a bundle of rags, and she inched closer, ready to bolt. Sudden movement in the brush spooked her. She jerked back in alarm. A man's bloody, scraped legs were visible through his shredded trousers. Those and a pair of worn boots protruded from the tangle of vines and wild growth.

A rustler?

A chill slithered up her spine. She'd heard how ruthless those outlaws could be. But maybe this one was dead. Or dying.

Going for help crossed her mind, but he might not last until she got back. A fainthearted ninny would run, but

Marley was made of sterner stuff. Her hands trembled as she touched him.

"Mister, are you hurt? Come out where I can see you." She braced to run if he reached to grab her. It occurred to her that he might've frozen overnight. The chill had come down from the north last night with little warning.

"Hey, mister." She nudged him with a cautious toe.

The man gave a loud groan and rolled over by degrees. Marley's tongue worked in a suddenly dry mouth, and she stumbled backward, staring at his badly mangled body. Her heart pounded like a team of runaway horses. How could a man still breathe with a face so swollen and bloody? He tried to open his eyes, and Marley was grateful that he couldn't. The sight sickened her enough without the thought of seeing empty sockets behind those lids. Anyone who'd beat a man this badly surely wouldn't hesitate to add that sort of cruelty to the list.

"Help," the man croaked.

A brief glance noted the lack of a gun belt or weapons.

"I don't know who did this, mister, but they sure meant to kill you. Whether you're friend or foe, I can't be sure, but we'll sort it out after I get you to the ranch." She gripped the shredded mess of his shirt, not surprised that a section came off in her hands.

The stranger must outweigh her by a hundred pounds. Scraped flesh, visible through the rips and tears, suggested not an inch of fat on his long, muscular body.

"Can you walk a little, mister? You're too heavy to lift but I'll help you to the buckboard. It's no more than half a dozen steps."

The stranger attempted to rise without a word, only to fall back. Marley got behind him and pushed and slowly got the man to his feet. He shivered uncontrollably.

"Put your arm around my shoulders," she said.

He gave a loud cry of pain but he did as she asked, leaning heavily on her and half-dragging his feet. One agonizing step at a time, they inched toward the bed of the buckboard.

His teeth chattered from the cold, blood covered his face, and she kept urging him to put one foot in front of the other. They finally reached the wagon, and she tried to ease him up into the bed, but despite her care, he fell with a thud onto the boards. His scream pierced right through her. She reached for a blanket she'd thrown in that morning just in case, and as she tucked the heavy wool around him, she noticed he'd lapsed into unconsciousness.

Marley stared at her gloves, slick with blood, but the only thing she had was her dress to wipe them on. Several hundred yards down the road, she spied a flat place to turn around.

She mumbled a prayer as they raced toward the ranch. The pair of chestnuts hadn't had such a workout in quite a while. She sped into the compound amid a cloud of dust, sending men running from everywhere.

Her father reached her first. "What's wrong? Are you hurt?"

"No, not me. I found a man on the road. He's in bad shape." Marley hopped to the ground. "He needs a doctor. Bleeding something awful."

Duel McClain glanced into the buckboard. "That's putting it mildly. Doc Henby is out of town and won't be back for two weeks." He grabbed a ranch hand. "Get my wife." He turned back to Marley. "I don't know where we'll put him. Every nook, cranny, and spider hole is occupied." He heaved a sigh and rubbed the back of his neck. "The bunkhouse is also full and spilling over."

Marley met his gaze. "I have room. It makes sense to take him to my house anyway. He'll need care, and I can sleep on the sofa."

He hesitated. "I don't know. Are you sure you can handle this?"

"Papa, I'm a grown woman."

"Even so, we don't know who he is, and rustlers are running rampant over this entire area. He could pose a danger to you."

A gurgling noise came from the stranger's mouth, and

blood oozed from between his lips. They had to act. Duel turned to the ranch hands clustered around the wagon. "Carry him to Marley Rose's house for now. We'll figure the rest out later."

Marley raced ahead and held the door, then stood back as they carried him inside and gently laid him on the bed. A nice fire in the fireplace kept the dwelling warm, but still she placed a quilt over him.

She didn't know who the man was, but he must have had a powerful lot of enemies. His clothes were in tatters, and he had injuries every place she looked, especially his poor face. An entire strip of skin was gone along one side.

Mitch, the ranch hand Duel had sent off to find her mother, rushed into the room. "Boss, Miz Jessie can't come right now. One of the kids cut himself and blood's everywhere."

Duel turned, resting a hand on her shoulder. "Marley Rose, put on water to warm in your kitchen and fetch supplies for this man from the main house. See if you can help your mama while you're over there."

"Yes, Papa." She rushed to the kitchen, filled a pail with water from the pump, and put it on to heat. That done, she hurried toward the ranch house.

Her mother sat at the kitchen table, holding five-year-old Benji's arm raised over his head. Blood had soaked his shirt and her mother's apron. The boy was sobbing.

"What happened, Mama?"

"Benji was playing with a knife and sliced his hand open. I'm trying to get it stop bleeding so I can put some stitches in it." She spared Marley Rose a worried glance. "What's going on over at your place? Mitch just said you'd brought in a stranger who was badly hurt."

"I found a man on the road on my way to town. Not sure exactly how bad he's hurt, but there's a lot of blood. We need cloths and bandages."

"Go get the box that has all my medical supplies." Jessie shifted Benji and glanced toward a baby's weak cries that came from a nearby crib. The child was one of the new three-month-old triplets that Jessie had taken in after their mother had died in childbirth. Their father had quickly enlisted in the frontier army, not wanting to shoulder the burden of his offspring's care.

"I'll see to her, Mama." Marley patted the small back for a few minutes until the baby quieted, then rushed to the cabinet in the corner of the kitchen where her mother kept ointments, bandages, and the like. Between the children and accidents with the men on the ranch, the room often became a makeshift doctor's office. Resting a hand on a box filled with what they'd need, she shot Jessie a questioning glance.

"Go on," Jessie said. "I can handle this little guy. I have a feeling your patient needs you worse."

Marley grabbed the box and headed for the door.

"I'll be out after I tend to these children." Jessie lowered Benji's arm to look at his hand. "For now, you'll have to fill in for me. Seeing as you're as skilled as I am by now, that shouldn't be a problem—so long as you're fine with it?"

"Yes, Mama. I'll do my best." Marley rushed back to her little home. The water wasn't hot enough yet, but it would have to do. They couldn't afford to wait. Taking the pail from the stove, she carried it into the bedroom. Her father had stripped the man and covered him again with the quilt. The stranger lay so still, with his eyes closed. His croak for help back there on the road echoed in her head. She hadn't heard him speak another word and maybe she never would.

"Is he still unconscious?"

"Yep. It's a blessing." Duel took the pail from her. "You can help with some of this, then I'll finish."

She dipped a cloth into the tepid water and gently washed the blood from the stranger's face. He was nothing but a mass of cuts and bruises, with skin peeled away on arms that seemed to have taken the brunt of whatever had befallen him.

Duel gently applied some ointment to what appeared to be deep rope marks around their patient's chest.

"Papa, what do you think happened to him?"

"I once saw a man after he was dragged behind a horse. This is what he looked like."

Her father's quiet words struck fear in her. "Did he live?"

"A few days."

A heavy ache filled her chest, bringing tears to her eyes. She couldn't bear to think of this stranger's hopes and dreams dying before he got to fulfill them. From what she could tell, he appeared no more than a few years older than she was. His hair, the color of an eagle's wing, was a bit long but not shaggy. She got the impression he took pride in his appearance. More telling was his face. The hard lines and older scars indicated a life that had already been unkind. She placed her hand over his heart and felt the steady beat of a fighter. She imagined what he must look like whole and healthy. Surely, his high cheekbones and strong jaw marked him as a man who would stand up for his principles no matter the consequences. Maybe that's what happened. The black fringe of his dark lashes was barely visible because of the swelling, but she prayed he'd open his eyes soon. Then she'd know for sure if they had a blind man on their hands.

Her father rinsed out the cloth he was using and shot her a worried glance. "Honey, I really don't know about you taking on his care."

"Who'll do it if I don't? We have no one else. Mama's busy with the little ones, and the men have those rustlers to chase. Besides, the men can barely doctor a shaving nick. I'm the only one with the time and knowledge. Mama taught me well."

"I suppose you make a good argument. But I'll never forgive myself if I put you in harm's way."

Marley went to her father and slid her arms around him, laying her head on his chest. "I think you look for things to fret about when it comes to me or the children."

"You're right."

"This stranger doesn't appear to have a mean look about him. Besides, when he wakes up, he'll be too weak to hurt me if he's that kind of person."

Duel tightened his arms around her. "What about who-ever did this? They might get wind he's alive and come to finish him off."

"Then you can order the men to stay close." She pushed out of his arms and returned to their patient. "I'll be fine."

"All right. I'll hush."

"I wonder if he has family." She tried to brush back his hair only to encounter a sticky, matted mess. Once things had settled some, she'd wash it.

Duel shifted beside the bed. The black Stetson he wore shadowed his amber eyes, the color of whiskey, so unlike her dark ones. Hers weren't anything close to her mother's blue shade either. She'd often thought it odd that she bore little resemblance to either parent. Maybe she was some kind of changeling child.

"If he wakes up, we'll find out about kin, and I'll get word to them." A cowboy came through the door and motioned her father aside.

Though they spoke low, Marley caught the word *rustlers*, then something about stealing them blind. Worry on her father's face shot fear into her. Was this man lying in her bed involved in something so awful?

She raised her patient's chin to wash the blood from his throat and noticed the thin cut from a sharp blade that ran from under one ear right across to the other. She sucked in a breath.

No matter if he did have a hand in the rustling. He didn't deserve this. No one did.

Who was he, and who hated him so much that they'd try to end his life in such a horrific way?

Three

MARLEY SAT BESIDE THE BED ALL THROUGH THE FIRST night. If her stranger passed on, he needed someone to hold his hand. The man deserved to know that at least one person cared. What little sleep she got came by resting her head on her arms on the quilt next to him, where any movement would wake her. But the man lay motionless and quiet, so still she'd occasionally put her cheek to his mouth to see if he breathed. Mourning doves cooed outside the window at daybreak, the sound making chills dance up her spine.

She pushed back the curtain, and four gray birds perched on the ledge. They paid her no mind, continuing to make their mournful sound.

A glance at the stranger showed no change. She laid a hand on his chest. "I'm not going to let you die. Get that through your head right now. I didn't find you just to bury you."

Marley leaned over him and patiently sponged tiny amounts of water into his mouth, massaging his throat to make it go down. Keeping one eye on the bed, she fixed herself some breakfast, making a list of all the things she should do. Changing his bandages and checking for infection would come first. She'd helped her mother treat the cowboys over the years, and knew what to look for. Keeping the infection down would give him a chance to survive.

Her father stopped by and stood over the bed, holding

his hat in his hands. "His color seems a little better. Has he woken up yet?"

"No. He hasn't even moved. Except for his shallow breathing, I'd think he's dead."

"I wish you didn't have to shoulder this by yourself. Are you sure you want to?"

"I'm sure, Papa. We've been over this." Maybe her need to fix this stranger was because she had been the one to find him, and that made this connection so strong. All Marley knew was that she had to be the one to care for him.

"Your mama said she'd be over after she got the kids off to school."

"Lord knows Mama has her hands full, but I welcome her assessment." Marley changed the subject. "Are you heading out to look for the rustlers?"

"I am." Fire flashed in her father's eyes. "If I catch the thieving bunch, I might be tempted to take the law into my own hands."

"You know you won't, even as much as you want to." Marley had never seen him kill anyone outright. He was the fairest man she knew, and he let the law and the court handle criminals.

He sighed. "I know. But I think I'd sure be tempted this time." He laid a hand on her shoulder. "I need to go. I don't know when I'll be back but—"

"I'll be fine," Marley assured him. "I'm not some spineless little girl who wrings her hands and waits for someone to ride to her rescue."

Duel laughed. "Don't I know." He hugged her, put on his hat, and left.

After washing her dishes, Marley warmed water and gathered the salves and sterile strips of cloth. The doves continued to coo outside the window, almost as if they were keeping watch over the stranger. In all the time she'd lived there, she'd never seen the birds crowd right up on her narrow ledge before.

She removed the bandages on her patient's chest and

dipped a cloth into the water. Very gently, she washed away bright-red blood that had seeped from some of his wounds. There was no new redness and no sign of infection, thank goodness. When she had cleaned them and the slice around his throat, she reached for the healing salve.

Her fingertips glided over his muscles and across his broad chest. His body was hard and lean, and showed the effects of backbreaking work. She lifted his hand, noticing calluses lining his palms and fingertips. More signs of strenuous labor.

Listening to the doves through the windowpane, she stared at his horrible injuries and found tears lurking behind her eyelids. She laid a hand on his chest over his heart that beat weakly.

How could anyone have been so cruel?

She leaned close to whisper in his ear. "Get well soon."

The next hour found her unwrapping the bandages and applying fresh ones. The front door opened, and Marley turned, listening. A thumping noise followed, not the greeting she expected, and she went to investigate. Her mother was attempting to lift one of the children's wagons over the threshold without waking the triplets inside.

Once they'd freed a wheel, Jessie McClain glanced up. "Thank you, Marley Rose. I thought the wagon was a good idea but found otherwise once I got here."

"You didn't have to come, Mama. I have things under control."

"I know." Jessie smiled and pushed back the red strands of hair that had fallen forward in the exertion. "I just wanted to see how the man is doing."

"Come see for yourself," Marley invited. "The babies will be all right here in the parlor. We'll hear them if they wake up." She didn't like her mother's tired eyes. She never got enough sleep these days.

Jessie followed her into the bedroom. "I think I'm getting too old to take care of babies."

"What does Papa say?" Marley herded her mother into

a chair and returned to her task of bandaging the stranger's wounds, carefully applying one new linen strip after another.

"He gripes a little but he gets up during the night to help feed them." Jessie chuckled. "Somehow, he can't quite get the hang of changing diapers. He seems to have forgotten all he ever knew when you were little."

"Mama, you need to stop taking care of so many children. It's wearing you out."

"Who'll do it if I don't, Marley Rose? The need is so great, and folks don't step up like they once did."

Marley covered her mother's hand with hers and met Jessie's weary blue eyes. "You're overworked, Mama. You can't keep doing this. Your health will suffer and then Papa will leave you no say in the matter."

"I know. I'll try to get more rest when the babies take naps." Jessie swung her attention to the man in Marley's bed, her quick eyes taking in the wounds that Marley had yet to rebandage. "I don't see any infection setting in. That's good. Did you get out all the dirt and small rocks that might've been deep in the cuts?"

"I think so. I've washed each one very well several times."

"Good. The cut around his throat isn't very deep, but it looks painful." Jessie leaned over for a closer examination. "Why would someone torture a man this way?"

"He has old welts crisscrossing his back," Marley said softly. "Whoever he is, he's had a hard life."

"It certainly appears that way." Jessie shot Marley a strange look. "Don't let yourself get too close. If he survives, he'll more than likely up and leave. He could be a drifter, and those never stay in one place long."

"I'm just taking care of him as I would any hurt thing that came my way. I think we should keep an open mind until we have reason to think badly of him." Marley rose and went to the window. The doves were still there. Were they waiting on something? She reined in her thoughts. "It's not like you, Mama, to voice such negativity. What's wrong?"

"I just worry about you, dear. Women in your position,

those who fear life has overlooked them—they tend to leap before they think. I don't want to see you get hurt."

Marley finished the last of the bandages and pulled the quilt over the unconscious stranger. "He's an injured man, that's all. Besides, he might not make it, so your worries could be in vain."

One of the triplets woke up, and Marley followed Jessie to take care of the babe. When a second began to cry, Marley lifted the small boy from the wagon. She and her mother sat and talked a bit, then Jessie rolled the little babies back to the house in the wagon.

The doves made even more noise, flapping their wings against the window when she returned to the bedroom.

Marley leaned over her patient and again placed her mouth next to his ear. "I'm not giving up on you. Fight to live. I'm waiting. The doves are waiting. I want to know your name."

Four

Fire shot through Roan Penny from head to toe. He must not have been dead, because there wasn't a part of him that didn't burn or throb. Surely dead people didn't feel such agony. If only he could force his eyes open. He felt them fluttering, but they seemed to be weighted down. Maybe the bastards who caused all this had returned and sewn them shut.

Panic raced through him. He needed to see, to find out where he was and what kind of danger he was in. Why were the doves mourning so? Were they warning him? He had to get up. He tried to move, and a sharp cry burst from his throat.

A sudden hand on his chest offered comfort. A woman's voice murmured, "You're safe. No one will hurt you here. Sleep and let your body heal."

Water dripped into his parched mouth and moistened the lining. The faint scent of rosewater surrounded him. Roan relaxed and let himself drift. He was safe. The kind voice had said so. It was men he had to be wary of. Almost every man in his life had beaten him down, but the women had shown him softness...until they went away. They always went away.

He had no idea how long he'd slept, but when he awoke again, he found he could force his eyes open. A glance at the wooden ceiling told him he was in someone's modest house, not a saloon with its tin or a barn with rafters.

Movement beside him drew his attention, and he turned his head, the pain from the effort sending a sharp intake of air whistling through his teeth.

Through his swollen eyelids, he could make out a woman. And he had no problem noticing the pistol she held on him. He stiffened, wishing he knew where he was, who she was.

"I'm glad you're awake." She laid down what appeared to be a pencil and he heard a book softly closing. He gathered she'd been writing something. She leaned forward, the gun in her grip. "You must have a million questions. So, I'll start by telling you that I'm Marley McClain, and you're on the Aces 'n' Eights Ranch. How are you feeling?"

Like hell, but he didn't think that would be appropriate to say in front of her. Instead, he managed, "Alive."

"Who are you?"

He worked his tongue, his mouth as dry as dead leaves, and pointed to what appeared to be a cup on a small table. He could see little beyond shadows and outlines. Was this the best his vision would ever be from now on? If so, it would make his task a hundred times more difficult. She helped get the water to his mouth with her free hand, and he didn't think he'd ever tasted anything as refreshing. He drained the cup and laid his head back on the pillow.

"Roan. Roan Penny," he rasped. "You don't need that gun, ma'am. It's not like I'm in any shape to hurt you. How long have I been here?"

"Two days." Sounds suggested Marley laying the gun down on a plank floor. "It pays to be careful. We're dealing with rustlers around these parts. Are you involved in cattle theft?"

It took him a second to process that he'd lost two precious days, and another to comprehend her question. "No."

"Do you know what happened to you, Mr. Penny?"

He closed his eyes and saw the hooded men, the flash of fire, Mose lying dead. He heard that raspy snarl in his ears that had warned to never return to San Saba County. He had news for them when he found them again—no one was going to tell him where he could go.

"Yeah, I know," he said quietly. "Could I trouble you for more water?"

She refilled the cup and held it to his lips; the scent of roses that followed her reminded him of wild ones that had grown next to Mose's cabin.

"I'm sure you're starving." She rested a hand on the bedcovers. He wished he could see her better. "I'll get you something to eat. My mother put on some hearty soup this morning."

"What time is it?" Roan couldn't tell, little light coming through the windows.

"Midafternoon. The skies are dark and gloomy." She was silent a moment. "Do you have anyone who'd be worried about you?"

"No." No one who cared whether he lived or died.

"What is it that you do, Mr. Penny?"

"Whatever work I can find. Can you call me Roan, miss?" Roan tried to sit up but the effort was useless, and he dropped back to the pillow. Pure agony riddled his body and filled his brain with thick mush.

Marley put a hand on his chest. "Lie still and rest. What are you searching for, Roan?"

"Answers." He had a group of murderers to find, and he wouldn't rest until he did. But the main thing he'd tried to find ever since he'd turned twelve was a place to belong, where someone welcomed him. Mose had, but now he was gone. Roan inhaled sharply. "Everyone alive is searching for something or another."

"I never thought about it that way, but that's very true." She turned when the door opened and what appeared to be a small boy crept inside. The shadowy figure went straight to Marley, and Roan wondered if he belonged to her. She hadn't said whether or not she was married.

"Mama Rose, what'cha doin'?" the boy asked. Roan could barely make out the boy's light-colored hair and slight build.

"Matthew, I told you, my name is Marley Rose not Mama Rose." She lifted the hair from his eyes and kissed his forehead. "I'm tending to this man here, sweet boy. His name is Roan Penny. Can you tell him hello?"

"Hi, Mr. Penny." The youngster stood next to the bed, squirming. "What'cha doin' in bed for?"

"He's hurt, honey." Marley lifted the boy into her lap. "And before you ask—I don't exactly know how it happened. Maybe Mr. Penny will enlighten us soon."

Her voice felt like smooth silk rustling over him, and Roan didn't think he'd ever forget the musical sound. He wished he could make out her features. Between the way his face was swollen and how bad his eyes were watering, he couldn't see much of anything.

"Will you get all better, Mr. Penny?" Matthew asked.

"I sure plan on it." Roan wasn't about to stay in bed much longer. He'd wasted too much time.

"Did you fall down and hurt yourself?"

"Hush, Matthew," Marley scolded. "Don't ask so many questions."

"It's all right," Roan said, his voice hoarse and raw. "The boy's just curious. Matthew, some very bad people didn't like me being friends with a certain man. I was lucky and survived, though I'm not so sure they meant for me to." That was all Roan was saying right now. He didn't like talking about his circumstances. "Is Matthew yours?" he asked, changing the subject.

Her tinkling laugh made him want to smile, even though it was too painful. He blinked hard several times and was finally able to make out the woman's cloud of midnight hair. He guessed she'd have dark eyes and the coloring to match. Could be Spanish—a good many in this part of Texas were—but she had no accent.

"Matthew is one of my adopted brothers," she said.

"How old are you, Matthew?" Roan asked.

The kid giggled. "I'm big. I'm this many."

Roan guessed he was showing him with his fingers.

"You sure are. Only I can't see that good right now. Can you tell me how many fingers you have up?"

"Six."

Roan winced. He had only been a year older than Matthew when his father had first told him he was worthless. That moment would never fade, staying as crystal clear now as it had been years ago. He and his father had stood at his mother's deathbed, and even though he was a child, Roan had known she would never hug him again.

Blackie Culpepper had stared down at him with eyes as cold and lifeless as a piece of steel. "From now on, your name is Roan Penny. You know why?"

"No, sir," Roan had said, wiping his nose on his shirtsleeve.

"Because you'll never be worth more than a penny. Remember that, boy. You're never going to amount to a tinker's damn. What is your name?"

"Roan Penny," he'd answered.

"I've given you to old Widow Harper. Pack your belongings."

The next time he saw his father, Blackie had a bandana covering his mouth and nose and was holding up a bank in Amarillo. And the last time, Blackie was laid out in a rough-hewn coffin on the street outside the bank in Sweetwater, wearing a sign that read *Outlaw*, and had a hole in his heart.

Roan had just turned seventeen, and he'd spared Blackie a single passing glance before hurrying on. It had felt like lucky stars then, not a bad moon, that had made Blackie give him up.

"Ahem," Marley coughed, bringing him back to the present. "Matthew wants to know how old you are."

"Sorry." Roan released a troubled sigh and rid himself of the painful memories. "I'm way older than you, Matthew. I'm not sure you want to know by how much."

"Yes, I do," the boy argued.

Marley leaned toward Roan. "He won't hush until you tell him, I'm afraid."

"I'm twenty years older than you, Matthew."

"Wow, that's real, real old!" the boy exclaimed. "Are you married and have little boys like me?"

"Nope." Roan tried to chuckle, then winced at the pain. He had barely started to think about what kind of life he wanted. He'd barely given thought about the kind of woman he'd take for a wife. He glanced at the outline of Marley's shadowy figure. The lady had such a comforting, tender touch. He'd like such a wife, one who'd ease his loneliness and stand next to him when the storms came.

His stomach growled loudly.

"Oh my goodness, here we are talking away and you're starving." Marley jumped up. "I'll get you that soup."

"Coffee too?" Roan asked hopefully. "I could sure use some."

"Of course. Come, Matthew, Mr. Penny needs to rest."

If she left and he drifted off, she might not wake him, and his stomach was already chewing on his backbone. "Please, can you leave the boy? I don't want to fall asleep."

"If you're sure."

"I am."

She put Matthew in the chair and told him to be good, then left the room.

Roan turned to the outlined figure of the kid. "What do you want to talk about, Matt?"

"My name ain't Matt," the boy said with a giggle.

"I thought since you're six years old we could talk man-to-man. Do you drink whiskey and smoke yet?"

"Nope. They won't let me."

"How about a girlfriend. Do you have one?"

"No." Peals of laughter filled the room.

"Matt, is there a gun by your chair?" He was concerned about that, even though he didn't think Marley would be careless.

"Nope. Mama Rose took it with her."

"Okay, that's good. I just don't want you to get hurt." Kids' lives were cut short too often, and this one needed a chance to grow up.

To fill the time, Roan got Matthew to tell him about the ranch and the couple who'd adopted him. Through the eyes of a child, he found out how big these people's hearts were. They'd taken in a whole slew of kids just like Matthew, kids who'd had no one, and given them not only a home but love.

"I love my Papa Duel. He's the bestest one in the whole world." Matthew's voice lowered. "Even when I get in trouble, he don't whup me. An' Mama Jessie, she don't get mad either. I don't like to get spankings. They hurt real, real, real bad."

"You know, I didn't like whippings either." Roan struggled to block out the memory of a dark barn and the pain that had always come to him there.

"Did those men hurt you because you were bad?"

"I didn't do anything wrong. They did this to me because they wanted something someone else had."

"Did you shoot 'em?" Matthew sniffled and, from what little Roan could see, wiped his nose on his sleeve.

"Wounded one."

"Are you gonna kill 'em when you get well?"

Roan didn't feel comfortable talking about this with the kid so he said nothing. But he was sure going to try. They had to pay for what they did to Mose. He didn't want to take their lives, didn't enjoy the thought, yet if it came down to that and there was no other way, he knew he would. He'd talk to the sheriff in San Saba first. But if the hooded gang was too powerful, the sheriff might refuse to do anything. Hell, they might even be paying the sheriff to look the other way.

"My Papa Duel says that we can't turn a blind eye to wrong things." Matthew scooted from the chair and placed both elbows on the quilt covering Roan. "Are you blind in your eye, Mr. Penny?"

"No, I don't think so." But his head was pounding.

"I cain't even see your eyes. Did those bad men pull 'em out?"

"Of course not." Roan almost regretted asking for Matt to stay. The kid had a million and one questions. "Have you ever played the quiet game?"

"Nope."

"Let's play it. It's easy—the first one to talk loses."

"Okay. I guess." Though Matt's features blurred, Roan saw him put his fingers to his mouth and pretend he was buttoning his lips.

Silence finally fell over them, and Roan could think. He needed to bury Mose, and he'd already lost two days. The animals would have gotten to him by this time. Were the riders who'd killed him connected to the rustling going on around Aces 'n' Eights? He wouldn't put anything past those murdering bastards. Anyone who'd empty his gun into a man point-blank and then drag another would be capable of anything.

He couldn't place the ranch's location in his mind, but he hoped he was within walking distance of San Saba. Even then, he was in a weakened state. The food might give him enough strength to ride, but first he'd have to find his clothes and borrow a horse. God willing, that gang hadn't found his mare, Shadow, in the cane breaks where he'd staked her out with Mose's mules. Shadow was the only thing of value Roan owned, and to lose her would hurt as much as losing Mose. The gray mare was family.

And if the riders had killed her as callously as they had Mose…

Either way, he had to do something. Sometimes a man had to take a stand and find justice. Even if little was to be had for honest men like Mose Mozeke.

Five

Marley returned a short time later with the soup and coffee, amazed at the quiet. Matthew never seemed to run down. "I hope this will tide you over until suppertime."

"I'm sure it will. Right now I'd be grateful for a piece of dried-out shoe leather." He struggled to pull himself to a sitting position, but his arms gave way and he collapsed back onto the pillow.

"Here, let me help you." Marley set down the tray. Putting an arm around him, she managed to prop him against the headboard, then fluffed the pillows and straightened out the bedcovers. "There," she declared.

"My Mama Rose knows how to make things all better," chirped Matthew.

Roan lifted his gaze to hers. "I can see that."

"Has Matthew been too much of a bother?" Marley sat the tray on his lap and wasn't surprised at all to see him go for the coffee first.

"I played the quiet game," Matthew said, fidgeting.

Marley chuckled. "How did that go?"

"Pretty well actually." Roan set down his cup and dipped the spoon into the soup. A taste brought what appeared to be something close to a half-formed smile. "This is real good."

"My name is Matt," Matthew announced. "And I'm going to be just like Mr. Penny."

"Oh, you are?" She shot Roan a questioning glance.

He took a drink of coffee. "Don't look at me."

The look that passed between him and Matthew was one of conspiracy. She was glad that Matthew had found a new friend.

Roan ate, and noise drifted in from outside.

"Who are all those kids out there?" Roan asked.

"They belong to my parents. They're playing, but if the racket bothers you, I'll make them go elsewhere. It sounds like an army when they start running and chasing one another."

"They're fine. How many are there?"

"Including me, a baker's dozen right now." Marley sat down and lifted Matt into her lap. "My mother seems to have a special sense for lost or orphaned children. She somehow finds them all and brings them here."

A strange look crossed Roan's eyes. "She must have a generous heart. I assume they don't all live here with you."

"No, they live next door with my parents." She kissed the top of Matt's head. "Theirs got too crowded, so my father built this one for me. I like being on my own."

She sat there until Roan finished and asked him if he needed help lying back down.

"I can manage. It takes fewer muscles to fall than to get up."

Marley nodded. "Matt, we have to let Mr. Penny rest now. Come along."

The boy tugged on her dress and gave her a hopeful look. "Will you tell me a story?"

"Tonight, when I put you in bed."

"But can you now? Please."

"I'm too busy now. You'll have to wait." Marley glanced at Roan, who seemed interested in their conversation. "He loves for me to tell him stories and never gets enough."

Roan met her gaze. "Do you read from a book or make them up?"

"Some of both actually."

Ever since she was a little girl, Marley had loved telling

stories. Writing and illustrating children's books had always been her dream, but she had other passions as well. When she found time, she also loved to paint the rugged landscape and could get lost for hours mixing and splashing the colors on a canvas. But frustration twisted inside her. She didn't know the first thing about how to make her passions a reality, and these days she had too much work to do to even spare it a thought. "I should help my mother. I'll be back with your supper." She collected the tray and shepherded Matt toward the door.

"I can't thank you enough, Miss Marley," Roan said softly. "You're an angel."

Marley gave him a smile. She was glad she'd decided to go to town two days ago, and not just for his sake. For a long time now, she'd been yearning for something more than wiping kids' noses and tending to scraped knees. Wherever Roan Penny came from appeared to be hard on a man's health. Maybe he would stick around for a little while.

༺࿓༻

Later that evening, after helping her mother with supper in the big house, she carried another tray to Roan. Tending to him gave her a sense of accomplishment, and his arrival had broken the monotony of her days.

He was showing improvement since he'd awakened earlier in the day, and maybe that was a sign that they'd be able to get more answers out of him soon. She wanted to know more—where he lived, what exactly had happened to him, but he was saying little. He'd given a vague explanation about bad men, and she knew there was more to the story. Lots more.

Hardy Gage, one of the ranch hands, held the door for her. He'd been out since before dawn, probably tracking the rustlers her father had spoken of, and only just ridden back in. Worry landed in the pit of her stomach. She hadn't seen her father this upset and angry in a long while.

The aging cowboy wore a lot of salt in his pepper hair. He gave her a wide grin that showed missing teeth. "Miss Marley Rose, I do believe you get prettier every time I see you."

"I'll bet you tell all the girls that, Hardy." She glanced up at the lean man with a smile. He'd worked for them ever since she could remember, and as far as she was concerned, he was part of the family. Hardy was one of those men who never saw a stranger, and he was one of the finest people she knew.

He glanced at her from beneath those shaggy brows that had grown together to form a solid gray line. "Nope, only the ones that I helped raise."

They stepped inside the house, and Hardy stared and whistled. "Hell, a piece of dirt don't dare find its way inside here! You keep this cleaner than the inside of a church."

"Oh hush, you're not the one living here."

"I'm sure grateful for that. But what I want to know is why you've been cleaning the bunkhouse again. I've told you a hundred and fifty times to leave our place alone. Men like mess and clutter. We don't want our place all girlied up to where me and the boys can't find a blooming thing." He waved his arm. "Go girly up your own stuff and keep your hands off ours."

"I swear, you sound like a grizzly finding someone had beaten him to the honey. I had to rake the bunkhouse out. The place was a pig sty." They entered the bedroom. Roan was already sitting up and wearing a pair of long johns that her mother had brought him earlier, with a sheet over his lower half. They'd originally belonged to Caleb Butler, another of Marley's adopted brothers. He'd enlisted in the army and was one of Teddy Roosevelt's Rough Riders. He'd made the ride up San Juan Hill last year, and they'd all burst with pride for him.

"Looks like we'll have to invest in a good padlock," Hardy grumbled.

"Stop the bellyaching before I throw something at you, and come meet our guest. He got himself banged up a bit."

Marley led the way to the bedroom. "Roan Penny, meet Hardy Gage, one of our ranch hands."

Hardy let out a long whistle. "Someone must've thought hell needed paving but was out of pitch, so they used your hide instead."

"Something like that." Roan worked to smile but evidently found it too painful. He shook hands instead. "Gage, help me find my pants and get me to the table. I've had enough of this bed."

Marley shook her head. "You're too weak. Please stay there."

"No dice, Miss Marley. Gage?"

"I reckon a man knows when he's had enough coddling," Hardy said. "I don't see any pants, though. Marley Rose, where's the man's clothes?"

She threw up her hands. "Oh, for heaven's sake! They're on the trunk at the end of the bed. I just hope you know what you're doing, Roan."

Hardy grunted and pushed her out the door, shutting it. She had nothing left to do but sit everything on her small table and wait for them to open it again. A short while later, the two men emerged, Roan's arm draped around Hardy's neck. He dropped into a chair, overexerted by the few steps.

Marley sat a cup of coffee in front of him. "Steak and potatoes tonight. I hope the meat is how you like it. I made the apple pie."

Roan glanced up through his swollen slits. "It'll be perfect no matter how it turned out."

"Where's mine, darlin'?" Hardy asked. "I'm near crippled after repairing miles of cut fence."

"Oh, stop." Marley tried not to hover over Roan but stood ready to help if he needed it. "Did you find any sign of the rustlers?"

"The cattle took care of the tracks, and we lost all sign of everything at the river."

"They swam them downstream?" That appeared a little

odd to her from what she knew of rustlers, but that would sure wipe out a trail.

"Yep. Boss is mad as hell. I'd stay out of his way." Hardy swung to Roan. "Nice to meet you. I'd better get some grub before it's all gone. Either me or the boss will come to help you back to bed."

"Thanks, Hardy," Roan said. "Good luck finding the rustlers."

Finally, they were alone. Marley sat down in the chair next to him. "How is your steak?"

He glanced up and said softly, "Best I've ever had."

"But you haven't taken a bite yet. How do you know?"

"I've pretty much been on my own since I was twelve, Miss Marley. Anything I don't have to cook is pure heaven. Besides, the smell tells me I'm in for a treat." He picked up his fork. "Go eat. I can do this by myself."

"I'll keep you company if you don't mind. I prefer to wait until the crowd thins out, then I eat and clean up the dishes."

He cut off a bite of steak and stuck it in his mouth. He closed his eyes and paused for a second as though to savor the taste. "This is perfect."

"I'm glad you like it."

"Why did Hardy Gage say that about you cleaning?" he asked, chewing.

"I suppose there's no harm in you knowing." She wrinkled her nose and sighed. "I have this need for keeping things neat and tidy. I get teased a lot."

She didn't know how to take Roan's stare, but the intensity made her pulse race. Or maybe it was the way a few wispy pieces of hair curled over the neck of his long johns.

Finally, he said, "Should I be worried? I mean you might take a notion to tie a dish towel around my neck to catch the crumbs I drop."

"Good heavens no. I won't bother you. I promise." But before she knew it, she leaned to pick up a paper fragment on the floor, a corner of a page from her notebook.

Roan shook his head. "I see what they mean."

Oh dear. She sat on her hands. "You truly did enjoy Matthew's...Matt's...company?"

"The boy's extremely bright. He gave me a feel for this ranch."

"I have to say, he idolizes you now. I don't know what you two talked about, but you completely won him over." She glanced at Roan's plate. Judging by how fast the food was disappearing, he'd been starving. No telling how long it had been since he'd eaten his fill.

Roan laughed. "I'll take the blame for the name change. I started calling him Matt when I was teasing him, and I think it stuck. I might've taken things too far. I just wanted him to feel special, you know? Kids don't get to feel special very often. From what I gather, he's not had it easy so far. He talked about getting whippings, and since he flat assured me that doesn't happen here, I could only assume it was before he came."

"Poor kid. Mama found him sleeping outdoors with the dogs. His mother had died and someone shot and killed his no-good father—his body was still slumped over the kitchen table. I think the smell had driven Matthew outside. Why are so many kids left alone in the world?"

Sorrow rippled across Roan's face. "When you figure that out, I'd like to know." He stuck another bite into his mouth.

Marley rose to get the coffeepot, and when she leaned to pour, her hair dangled, brushing his shoulder. Roan shifted in his chair and tried to give her a smile. She didn't think it made him uncomfortable but she needed to watch that or he'd get the wrong idea.

He had almost finished when the door opened and Marley's father strode in. "Did you eat, Papa?" she asked.

"Not yet. I wanted to check on our patient. I have to say I'm glad you came around. We were worried about you." Duel pulled out a chair, and Marley poured him a cup of coffee.

"Sorry to worry anyone." Roan laid down his fork. "Thank you for taking me in, sir."

"I'm not sir. I'm Duel. And I never was much good at letting people die." Duel propped his elbows on the table. "I'd like to hear what happened and why someone came near to killing you."

Marley leaned forward a bit so as not to miss a word, moving back to her place when her father scowled. He let her know when she got overzealous, as she so often did. She reckoned she could hear well enough where she was, but her gaze never left Roan Penny's pitiful face.

Roan grimaced. "I reckon some people took exception to me breathing the same air. I was staying with a farmer friend of mine when a half dozen hooded riders galloped up to the cabin. They accused him of being a squatter and wouldn't listen to his assurance that he had a deed." Roan paused to gather himself. "They shot and killed him, then laid into me when I tried to fight back. Then they roped and dragged me behind a horse."

"How did I find you on our road?" Marley asked. "San Saba is thirty miles away."

"After they finished teaching me a lesson—as they called it—they threw me on the back of a horse, and best I could tell, we rode most of the night. I was in and out of consciousness." Roan stared out the window into the blackness. "They warned me that if I ever go back, they'll kill me." His bruised jaw was squared when he swung his glance to Duel. "I'm going back even if I have to walk so I can bury Mose Mozeke. Then I'll get my horse, presuming they haven't shot or stolen her. After that, I don't know."

"You don't have to walk, son. When you feel up to traveling, I'll loan you a horse. But on one condition," Duel said.

"What's that?"

"I'm coming with you. Whoever did this may be lurking around, and you're in no shape to give them a fight. So I'm giving you no choice. You want a horse, you get me along with it."

Marley glanced from the set lines in her father's face to

Roan's irritated scowl. Duel's eyes flashed, and it seemed like he was burning for the chance to get a little justice. She hadn't seen that kind of anger in her father for a long while now. The rustlers bore at least part of the blame.

Her gaze shifted to Roan and his obvious struggle with the choice Duel had given him.

"That's the deal?" Roan asked tightly. "I can do this by myself."

Duel McClain leaned back in the chair and stretched his long legs out in front of him. "Those are my terms."

Roan was quiet a minute as he mulled everything over. "I want to leave in the morning."

Marley's breath caught. There was no way he'd be able to ride any distance, never mind thirty miles.

"Nope. You're not up to it yet." Duel leaned forward again and propped his elbows on the table. "You can't even sit in a chair good, much less a horse."

The minutes ticked by in silence. Finally, Roan said quietly, "Begging your pardon, sir, I don't think you know me well enough to say what I'm able to do. My friend is rotting in the sun. Nothing else is important."

"I reckon not. Something like that, they'd have to chain *me* to keep me from going." Duel straightened and stood. "All right. We'll leave the moment you've recovered enough not to fall off the horse. Get some rest, son. You can't fight your way out of a paper bag right now. Do you have anyone I should let know?"

"Nope."

"Who claims that your friend was a squatter? A rancher, the railroad, who?"

"Some men came one day and said a rancher named Simmons sent them. They never asked to see a deed or anything. Nor did they produce one. They just snarled that the land belonged to Simmons. Funny thing though, there is no rancher by that name."

Marley's heart thudded against her ribs, and her blood turned to ice.

Anger deepened the lines of Duel's face. "Not the first time this has happened. It's outright theft. And now this group has added murder to the list. Doing something about it will be hard." Duel hooked his thumbs on his gun belt. "The commitment on your face tells me you won't rest until you set the record straight. I'll help you all I can."

"Before you go, I have a question for you. Your daughter told me about the rustlers that have been bothering you. Hardy Gage said you tracked them to the river. Mind me asking whereabouts on the river?" Roan ran his finger around the rim of his coffee cup.

"Tracked the herd to Brown County, but we lost them at the Colorado. The bastards took three hundred head this time." Duel pierced Roan with a stare. "If you know anything about this, you'd best tell me."

"Wish I did. I'd like to say it was the same bunch that killed Mose, but the two things happened a long way apart. Could be henchmen of theirs, I guess. Made a two-pronged attack."

Fear crawled up Marley's spine. If the two crimes were related, if the rustlers were part of something bigger, they could be in for a fight like she'd never seen. She'd keep the children near just in case, and she wished she could do the same with Roan Penny. Everything inside her screamed that he wasn't ready. At least her father had insisted he recover more.

But then what? Something said Roan wouldn't be near enough ready to ride a week from now, yet she knew he couldn't afford to wait that long. His friend needed burying.

In the quiet of the room, she realized the doves had fallen silent as well. Their vigil must be over. But what happened now?

What would Roan find when he went back? Would he find his revenge—or his own death?

Six

THE FOLLOWING DAY, ROAN TRIED HIS BEST TO STAY awake longer, but sleep robbed him of much of the sunlight hours. Maybe it was guilt that he hadn't left to bury Mose or that he missed the friend's company, but he dreamed of him a lot. The old man was as close to family as he had, and an ache throbbed inside that he wouldn't see his smile or hear his words of wisdom anymore.

Finally, his dry mouth and empty stomach protested. The sound of Marley tiptoeing about the darkened room forced his eyes open.

"Could I trouble you for a minute, Miss Marley?"

"Oh dear, did I wake you?"

"No. What time is it?"

"Four o'clock in the afternoon." The sound of a closing drawer reached him. Marley moved to the side of his bed.

"Why didn't you throw some cold water on me or slap me good and hard? I need to get up and around." He tried to toss the covers back but found he was too weak.

"Roan, sleep was the best thing for you. You have to let your body heal or you'll never make it to bury your friend. Are you thirsty? Maybe you can eat a bite to tide you until supper."

"Do you have any coffee? If not, I'll take a glass of water. And maybe a fried egg."

"It'll only take a minute. Would you like to sit up while I fix it?"

"I hate to be such a bother, but it would be nice to sit up."

She put her arm through his up by the shoulder and pulled. Together, they propped him against the headboard, but he was drenched in sweat by the time he got situated. He was appalled by the amount of strength he'd lost. Duel was right—he couldn't fight his way out of a paper bag.

"There. I'll be back with some food and that coffee." She raised the shades to let in the light, then left the room.

A windmill creaked beyond the walls of the house. He'd always loved the sound. His vision had cleared some, and he could make out a few things in the room that clearly defined Marley's space. An easel in the corner. Several paintings were on the wall—landscapes best he could tell. Frilly curtains on the windows. A pretty quilt covered him. A glance at the chair beside the bed revealed some kind of book lying open as though she'd been interrupted. He recalled a rug of some kind being on the floor when he'd gotten up yesterday. The lady appeared to have made her space comfortable.

Roan again dozed until the sound of footsteps awakened him. It made him mad that he couldn't stay awake for two minutes.

"Here's your coffee. I'll bring the food when it's ready." Marley handed him a cup. Their hands brushed when he took it, and he felt a jolt at the contact. "I'm glad you took our advice to heart. Getting rest is the only way you'll be able to do what you must."

"Yeah, but it doesn't make lying here any easier. Buzzards and who knows what else are picking the flesh from my friend." Roan blew on the coffee and took a sip, finding the liquid exactly what he needed.

"You'll get there soon. Try not to let it prey on your mind."

Yeah, well, that was easier said than done.

He changed the subject. "Judging from what I can see, you've made a nice home here."

"Thank you. I like having my own space."

"I noticed the easel. Yours?"

"Yes, but I don't get to paint very often; therefore, I'm not very good. I do love mixing the colors together and seeing what comes out on the canvas." She glanced at the door. "I need to get back to the stove. We'll talk in a minute."

He closed his eyes in the silence and let his mind drift to another who liked to paint. The Widow Harper, the woman his father had given him to, had also loved to paint landscapes. She loved life and colored her lonely world with beauty and kindness. He missed her. Everyone he developed a fondness for had vanished from his life.

Marley returned with a plate of eggs and toast. "This will be light on your stomach."

"Thank you." He tried to give her a smile, and he hoped she recognized the attempt at least. "Anything is welcome. I'm sorry if I've taken you from something else. I'm sure you have many things you'd rather do than sit by such a sorry-looking sight as I am."

She lifted the book on the chair and sat down. "I'm not complaining, and neither is anyone else. Tell me about this friend of yours, Mose. What was your life like with him?"

While he ate, he told her about Mose and just how much the man's friendship had meant to him. He found Marley easy to talk to. She asked a few questions, and he ended up saying far more than he'd intended.

Before he knew it, he'd practically cleaned his plate of the delicious food. Marley opened her book and scribbled something on a page. A thoughtful pucker appeared on her forehead as she wrote. He liked her brown eyes. Brown reminded him of the soil, necessary for growing things—whether crops or nurturing a soul. There was something wholesome and honest about the color.

"I'm curious about that book. What are you doing?"

"Writing a story for Matthew... I'm sorry, Matt." She flashed him a smile. "He does love my feeble attempts."

"How many have you written?" He filled his mouth with more eggs and toast.

"I think there's a dozen in this book. I have two more that are full. Most are very short and can be read in their entirety at bedtime. Nothing will probably come of them, but I enjoy letting my imagination take hold and run." She tapped the pencil against her cheek. "Writing completes something inside me as nothing else does. I know this sounds silly."

"Absolutely not. You appear to be a very creative person, and you should take it seriously." And beautiful to boot, the best he could tell. He'd gotten a good look at her when she'd helped raise him to a sitting position. The ends of her dark hair had tickled his cheek, and he'd fought the urge to touch a strand.

But what drew him to her most was her kind heart.

"I do try, believe me. But what use is it? What will I ever do with it other than read to Matt? Lord knows, no one else probably will."

"You should try to publish them."

"How? I don't know the first thing about that." She released a sigh and shut the book.

"Just don't give up on your dream." Roan laid down his fork and wiped his mouth. "I've been meaning to apologize."

"What for?"

"I'm sorry I stole your bed, Miss Marley. If you can direct me to another, I'll gladly give it back."

Marley laughed. "Nope. It's yours for as long as you need it. I'm sleeping fine on the sofa. Would you like to listen to some music? I have a phonograph I can bring in here."

"Anything to stay awake." He chuckled. "Fair warning, I'll probably fall asleep in the middle of a record."

"I'll take my chances."

She took his tray and disappeared through the door. He cursed his poor vision that he couldn't see her curves. Something told him that she cut quite a figure. One thing he already knew by the sound—she had a no-nonsense stride.

And he couldn't even admire it or her figure. Hell!

But he had seen her brown eyes when she'd leaned close, and they were real pretty.

❧

The next morning, Marley commandeered Hardy Gage and Judd Hanson into helping Roan outside into the sunshine. She gathered a pan of warm water, a towel, and soap to wash his hair. He'd already agreed and seemed to look forward to it. But he rested his head against the back of the chair as though it was too heavy to hold up.

Matthew came running. "What'cha doing, Mr. Penny?"

"Your Mama Rose is going to wash my hair, little man."

"Can I watch?"

"I reckon so, but it's going to be boring," Marley warned.

"Hey, Matthew, want to come with me an' Judd?" Hardy asked. "Molly had her kittens."

Judd picked up the cajoling. "They're awful cute I hear. But if you don't want to—"

"I do! I do!" The boy jumped up and down, clasping his hands together.

Marley breathed a sigh of relief. She wanted a few minutes alone with Roan. She wasn't even sure what to say, but she'd feel better not having little ears listening to each word.

"Are you sure you don't mind doing this?" Roan opened his eyes. Even though it wasn't very wide, given that they were still swollen, she saw a small improvement. "This sun is exactly what I needed, but I may fall out of this chair. It's sure making me awful sleepy."

"I'll catch you." Marley bit her lip. That sounded way too forward. "I mean, I won't let you hurt yourself."

"I'll hold you to that." Roan chuckled. "Not that anyone would notice new bruises."

"Lean back into the warm water." The pan, resting on a high table, was the right height and allowed Marley to use both hands. "I'll try to be gentle, but the dried blood may need to soak a bit."

"I hate for you to have to tackle this job, but I'm as weak as a newborn babe. It tires me to move any part of my body."

"That's why you have to rest more before you ride out, and besides, I don't mind one bit. When I finish here, I'll shave you."

Roan cut his eyes to her. "Shave me? Have you done that before?"

"Often ranch hands get hurt and can't groom themselves for whatever reason. I've gotten very skillful at shaving men. There's no need to be nervous."

"If you say so, Miss Marley. It will feel good to get this stubble off."

"Just close your eyes and think about a place where your soul can be at peace." She reached for the soap and lathered it to a thick foam on his wet hair, then very gently began to wash out the matted blood.

His eyes closed, Roan let a rumble of appreciation escape. "This is heaven right here. You have a most gentle touch, Miss Marley."

"Thank you, but I'm plain Marley. Like my father, I've never been big on formality. We're ordinary people here."

"I noticed that by the way you treat your ranch hands like family."

Marley chuckled, massaging his scalp. "That's because they are. They helped raise me and now these other children."

She kept him entertained with tales of her parents and the children they'd taken in. He seemed truly interested, as though the McClain family was a rarity. Maybe they were where he came from. She washed his dark strands until they gleamed, then collected her shaving items.

Roan sat up and touched his hair. "I can't thank you enough."

"I'm glad I could do it." Finding him on that lonely, cold morning had changed her life in a lot of ways. She loved his touch and how his voice changed when he spoke passionately about certain topics. He'd done things she'd only read about. He was smart and had a great sense of humor.

Roan Penny was the first man who'd ever truly interested her. And now he was set to leave. She probably wouldn't see him again.

Somehow, she found the thought unbearable. Roan had brought life into her monotonous days. She couldn't go back to merely existing.

❧

Roan soaked up the sun's warmth and leaned his head back, his eyes closed. Marley wrapped a warm towel around his face, leaving his eyes and mouth open, readying to shave him.

She rested a hand on his shoulder. Her touch gave him such a calm feeling. "I'm going to be very careful and avoid the cut around your throat. If I cause you pain, let me know right away."

"You can be sure of that. But it's such a shallow cut it doesn't bother me much."

While the moist heat softened the stubble, she told him about a new story she'd written about a boy and his pet horse. He could listen to her talk all day. Her voice had the same musical quality he'd noticed at the outset, and as she spoke, passion filled her words.

"You have a real gift, Marley. You have such a vivid imagination."

"Thanks, but I just write what's in my heart. I don't know any other way. I think we're ready to proceed." She removed the towel and lathered him up, then carefully put the razor to his jaw.

He closed his eyes and enjoyed the pampering. His thoughts wandered to this ranch, the McClain family, and to Marley. They'd shown him there were still kind people in the world.

The razor strokes were smooth, never hard or jerky. Marley's skill amazed him. Was there anything she couldn't do? He lay back, soaking up the sounds of the windmill, horses nickering in the corral, and the light scrape of the razor against his jaw. Except for Marley's closeness, he could have dozed off.

But Marley made sleep impossible. The faint scent of something flowery encircled his head. He relaxed and enjoyed her presence, wishing he could tell her how much sharing these days meant to him.

Still, what use would it be to voice feelings that couldn't go anywhere?

His thoughts drifted until he felt her lean over him, felt a strand of hair brush his shoulder. He opened his eyes to find himself staring into her pretty brown gaze just inches away. For a second, he barely breathed, for fear it was a dream and she'd vanish.

Her close proximity did strange things to his heart.

Dark curls framed her face, and her eyes glistened like diamonds shimmering in a stream. Air got trapped in his lungs, and the wanting was so powerful, it sent throbbing pain through him.

Like a man wandering too long alone, he reached to capture a strand of hair between his thumb and forefinger. The texture was like satin, and he couldn't move, couldn't think, couldn't speak. Her soft breath whispered against his newly shaved cheek, and unexpected hunger rose.

Awareness sizzled between them. He became acutely conscious of the length of her eyelashes, her heartbeat, the pulse in the hollow of her elegant neck. He'd long searched for a woman like Marley, never once thinking she existed.

Her mouth was so close. Just a slight move forward…

But to what end? He wouldn't tease her, make her think they could have more when, in truth, they could have no future at all.

Marley Rose McClain was everything a man like him could never have, and to even wish for a life with her was a big mistake that could only lead to bitter disappointment. Best to remember his place and that he had nothing to offer—not to her or to any woman.

But maybe, for just a moment, he could pretend.

"You have the silkiest hair I've ever felt." His voice was low and full of yearning. He released the strand and brushed a finger lightly across her cheek. "I'm afraid you got a poor bargain when you patched up my rotten hide."

"Let me be the judge of that. There is nothing wrong with your hide."

Her soft statement wound around his heart like a stubborn trumpet vine.

She adjusted her angle, cleared her throat, and moved back a fraction. Her attention once again on his jaw, she applied the razor's edge to his stubble. "I'm glad I found you," she murmured.

"Me too." Roan glanced away, feeling the need to apologize. "I'm sorry. I don't know what came over me. That was no way to repay your kindness."

"Good heavens, Roan. You didn't do anything wrong. I like being with you. Over the time we've spent together, I like to think we've become true friends." She lifted the razor and wiped it with the towel.

Friends. Well, that put him in his place. He should thank her for reminding him. He would, if he didn't think it would make things awkward. She'd been so kind to him— he was honored to have her friendship.

"You're easy to be around, Marley, and I've enjoyed being with you more than you know." He'd remember this time for the rest of his life. When he sat around a lonely campfire, he'd recall Marley McClain and how tempted he'd been to kiss her.

A minute later, she wiped away the remaining shaving cream and handed him a mirror. "What do you think?"

"You've worked a miracle. I feel like a new man and, except for the bruises and black eyes, I look almost human."

She stood back with a smile. "I think you're very handsome."

That was one word he'd rarely heard spoken about him. That she thought him pleasing to the eye made his heart flutter, and he worked to wipe a foolish smile from his face.

In the comfortable silence, he found peace that had been missing from his existence.

Roan thought about that as he sat with her in the sun, listening to the lazy windmill, imagining a life here for real— the place of belonging he'd searched for. He watched Marley scribbling in her storybook, a grin curving her lips. She was an amazing woman with so much to give the world.

He had nothing to offer except bad luck—and grief to Mose's killers.

But if one day he had the opportunity again to ride near the Aces 'n' Eights, he would stop in a heartbeat. For sure, the lovely Marley McClain would fill his dreams for a long time, her gentle touch lingering in his heart.

Seven

TWO DAYS LATER, THE CHILLY MORNING AIR HELD A BITE TO it as Roan pulled himself into the saddle of his borrowed horse. His body screamed with pain, and it was all he could do to stifle a groan. Even in the saddle, he tried to pretend every muscle wasn't quivering like a horse ridden too hard. Sweat popped out on his forehead from the exertion.

While he took control of his rebellious body, he also took a last look around the large compound. His gaze swept to the bunkhouse, corral, barn, and the two dwellings. Another building appeared to be a small smithy. He thought it odd that the kitchen of the main house faced the compound. That was the entrance everyone used rather than the front of the house. That said they were casual people.

It was pretty here. And peaceful. Trees, tall and thick, grew on each side of the gate.

Movement caught his attention as Marley strode from the headquarters. She smiled up at Roan, gripping her shawl tighter around her. "Will you come back, Mr. Penny?"

Roan stared at the dark hair that curled possessively around her shoulders, remembering how silky it had felt when he'd touched it. She was beautiful, possibly the most beautiful woman he'd ever seen, and had kind ways. Whoever married her and lived on the Aces 'n' Eights would be a lucky, lucky man.

"Would you care if I didn't, Marley Rose McClain?" He found himself unable to move from her dark gaze.

Her face turned somber. "A great deal. It would pain me if you didn't—if I never knew what happened to you."

Proof that someone cared about him shattered his inner calm. He hadn't expected to find that anywhere, not truly. But especially not with this woman.

"I'm not sure of my plans. I guess it depends on what happens when I get to Mose's." He glanced down at his clothes. Everything he had on—from his wool shirt and trousers to the thick jacket and hat—was borrowed. "Appreciate the clothes."

"You're welcome. Nothing much was left of those you came with." She rested a hand on Matthew's shoulder. The sleepy-eyed boy had stolen from the house to say his farewells.

"Bye, Matt," Roan said. "You take care now and don't chase after too many girls."

"I won't, Mr. Penny." Matthew giggled, then asked, "Are you still blind in your eye?"

"A little, but it's getting better." Roan could see Marley a whole lot clearer. He wished he knew how to tell her what her kindness to him had meant. Maybe the letter he'd left for her would suffice.

Jessie McClain handed her husband a heavy burlap sack. "Here's some food, honey. Come home safe."

Roan watched Duel's lazy smile and saw the couple's gazes lock. How would it be to have a wife to love him like that?

"I intend to, darlin'." Duel pulled Jessie close and kissed her.

Roan watched Jessie curl her arm around her husband's neck, then he quickly turned away to give them privacy. Though he'd been young when his mother died, he had no memories of his father showing her a speck of consideration, much less love. Duel and Jessie's passionate kiss and their little furtive touches only sharpened the contrast to the stark bleakness of Roan's life. Mose had rarely spoken of life with his wife, but the few times he had, reverence had filled his voice. This must be what the lonely man had tried to explain to Roan.

This sort of love was the farthest thing possible from the brothels where Roan had sometimes gone when the long, lonely nights clawed at him. He'd only done it a handful of times, repulsed by the cheap perfume and fake laughter. Afterward, he'd gotten drunk on rotgut whiskey, trying to forget the sadness that washed over him.

"I'll be back before you miss me," Duel told Jessie.

Jessie's satisfied sigh told Roan he could safely look again.

"Now get on up there, honey," Jessie said. "The quicker you leave, the quicker you can ride back." She turned to Roan and reached up to shake his hand. "Mr. Penny, it was a pleasure. I hope you'll ride back with my husband. You're welcome here."

"Thank you, ma'am. And also for patching me up," Roan answered.

"You should still be in bed, but I reckon you know what you're able to do."

"Yes, ma'am. I'll be fine."

"Keep a candle burning in the window, Jess." Duel patted his wife's bottom and mounted up.

"I always do, dear."

Somehow, Roan didn't think her words pertained to tallow and flame.

"I hope you get your friend buried without any trouble." Marley reached to shake Roan's hand. "I'm just glad my father is going along."

He was too, even though this was his fight and not Duel McClain's. Still, Roan was practical above all else and knew he was in no shape to take on the hooded gang by himself just yet.

"I can't very well talk to him unless I go, Marley Rose." Duel glanced at Roan.

The words ran through Roan, sparking his curiosity. He hadn't known the big rancher long at all, but he'd already learned that the man divvied up his words in fits and starts, not speaking until he had something to say. Whatever it was could bear hearing. Mose had taught him that it paid to listen to wise elders.

With Marley, Jessie, and a few of the children waving as they left, they rode out toward San Saba County.

Roan loped beside Duel's black gelding, trying to lessen the jolts to his battered body. "You have something in mind, sir?"

"I answer to Duel. It'll wait a bit I reckon."

The informal use of first names reminded Roan of Mose, and look what had happened to him. "I prefer to keep things as they are."

"Whatever suits you, son."

They rode east, cutting a trail along the Colorado River before turning south. An hour later, they stopped at a wide creek to rest the horses. Roan clamped his lips together to keep a sharp cry from escaping when he dismounted, then stumbled away from the water's edge to lie in the shade of a live oak. The ride was giving his battered body another beating, and he'd be hard-pressed to continue.

Duel dropped to the ground and made himself comfortable against the same tree trunk. "Come work for me," he said out of the blue.

The offer stunned Roan. "Pardon me, but you don't appear in need of another ranch hand." From what Marley had said, the rancher already had a full bunkhouse.

"You're wrong. One up and quit yesterday, rode out last night. And Hardy Gage is getting up in years, even though the stubborn cuss won't admit it." Duel removed his hat and wiped his forehead with a faded bandana. "I can use a man like you who's willing to work. It would sure help me out."

Working cattle would be a welcome change from planting crops that shriveled and died under the Texas sun. He had an obligation to Mose first, but even so, the offer intrigued him. And working on the ranch would let him get better acquainted with Marley Rose. He had an idea of how to help get her books in print.

"You'd trust a hard-luck drifter? I've been between hay and

grass all my life, sir." And had learned to make do with the little he had. Still, what was wrong with being flush for a while?

"I'm a good judge of character, and you remind me of myself when I was younger. A little over twenty years ago, after burying my first wife, Annie, and my stillborn son, I saddled my horse and drifted from town to town. I didn't have two cents to my name or much care about staying alive. In fact, I prayed to die. Thank God I found Jess, and she and Marley Rose gave me a reason to live again." Duel glanced toward a gaggle of geese dropping from the sky onto the water downstream. Roan followed his gaze to the birds taking their rest before they resumed their flight south for the winter.

Maybe that's what he needed to do. Take a break and work on the Aces 'n' Eights while he regained his strength.

"Mind if I think on your offer? I have a friend to bury first, then I'll go from there." One thing at a time was all he could promise.

"Sure. Take as long as you want." Duel opened the burlap bag beside him and handed Roan a cold biscuit and a slice of ham before reaching for his own.

Roan watched the rancher carefully. Duel appeared rock solid in everything he did. Roan had seen a few men like him and always admired them. They had honor and decency. Duel sure as hell wasn't like Blackie Culpepper, his outlaw father. McClain would fight to keep every single one of his children. That was the right kind of man in Roan's book.

Soon it was time to ride. The rest wasn't near long enough, but Roan climbed back into the saddle, anxious to be at Mose's place. All sorts of things raced through his mind, mostly questions about what was laying in store.

Twilight was still an hour away when they reached the small homestead. Shadows of the burned-out hulk of the cabin writhed across the ground. Roan's gaze went to the figure of his friend, lying where he'd fallen. No one had had the decency to move him. Vultures feasting on the bloated figure shrieked in protest before rising reluctantly into the sky.

The stench of decayed flesh filled Roan's nostrils. He reached for his borrowed bandana and held it to his mouth and nose. Grief overtook him, and he knelt beside the still form of the man who'd taken him in and shared what little he'd had. Tears ran down Roan's cheeks, and his shoulders shook with sobs.

"Mose, I'm sorry it took me so long to get back. Judgment day is coming for those murdering scum, I promise you that." Roan wiped his eyes. "I won't rest until I get them all."

Duel looped the reins of his horse over a tree limb. "I reckon I'll find a shovel in the barn. We need to get him into the ground."

"Yeah." Roan shot a glance toward the barn, the only structure left standing. Thick memories circled him like bees buzzing around their hive. Every second of the attack came back with crystal clarity. The face of the one man he'd seen. The smell of fear and despair. The voices he knew he'd recognize again. He finally stood. It was time to get to work.

Duel plucked a Bowie knife and hat from the dirt. "These yours?"

"Yeah, thanks." Roan wiped the dried blood from the knife on a thatch of nut grass and stuck it into his boot. Then adjusted the hat on his head.

While Duel headed to the barn, Roan went to his horse for the blanket he'd brought from the ranch. He wrapped Mose in it and secured it with a length of rope.

Duel emerged with a shovel and a piece of an old quilt. "I don't know why this was in the barn, but maybe it meant something to your friend."

Roan closed his eyes as memories swirled of the way Mose had thrown his wife's quilt around his thin shoulders the night before the raid, saying he felt her near. Roan tucked the memory away and went to take the quilt sewn by Mose's wife's hand. "Mose would want to be buried with that."

After wrapping the quilt around the blanket-clad body, they eased Mose over the borrowed horse and walked toward the family cemetery. A little while later, as the shadows deepened, they laid the gentle man into the newly dug grave beside his wife and children and covered him with dirt. Roan imagined the happy reunion that had taken place when Mose flew up to his family that terrible night. He could almost hear Mose's deep laugh that had seemed to come all the way from his toes.

Thinking of Mose's happiness instead of the way he'd died made the day a little more bearable. Almost.

He and Mose had shared happy times. They'd read each other's moods by the look in their eyes, not by words. Roan knew he'd never have another friend like Mose Mozeke. So he remained with his head bowed and told him how much his friendship had meant.

Duel stood reverently until Roan finished, then put a hand on his back. "It'll be dark soon. How about we make a fire, get coffee boiling, and eat something?"

"I have to find my horse first—if those riders left her."

"I'll help you look. Where do you think she might be?"

"Antelope Creek. She loves the wild rye that grows along the banks. I left her there with Mose's mule. That ornery mule never would go in the barn, so Mose usually let it roam around."

"Lead the way. We'll find them if they're there. At least they won't be hungry."

Roan tugged up the collar of his jacket and set off for the creek, with Duel beside him. The ride and then the burial had sapped his strength. If he didn't lie down soon, he'd fall. But the creek wasn't far, and they were soon there.

The mare began snorting and raising Cain before Roan even got near. Roan hurried his pace when Shadow came into view, ignoring the driving pain. He threw his arms around her neck and pressed his face against her hide. That horse was pitiful looking, but to his eyes, she was the prettiest animal he'd ever seen. A thatch of dark-gray mane fell over her eyes, and one ear lay folded over where it'd been damaged before Roan got her. Shadow's dappled gray body quivered, and she nickered softly in welcome.

"You're not much to look at, girl, but I'll sure claim you," Roan said. She was worth little to others and probably wouldn't get a second glance. Maybe that's why the raiders had left her.

Duel must've sensed that Roan was hurting too badly to swing up on his own and helped him onto Shadow's back. Roan rode her to the burned-out cabin while Duel brought the other two and the mule.

Later, after they'd eaten, Roan lay next to the fire, satisfied with the outcome of the journey. He'd taken care of Mose, found his hat, knife, and horse. Tomorrow, he'd look for his Colt among the ashes.

His glance slid to McClain, sitting by the fire on a stump, holding a cup of coffee. "Thanks for coming, sir. I was in no shape to do this alone."

"Glad to help."

That the man had dropped everything to help a stranger, in the midst of dealing with losing his cattle, amazed Roan. He'd imagined men like Mose were too rare to find another, but it looked as if—in this, at least—his luck was holding steady.

Duel rose and stared out toward the town of San Saba. "Some real bad stuff started here in 1880, and lasted until three years ago when the Texas Rangers rode in. A mob of men who hated former slaves and white abolitionists ruled the town. They lynched and burned and took whatever they wanted. By the time it was all said and done, a whole lot of people died."

"I didn't hear anything about that." Roan's ears perked up. "Do you think what happened here was connected?"

"There are always pockets of resistance after that type of hate burns into a man's soul and can change him into someone he doesn't know. There's bound to be resistance by broken men unwilling to change." Duel turned. "Mose's killing has all the markings of the same type of crimes that occurred back then. That mob wore hoods too. I think it's possible the two bunches could belong to the same faction." He released a troubled sigh. "God help us if it's a new group."

The rancher's words chilled Roan. "You should be safe, seeing as your ranch is in McCullough County."

"Son, no place was safe back then. The war—and that's exactly what it was—spilled over into every county around. It might still be raging hot if not for Walter Early and Sheriff Charley Bell of Brown County. They stood up to the group of terrorizing bastards. They were the ones who called in the Texas Rangers and quelled the violence. Yep, it was bad stuff."

Long after Duel climbed into his bedroll, Roan lay there, listening to the sounds of the night, reliving his own horror. The carnage and the flames flashed through him like jagged bolts of lightning each time he closed his eyes.

Mob rule left no one safe.

Surrounded by the heavy night shadows, Roan glanced toward the house and thought he saw Mose smiling in the blackened doorway. Maybe he was trying to tell Roan not to worry, or reassure him that he was in a better place now, free from pain and loneliness. Or it could have been nothing more than a trick of the light.

One thing Roan knew. Mob rule or not, he was hell-bent on making them pay.

Eight

MARLEY SAT AT A NEWFANGLED SINGER SEWING MACHINE
the following morning, trying to figure out why her bobbin
thread kept breaking. Truth to tell, her thoughts were more
on the letter that Roan had left on her bed with a late-
blooming rose on top. He'd thanked her again for saving
his life and then spoke of never forgetting her. The part
that filled her thoughts had seemed to come from his heart.
She'd memorized the words.

> *People's paths sometimes cross for seemingly no*
> *reason, only to realize the significance later. You*
> *gave me hope that I had long lost. It crowds out*
> *despair, and I will always carry you in my heart.*
> *When loneliness sets in, I'll recall the conversations*
> *we shared and times spent together. I wish you*
> *every success and happiness that life has to offer.*
> *Follow your dreams and don't get discouraged. I*
> *hope you think of me fondly as I will you.*

Though she'd risen early and thrown herself into her
chores, nothing kept worry at bay. Her constant thoughts
were on her father and Roan. She sent up a silent prayer
for their safety and hope that everything would turn out
all right.

She finally rose with a sigh and went next door. "I'm having a difficult time focusing today, Mama."

Her mother glanced up from feeding one of the babies. "They'll be all right, Marley Rose. It doesn't do a lick of good to fret. Your father knows how to take care of himself, and I suspect Mr. Penny does also."

"Sometimes things happen beyond a person's control." Marley stood at the window, looking out. "What do you think about him?"

"I like the man very much. He has kind eyes and a beautiful smile." Jessie glanced up. "But don't go losing your heart, Marley Rose. Roan Penny is a handsome man with caring ways, but he may not be looking for a place to settle down. And what do we really know about him? Take this slow."

"We've been over this, Mama. I told you that I'm not pinning any hopes on him."

"I've seen how you stare at him and how he looks at you. Your father and I have kept you too sheltered. You don't know how easily a man can charm a woman and make her do crazy things," Jessie answered softly.

"There's no worry there. I'll probably never see Roan Penny again." But Marley's heart desperately wanted him to return. His touch still burned on her.

Roan was digging around in the rubble of what was left of the house when Duel found him, still looking for his holster and Colt.

"I'd best get moving if I don't want to be late getting home," Duel said. "Have you thought about my offer?"

Roan stared through the hole where the doorway had been, his gaze trained on the rolling hills Mose had given his life for. "I intend to seek justice. I can't do it from your ranch."

"Wouldn't expect anything different. But here's something for you to chew on. These things take a while and are a whale of an undertaking for one man alone." Duel pushed back his hat. "It's always been my experience that it's wise to bide your time on revenge. Let the confrontation come at a time and place of your choosing, not theirs. And in the meanwhile, you'd have a paying job, food, and shelter, and can regain your strength for a proper fight."

"I won't have the bastards think I tucked tail and ran. That's not a message I want to send," Roan argued.

"Who cares what the hell a group of murderers think? You don't have to prove anything as long as you know who you are."

"Begging your pardon, but I've never given anyone reason to think I'm weak or incapable, and I don't intend to start now." Roan noticed a glint of silver among the ashes. His Colt. He dug it from the rubble, but the fire had baked the leather holster the gun was in. He wasn't even sure the gun would ever work again.

"Son, I suspect you've had to fight all your life for every speck of ground. It takes courage to keep getting up each time someone knocks you down. Only a fool would call you weak. All I'm saying is this—retreat for the moment. Devise a plan, then come back. I guarantee you'll get a lot more satisfaction. Choice is yours though. I've got to ride." Duel stuck out his hand. "If you need help, you know where to find me."

Roan stuck his Colt into his waistband and followed Duel to the horses. Before they reached them, two riders, bandanas covering their mouths and noses, burst from the wooded growth.

"You're trespassing on private land," the man with long, light-colored hair snapped.

The voice indicated someone around Roan's age. In fact, both seemed young. Anger boiled inside Roan. "I came to bury my friend. The devil take you and the rest giving the orders! This land doesn't belong to you." He slid his Colt from his waistband before the two riders could blink. Their eyes widened, and they shifted. "You caught me by surprise the other night. I assure you it won't happen again."

A gust of wind whipped the other horseman's sandy hair. "You were told not to return. We meant it."

Duel pointed at him. "You come a little late to tell a man where he can go. As you can see, he's a mite riled. Unless you can produce a deed, I suggest you get off Mozeke land."

"It's in the process," the blond rider shot back. "Who are you, mister?"

"Duel McClain of the Aces 'n' Eights. Maybe you've heard of me."

Roan watched a light dawn in their eyes and their nervous glances. He kept his gun trained on the two.

Duel narrowed his eyes and hardened his voice. "Maybe you're the ones who rustled my cattle. You know what we do to rustlers, don't you?"

"You can't blame that on us."

"But I'm guessing you know who did it." Roan's finger tightened on the trigger. "You'd better speak up before he reaches for his rope. A man like McClain doesn't have much patience."

The two men's eyes widened with fear. The sandy-haired one opened his mouth to speak, and a shot rang out. At the same moment, a flock of pigeons flew from the barn. The rider toppled, falling from his horse. Roan took cover behind a tree, and Duel dove into the brush. The second rider whirled and galloped into the woods.

"Did you see where the shot came from?" Roan asked, scanning the area for movement.

"Nope. I was watching the two riders." Duel removed his hat and lifted his head for a look.

"Evidently someone didn't want them to talk." Roan cursed the blurriness still affecting his eyes. "I think he must've been nearby. Close enough to hear the conversation. The shot scared those pigeons from the barn. Could be where the shooter hid."

"Yep," Duel answered.

They waited for several minutes, listening to the sounds

around them. When no other shots came, they emerged from their cover.

Roan knelt over the body of the downed rider, staring at the perfectly placed hole between his eyes. He removed the bandana. The pimply face showed him to be very young, and Roan didn't recognize him.

Duel rifled through his pockets, finding only a bent harmonica, a bag of marbles, and a cold biscuit.

What was going on here? Counting the boy Roan had unmasked on the night of the attack, and then these, they were all only half-grown. Was it the work of a gang of fresh bloods? Though there had been the rider with the gravelly voice. That rider had definitely been older, and he'd appeared to be the one in charge.

"McClain, do you think I might've been the target?"

"Nope, you weren't standing close enough. And the shot came just as this man opened his mouth to spill his guts. The shooter wasn't aiming at you." Duel swung to his feet and stared at the barn. "The gunman was *facing* the riders, not behind them." He drew his gun and strode toward the structure. Roan hurried to catch up, though his gut told him the shooter had already vanished. Maybe he'd left something behind that could identify him.

A cat raced for a hiding place when they entered the barn. In the loft, they discovered a matchstick, the leavings of at least half a dozen cigarettes, and an empty Bull Durham sack. No telling how long the shooter had been sitting there watching. Maybe he'd slept there too, only yards away from Roan and Duel in their bedrolls. The hair rose on Roan's neck. Whoever it was could've killed them at any time.

If that was so, what had stopped him?

Roan glanced around, looking for any other clue. "He was up here a while, watching us. I wonder why he waited so long to make his move? Any thoughts, McClain?"

"Definitely here since early morning," Duel answered. "I doubt he slept here, or there'd be more telltale signs."

"I guess we might as well head down. I'll tote that body

into town to the sheriff." Roan moved to the ladder but paused. He picked up a long silk thread—red—from bits of hay and dirt. "What do you make of this? It certainly isn't anything Mose would've had. A woman?"

Duel took it and scowled. "Has to be from a woman."

The mystery deepened. "No women ever came to visit Mose and me." So who? Roan puzzled over it all the way back to the man lying on the ground. He glanced at Duel. "I don't suppose you could spare an hour to go into town with me. It would be just like this bunch to accuse me of firing the fatal shot."

"I can spare the time."

They put the young man over his horse and rode toward San Saba.

Duel broke the silence. "Where did you learn to handle a gun like that? You're fast."

"Just practiced a little," Roan admitted. "It pays a man to be good with any weapon he carries, otherwise it'll get him killed. I'm not ready to die."

"I assume you're just as skilled with that big knife you carry."

"I do all right. I stabbed one of those hooded riders with it the other night." Roan explained about leaving his holster and Colt inside Mose's cabin, and what it had cost him. "If I'd had it on, I could've made a difference."

Duel studied him. "Maybe or maybe not. Don't second-guess yourself."

They rode a little farther before Roan spoke. "Is that job still open?"

"It is." Duel allowed a grin. "Glad to see you changed your mind."

There had been a lot of wisdom in Duel's advice. He had to be smart about this. There was nothing left here except retribution, and that would come later. After he came up with a plan, at a time and place of his own choosing.

When the gang least expected it.

He'd haunt their dreams and take his revenge very, very slowly.

Nine

THE SIGN HANGING ABOVE THE SHERIFF'S OFFICE CREAKED in the wind, and a dog barked in the distance. Other than that, San Saba was eerily silent.

Roan and Duel found the wavy-haired Sheriff Coburn sitting on the boardwalk outside his office, reading a newspaper. Coburn looked younger than Roan, and he didn't bother to glance up when they stopped at the hitching rail with the dead man draped over his own mount. Roan had heard rumors about the sheriff's skill with a gun, and the man was reportedly mighty anxious to prove himself, locking up or burying anyone who crossed him.

They both dismounted. Only then did Coburn spare them a look.

"We have business with you, Sheriff." Roan motioned to the body on the horse. "This man tried to run us off Mose Mozeke's land. He was about to tell us who killed Mozeke when a shot rang out from the barn and struck him."

"I'm supposed to just take your word that's what happened? I wouldn't believe you if you said the sky is blue." The sheriff's hard words could've frozen a piece of iron. "You were living out there with the mangy squatter."

"Mose had a deed. That land legally belonged to him and everyone knows it. I guess that doesn't count around here." Roan swallowed the rest of what he wanted to say, knowing nothing he said would make a difference. He glanced at Duel and noticed how the rancher shifted, drawing the sheriff's attention, quietly letting his presence be known without uttering a word.

"Things will go smoother with the troublemaker dead," the sheriff snarled.

Anger blazed through Roan. "I see you know about Mozeke's death."

"I know everything that goes on in my county." The sheriff turned to Duel. "Who are you?"

Duel rested one foot on the edge of the boardwalk. "Duel McClain. I own the Aces 'n' Eights spread over in McCulloch County. Maybe you've heard of me. I've got a bunch of rustlers stealing my cattle. I don't suppose you know anything about that either."

"Nope. Not my problem."

"What are you going to do about Mozeke?" Roan asked. "Masked riders came onto his property and killed him outright."

Sheriff Coburn shrugged. "Give the riders a medal? From the looks of you, it appears they gave you a beating for interfering. And don't bother making a complaint, because it won't do you any good, Penny. I heard you don't know their identities."

Who exactly told Coburn that? The whole thing left Roan with a sour taste. He burned with an itch to slam a fist in the sheriff's weak jaw, but he took a deep breath instead and strode to the body they'd brought in. "Do you know this man?"

Coburn moved closer to look. "Yep. That's Maxfield's son, George. Rube's going to come after you with guns blazing, Penny."

Who was Rube? Roan had never heard the name.

"Look, Sheriff," Duel said hotly. "We didn't do this. Anyone who says otherwise better be prepared to stand behind the accusation." He took a step forward. Coburn backed up and rested his hand on the walnut grip of his gun.

Roan spoke up. "We just wanted to do the right thing, but I can already see that was a mistake. We should've let him rot on the ground like those hooded murderers did to Mose."

Rage mottled the sheriff's face. "Get out of my town before I throw you both in jail!"

"A pleasure." Roan untied Shadow and mounted. Duel did the same, and they galloped toward fresher air. One thing at least, Roan's question had been answered. The law wasn't on Mose's side, and no justice was to be found there. It was entirely up to Roan.

Marley heard riders just after dark. She flew to the window of her small house and watched her father and Roan head to the barn. He'd returned. Her heart fluttered as she raced out the door. The sight of his proud shoulders and the chiseled set of his purple-bruised jaw took her breath from her chest. The slowly healing mass of blood and bruises was becoming a strange patchwork quilt of his honor and courage. She remembered the scars she'd seen on his back, marks that bore witness to someone's long-ago rage.

Roan had already removed the bridle and was slipping a halter on an unfamiliar dappled gray mare, while her father took care of the other animals.

"You're back after all." Marley noticed the half smile on Roan's weary face when he glanced her way. "I'm glad you changed your mind."

"Got an offer I couldn't refuse." He met Duel's gaze. "Your father offered me a job."

"And?" She watched Roan bend to uncinch the girth. When he stood, her hands collided with his. A delicious shiver ran through her. He, on the other hand, appeared completely unaffected by their accidental touch.

"Gave me a comfortable bed in the bunkhouse, even though my legs will probably stick off the end."

"And?" she prodded.

Roan walked around his mare and rested an arm on the saddle. "Look, Marley. If you're fishing, maybe you should use better bait."

Heat rose to her face. She'd been too nosy again. Darn it, when could she learn to hold her tongue? "I'm glad you're staying," she finally said.

"It's only temporary." His eyes met hers in the dim light, and she felt as though she stood in the middle of a lightning storm. "I'm moving on as soon as I'm able." He struggled to lift off the saddle and heaved it over a rail. Judging by the white line around his mouth, the task appeared to take what little energy he had left.

She grabbed the gray horse blanket and laid it on the saddle. Temporary was better than nothing, even though disappointment wound through her. "Maybe you'll change your mind." Anything was possible.

He wearily wiped his eyes. "I don't see permanence in my future."

Because he'd never had any or because he didn't want it? What man would be satisfied moving from place to place? She thought of the letter he'd left and the longing in the words. She'd just have to show him the advantages of staying put.

Marley ached for him and all he'd suffered. She said quietly, "You're about to drop. I can help you make this go faster."

"I already have it, but thanks for the offer, Marley."

"Matt's been pestering us half to death, wanting to know when you'd be home." She gave him a smile. "I guess you know you've put ideas in his head. Next, he'll be sneaking behind the barn to drink whiskey and smoke."

"No need to worry. Matt's just a little kid."

She laughed. "He's a boy with big ambitions." She changed the subject. "Did you have trouble at your friend's farm?"

Roan's arm brushed against hers as he led his mare to a stall. "Depends on your definition of trouble."

Worry twisted into a knot in her stomach. "I gather things didn't go well."

"I did what I went to do, then this morning, two riders challenged our right to be on Mose's land." He attached the heavy rope across the stall door. "One got shot and died. Not by our hands, though. From someone hiding in the loft."

Marley gave a cry and grabbed his arm. "Was this person shooting at you or my father?"

"I don't think so." Roan hung the tack on a hook on the wall.

Duel paused in brushing his black gelding. "The man's beat to a frazzle and hurting, Marley Rose. The ride about did him in. He can use some food and a bed."

Heat rushed to Marley's face, and she mentally kicked herself. One day she'd learn to behave like a proper lady. "Of course. Mama is keeping supper warm for you both. I guess I'll run along." She reined in her happiness at seeing him and turned toward her home.

"Wait," Roan called. "Will you walk with me?"

"Sure. You're probably still unfamiliar with things. After all, you've not eaten at the main house before." She grinned. "Just be prepared for a huge dose of hero worship. Unless I miss my guess, Matt's looking out the window right now. I'll do the best I can to keep him quiet."

And herself too. She was babbling, but she couldn't help it. He'd asked for her company.

He offered his elbow and Marley took it. They strolled toward the main house, with her skirts swishing against his leg. The brisk fall air and the fragrant smell of the fireplaces added to the feeling that everything was all right. Roan had returned. Maybe she could convince him to stay—for his own health if for no other reason.

Unsure of what to say, she studied his bruised profile. "I found the letter you left. Our paths did cross for a reason, and I'm glad I could give you hope as well as treat your wounds."

"I never intended to come back, or I wouldn't have left the letter," he said low. "I thought you had a right to know how your kindness and companionship touched me." His gaze sought hers, and she saw something in the depths that said he didn't think he had the right to have someone care. "I haven't had much of that in a while, not from a lady."

"Roan, on the third Saturday of every month, there's a dance in town. When you fully recover, maybe you'd like to go sometime?" She rushed to add, heat flooding her cheeks, "It would be good to go with a…with a friend."

He was silent for a minute. "Remember, this job is only temporary."

"I understand." Her hopes fell and she dropped her gaze.

The lines of Roan's face deepened. He shifted his stance, then let out a deep sigh and muttered something she couldn't make out. Maybe he couldn't allow himself to accept even a moment of fun or let anything steer him from his commitment.

Finally, he met her gaze, speaking softly. "If you don't mind teaching me, I'll try to learn to dance. Just in case I'm still around."

Marley's heart thudded against her ribs. "Waltzes are easy. Mostly, you just shuffle your feet. I know you'll be a natural." It was the ones who appeared to have a board in their spines and wouldn't bend to save their lives who couldn't learn. Roan didn't appear to be like that.

"I'll just have to take your word for it." He glanced at the sky. "Look up."

She did and gasped. The sky was alive with shooting stars. "I've never seen anything so beautiful."

"It's a meteor shower."

"A what?" She'd never heard the term.

"Meteors. They're particles of frozen rock that burn up as they fall to earth," he explained softly.

"Where did you learn that?"

"The widow who raised me was an old schoolteacher, and among the things Mrs. Harper taught me was astronomy. We'd watch the night sky, and I learned the names of all the planets and constellations. She died when I was twelve, but I haven't broken myself of the habit of watching the skies." Roan's voice turned wistful.

"You must miss her something terrible."

"I do. She was full of interesting information. Mrs. Harper was ancient and couldn't get around very well, and at first I hated living with her, but I came to love her."

Marley wanted to ask what happened to his parents, but she didn't want to pry. He'd tell her in his own good time as they got better acquainted. She pulled her gaze from his face and glanced again at the sky.

"I think I like shooting stars better then shooting meteors. Just has a better ring to it," she said. Looking up, she became unsteady and began to sway.

Roan reached for her, his breath teasing the hair at her temples. "You can call them stars—or anything you like," he said huskily.

The sensation of falling again came over her even though she was anchored to this man who knew about so many things.

"I like being correct when possible," she managed to whisper, taking his elbow again.

He hesitated, visibly struggling between desire and restraint before saying, "Marley, I don't know what life holds for me, and I never want to lead you on or hurt you. I value your friendship too much for that."

"We just go where life leads us. None of us have a map. Let's just enjoy the time we have together and not worry about the future. No promises, no regrets. Deal?"

He gave her a tired smile. "Deal."

They strolled into her parent's kitchen, and kids came from everywhere, all curious about this tall drifter with the devastating injuries.

Jessie hurried in after them. "Shoo! Mr. Penny needs to eat in peace without you watching him take every single bite."

"But Marley Rose gets to stay," argued Allie, one of the older girls.

"She's different—she's helping me, and besides, she's the oldest." Jessie put an arm around the fifteen-year-old and kissed her cheek. "Honey, can you keep the little ones occupied until Mr. Penny finishes eating?"

Matthew quietly stole next to Marley and hid behind her dress. The sweet boy knew Jessie would find him, but Marley didn't have the heart to tell on him.

Allie's loud huff filled the room. "I guess, but it isn't fair."

"You're going to find that not everything about life is fair," Jessie answered. "Mr. Penny, take a seat at the table and Marley will get your plate from the warming oven."

"Thank you, ma'am," he answered. "But please call me Roan. I'm not a mister anything."

"Okay...Roan." A baby's cries came from farther inside the house, and Jessie grabbed a baby bottle from a pan of water. "When your father comes in, tell him I'll be back."

"I will, Mama," Marley said, setting a plate of meat and potatoes in front of Roan. Matthew still hid behind her, and when she sat down, the boy climbed into her lap. She gave him a stern look. "Matt, say one word and I'll make you leave."

"I promise, Mama Rose." He placed his fingers to his lips and buttoned them.

Roan ruffled the boy's hair and winked. Before long, Matt slumped back against her, sound asleep. Marley kissed the boy's cheek, and she and Roan talked low about his trip. He'd been a very lucky man to have missed the bullet and jail also.

The door opened and Duel strolled in. Marley gave him her mother's message, but before she got it all out, her mother ran into the room and directly into Duel's arms.

Marley wanted a love like her parents had. They were a set of magnets, clinking together every time they got close. She watched them hug and laugh, and her heart warmed. She imagined they'd shared a lifetime of not only private talk, but more trials than anyone could list.

She studied the dark stubble already along Roan's jaw, thinking she'd never been drawn to anyone like she was to him. The ends of his hair brushed the collar of the borrowed linsey-woolsey shirt. The shirt buttons sat open at the throat, revealing a powerful neck. His swollen eyes and bruised face still made her heart ache, and she was suddenly very grateful she'd found him on that lonely road.

His perfectly shaped lips drew her gaze. They were full and masculine and marred only by the deep split on the bottom, compliments of someone's fist. His mouth suddenly twitched, and his eyes flicked to hers.

"The way you're looking me over, I wonder if you're thinking of buying me, Marley."

Caught! Heat rushed into Marley's cheeks. She glanced at her parents to see if they were listening, but they were lost in each other. At the moment, she doubted they'd hear a freight train barreling through the house.

The thought had barely formed when her mother whispered something in Duel's ear and released a soft laugh. "You make me forget we have children to tend to. I'll meet you upstairs."

Duel released her, stepped to Marley and took Matthew, then left with Jessie.

Alone at last, Marley turned her attention back to Roan. "I wasn't staring *at* you, Roan. I was just checking to see how you're healing, that's all," she mumbled. "And I've been curious about the color of your eyes. It's been hard to see them thanks to the swelling, and I only just noticed that they're gray." The color of gunmetal.

He was charming, gentle, and kind, but the determined set of his jaw said he could be a man to reckon with when the odds weren't stacked against him.

Roan laid down his fork and propped his elbows on each side of his plate. "You know what your eyes remind me of?"

"No."

"A doe. They're large and glistening. They reveal a lot about you."

"They do?" She prayed he didn't see too much. She had far too many imperfections.

A smile teased the corner of his mouth. "I know by looking at your eyes that you keep a lot of feelings buried inside, and it rips your heart out to see anyone suffer. I can also tell by the stern glance you sometimes give that you don't put up with much when it comes to the children. How'd I do?"

"Pretty well." She wouldn't tell him that he'd read her perfectly—so much that it scared her.

If she didn't watch it, he'd see her long-buried dream to be held. To be loved. To be seen as a woman.

Ten

WHILE HE HEALED, ROAN WORKED NEAR HEADQUARTERS, repairing things and generally making himself useful. Matt and some of the other children liked to hang around, and he'd taught them how to make wooden traps for small animals, though not the painful kind. He loved spending time with them and teaching them things. From everything he could gather, every child loved their life on the Aces 'n' Eights.

He gazed over the compound and beyond, thinking how fortunate he was. An old German proverb came to mind. *The heaviest baggage for a traveler is an empty purse.*

How true. His had weighed him down, and Duel McClain's proposition had been a godsend.

The kitchen door of the main house opened, and Marley stepped out into the early morning sunshine, a babe tucked in her arms. Roan's attention riveted on the beautiful woman and the pretty blue dress she wore.

Just like each morning on a school day, she stood beside the doorway and blew on a little silver whistle like a general in petticoats. An assortment of boys and girls of all ages and sizes filed out behind her. A boy and girl about ten years old stuck their tongues out at each other, then took off in a wild chase. Some older girls who looked to be around fourteen or fifteen linked arms and walked toward the gate, laughing. A cluster of boys around those same ages cut through the trees and disappeared from view. Matt and another boy hovered close to Marley until she sent them after the others.

Soon, he was going to have to make a list of all these children to keep them straight. It seemed he'd dropped into the middle of a kid explosion, flying at him from all sides. Strange how the children had all come from different wombs to arrive in the same place. While the home bore the markings of an orphanage of sorts, love and a sense of belonging filled every inch. None of the kids here bore the scars of an unwanted child.

As he was about to turn back to his job, a boy and girl somewhere around twelve years old rushed from the house. The boy had a pronounced limp, but as the two emerged, he pulled the girl's braid, then took off hobbling toward the gate as fast as his bum leg would allow.

"I'm gonna get you, Ethan!" the girl yelled, running after him.

"You children better not dawdle. You'll be late for school!" Marley called. "And someone watch out for these littler ones!"

Roan captured the moment, storing it away in his memory. This was what a real family looked like.

Marley headed toward him, a smile curving her tempting lips. "Getting those kids off to school is a monumental undertaking. I'm worn out and my day has just started." She shifted the babe in her arms.

"I don't know how you all manage so many." Roan returned her smile. "Which triplet have you got there?"

"Dan." She lovingly brushed the fuzz on the top of his head. "Mama's got her hands full with Edith and Joe."

"I can only imagine. You look very pretty this morning."

A blush colored her cheeks. "Thank you, Roan. I wonder if I could borrow you in about an hour. I need to visit a friend who can't get around very well."

"Sure. I'll have the buckboard hitched." The prospect of spending time with her made the day a whole lot brighter.

"I need to help Mama get the babies to sleep first. Two of them have the croup and aren't feeling well."

"Just say the word." His gaze followed her as she strolled back to the house. He'd never studied a woman when she walked, and he found watching Marley fascinating. Her dress swished from side to side in time with the rise and fall of her rounded hips. Watching her reminded him of the way a boat glided through the water, easy and smooth, without a fuss. He imagined she danced the way she walked.

A grin spread across his face. She'd announced at supper last night that they'd start on the dancing lessons today. He'd have a reason to hold her in his arms, feel her heart beating against his chest, and smell her fragrance drifting around him, holding the promise of paradise.

If only for a few minutes. Then he'd remind himself she wasn't for him.

An hour later, Marley put the last baby in the crib and slipped out the door. Excited tingles danced along her spine. This visit to Granny Jack offered a chance to spend a few hours in Roan's company.

Besides, with rustlers lurking about, it paid to have an escort. Or at least that's what she told herself as she carried the basket of goodies for the dear old lady.

The borrowed holster he'd strapped around his lean hips hung low. Maybe he was thinking of rustlers also. He wore his hat pulled down on his forehead, and she could barely see his eyes when he offered his hand.

The sun peeked from the clouds like a mischievous child when Roan helped her into the buckboard. "Thank you for going with me." Careful not to wrinkle her skirt, Marley moved it over to allow room, but the seat seemed to have narrowed when his knee rested against hers.

"I'm happy to lend my services." He lifted the reins and set the buckboard in motion. "How far is it to this friend's house?"

"Granny Jack lives down the road about two miles."

"Granny Jack? Whose grandmother is she?"

Marley laughed, shaking her head. "She's no relation—everyone calls her that. You'll like her. She lives alone and is quite a character. She's up in years and always looks forward to fall and my fresh apple cake and jars of apple butter. I try to visit once a week, and we sit and talk over cups of hot tea. Granny is full of homespun wisdom."

"It must get lonely for her."

"She has a houseful of cats, but I've found carrying on a conversation with animals that can only meow falls short of having someone real to talk to. Do you like cats, Roan?"

A quick grin flitted across his lips before disappearing. "I'm more a horse and dog kind of man myself."

"I kinda am too," she confessed. "The only cats we have are the barn variety. When I was young, I had a retriever I named Boobie, and he was very special. I sure miss him."

"Boobie? That's an odd thing to name a dog."

"Hey, don't laugh! It was pretty good, considering that I hadn't learned to talk very well. I was probably trying to say doggie, and that's what came out. I also had a goat named Cheeba. Don't ask where I got that." She paused a moment before sharing something she'd never told anyone. "This may seem rather selfish, but part of me wishes I could go back to those days when I had my parents all to myself. It's not that I mind sharing, and Lord knows those kids need so much love, but"—she looked away, trying to control the tremor in her voice—"sometimes it just gets to be too much. I get lost in the crowd."

"I can understand that." He pushed back his hat, and his gray eyes were somber as he took her hand. Marley warmed under his deep, searching gaze. "I haven't been there long, but sometimes I have to escape all that noise. Marley, what do you want to do with your life?"

Tears filled her eyes. What good did it do to dream? They never came true.

"Sometimes I wake in the night with this crushing fear lying on my chest, squeezing the life from me. I'm drowning in kids and work. I want so much more than this." Her voice cracked. "I have all these stories crowding in my head, and I love to paint, but when do I ever find a minute for myself? Sometimes I think I might lose my mind."

The harnesses jangled as the horses' hooves struck the packed road. Roan probably thought she was a pitiful whiner. She had plenty of food, a warm bed, and people who loved her. From what she knew, he'd rarely had any of those, so what did she have to complain about?

"You have to make the time. Marley, this is important to your survival. You have to feed your soul as much as you feed your belly. Believe me, I know."

"Tell me more about yourself, Roan. I sense sadness so deep it makes me want to cry."

"My life is not a pretty story. My mother died when I was seven, and my sorry-ass father gave me away. Blackie Culpepper was a drunk and an outlaw, only I didn't know about the robbing and killing until later. The day my mother died, he changed my last name to Penny because he said I wasn't worth a tinker's damn as a son, and he made me go live with the Widow Harper and rode off."

"Oh, Roan, that's horrible!" Such cruelty appalled her and raised her temper.

He gave her a wry smile. "It turned out to be a blessing. Like I told you the night of the meteor shower, the old woman he gave me to was kind and loving. Mrs. Harper fed my mind. She taught me courage and gave me honor. For a lost boy, that was huge. But one night when I was twelve, she went to sleep and didn't wake up."

Marley moved closer and curled her fingers inside his. "That's way too young to be on your own. What did you do?"

"At first, I slept outside a nunnery. I found some loose boards and made a place under the porch. A nun would leave food out for the wild animals, and one day, she discovered me eating from the dish. She took me inside and told me I had to be very quiet and stay out of the way or suffer Mother Agnes's wrath." He gave her a sidelong glance. "Mother Agnes was old and as strict and rigid as

Sister Frieda was kind. I lived in a small room next to the library. I read constantly and took long walks once a day after the sister had finished her chores."

"Bless Sister Frieda." Marley pictured Roan as a frightened little gray-eyed boy with such an uncertain future. "It's amazing how you found the right people to help you along. They were almost like stepping stones."

"Sister Frieda picked up where Mrs. Harper left off, and I developed a deeper understanding of the world. From her I learned that knowledge could keep me safe, so I soaked up everything."

The buckboard rounded a bend in the road, and they rode between rows of tall trees on each side, their branches overlapping and forming a bower that blocked out the sun's rays. This section of road always seemed so private, and today it felt even more so.

Marley was intrigued by Roan's life. "What kind of knowledge exactly?"

"It's a little hard to explain but I'll try. It's reading the landscape and knowing the places to find shelter. It's learning which plants are safe to feed a starving belly. But the most important of all is how to stay alive when others want me dead. Sister Frieda had escaped torture and captivity in her homeland and knew all about survival. She was one tough lady."

"I wish I could've known her. She sounds amazing. Why did you leave there?"

"They closed the nunnery, shipped everyone back East. But I had a sense of direction."

"Well, Sister Frieda deserves an extra star in her crown." Marley had a clear picture now of the man she'd saved and, even if he didn't know it yet, she was determined to be another leg of his journey. She just hoped the ranch proved more than a stopover. He needed a secure place. And she needed a friend.

How could his father have been so cruel to just change his name and give him away? He was just one year older than Matt—had just lost his mother and was probably terrified out of his mind. Her heart hurt for the child he had been. But she had to ask one more question that had been bothering her.

"When I brought you to the ranch and doctored you, I noticed a bunch of old scars on your back. Roan, who hated you that much?"

The clop of the horses' hooves filled the air as the silence between them stretched. At last, he said, "My father. He tried to whip some backbone into me."

She'd thought that may have been the case. "That's horrible. I'm so sorry."

"Enough about that. I'm curious—how did you become interested in writing children's stories?" he asked.

"I think I was born with stories in my head. I've always loved creating new worlds and filling them with interesting people." Marley picked at a piece of lint on her brown skirt and lowered her voice. "I want to make a difference in someone's life, to really matter."

"You already do. More than you'll ever know." Roan still held her hand and stared into her eyes. She wanted to look away but found he held her captive.

"Words are powerful weapons. The world needs more writers and creative people," he said softly. "We all yearn for things beyond reach, but your dream isn't. You have the tools and I see the desire burning in you. The only thing preventing you from reaching success is finding the hours. Stop putting everyone else's needs ahead of yours."

She let out a sigh and withdrew her hand. "I'll try. I needed to hear someone say that I'm not being selfish."

Noise on the road caught her attention, and she noticed a rider cantering toward them through the bower of overhanging trees. When he pulled even, the middle-aged man slowed to a crawl and leaned forward to peer intently at them. The hair on her arms rose. He resembled a scarecrow, the way the skin stretched tight over his cheekbones, and his nose was like a bird's beak. But it was the knowing, brown-toothed leer that unleashed a quake that shook Marley all the way to her toes. She'd never seen anyone who so unnerved her. Evil poured from him like water through a sieve.

Roan rested his hand on the butt of his Colt. "Do you want something, mister?"

Without a reply, the stranger smiled and tipped his hat.

As the man rode on, Roan asked, "Do you know him, Marley?"

"I've never seen him before." Shivers still ran through her from his sharp, piercing stare. It was almost as if he hated her. Who was he, and why did he seem to know her?

Roan swiveled in the seat for a glance back, and his warning froze her. "If he ever comes around, run as fast as you can for help."

She couldn't help turning for a look as well. "Do you suppose we'll ever see a day when folks have no need to arm themselves to the teeth when they step out their door?"

"Maybe when folks become more civilized."

"This is 1899 for heaven's sake! In three months, we'll celebrate the turn of the century. We live in a world of baseball, Barnum and Bailey, and chewing gum. We should have learned something by now."

The stranger turned, his stare burning into hers. She clutched Roan's arm and whipped back around, hoping that the blackhearted man would never cross her path again.

Eleven

MARLEY AND ROAN LAPSED INTO SILENCE. SHE KEPT glancing at him, wondering what he was thinking. From time to time he frowned, but she didn't break into his thoughts. She was trying not to pry. All she knew was that the hawk-nosed man had ruined their momentary closeness.

At last, Roan halted in front of Granny Jack's small house—little more than a lean-to—and set the brake. She thought his hand might've lingered on hers when he helped her down, but then again, maybe it was nothing more than wishful thinking. But she wasn't imagining the way his shirt tightened across his broad shoulders as he reached for the basket of goodies she'd brought.

Granny Jack hobbled painfully from her shanty to greet them, wispy tendrils of silver hair flying from the knot wound on top of her head. A herd of meowing cats in every shape and color trailed behind her. "If it ain't my favorite brain-picker. Who you brung with you, girl?"

"Meet Roan Penny, Granny." Marley took the basket from Roan. "Papa hired him to work for us."

Roan removed his hat and smiled. "Pleased to meet you, ma'am."

"Didn't expect gentleman callers." The woman's cheeks flushed, and her smile showed gaps in her teeth as she pumped his hand. "Marley Rose gen'rally comes alone."

Marley stooped to kiss the leathery, wrinkled face that'd seen plenty of sunshine over the years. The heavy jowls that hung like wet drapes from a willow rod gave the heavy-set woman the look of a coonhound, but the little topknot of silver fluff spoke of her waning years.

"Come on in, young man," Granny urged.

Roan shook his head and chuckled. "You ladies have lots of talking to do. If it's all the same, I'll wait out here."

Marley shot him an anxious glance. The stranger on the road had spooked him. Surely he didn't think the fool would come back? At any rate, he seemed prepared to keep watch and protect her. A nice, warm feeling crept up from the tips of Marley's toes.

"Got a nice cup of tea about ready." Granny pushed up the old pair of spectacles that somehow always slipped to the tip of her nose. They never seemed to do her much good, but she never took them off. "Care for some, Mr. Penny?"

He shook his head. "Appreciate it, but I'll pass."

The woman cackled. "Didn't really take you for a tea drinker. Don't have nary a drop of coffee or whiskey. Holler if you change your mind. I hope you got your sittin' britches on, because we're liable to take a while."

"Now, Granny, I promised I wouldn't stay long." Marley exchanged glances with Roan before helping the old woman into the one-room cabin that had been built from scraps. The shelf that held a few dishes was made from part of a chicken coop and still had the wire across it. The herd of cats appeared to have multiplied since her last visit.

One glance at the clutter and the cats lying everywhere and Marley knew she'd be hard-pressed to control her obsession to clean and pick up. Last time she'd visited, Granny had laid down the law in no uncertain terms, and Marley didn't want to upset the woman again.

"That's a right handsome young man out there, but someone sure whooped the tar outta him." Granny lifted the teapot from the wood stove. "I practically mistook him for another stray your mama'd wagged in, 'ceptin' he's a whole bunch taller and filled out."

"I did the wagging this time. I found him in a bad way, lying near the road. I thought at first he was dead." Marley picked up a yellow tabby from the chair and set it on the floor before taking a seat.

Granny Jack laughed. "Taking up your mama's habit, huh?"

"I couldn't do much else, could I? He was half-frozen and needed help."

"You did a charitable deed, girl. I thought you might come today, it being so sunny and all, so I already made the tea." Granny Jack filled two cups, setting them on chipped saucers before adding, "Stray or not, it looks like you've already taken a shine to that young man out there."

Marley rolled her eyes, hoping to hide her feelings. She wasn't ready to share them with anyone. "You know I have no plans for marriage. I'm going to be a children's writer. I have all these stories in my head just bursting to come out."

"Plans have got a way of changing, girl."

Not likely. Marley lowered her eyes and took a sip of the hot tea, watching Granny saucer hers. She always thought the practice of pouring a small amount of tea into a saucer first before drinking it a bit odd. Granny had explained that this cooled the hot liquid and prevented scalding her mouth.

"You and Mama are two of a kind. I only did what anyone else would've done. Anyway, Roan only has one thing on his mind and it doesn't appear to be me."

The woman chided, "You know you can't lie to your old Granny Jack, now."

"I have to be honest. He's just killing time until he heals. Then he's going to go after the men who killed his friend." Marley quickly related the events, the killing of Mose Mozeke and the two men who'd ridden upon them on his return. "A sniper took down one of the riders just as he was about to tell them something, and that rotten sheriff in San Saba almost blamed the death on Roan. I really think the sheriff would've thrown him in jail if my papa hadn't been there."

Granny Jack peered over the wire-rimmed spectacles and stroked the fur of the two cats now in her lap. "It's a good thing Duel went with him. Folks tend to back up when he's around. I never met a man who cast such a big shadow, and getting riled up probably did his blood good. Veins get rusty without some good ol' righteous anger to clean 'em out from time to time."

"Don't forget about Roan," Marley said. "He's cut from the same wool. I wish he'd forget about those bad people in San Saba."

"Honey, every tub has got to sit on its own bottom. We all have things to do and ways of doing them that sometimes don't make a lick of sense to anyone but us. I seem to recall you burning for some justice of your own when the papa of those triplets of your'n up and left them. You wanted to hunt him down and shoot him."

The old widow was right. She always was. Marley glanced out the thick window at the man who had occupied her thoughts of late. "That was different. Those were babies unable to care for themselves. Roan's obsession with finding the killers could put him in a grave, and they almost ended his life twice already. I'm terrified for him."

True that they hadn't known each other long, but she couldn't bear the thought of him getting killed. She could still recall his gentle touch on her cheek, when their faces had been so close the time she'd shaved him. The temptation so strong to kiss him.

"I don't know too much, child, and that's the truth. Lord knows I ain't got much book learning, but I can see that man out there has more guts than twenty men. The way he studies people, taking their measure, and the strong set of his jaw reminds me of my Mooney. Them kind don't know the meaning of quitting. He gets something stuck in his craw, and he's gonna work like the devil to pry it out. Even knowing they might end his life, he has got to fight for his friend. You'd do the same, and don't deny it."

"I know, but I don't like it. He doesn't have any family. I reckon we're all he's got, assuming he'll have us."

"A good bargain if you ask me." Granny saucered some more tea, and a black cat leaped onto the middle of the table, almost knocking over the cream. "What else is frettin' you, child?"

"Nothing. We're just discussing things." Marley idly began rearranging the dishes, wiping away crumbs and straightening the spoons.

"Stop that." Granny lightly slapped her hand. "Now, missy, you didn't drive all this way with the excuse of bringing me three jars of apple butter and a cake that I'd be better off without." A calico jumped into Granny's lap, nudging her hand for a gentle touch. "I read you like a book, so don't go claiming nothing's fretting you."

"Well, there's the rustling that's keeping everyone's nerves jumping. Even though Papa tries not to show it, I can see the worry deep in his eyes. A storm is coming—I feel it—and I don't know from where. And then on the way over here today, a strange-looking man passed us on the road, and he stared so intently it brought chills. When Roan asked him if he needed something, he just gave us this odd smile, didn't say a word, just tipped his hat and rode on."

"Dear heavens! Do you think he's involved with the rustling?"

"I don't know. He stared a hole right through me, paying Roan no attention—only me. The man had such deep hatred written on his face and in his deep-set eyes. I haven't been this shaken in a long time." How could she have angered him when she'd never met him?

Granny pushed up her glasses and covered Marley's hand. "We can't hide from trouble. It'll find us no matter what we do. Stand tall, girl, and don't let it knock you down. If it does, get right back up and fight."

"I plan to. I just hope I can weather this."

"You can. Child, you let your imagination run away with itself and live in a fantasy world three-fourths of the time. I don't know who that stranger was on the road, and nor do you. His intentions might've been completely innocent."

"I know. But this is different." Something in her gut said so, yet it was hopeless to try to convince Granny. Marley refilled her cup and leaned to kiss Granny's cheek. "Thank you for listening. I needed some of your wisdom."

"I've been around a long time, child, and learned a lot as I went. I've seen my share of joys and bitter disappointments too. You'll do the same. It's called living." Granny's watery gaze met Marley's. "You've got something else on your mind. You can't hide anything from me."

"I've given up trying. I must be an open book the way you always see through me. But how I feel doesn't make any difference—Roan insists he's only here temporary. Says he's a drifter and permanence isn't in the cards for him."

"I once met a man who had a bad case of wanderlust, and I shackled him good 'n' tight with the bonds of wedded bliss." She cackled. "Mooney Jack was as good a husband as you'll find. Sure is lonesome since the fool died and left me a poor, old widow woman."

"I'm sure it is. You were married for such a long time."

"Fifty-five years."

The wire-rimmed glasses fell from Granny's face and clattered to the floor. Marley crawled under the table to get them. "Why on earth don't you get a pair of spectacles that fit?"

"Don't have no need for any." Granny took them from Marley and put them back on. "These belonged to Mooney, bless his poor soul. After he passed on and I took to losing my eyesight a bit, I got 'em out of the drawer. Shoot! Weren't no need of getting my own when these were sitting there wasting."

"Not everyone's vision is alike. I doubt you can see much better with them."

"Can too. We took the same dadgum pills Doc gave us. What was good enough for Mooney was extra fine for me."

"You're hopeless," Marley said with a laugh.

"Not gonna argue with that, girl." The woman jolted

to her feet, sending the calico running for higher ground. "Let's cut that apple cake. It'll go real good with this tea, and you take some out to that young man." Granny rose and found a knife and two small, mismatched plates.

"Yes, he might like some." Marley took a small plate of the cake and a fork out to Roan.

He glanced up in surprise, a grin curving his mouth. "You didn't have to do this."

"I know, but we wanted to share. It wasn't right not to." She noticed how his large hand brushed hers, sending tingles through her when he took the plate.

"Thanks." Seemingly on impulse, he leaned in and kissed her cheek.

His lips against her skin made her pulse race and warmth flood her face. She tried her best to erase her silly smile but found it impossible. "We won't be much longer."

"No rush. Enjoy your visit. Granny Jack is my kind of people."

"Mine too." Her heart all fluttery, she hurried inside.

With pieces of cake in front of them, Marley's old friend leaned over. "Now tell me more about your Roan Penny out there."

"He's not *my* anything." But if things worked out…who knew what the future held? She put her fingers to her cheek and was hard-pressed to keep from smiling.

Granny took a big bite and murmured approval. "This apple cake is one of your best, child. Glad I don't have to share the rest with that brood over at your place. I'd have nary a crumb left. Let's get back to your handsome young drifter. Deny all you want, but I can see you're just about bursting to talk."

Marley told her about the night the sky exploded with shooting stars. "I'd never seen so many." She lowered her voice. "Roan leaned close, and for a moment I could barely breathe, the yearning was so powerful." She closed her eyes, remembering the way his breath had fluttered the hair at her temples like soft butterfly wings. She inhaled the fragrance

of the night swirling around them and recalled the way
his hand had anchored her. The closeness of his body and
the power that seemed to come from him lingered in her
memory like the taste of something rare.

"Shooting stars, huh?" Granny's eyes twinkled. "I pre-
dict the kissing won't be far off."

Delicious tingles ran up Marley's spine. The thought of
him actually kissing her lips filled her with longing. She let
out a loud sigh. "But he may die before he gets the chance."

"Men like Roan Penny and Duel McClain burn with
a powerful need to see justice done, no matter the risk to
themselves." Granny Jack stilled as she seemed to drift back
in time. "My Mooney Jack was such a man. About forty
years back, a gang roamed through here, killing and burning
and torturing. I remember how terrified I was. I can still see
Mooney standing alone, legs braced apart, in the middle of
that moonlit road with a torch that must've had a three-foot
flame. My, he was such a sight to behold! Mooney cussed a
blue streak and yelled fit to beat all. He promised he'd hunt
down every last one of them even if it took the rest of his
life and led him all the way to the gates of hell."

"What happened?" The story had Marley captivated.
She could picture the scene vividly in her mind and made a
mental note to put it into a story. Already she was painting
the scene on canvas.

"The gang laid real low for a while, but Mooney started
goin' out after dark and not coming home till morning. I
laid awake, fearful he was lying dead somewhere. Several
times he was gone a week or more. One by one, he found
those murderin', thievin' varmints and took them to jail."
Granny's jowls shook. "Several took a wrong turn and
landed in a grave instead."

"Oh, Granny, I wish I'd have known Mooney Jack.
Roan is just like him. So is my papa."

"Mooney was some kind of man, and I loved him to
his last breath on earth." Granny took another bite of cake.
"That's the kind of man you want. I'm thinking that out

there in the yard sits one. Grab hold of that cowboy an' don't let him get away."

"One thing I didn't tell you is he rides a gray mare. Poor thing is pitiful looking, but Roan loves it."

Granny slapped her thigh. "You don't say. That cinches it. He's a keeper."

They finished off their cake and made a new pot of tea. They'd been talking for quite a while, and Marley hoped Roan wasn't getting tired of waiting, but she had one more question for Granny Jack that had been preying on her mind for a while.

She took their empty plates to the dish tub to wash before she left. "I didn't realize you were here so far back. You've probably known our family since Mama and Papa married."

"Yep, sure have."

"Were you there when I was born?"

Alarm rippled across the old woman's face and left two bright spots on her cheeks. Granny whipped off her glasses and polished them on her apron until the round lenses sparkled. "Now, about Roan Penny standing guard out there…he's like an old dog with a bone. Right now, he's planning and setting a trap. I'll bet you anything, 'cause that's what I'd do."

Marley narrowed her eyes. "Why did you change the subject?"

Granny grabbed for her spectacles as they slipped off her nose. She caught them before they hit the floor. "Dadburned glasses!"

Desperate for an answer, Marley pressed harder. "Were you there the night I was born? It's a simple question."

"Well, not exactly. I sort of—" Granny held up a cat and rubbed the soft fur across her deeply lined cheek. "Don't you hafta be running along, child? I don't wanna make you late."

It was plain that the widow had no intention of talking about Marley's birth, though for the life of her, Marley couldn't figure why. She finally gave up and washed the dishes. And when she and Granny walked outside again,

Roan stepped from the shadow of the cabin and handed her his empty plate.

"That cake sure hit the spot, Granny Jack. Thank you." Roan kissed the old dear's cheek and she blushed, appearing pleased at the attention.

"Marley tells me you ride a gray mare. I once owned one. Never had a better horse." Granny cackled like an old hen looking for grain. "Course now I cain't ride anything wilder than a rocking chair. Come back again when you can stay longer." She hugged Marley and whispered loudly, "I like your man. If'n I was younger, I'd steal him from under your nose."

Heat rose to Marley's face. She glanced toward Roan. Twinkling in his eyes suggested he'd heard every word. She wanted to groan and find a hole to crawl into. Heaven forbid that any of their conversation had drifted beyond the cabin walls. Especially the part about kissing.

Granny took the dessert plate from Marley. "I haven't spent a finer afternoon. Come again whenever you take a notion."

"I will." Marley accepted Roan's warm hand and climbed into the wagon. The second she sat down, all her worries evaporated, and the cowboy beside her was the only thing to fill her mind. Maybe they could take the long way back. Some long, winding road where trouble couldn't find them.

Twelve

ROAN LAY IN HIS BUNK A WEEK LATER AFTER PUTTING IN a hard day. He was worn out, but his mind kept drifting back to Marley and their ride out to Granny Jack's. He'd seen quite a lot of her since then. He loved having her near. She was funny and kind, and he'd never seen a quicker mind. It was getting harder and harder to remember why their relationship could never go beyond friends.

Yet *friend* didn't exactly describe how he felt about her. Nor would it ever.

He had to find a way to either stay away from her or else get well enough to leave before he hurt her. But how, when he yearned with all his being to hold and kiss her?

The bunkhouse door opened, and Hardy and Judd strolled inside. They were arguing over a poster Judd held.

"Hey, Roan." Hardy pushed the handbill at Roan. "You're going to like this."

"What is it?" Roan sat up and took the poster and froze. It advertised a horse racing event at the county fair—in San Saba.

"It's the perfect plan," Judd insisted.

Hardy snorted. "Yeah, if you want Roan dead. That's enemy territory. Besides, he doesn't even have a horse that can win. That gray mare is plumb ugly."

"But she can flat run." Roan stood, his mind whirling.

"No better way to get a look at folks without really seeming to."

"Maybe I'd best check your hearing, son. Did you overlook the dying part?" Hardy asked. "Those bastards will silence you for good."

"They'll try." A muscle worked in Roan's jaw. "Doesn't mean they'll succeed."

Judd slapped him on the back. "That's the spirit. Me and Hardy and maybe some of the boys could go with you to even the odds a bit. How sure are you about that mare?"

"I'd stake my life on her." And Roan had, many a time. "She's nimble on her feet and fast."

"There you go!" A gleam filled Judd's eyes. "I'd love a chance to clean out that mess over there. I'm guessing there's lots of good folks who'd welcome that."

"Her pitiful looks could be a real advantage," Hardy drawled. "No one would expect such a plug-ugly horse to win the purse."

Roan glanced at the poster again and his hopes fell. "The entry fee is twenty dollars. I won't have that until I get paid at the end of the month, and the fair will be over by then."

Hardy rubbed his whiskers. "I reckon I've got a little something stuck in a sock under my mattress that I can loan."

"So that's where you've been keeping your stash." Judd gave Hardy a playful jab. "Wish I'd have known last month when I wanted to invite pretty Sally Ann Winslow to the ice cream parlor in town."

"Keep your paws off my money." Hardy narrowed his gaze and drew his one long eyebrow into a stern line. "If any comes up missing, I'll know you helped yourself. And if that's the hardest you can hit, I suggest you stay behind with the womenfolk when we ride to San Saba."

Judd laughed. "Just joking, old man. I've known about your money for a long time." He turned to Roan. "I have some put back too, and if you're needing it, it has your name on it."

"Thanks to you both. I'll have to think about it."

Roan slowly sat down. A disguise of some kind might fool everyone for a while and let him get the lay of the land. He glanced at the poster again. The race was in two weeks. Would he be ready by then? If he did this, he'd have to be. This chance was too important to miss.

Some of the other ranch hands drifted in, and they dug out the cards. Before long, the men were raising hell along with their antes. To escape the noise, Roan shrugged into his jacket and went outside. He strolled to the corral and leaned against the rail. The night was clear, a million stars twinkling overhead.

"I'm coming for you, you murdering hoodlums." His voice was as jagged as shards of glass. "As God is my witness, I'm coming."

He glanced up, deep in thought, mulling over the county fair, planning everything he needed to do to get ready. He had to be smart about this. To fail would make them come after him harder than ever.

Footsteps crunched behind him.

"Do you have some time for a friend?" Marley asked.

Her soft voice floated over him like a layer of expensive silk. Roan turned and was struck by the sight of the moonlight shining on her hair.

"I always have time for a pretty lady." He grinned. "Are you looking for an escape too?"

"How did you guess?" She laughed. "I helped Mama get the little ones to bed, and those kids wore me out. I needed some fresh air to relax. It's beautiful out here, with all these stars. But the thing I cherish most is the quiet. How about you?"

"The men are playing cards, and words were getting pretty heated." He settled his shoulder against hers, wishing he could find the courage to tell her how she made him feel. How deep pleasure wound through him just to have her next to him. And how afraid he was that fate would step in and leave him holding empty dreams. Best to silence the yearning. Somehow.

Marley glanced up, her eyes shining in the moonlight. "You're not a card player?"

"Life is a big enough game of chance without the need to wager hard-earned money." Roan drew in a breath, catching the edge of her fragrance mingled with the scents of the night. "Besides, I had some serious thinking to do." He pulled the folded poster from inside his jacket and held it out.

She took it. "What's this?"

"A horse race at the county fair…in San Saba."

Her eyes grew wide. "No. Surely you're not thinking of entering. Tell me I'm wrong."

"The men said they'll pitch in to raise the fee and go along to make sure any fight I get into is fair. How can I refuse their help?"

"By saying no. This is dangerous, and all the friends in the world can't stop a bullet. Roan, you almost died before. Do you want them to finish the job?" Her trembling hand brushed her eyes. Tears? Roan swallowed guilt. "And another thing," she went on. "You're still dealing with the effects of your other ordeal." She threw up her hands. "I'm not going to dig a grave. I'm just not."

She paused again, this time to still her quivering lips. "How could you risk your life this way? How can you do this to Matt? To me? I swear, I don't understand you. All of us care for you. I care. Why don't you care for yourself?" Marley sounded like the boiler of a train engine spewing and gushing hot steam. Just as he thought she'd settled down, she fired up again with another headful. "I'm through worrying about you! Just go ahead and get yourself killed!"

He gently took her hands and faced her, staring into her dark eyes. "I can't promise that I'll stay alive. I can only say that I'll be on guard for trouble. Despite what you evidently think, I do have a brain. At least half a one. I'm not going to waltz in there, daring that gang to shoot me. I'm going to devise a plan and move carefully."

"That's smart to think through it first."

"I don't know exactly how for sure, but I'm going to

root out each rider who was there that night and make them pay. Mose deserves to rest easy in the grave."

"And what do you deserve, Roan?" she asked softly.

That was hard to answer. He'd deserved more than Blackie's whippings, the name-calling, and watching everything and everyone he cared about turn to dust.

"This isn't about me."

"Isn't it?" she cried. "For me it is."

He released her hands and brushed back her silky hair. "There are some things a man has to do in order to look at himself in a mirror. This is one." He kissed her smooth forehead. "I don't want to fight with you. There's too much fighting in this world as it is." He turned to go back inside.

"What *do* you want?"

"To kiss you," he answered softly before he could remind himself again that the best thing he could do was to saddle up and ride. The pull was too strong, and he didn't have that much strength to walk away. He swung back around to face her. "Heaven help me, I want to taste your lips. I have wanted to ever since I woke up to find you sitting beside my bed."

"Then do it," she challenged before softening and stepping close enough that he couldn't escape the sweet scent of her. "Hold me, Roan." Marley slid an arm around his neck. "Hold me and kiss me. Life is too short, and we may not get many more chances."

Her tilted head, lowered eyes, and mouth that begged to be kissed made him forget everything except hunger for her. He didn't know what would happen when the kiss ended and she wanted more than he could give, but he couldn't keep his mouth from crushing against hers. Burning need silenced the voices in his head. He put his hands around her slender waist and pulled her closer. She fit against him as though a carver had whittled her especially for the shape of his body.

The tiny cry that escaped her fueled the heat scorching everything inside. He nibbled on the edges of her lips, savoring, exploring, teasing the velvet warmth of her mouth. Strange how a person never knew how something tasted until he sampled it for the first time. Fair to say he'd never tasted such sweetness and desire. Something had told him her kisses would uproot everything inside and leave him a mass of quivering jelly, and that's exactly what Marley did.

Heaven help him. He crushed her to him so tightly he could feel the wild beating of her heart next to his. Daring to run his hand down her luscious curves, he deepened the kiss, wishing, praying, hoping it would never end.

The fact that Marley didn't push away told him she wanted this as much as he, and so did her whispered plea to hold her, kiss her.

Mystery and desire. Passion and promise. Marley Rose McClain tasted of hope.

She melted in his arms, her breasts crushed against his chest, and clung to him. Roan's hands wandered down her back, her waist, and ended at those flared hips that drove him beyond insane. Little mewling sounds squeezed from her throat, seeming to beg him not to stop. A shiver of pleasure ran up his spine.

When the need to breathe drove their lips apart, she stared up at him. "I've never known anyone like you," she whispered against his cheek. "No one has ever made me feel cherished before."

"They must be imbeciles," Roan muttered hoarsely. "Or blind as bats."

Anyone should have been able to see the special woman she was.

He took her face between his hands and lightly kissed her lips. "I shouldn't have done this, and your father would have my hide if he knew, but I can't say I'm sorry."

The moments they'd just shared were the best he'd ever spent, and he'd be damned if he would apologize.

Marley caressed his jaw. "No promises, no regrets."

Roan released her. "Run far away from me. I'll only cause you hurt."

"I can't," she whispered, running her fingers along his arm. "It's too late."

"Nothing is too late. I'm not the kind of man you need."

"Sorry, but you don't get to determine that." Marley ran a fingertip across his lips. "What are you searching for, Roan?"

A pot of gold at the end of the rainbow? A place to belong? The kindness of strangers?

"One day I'd like to have a small plot of ground to call my own," he answered softly. "A place where I can lay down roots so deep no one can ever yank them out."

"What will happen then, when you've reached the end of your search?"

"I'll find peace and sleep a dreamless sleep."

"I hope you get that. One day you might just own more than a gray horse and a holey pair of boots."

"Yeah, maybe." If he was lucky enough. Roan stuck his hands in his pockets to keep from reaching for her again and glanced up at the stars. "You noticed my footwear?"

"They'd be pretty hard to miss," she drawled.

"I'll have you know these boots and I have walked many a mile together." He tried for a teasing tone but seemed to fall short. "Bet you didn't know that once boots mold to a man's feet, they won't fit anyone else."

"I imagine that takes a pretty long while."

"Years." He was having trouble keeping his gaze from the long column of her throat and the hollow where her pulse softly beat. He itched to pull her close, to wind his fingers in her hair, and speak the words she wanted to hear.

He should go back into the bunkhouse and stop pretending things could ever be different.

His father's voice grated inside his head. *You're worthless, boy. Not fit to shine my shoes. I curse you.*

Roan closed his eyes to block out Blackie's face. "Marley, I never dreamed a woman like you existed, but you're too beautiful, too talented, too smart to get tangled up with a common ranch hand who's trying to buy trouble. I'm not a character in one of your stories that you can fix."

"You don't need fixing. I wouldn't change anything about you." Her voice broke, and Roan called himself every name he could think of.

"I wish—" The door to headquarters swung open. Just as well.

Duel strolled out with his arm around Jessie. Roan quickly put plenty of space between him and Marley. It worried him a little that the man headed directly for them. Had Duel seen them kissing?

"Nice night, sir," Roan called. "Not a cloud in the sky."

When Duel reached them, he wore a big grin. "So it is. Marley Rose, your mama and I are going to look at the stars. The babies are asleep under Allie's watchful eye, but stay close in case she needs help. The girl's a little scatterbrained at times."

Jessie patted his chest. "Now, honey, she does her best."

"I know." Duel pulled his wife a little closer. "Marley Rose, we won't be gone long."

"Okay, Papa." She grinned. "You two have fun."

Roan watched them stroll off arm in arm. Something told him they wouldn't give the sky one glance. He leaned against the corral rails. "I should probably go inside."

"Please, just a little longer." Bright spots of color stained her cheeks. "Would you like to begin your dance lessons?"

She had dangled a carrot in front of him. Good sense told him no, but his heart said dance lessons couldn't hurt. She would be the teacher and he the pupil.

"Just for a few minutes." He straightened, hoping this wasn't a mistake.

She showed him the basic steps. "Let your body move with mine and follow what I do."

He opened his arms, and she walked into the circle without hesitation. Her slight form pressing against him aroused a hunger so deep it shook him. Damn that carrot. "This is a mistake. I shouldn't."

"Shouldn't what? Find any enjoyment?"

Shouldn't let her closeness open the door he'd closed.

In answer to her murmured question, Roan curled his hand around hers and brought it to his chest. "This feels… It's nice."

"See, I told you," Marley whispered. "I just wish you didn't have this cloud hanging over your head. I feel danger lurking around us, and it scares me. Oh, Roan, I wish you weren't going to race in that fair. You could die, and I don't think I could stand it if you did. I'm afraid for you. For us."

"There's risk to everything. I can't let them win. All my life, people have been taking from me." He couldn't control the muscle quivering in his jaw. "I won't let them take anyone or anything else. The price is too great."

"I understand, or least I'm trying." Marley looked up at him. "Granny Jack says that every tub has to sit on its own bottom."

Roan chuckled. "She does, huh?"

"I told her about your determination."

"She's a very nice lady and one I'd like for a grand-mother if I could choose."

"Are you sure you've never danced?" Marley asked softly.

"Positive."

"Because you're already doing it—even without music."

She'd probably think him looney to know he was simply moving to what he heard in his head and hoping for this time with her in his arms to never end. He placed his lips to her temple and inhaled deeply.

A small voice suddenly said, "Mama Rose, I need you."

Marley glanced down. "Matt, what are you doing out of bed?"

"I wasn't sleepy, and I…I need you to read me a story." Matt took her hand. "One from that special book of yours, the one you said was a secret."

Roan dropped his hold. "Go take Matt on an adventure. I have to go anyway."

Another minute with her curves against him and he'd do something he shouldn't. There was only so much tempta-tion a man could stand before he broke.

Matt tugged on her hand. "Let's go read some more about that little boy that's just like me."

"You haven't even spoken to Mr. Penny. Mind your manners," Marley gently scolded.

"Hi, Mr. Penny." Matt looked at him, pushing the hair from his eyes. "Now can we?"

"Go on." Roan brushed her soft cheek with a knuckle. "Your stories bring the boy so much enjoyment. Someday I hope you let me read them."

"Only if you promise not to laugh. Come along, Matt. I'll read you a story, but only one. Then you have to go to sleep."

Roan's throat tightened as his gaze followed them into the house—the woman with a dream and a little boy who worshipped her. Marley couldn't know it, but she was kinda like his Sister Frieda. Both had come along at the right time on his journey.

Except he'd never once thought about kissing the kind nun.

Thirteen

SEVERAL EVENINGS LATER AS THE SUN GAVE OFF ITS LAST golden rays, Roan took Shadow for a hard run across the pastures. He'd started to make a point of doing it each day since deciding to enter the race. Nerves tightened in his stomach for several reasons. One was the trip to San Saba and the uncertainty of what that might bring. But the biggest cause of nerves was Marley. He'd made a point of avoiding her since the kiss, but he didn't know how much longer he could.

The pretty lady didn't seem inclined to take his advice, and he didn't want to be cruel. That wasn't him.

Maybe someday he'd have more to offer, but for now, all he had was his strong back and willing hands. Not enough for a fine woman like Marley Rose McClain.

The mare ate up the ground, jumping stumps and creeks with ease. The wind blew back Roan's hair and filled him with exhilaration and a sense of being one with the animal.

Shadow would be ready in no time, and she stood a good chance of snatching the purse. And that was only the first victory he'd take. Roan's thoughts were on finally finding Mose's killers as he topped the hill—and right into a painter's easel. Pieces of the wood went flying as Marley McClain yelled and leaped out of the way.

A hard left jerk on the reins helped him narrowly miss

plowing into her horse. He gulped in a harsh breath that stung his lungs.

"Did the mare brush you?" Roan asked, jumping off Shadow before she'd stopped. "Did I hurt you? Talk to me." He was afraid to touch Marley for fear he'd make things worse.

Why wasn't she replying? He could understand the dark glare, though. No mystery there. The last thing he'd wanted to do today was plow into the boss's daughter. Thank God she didn't appear to be bleeding.

He called himself an idiot and cursed the telling silence as he quickly gathered the splintered legs of the easel. But the question was what to do with them now. He glanced at Marley as she picked up a canvas from the ground. She had yet to utter a word, and her silence was deafening. If she'd just tear into him, he'd feel better.

"If you want to kick my rear end, I'll bend over." Roan finally laid the broken easel on the ground. "I didn't see you in time to stop. I'm sorry."

He gave up on trying to figure out the right thing to do and pulled her and her painting close. She trembled from head to toe, and the fact that she hadn't hauled off and hit him must have meant she hadn't recovered from the shock. He rubbed her back and stiff spine.

"What were you doing? You could've killed me!" she finally yelled in his face.

"Believe me, I know just how close I came. I was practicing for the race, and the hill blocked you from view." He pushed back tendrils of hair from her beautiful eyes. "If I'd hurt you, I couldn't live with myself."

"I found myself with some free time and came out here away from everyone to paint." She glared at him. "It was peaceful until"—her gaze went to the splintered wood—"this."

"I'll buy you another easel as soon as I get paid." Thank goodness the mare hadn't planted her hooves on the canvas, or his butt would be in a bigger sling. "I promise. Is the paint on that dry? I don't want you to get it on that pretty dress. I love that shade of blue. It looks real good on you."

"Compliments aren't going to get you out of this." Marley stepped back, clutching her masterpiece and tapping one foot. "I never expected to get trampled to death on my own property."

"Technically, it was just the easel, and you're unharmed." He peered closer. "Aren't you?"

"Relax, I'm fine." She hadn't eased her grip of the painting. She acted like he was about to snatch it from her.

"I don't see your paints." He nudged aside the clumps of silver beard grass with the toe of his boot. A frightened rabbit leaped out and scurried for other cover.

"Stop looking. They're safe in my saddlebags. I'd already started packing up before my brush with death."

Leave it to a writer to exaggerate. Still, he should've been more careful.

"How can I make it up to you?" He moved to her side and touched her arm. "Tell me and I'll make it happen."

She relaxed a little, and a smile teased the corners of her mouth. She tilted her head. "I would say stop avoiding me, but right now, a kiss comes to mind."

Of course, nail him to the wall. He couldn't very well refuse. He'd make it brief. It wouldn't mean anything and would smooth ruffled feathers.

He pressed his lips to her cheek and backed away.

"No, sir. That was not a kiss. You'll have to do much better."

"You are a stickler for doing things right, Marley." He couldn't even pretend to be reluctant, no matter how he kept calling himself a fool. Roan all too happily captured her lips and drank of the sweetness he held in his dreams each night.

Liquid fire raced through his body. He didn't need to stand in a storm and dare lightning to hit him to know this kiss held equal power. His heart beat loudly in his ears, and his knees wobbled.

Marley clung to him with one hand and her painting with the other, throwing herself into the kiss.

Damn, the lady knew how to get under his skin.

It was all he could do to release her and step back. "I should probably get you home. Supper will soon be ready." He thumbed back his hat. "Why is it that you escaped kitchen duty?"

Work on the Aces 'n' Eights never ended—especially not for Marley and her mother.

Marley tilted her head and smiled. "Mama shoved me out the door and ordered me to have some fun. She said she had enough help. I wonder what's going on with her. She's never done that."

"Anyone's guess." Maybe Jessie had finally realized her daughter was buckling under the load. Whatever the reason, he was glad to see it. He motioned to her painting. "Can I see that?"

She shielded it against her, biting her lip. "I've never shown my paintings to anyone."

"I just want to see what you captured, satisfy my curiosity."

"I'll show it to you on one condition. Tell me why you've been avoiding me."

Roan glanced away and shifted his weight. "Marley, it's best this way. I don't know how to make you understand that I can't give you what you want, so don't wait for me to change. I can't."

"We can still be friends." Marley raised her chin. "Or did you decide against that also?"

The hurt in her eyes almost undid him. Pain stabbed his heart. She'd saved his life and this is the way he repaid her?

"We will always be friends." Until she found she couldn't, then he'd find the strength to ride out of her life. He took her hand. "Look, I'm about to stick my head into the lion's mouth. I don't know if I'll survive. I don't know what the future holds for me." He flashed her a wry grin. "My future is a bit murky. I can't, I won't, ask you to share it."

She studied him for a long minute before letting out a sigh, then nodding to herself. "I'm glad we're friends at least. All right, fine. What do you think of my painting?"

Glad to change the subject, Roan studied the work of art. In the dying orange and purple light, he took in all of her painstaking work. For someone untrained, she had real promise.

She clasped her hands together in expectation. "What do you think?"

"It's good, Marley." He tilted it this way and that. "You have a great eye for color and blending shades together to add depth. You do have a wonderful gift."

Her face fell. "But? Let me have the rest," she managed tightly.

"I don't know much about painting. I think it's good."

"I don't want good. I want great, beautiful, fantastic, stunning." She chewed her lip.

"Maybe it's a little *too* perfect and there's not enough detail."

"What do you mean?"

"You don't paint from your heart." He pointed to the vegetation. "You paint with your eyes. Shadows should dance where the fading light hits them. Over here where you have the herd, you missed the covey of quail next to these bushes."

"Oh dear, I didn't even see them."

Roan handed her the canvas. "Who am I to criticize?"

"You're not. You're helping me. Did you learn to paint?"

"Not really. Sister Frieda liked to though, and she taught me a few things."

"Such as?"

"Maybe put red berries on the possum haw. You drew that rock perfectly but left out the armadillo resting next to it." He moved his finger to the sky above them, then to her painting. "Add the line of darker clouds here that warn of colder weather bearing down from the north. Like your stories, it's the little details that make a person feel as though they're standing in the middle of the scene."

"In other words, I stink."

With a finger under her chin, he lifted her eyes to his. "Not at all." She was so close he could kiss her again. Before he let himself get lost, he glanced toward the sun sinking below the horizon. "We should go."

Marley put the painting in her saddlebag and thrust her foot into the step he made with his hands to help her mount her horse. Roan swung into his saddle, and they headed toward headquarters. He glanced at her, glad that her anger at him seemed to have faded. But from the tight line around her mouth, it seemed as though she struggled to contain something she wanted to say.

The silence stretched, broken only by the sounds the horses made.

Finally, Marley spoke. "How do you know about so many things?"

"I owe that to both Mrs. Harper and Sister Frieda." He grinned. "Mrs. Harper especially wanted me to be well-rounded. In truth, I think she viewed me as a special project and certainly attacked the job with zeal. Not too many twelve-year-olds know about astronomy, science, and the arts."

Marley laughed. "I can vouch for that. If they can read and cipher, they're doing well. Shoot, I don't know about any of those subjects, and I'm twenty."

"You don't live with a schoolteacher either," he pointed out.

"Very true. I wish I had your learning though. You're truly a pupil of the world and sometimes I think that's the best kind." Marley leaned to stroke his mare's neck. "Shadow has such a sweet way about her and I can definitely testify that she can run. She flew over that hill like a streak of greased lightning. I think you stand a chance of winning." She laughed. "But I've heard all my life to never bet on a gray horse. Something about them being bad luck."

"Then I have an advantage already. But winning the race isn't the real reason I entered. It just provides an excuse for being in town. It gives me a shot at finding the men who killed Mose." Pray to God he did. He itched to settle the score and to learn who had left the long, silk thread he and Duel had found in the barn. If it did belong to a woman...that changed things.

Still, no way would he believe a woman was involved in murder. There had to be another explanation. Maybe she'd been there against her will. Now that he could definitely believe. This group was as ruthless as he'd ever seen.

Marley's chestnut wandered closer to Shadow, and Marley's leg brushed Roan's, the contact jolting him. He closed his eyes for a second and soaked up the warmth before he inched away and gazed out across the rolling landscape.

These two weeks since he'd arrived in the back of Marley's buckboard had brought much-needed peace. The land offered a silent balm to his ragged soul. Duel McClain was easy to work for. In the quiet times when Roan's thoughts seemed to be loudest, he wished Blackie had been like Duel, instead of mean clear to the bone. He'd missed having a real father. A family.

Roan dragged his thoughts back to Marley. "How long have you been interested in painting?"

"Most of my life. Even as a little girl, I drew pictures. I didn't learn to paint until a few years ago, though. A man came to Tranquility selling Arthur D. Winston paintings. Have you ever heard of him?"

"I can't say I have." Roan couldn't hold back a grin. He loved hearing Marley talk about her childhood and, hearing the excitement in her voice, pictured her with pigtails and freckles.

"Anyway, I bought one. I have it hanging in my parlor. I dearly cherish that painting. You might've seen it."

"Since I'm unfamiliar with his work, I couldn't say. But the stories you wrote and illustrated for Matt—did you know that you could make a lot of money doing that? Even illustrating for other writers."

Her eyes widened. "How would I find someone who's looking for them?"

"I seem to recall an advertisement in the general store in San Saba. I'll make a point to go by and see if it's still there."

"Roan, my whole life began to change when I found you. I think it was fate."

He met the dark pools of her eyes, wanting to tell her that fate had never been too kind to him. Born under the waning moon on Friday the 13th had sealed his fate. But maybe not entirely blocked good luck. Marley had found him and saved his life. That had to count for a lot.

"Granny Jack believes everything happens for a reason and there are no coincidences," Marley Rose went on. "I think so too."

They reached the barn, and Roan dismounted and helped her down. He wished he could freeze these moments of bright hope and save them for when he needed them most.

Matt suddenly popped up, grinning, from behind a bench bathed in shadows. "Hi, Mr. Penny."

"You don't have to keep calling me 'mister.' Can you call me Roan?"

"Nope. Mama Jessie said I hafta use 'mister' and 'missus' when I speak to grown-ups. If I ain't polite, I'll have to sit in the naughty corner." His grin showed a missing tooth on top. "Bet you don't know what I have in my pocket."

Roan put a finger to his jaw and cocked his head sideways. "Let's see. Is it a horned toad?"

"Nope." Matt came closer and gazed up in that funny little way he had that made a lump block Roan's throat. The kid seemed happy, yet deep sadness lurked behind his eyes. He was like an old man who'd seen too much darkness in his life.

"How about a smooth rock you found on the way to school?" Roan asked.

The boy giggled. "Nope. You're a really bad guesser, even if you can see better now."

"You're probably right about that," Roan said with a chuckle and ruffled the boy's hair. Marley stood watching their exchange, and Roan winked at her. "I've got it this time. You found a lucky penny."

"Ah, darn it, how did you know?" Matt dug around in his pocket and pulled out an old, crusted coin. He handed it over.

Roan made a big production of studying the cent piece, turning it this way and that and holding it up to the light. "You know what this is, don't you?"

Matt dragged a sleeve across his nose. "It's a penny."

"Not just any penny. This dropped from a pirate's pocket. Why, I'll bet he was probably on his way to bury some loot when it fell out on your road."

The boy's eyes opened wide. "Really?"

"I'll bet anything." Roan loved playing this game. The sadness had vanished, and Matt was now full of a child's wonder. Roan dropped to one knee and whispered, "It might've come from Jean Lafitte himself. See this little divot? That's the mark he used to put on everything."

"Oh boy! I have pirate treasure." Matt squeezed his hands together with excitement. "Did you hear that, Mama Rose?"

"I did. You're a lucky little boy," Marley said. "You have something no one else in the whole wide world has."

"It's our secret." Matt grinned up at her. "Will you write a story about it and read it to me at bedtime?"

"Honey, it's a little late in the day for writing it down. I have supper to fix." She knelt to give him a hug. "I'll tell you what though. Mr. Penny will give me all the details, and I'll tell them to you at bedtime."

"I love you, Mama Rose." Matt threw his arms around her. "You're the bestest mama I ever had."

"You're a sweet boy, and I love you too." She stood. "Now go wash up. With soap too," she added sternly.

Roan watched the pair, and his heart swelled. What Marley was giving Matt couldn't be measured in money. He handed Matt the penny and watched him scamper off.

He quirked an eyebrow. "I know all the details?"

"Sure." She grinned. "Anyone who hung the moon for a lonely little boy knows about Jean Lafitte and his loot. Tell me, what was he doing so far from Galveston?"

"Anyone knows that. He was visiting the woman who occupied his dreams." Roan tweaked the tip of her nose.

"And when he got there, he spirited her away with him to his pirate ship."

"Then what?" she asked in a breathless voice.

"They sailed to a hidden private island where no one could find them, and she wrote stories all the time." *And they lived happily ever after*, he added silently. Just Marley and him, where bad people could never find them, and nothing—not even the search for justice—could ever keep them apart.

Fourteen

ROAN ROSE FROM THE SUPPER TABLE. "THANKS FOR THE meal, Miz Jessie. I never had better."

Jessie McClain smiled. "I'm so glad you liked it, Roan."

He made it to the door, where Duel caught him. "Can I have a private word?"

"Sure." Roan glanced at Marley, and she shrugged her shoulders. Well, he'd soon find out what her father had to say.

The men's boots crunched on the small rocks and hard-packed ground as they strolled toward a bit of blessed quiet. They both propped their feet on the bottom rail of the corral and rested their weight on the top rung, nothing more than a few owl hoots breaking the silence. A full moon shone overhead. He relaxed. No waning moon for about two weeks. That was good.

"I heard you're getting ready to leave." Duel sounded resigned and a bit sad.

"Yes, sir." Roan stuck a match stem in the corner of his mouth. "I need to get about the business of finding Mose's killers."

Duel faced him with a hard stare and reached into his pocket for his sack of Bull Durham. He rolled a cigarette and lit it. Roan worked to resist fidgeting and stand his ground. The rancher sure knew how to intimidate, and Roan would hate to cross him.

"I like you, Roan. I did from the start when Marley brought you to the ranch more dead than alive. You have strength and courage in spades. I admire you as a man and know they don't come any better than you. You're the kind of man I would want for my daughter, and I think a good portion of why is because you don't quit when the bridge washes out from under you."

The news of Duel's assessment of his character surprised Roan a bit. He hadn't known the man felt this way about him.

"No, sir." Roan moved the match stem to the other side of his mouth. "I never saw any value in quitting. A man who can't keep going is a dead one. This land is unforgiving, and it either makes men tough or they fill the cemeteries."

The tip of Duel's cigarette glowed red when he inhaled the burning tobacco. Smoke curled around his head. "You've had plenty of hard times, and you're going to see many more before your job in San Saba is over."

"I reckon so." Roan turned toward the house and thought he saw Marley in the window. Maybe not though. "I appreciate the job and a place to stay until I got on my feet."

"Happy to do it. What are your intentions toward my daughter?"

For a moment, Roan froze. So this was about her. "I can assure you that my feelings for Marley are real. I'm sure you've noticed how close we got, but I don't have one thing to offer her, and I won't act on my feelings, you can be assured of that."

"If I didn't believe that, we wouldn't be having this conversation. I'd have kicked you off the ranch in nothing flat. But there is one question in my mind."

"What's that?" Roan tried not to notice the sinking in his belly.

Duel's eyes pierced him. "Are you going to come back once you get this thing in San Saba settled? You keep saying this job is temporary."

There it was in a nutshell—everything boiled down to

one question. Roan searched for a clear-cut answer, finding none. There were too many ifs where there should be only one big yes. "I honestly don't know, sir, and doubt I will until the time comes. But who's to say how this mess in San Saba is going to go?"

"Exactly. You bring danger to my baby girl, Roan, and you and I will have big problems. I'm not going to have her hurt, by your hand or someone else's. If you let her believe you have a future together and then ride out, it'll break Marley Rose's heart." Duel's voice cut like steel. "If that happens, you'd best hope I never find you."

Roan didn't flinch from Duel's hard eyes. "I'd expect nothing less."

"Do you love her?" Duel prodded.

The spit in Roan's mouth dried. He felt like a bug pinned under glass. That depended on the definition of love. It sure wasn't what he'd seen between his mother and Blackie. Roan thought of Mose and how he'd spoken of love for his wife so binding even death couldn't sever it. That must be the truest form of love and what Roan wanted some day.

"Honestly, sir, I don't know." Roan gazed up at the stars, hoping to see an answer written there. "We barely know each other. I don't have many worldly goods, and I figure that's a drawback when it comes to looking for a wife. But you won't find a harder worker or one who has greater respect for your daughter. I've never drank much or smoked, and never curse around womenfolk. I know I can't offer her or anyone much of a life right now. I hope to change that."

"I see your mettle and I admire you. If you'd said you love her, I'd tell you flat out to get lost." Duel allowed a flicker of a smile. "Come to me when you decide to stay on, and we'll talk again. You're a good man, but I can't let you hurt my daughter."

Roan breathed a sigh of relief to have the probing ended. Yet Duel was being right and fair. A father had to protect his child to the best of his ability, especially against a man who already knew he wasn't marriage material.

The conversation moved to children. "I never expected to have so many." Duel took a drag of his cigarette. "After Jessie found out she couldn't have any…uh, more, she was crushed. She desperately wanted a houseful, so I didn't say anything when she started bringing in kids who needed a home. I had a lot of love to give, but I thought Jessie's need would taper off at some point, not increase."

Confusion washed over Roan. He must've heard wrong. It sounded like Duel had said that Jessie couldn't have any kids. But that had seemed more like a slip of the tongue. Marley certainly thought she was their daughter, even though…she didn't resemble either her mother or father.

Maybe Marley was Duel's daughter by his first wife. Yes, that must be it.

Duel let out a long sigh, threw his cigarette to the dirt, and ground it out with his heel. "I love that woman more than anything or anyone on earth, and I suppose living inside a tornado is a small price to pay. Jessie completes my life, and she certainly saved me." He swung his gaze to Roan. "You'll see what I mean one day."

"I hope so." Roan swallowed the question hanging on the tip of his tongue. It wasn't any of his business if Marley was Jessie and Duel's true daughter or not.

Duel folded his arms on the rail. "About this race coming up—what is your plan?"

"Get close to the other racers, onlookers too, and try to spot the face I saw that night when the hood came off. And if I hear it, I'll also recognize the voice of the one who was in charge that night. His voice was odd."

"In what way?"

"Gravelly. Rough sounding. Low. Scary." The memory was lodged deep in Roan's soul.

"What's your plan when you find these men? Or have you thought that far?" Duel asked.

Roan had thought about it all right. He'd done nothing but think about the moment he would come face-to-face with the killers. "I'm going to capture them however I can.

It won't be easy, and I'm prepared for a fight. I'll take them to jail in another town because clearly the sheriff of San Saba has been bought off. I saw it the day we rode in to deliver that body."

"I saw it too. You're wise to get the men out of San Saba once you find them." Duel laid a hand on Roan's back. "Be ready for trouble. Stands to reason the whole town is likely on their side. You may have to put a bullet in the men you catch instead of carting them away. I wish I was going with you, but I can't afford to leave. I have to catch these rustlers before they ruin me."

"I understand. I'm thankful for the men you can spare. Judd, Hardy, and the other hands will be a big help." Roan was glad he didn't have to go alone, but he would have if he'd had no other choice to right this wrong.

"Don't mention it." Duel faced him. "Glad we had this talk. I'd better get back. Jess might need help, and I gen'rally read a story to the kids before they turn in."

The night closed around Roan as he watched the big rancher head toward the kitchen door. Marley appeared at a window, staring out.

There would be no moonlit kisses tonight.

No private touches.

No talk of the future.

Still, if and when he returned in one piece, he meant to ask Duel for permission to court her. Marley Rose McClain seemed to need him, and he for sure needed her.

All he had to do was find a way to be worthy.

But would fate snatch her from him—just like it had everything else he'd ever wanted?

❧

Marley finished the dishes and put everything away. In a moment, she'd go up and tell Matt the story of the pirate and how he'd dropped the penny on their road on a moonless night. But right now, her nerves were jumping worse than hot grease in a skillet as she kept glancing at the door. What were he and her father talking about?

The knob suddenly rattled, and the door swung open. Her heart pounded as she whirled, her gaze colliding with her father's.

His glance told her nothing. Her heart lurched, and she could barely squeeze the question from between her lips. "Did you run him off?"

He barked a laugh. "Now why would I do that? Roan is a fine man and an excellent worker. He knows he has to make some changes in his life, though, to get what he wants."

Frustration and anger twisted in her stomach. "He's had such a hard life. I care for him, Papa."

"I know you do. I see it in your eyes, and it's my job to protect you, Marley Rose. Roan could end up hurting you, and I'm not having that." Duel went to the stove and shook the coffeepot, frowning to find it empty.

She gripped the back of a chair, fighting down angry frustration. "I've told you repeatedly that I'm a grown woman. I know what I want and I'm capable of making my own decisions. I've asked you to drop the Rose part of my name—that belongs to a *child*—yet you persist. I do as much around here as anyone, but you still treat me like a little girl who doesn't know her own mind."

Duel tried to put his arm around her, but she stepped back. If she didn't stand firm, he'd twist her around his little finger before she knew what was happening.

He let out a heavy sigh. "When you have children of your own, you'll understand the role of a parent. Often my decisions are unpopular, but they're because I want to shield you from hurt."

"You can't always do that," Marley pointed out. "Things happen beyond your control. You can't keep me in a box and set it on a high self."

"And that keeps me awake at night." Duel waved his arm toward the door. "I wish you could see the dangers that are out there beyond this ranch. There are people who would hurt you for no other reason than that they can. Or to get back at me for some slight."

Marley raised her chin. "You say you don't want Roan to hurt me, but what about you? I care for him, Papa. Do I know if what I feel will last? No, I don't. I just need a chance to find out and to spread my wings a bit. If you keep a bird in a cage, it'll eventually die. Don't you see?"

"She's right, honey," Jessie said from the doorway. "No one wants to be caged. Not me and not Marley."

"Gang up on me, will you?" Duel growled. He went to Jessie and pulled her into his arms. "For the record, I told Roan that he's welcome here, and when he decides if he's staying, we'll talk again. Right now, he doesn't know much of anything except that he burns to see justice done for his friend. He's got to settle this thing with that gang over in San Saba before he can start to make a true life for himself."

Her father's words made sense, and he hadn't closed the door on her and Roan like she'd first thought. She glanced at her mother and father, who were once again lost in each other. They'd already forgotten about her.

Marley quietly left and climbed the stairs to the room where a little boy was waiting. She had to be patient and focus on the things she could control.

Like the pirate story. She didn't need a crystal ball to know that Jean Lafitte would turn into a man with startling gray eyes and lips that could light a fire inside her. And if he should appear outside her window to whisk her away, she'd not waste a second in letting him.

Fifteen

THE NEXT FEW DAYS PASSED QUICKLY FOR ROAN. DUEL HAD sent him out to the site of the latest cattle theft, where he and five other ranch hands worked on getting the last long section of fence back up. He rode with the others to guard against more rustling but saw no sign of the thieves. The two oldest McClain boys had raised a fuss about coming along, but thankfully, Duel had kept them behind. This was too dangerous and no place for untried young men who'd only just begun to shave. His thoughts drifted to the young boy riding with the group of marauders who'd killed Mose. And the other shot dead in front of him by the person in the barn.

The last hadn't even had a chance to live yet. The other might if someone got him away from the gang. Roan would if he had an opportunity. But why were they with that bunch?

He missed seeing Marley but was grateful for the space between them. Yet, each night, he lay on his bedroll on the ground, gazed up at the dark sky, and found her face among the multitude of twinkling stars.

Each evening, he took Shadow for a run to keep her in shape. The men said they'd never seen a faster horse.

Four days out, trouble rode toward them in the darkness. The shaking ground and terrifying noise of pounding hoof-beats brought back a rush of memories of the last time death had come to visit. Roan inhaled a sharp breath, snatched up his rifle, and kicked out the campfire. He took cover behind the lacy foliage of a cedar tree, determined to hit his targets.

Black-hooded riders spilled through the gaping hole in the barbed wire like hungry wolves, whooping and cursing, emptying their guns at them as they came. They weren't after cattle this time—these night riders had killing in mind.

Bullets kicked up the dirt around Roan and the cowboys. There must've been at least eight marauders. He steadied his aim and fired at the lead rider. The black night kept him from seeing if he hit the man, but a loud yell told him he had.

Roan ratcheted another cartridge into the chamber and swung to another rider. His aim was good. This time the attacker fell from the saddle.

Once all the riders were through, they circled and took another run at the ranch hands. When one man came near, Roan grabbed his ankle, yanked him from the horse, and slung him to the ground. He sat on the man's chest and snatched off his hood. The scared eyes of another young boy met his.

"Who are you?" Roan yelled. "What do you want?"

Before the kid could open his mouth to speak, someone struck the back of Roan's head. The stars fell from the sky, exploding around him as he crumpled over.

When he came to, Hardy Gage was bending over and slapping his face. Though his head was splitting open, Roan sat up to find the hooded riders were gone. "Who the hell hit me?"

"One of our visitors. They had me pinned down, and I couldn't help."

"Dammit, Gage, they got away again. But I know I wounded one and maybe killed another this time."

"He's over there by our bedrolls." He helped Roan to his feet. "Ain't gonna be doin' much talkin' though—he's dead."

Roan stumbled over to the prone man. Someone had removed his hood, and he stared up with unseeing eyes.

Roan didn't recognize the face, but he'd take a closer look at daybreak. If only he could catch one alive!

"This has all the makings of a traitor in our midst."

"What are you sayin'?" Hardy Gage growled above him. "Do you think we'd betray the boss? I've been with him for twenty years or more. I'd give my life for him."

"Calm down," Roan snapped. "I'm not saying it's you. I know it's not. But it's someone."

"I always thought it strange that Wes Douglas up and quit for no reason when you came." The statement came from Mitch Joel. Everyone turned to stare.

"You know, that was a bit odd. Wes's excuse for riding out was pretty flimsy," Gage said.

Roan glanced up. "One thing for sure, someone is feeding them information. These rustlers know where to be and when."

Judd squatted beside him. "From your description of those hooded riders who killed your friend, these were very similar."

"They are." Roan glanced at the group of cowboys. "Looks like they answered our questions for us. There's no doubt the rustlers and the killers are the same group. Dammit! What are they trying to do?"

"Don't know. But they hit one of our men."

"How bad?"

"Just a flesh wound." Judd grinned. "Probably get out of stringing fence for a few days."

"Glad it's not serious. Did you see what happened to the man I was sitting on when the other smacked the back of my head?" Roan reached into his hair and found a big lump on his scalp. "I saw his face for a second, and he was just starting to say something."

"Yeah," Hardy said. "One of the other riders yanked him up, and they got on a horse and lit out."

"Why they're all so young? I'd give anything to know." Roan stared into the thick blackness.

They sat around for the remainder of the night, afraid to go to sleep for fear the riders would return. By dawn, it was clear the attackers had planned to hit hard and fast, then ride like the devil for safer territory. Some of the men climbed into the saddle to try to pick up a trail.

Roan knelt next to the dead young man and stared at a large bruise on his jaw. He lifted the boy's hands and noticed the knuckles on both left and right were raw. He'd fought someone not long before they'd attacked. Had he been trying to leave the group and been forced to go on the raid?

Or maybe the boy had simply had a tussle with someone and Roan was overthinking this.

The boy's pockets yielded few clues—a spinning top and a little wooden dog that someone had whittled. He couldn't have been more than fourteen, if that. A lump formed in Roan's throat. The whole sum of this kid's world was measured in these toys. Only this time, along with the bits and pieces of a life cut too short, Roan found a map of San Saba County folded up in a small square. It showed four large *X*s. One was over Mose's farm. In the lower right corner were the scribbled words *For Mom*.

What did the map have to do with the boy's mother? Was it even his own mother?

Maybe she had lost their land, and in some crazy way, the kid was hoping to get it back. But that didn't explain all the other raiders. What was their interest?

He examined the boy's clothing. His shirt had been made from a flour sack, patched at the elbows and near the tail in front. A piece of rope cinched up his pants. The kid's trousers were also patched. The clothing indicated someone who had nothing—someone very much like Roan. He looked away for a second, struggling to get control of his emotions.

Finding nothing else helpful, Roan stood and showed the other cowboys the map. They shrugged and shook their heads, not even hazarding a guess at what the two words meant.

"Reckon we'd better get the body to the ranch." Roan slapped his hat against his trousers. "Boss needs to know what happened and probably try to find his kin." If the boy had any, and from the looks of him, that seemed doubtful. Except maybe for his mother.

Hardy nodded. "The poor kid's gonna start smelling soon."

As they scattered to pack up, Judd hung back. "Some of us should stay until Boss decides what to do. If we all leave, those killing varmints might come back."

Roan shook his head. "They come if we're here, and they come if we're not. Doesn't seem to make much difference to them. What do you think they were after?"

"Not the cattle this time." Hardy rubbed his whiskers. "I think they meant to kill us."

"I do too," Roan admitted, wishing he could've seen their faces. "But why us? And why turn around and leave before trying to finish the job? They had us outgunned. We don't have any money, so robbing was out. They had to be sending a message, letting Boss know that they could do whatever they wanted, anytime they felt like it."

"Who the hell knows? Maybe they like killing. I just don't feel right about leaving," Judd said.

"I guess this means no one from the ranch is going to San Saba with you." The breeze ruffled the red bandana tied around Hardy's neck. "More than likely, Boss will want to keep us here. Sorry, Roan."

"Don't worry. I'll be fine." Even alone, he still had to go. And besides, he'd promised to get Marley the information about that book publisher from the mercantile.

No matter how he had to do it or whether he lived to watch it come true, he meant to see that she, at least, reached her dreams.

❦

Who was the dead man tied to the horse that Roan was leading?

Marley had just gotten the children off to school. She raced from the house, her heart thundering in her ears like a herd of walleyed longhorns. At least it wasn't Roan, and knowing that brought some measure of relief. She yearned for a private word, but there were too many ears. His weary eyes met hers, then flicked over to her father hurrying from the direction of the corral.

"What happened?" Duel grated his teeth as though steeling himself. He strode to the dead body to look at the face as the men dismounted.

Roan pushed back his hat. "Hooded men rode in about midnight with guns blazing. We barely had time to take cover. I know I hit some. Maybe this one carries my bullet, but it's anyone's guess. After they rode out, we found this boy dead in the dirt." He paused a second before adding, "He's young, like the other one at Mose's farm."

Marley stood on the fringes and took in Roan's haggard appearance, his tired eyes. She longed to kiss him, to feel his heartbeat under her palm, and to offer him comfort, but she could do none of that.

Duel bit out some muttered curses. "And the condition of my hands?"

Hardy spoke up, "Pete here got a flesh wound. They struck Roan over the head and knocked him out."

Marley sucked in a breath. He could've been killed.

Roan waved them off. "I'm fine."

"Hardly hurts, Boss." Pete held up his arm with a blood-stained bandana tied around the upper portion. "Hardy insisted I need to get it looked after."

Jessie hurried from the back door of the house, wiping her hands on her apron. Her voice shook with fear. "What happened?"

"Pete needs tending, darlin'." Duel's eyes softened as he spoke to Jessie. "If you can't spare the time, maybe Marley can do it. She's getting good at doctoring folks."

"Yes, she is, but no one needs me right now." Jessie took Pete's arm and told him to come with her.

"I found these in the boy's pockets, sir." Roan handed Duel everything he'd found. "I'll be curious to know what you think of the map."

A map? Marley pressed closer and peered around her father. The large Xs puzzled her, and the words in the lower corner were too small to read from where she stood.

Duel frowned at it for several minutes. "Roan, do you think this was the same bunch who killed your friend?"

"They wore the same hoods, and like before, galloped in without a warning. At least a few of those first raiders were young, just like this dead one and the other at Mose's. Though I have no proof, I do think they're the same group." Roan smiled at Marley, and she returned it, grateful for his notice.

"What the devil do they want besides every last bit of my cattle?" Duel stared in the direction of San Saba.

"I wish I knew, sir," Roan answered. "What are we going to do with this kid?"

"I'll take him into Tranquility and speak to the sheriff. He can deal with finding and notifying any kin." Duel swung around to Hardy. "I hate to send you back out there, but I'd like you and the boys to guard that section of the ranch. I doubt it'll stop the bastards, but at least maybe they won't keep stealing me blind."

"All right, Boss. I'll have some coffee and hightail it back," Hardy said. "Boss, this is just a theory, but I have to tell you anyway. Me and the men think Wes Douglas has gone over to their side. He quit too suddenly and for no reason. And it was just as Roan came."

Duel was silent for a moment, staring at the ground. "You might be right. I had a strange feeling about that. He knows the workings of this ranch, and that could explain a lot." He swiveled back. "Roan, I'd like to have you ride into Tranquility with me and tell your story to the sheriff."

"Sure." Roan hesitated. "In case you forgot, I leave for San Saba tomorrow morning, sir."

"I didn't forget." A wry smile formed on her papa's face. "I can't send any of the hands with you like we'd talked about. Just can't spare them."

A cold hand gripped Marley's heart. Roan had to have

help. If he went alone, they could kill him. She struggled to draw a breath.

"I understand. I didn't figure you could. I'll be fine." Roan started toward the kitchen with Hardy to get coffee.

Marley swung into step beside Roan. "What are you going to do now?"

"Nothing." His gray eyes hardened. "I've been alone most of my life. This is my fight anyway, not theirs."

A little cry escaped her, and she clutched his arm. "You're crazy. That's just asking to get hurt." Or worse.

He faced her and smoothed back her hair. "I probably am, but I refuse to live my life in fear. And as you've noticed, I'm pretty hard to put in a grave. Please don't worry about me."

"Too late, cowboy." She heard Granny Jack's voice in her ear, reminding her that every tub had to sit on its own bottom. Her jitters eased some, and she remembered saying, no insisting, that she was not going to bury him. Such hasty, angry words. She knew if someone brought him back to the ranch draped over a horse or in a wagon, she'd dig the grave herself.

And she'd cry her eyes out for the man whose father had told him he was worthless. Maybe he believed that. Maybe that's why he took these chances. Damn Blackie Culpepper.

She turned to hide her tears and hurried toward the house.

In the kitchen, she poured both men hot coffee. "Would you like some food with that?"

Roan glanced up and smiled. "Not sure I can spare the time. Your father's in a hurry."

"Well, I sure can," Hardy said. "I'm so hungry I could eat a skillet full of skunk eggs."

Marley laughed. "You've been trying to pull my leg with that since I was a girl, Hardy. I'm wise to you."

"Shoot! You figured me out. But go ahead and fix me a whole mess of hen eggs."

While she prepared breakfast, she listened to him and Roan.

"I wish we could pick up those riders' scent. If we could just confirm that they came from San Saba County, it would settle a lot in my mind." Roan took a drink of coffee and reached for a cold biscuit from a plate in the middle of the table.

Marley handed him a piece of warm bacon to eat with it. She stared at him, admiring the strength of his jaw and his icy gray eyes. She'd once seen those same gray eyes smolder with desire, shivered as his lips found hers, felt his strong arms around her, blocking out the world. His original bruises, compliments of the hooded gang, had all but vanished in the two and a half weeks since he'd been there. They shouldn't draw any attention in San Saba.

The two men talked about the horse race at the county fair.

"What about your disguise when you leave in the morning?" Hardy asked.

Roan frowned. "I haven't thought much about it. I don't have any clothes except what I'm wearing, and another set just like them. Any suggestions?"

"I do," Marley said quietly. "You'll need to appear well dressed and project yourself as a successful, educated man. A three-piece suit, a string tie, a new Stetson and boots. Those plus a fresh shave and haircut will hide your identity. The sheriff and others only know you as a poor drifter."

Roan snorted. "Where do you think I'm going to get those? I'm not a magician."

"She's right. Think about it." Hardy leaned, propping his elbows on the table. "It's perfect."

"You're both crazy." Roan finished the last of his coffee, stood, and grabbed his hat.

"Leave everything to me." Marley touched his arm and felt the muscles rippling underneath. "Do you mind if I ride into town with you and Papa?"

His well-formed lips turned up in a smile. "That's a strange question. Why would I mind? Better hurry though. I have a feeling your father won't wait."

The minute he moved to the door, Marley darted into the next room to find her mother. A minute later, with Jessie finishing the preparations for Hardy's breakfast, she raced toward the barn but drew up short when Roan led out her saddled horse.

"I saved you some time," he said.

"Thanks, I appreciate it." She accepted his help mounting, and a few minutes later, the three of them rode out and headed toward town.

Marley took advantage of the ride to tell her father about her plan for Roan's disguise. "He'll be hiding in plain sight. No one will expect a man of means."

Duel was quiet a moment before answering. "I think that's a great idea, Marley Rose. When we finish our business with the sheriff, we'll go to that fancy new clothing store."

"You'll subtract the cost from my wages," Roan said firmly. "It's that way or not at all." He paused, then asked, "Describe Wes Douglas. Just in case I run into him in San Saba."

Marley pictured the man in her mind. "Stocky with brown hair that's a lot lighter than yours, almost blond."

"Wes is late twenties, I'd say." Duel thought a second. "He has a scar on the right side of his neck caused from a bullet wound he said."

"Papa, don't forget the way his chin just kind of runs in with his neck. He really doesn't have a defined chin." Marley glanced at Roan. "You won't have any trouble recognizing him if you cross paths."

Roan chuckled softly. "I think I have a clear picture in my mind. Thank you."

Tranquility bustled with people, wagons, and animals, and the group soon halted in front of the sheriff's office.

"Who you got there, McClain?" Sheriff Bagwell hurried from the barber adjacent to his office. The middle-aged man yanked off the cape from around his neck and swiped at the shaving cream on his face but mostly left it smeared.

"Hey, come back here!" yelled the barber from the door.

"No time," Bagwell answered, increasing his stride. "Got a dead man out here."

"Sheriff, he's not going anywhere," Duel said. "Reckon he can wait."

Truman Bagwell shook his head and lowered his voice. "You saved my hide, McClain. Jed was trying to pawn off his old-maid sister on me."

Duel barked a laugh. "He's been trying to do that for years, Truman. What's the problem now?"

"I'm running out of excuses, that's what the problem is." The sheriff turned to Marley. "Miss Marley Rose, you're sure a sight for sore eyes. I think you get prettier every day. If I was little younger, I'd come calling."

"Why, thank you, Sheriff. If I was a little older, I'd take you up on it." Marley had always seen Truman Bagwell as a handsome man, what with his sandy hair and those twinkling eyes that saw humor in almost everything. In all the years since she'd known him, she'd never seen him downright spitting-mad angry. An even temper was a fine quality in anyone.

Roan almost never got mad, and he was very patient with the kids, even when they were all clamoring for his attention.

"Truman, if you come to the ranch, it'd better be to play our weekly game of checkers," Duel growled, narrowing his eyes.

"Relax, McClain. I'm too old and set in my ways to think about taking a wife. I imagine I'd have to train her, and Miss Marley doesn't appear the easy kind to break in."

Marley laughed. "You're not wanting a wife; you're wanting a saddle bronc. I'm too wild and wooly for you, Truman."

"Guess you're right, Miss Marley." The sheriff scowled at Roan. "Who are you?"

"Roan Penny, a new hand at the Aces 'n' Eights," Roan answered, sticking out his hand.

Marley admired the way Roan carried himself. He answered questions directly, without shame, and in a deep, strong voice that left no doubt in anyone's mind that he could handle any situation.

Duel rested his foot on the step to the boardwalk. "Roan brought the dead man to the ranch this morning."

Bagwell's mood became somber. "Give me the facts."

"I sent Roan and some of my hands out to the east

section to mend cut fences four days ago. The rustlers are stealing me blind. Last night, a bunch of black-hooded bastards rode through with a barrage of gunfire and wounded one of my men. One of my boys managed to shoot this one."

The sheriff lifted the dead man's head, and shock rippled across his face. "He's still wet behind the ears. Can't be more than thirteen or fourteen, McClain!"

"I know." Duel pushed back his Stetson. "I'd give anything to know what he was doing there. I'm not sure, but it appears a new gang of young riders has popped up."

Worry filled Bagwell's eyes. "Do you think they're leftovers of the San Saba mob?"

"Maybe. It sure wouldn't surprise me," Duel answered.

Bagwell mumbled something that sounded like a curse. Marley could tell he was shaken. "Then why did you bring the dead man here and not to the San Saba sheriff?"

"Several reasons. The biggest being I'm not positive that this dead rider came from there. Another is that Sheriff Coburn would accuse us of killing the man, but Roan can tell more about that."

"Penny, tell me every single detail about the riders, and don't leave out anything," the sheriff ordered.

"Let me back up just a bit, if you don't mind, because I think it's all related." Roan told him about the cold-blooded murder of Mose and afterward how the riders dragged Roan into McCullough County. Then he laid out how he and Duel got attacked when they went to bury Mose and the young man who died there and moved on to the previous night. He ended with a quiet request. "If no one claims the body, let me know. I'll pay for the burial."

Marley was proud of Roan's thoroughness in relating the details. He'd been through so much yet hadn't gone bitter or hard. How his father could've given him away was beyond her. She'd like to find Blackie Culpepper and deliver stinging blows to his face.

Roan was worth five hundred Culpeppers.

He'd saved her as much as she had him. In a way, he belonged to her now—if she could just keep him from dying.

Sixteen

Nerves set in a little before dawn the next morning, while the roosters were still sleeping. Roan got out of bed and dressed in his normal clothes. He combed his hair in front of a small mirror, then glanced at the new suit and white shirt still wrapped in brown paper. At his insistence, Duel had deducted the cost from his wages. Roan had never taken charity in his life, and he wasn't about to start.

Made things much simpler that way.

He slid his feet into his old boots, refusing to even consider a new pair, though he'd conceded to the purchase of a new hat. He adjusted the black Stetson on his head and buckled his gun belt on. Roan tucked the borrowed entry money from Hardy, Judd, and the men into an inside pocket of his coat. Then he grabbed the bundle of new clothes and let himself out into the black silence.

Though he yearned for a cup of hot coffee, he strode toward the barn, where he lit a lantern. Shadow poked her head from the stall. One ear perked straight up, the broken one laid over. She nickered softly and nuzzled his hand as though saying she was glad to see him.

He'd ride away in a moment, aware that he might never again see the woman who'd stolen his need for air. He blinked hard, glad he hadn't told her that he carried her in his heart.

Getting up so early and escaping goodbyes was best. For them both.

A minute later, he led Shadow out and threw a saddle on her back. He'd bent to cinch it under the mare's stomach when a noise alerted him. Roan straightened.

"I hoped to catch you." Marley stepped from the shadows cast by his lantern. "Why aren't you wearing the new clothes?"

"I'll change down the trail before I get to San Saba. You should be in bed."

Her voice sounded husky. "I couldn't let you go without a goodbye. I knew you'd try to skip out without one though. I've learned a lot about you, Roan Penny."

His heart gave a funny little lurch. He wanted to take her in his arms and dare anyone to tear them apart. But he couldn't. "That so?"

She walked toward him in a tantalizing stroll that made her hips sway. "I know you'd die trying to be fair. To me. To you. To everyone. But I'm tired of denying what I feel. I told my father how much I care for you."

"Bet that went over well."

An exasperated sigh left her mouth. "He already knew, Roan. He's awfully observant."

"He's only looking out for your best interests, Marley. He's not doing it to be mean but to keep men like me away from you." Roan turned back to the task of tightening the cinch and steadied his heart. "And he's right about me. What good can come this?"

"Tell me that you don't care for me, and I won't bother you again." Marley pressed her face against his back. "You are the gentlest, most honorable man I know. Tell me that what we have doesn't mean one blasted thing to you."

Heaven help him. Roan closed his eyes against the pain, unable to speak. He relished the feel of her face between his shoulder blades, her arms around his waist, burning her touch into him. He hadn't the strength to lie, to deny his heart.

Unable to bear the torture any longer, he whirled and crushed his lips to hers.

A hunger so powerful that it hurt to breathe spread through him, rushing along his limbs and touching off a whirlwind inside him. He stood in the storm and let the emotion wash over his body, healing his ragged spirit and muzzling his fear.

A moan escaped from him. His heart beating like a thundering herd of buffalo, he held Marley so tightly against him that he expected her to complain. If he could somehow open himself up and draw her inside, he would. He'd protect her with every bit of strength he had and carry the beautiful woman with him forever.

Dear God, he wanted her. Wanted her more than anything in the world. His hands roamed over her curves, memorizing every indentation and soft swell. She seemed to be learning every inch of his body as well, and the way she clutched, kneaded, and caressed him spoke of a great need of her own.

The very air seemed to vibrate with this craving that swept through him. His senses filled with her, Roan deepened the kiss and backed her against a worktable where they repaired harnesses and saddles. Tightening his grip, he lifted her onto the planks. She knocked off his hat as she reached for him, and it tumbled to the floor. He ran one hand up her leg above her low stocking and didn't think he'd ever felt anything so soft, so satiny, so enticing.

His heartbeat roared in his ears and drowned out everything except this overpowering desire for her.

How long they stood wrapped in each other's arms, he didn't know. He was barely conscious of where they were or of the dawn breaking. Men and children would spill out any second and find them.

It took everything he had to remove his hand from her leg and break the kiss. He tenderly brushed a tendril of hair from her eyes and studied her dark eyes. "You're like those shooting stars we watched. You blaze across a man's life with such a streak of color and pageantry it steals his breath. You're my Texas star, Marley Rose McClain. That is if you don't object to the title."

"That's beautiful. I've never been compared to a shooting star before."

"Well, you are. I don't know what the future holds or if I'll ever see you again," he mumbled against her mouth. "Keep shining, Texas Star, for as long as you live."

Marley's gaze met his, and she ran a fingertip along his jawline. "No promises, no regrets."

"None." The rooster finally crowed, reminding Roan he'd best hurry. He grinned. "Maybe you'll write a story one day about me and how you saved my life one frosty morn. Just don't read it to Matt. It might give him ideas."

Tears bubbled in her eyes. "You'd better come back or I'll come looking for you."

"You will, huh?"

"I'll brave a den of snakes and go through a hail of bullets to get to you, and you can count on that." Marley straightened his collar and picked a piece of lint from his coat. "You're a handsome man, Roan Penny. Women are going to chase you, but it doesn't mean you have to let them catch you." Her voice broke.

Roan swallowed a lump in his throat. This was tearing him up inside.

With a cry, she tangled her fingers in his hair and pulled him close for another kiss.

"I'll pray for you, Roan," she whispered against his mouth.

"Save your prayers for those who believe in their power."

Before the banked fire had a chance to flare again, Roan stepped away from her and issued a stern warning. "Don't come after me. I mean it. You don't know the danger waiting in San Saba. If they knew I cared for you, they'd kill you as easily as looking at you. Promise you'll stay here. You have to promise not to come after my sorry hide. Go on with your life."

Marley shook her head, her dark eyes large in the low light. "I can't do that." She reached behind her and brought out a burlap sack. "This isn't much, but maybe it'll silence your hunger pains later."

"Thanks." He touched her passion-swollen lips. "Goodbye, my Texas Star." Before he could voice more that was better left unsaid, he picked up his hat from the floor and reached for the reins. Adjusting the Stetson on his head, he swung up onto the gray mare's back. Keeping his eyes ahead, he rode out into the frost-covered blackness.

A shiver had him tugging the collar of his coat up around his ears. Damn, he wanted a pot of hot coffee! He'd build a fire down the road and make some when he stopped to change. Maybe it would help him forget Marley Rose McClain. Except he knew it would take a lot more than that to put the beauty out of his mind.

Though, if he couldn't focus on the task at hand, he wouldn't live long enough to ride back.

The morning chill seemed to have crawled inside his skin. Roan jumped at every noise. Once he swung around when he felt someone following but saw nothing.

A layer of frost still lay upon the ground an hour down the road. Unable to silence the grumble of his stomach, he stopped to make that fire he'd promised himself and boil coffee. Once it was ready, he opened the burlap sack Marley had packed and found thick slices of ham along with a loaf of fresh-baked bread. Roan wondered if she'd cooked all night.

As he ate, he let his thoughts drift to the woman who made him dream of a life with her by his side. Every waking moment was filled with thoughts of her, teasing him, testing his strength. He remembered when he'd first returned to consciousness to find her sitting beside him with the gun pointed at him. And he recalled a few hours ago when he'd kissed her and said goodbye.

One memory held happiness—learning that he'd survived and had been found by a friendly face. The last was full of nothing but sad longing.

No promises. No regrets, she'd said.

"Yeah right," Roan muttered sourly. "Speak for yourself."

If he survived this, he was going to make a lot of changes. He'd become someone worthy of the dark-haired beauty who'd stolen his heart. Someone Duel had no objection to.

A limb cracked. He jumped and whirled, pulling his gun. "Who's there?"

The sad cooing of mourning doves filled the air. It must've been an animal, but to make sure, he poked around. Ten minutes later, he packed up. A couple of other times, he felt eyes watching but never saw anything.

"You're crazy as a loon, Penny," he mumbled low.

Five miles from town, he changed into the new clothes. He buttoned the gold brocaded vest, running his fingers down the expensive material. He'd never owned, never even dreamed, of wearing anything so fine.

Roan arrived in San Saba two hours before sundown. The stores were packed, and a huge banner advertising the county fair and horse race hung across the street. People milled up and down the boardwalk like a bunch of ants. Roan relaxed. With this many visitors in town, maybe they wouldn't pay him any notice. He went straight to the livery and left his mare in the care of the owner, an old man with a long, white beard by the name of Jessup.

"Don't worry none about your mare." Jessup winked. "I'll take real good care of her."

Roan liked the honesty in his eyes. "Obliged."

Even if the hotels had any vacancies left, Roan couldn't afford a room, so he secured a spot in the loft of the livery from Jessup. A bed on some fresh hay would do just fine. He staked out a corner with his saddle and bedroll and went out into the street.

He pulled his Stetson down low and caught a man walking by. "Could you tell me where to register for tomorrow's horse race?"

The man looked him up and down through narrowed

eyes. "Go to the fairgrounds and you'll see a tent with a sign in front. Where are you from, mister?"

"The Aces 'n' Eights Ranch."

"Well, good luck. You'll need it." The stranger moved on up the street, and Roan watched him hurry into the Bull's Head Saloon.

The fairgrounds were easy to find, and the short walk gave him time to look around, hoping to spot Wes Douglas or anyone he recognized. But he came up empty. He couldn't help wonder if Sheriff Bagwell had brought the dead kid's body in yet. Most likely the lawman would telegraph first to find out if the boy had kin in San Saba though. Roan hoped someone claimed the boy. Everyone deserved a decent burial and maybe a tear or two.

Who would shed a tear for Roan? Marley McClain?

Roan frowned. He didn't want her crying for him, didn't want to cause her grief.

As the man had predicted, the tent was easy to find. It appeared the big purse had attracted a lot of risk takers. Roan took his place in line. By the time he made it inside, ten more were behind him. He glanced around the tent. A man with a goatee sat in the middle at a desk, taking names and money, and a large man stood directly behind him with his arms folded. He wore twin revolvers. The bodyguard most likely.

A couple to the left of the table drew Roan's interest. An auburn-haired woman stood with a tall, thin companion. Roan moved closer for a better view, and shock ran through him to find himself staring at the hawk-nosed stranger who'd passed Roan and Marley on the way to Granny Jack's. Who the hell was he?

The hair on the back of his neck rose. Bathed in shadows, the tall man's cheeks appeared even more sunken and his skin stretched tighter over protruding facial bones. Roan couldn't hear the scarecrow's voice from where he stood. He had to know what it sounded like.

But the man with twin revolvers was staring a hole through

Roan. He couldn't make his interest so obvious or he'd get shot. He reached into his vest pocket for a silver dollar.

Turning his gaze to the line stretching behind him, Roan let the coin slip from his hand. The heavy silver piece rolled in the right direction, stopping just inches from the man's boots. Roan hurried to pick it up.

"Virginia, you worry too much. It'll be all right," the man grated out.

The gravelly voice sent chills through Roan. It was the same he'd heard the night of Mose's death, giving the order to burn the cabin.

What would a lowlife like that be doing with a pretty lady? He made a note of her name.

The goateed man at the table barked an order to get back in line or get out. Roan pocketed his coin and complied but kept his gaze riveted on the two. Judging by their body language and low tones, they were angry and arguing about something. When the women spoke a bit too loudly, they both glanced around to see if anyone had heard.

All too soon, Roan reached the sign-in table, and it only then occurred to him that he couldn't use his real name. His father's? He wouldn't give a dying, smelly skunk his father's name. Out of the corner of his eye, he spotted a fellow contestant fishing a bag of Bull Durham from his pocket.

"Your name?" the goateed man snapped.

"Jack Durham."

The man glanced up. "You're dressed awful fancy. Ever race a horse before?"

"I assure you I have. Won a bunch too, but I don't know what that's got to do with anything."

A young man limped into the tent and up to the desk. "Bartender over at the saloon sent me, Mr. Quinn. Your son Willie got hisself in a fight."

"Is he winning?" Quinn asked.

"He's out cold, sir."

"Then pour some water on him or get the doctor," Quinn snapped. "I'm too busy."

"Yes, sir." The boy limped out.

Mr. Quinn turned back to Roan. "Color and name of your horse?"

"Shadow, and she's a gray mare."

Tittering commenced behind him. Roan slowly turned. His steely glare quieted the bunch.

Quinn squinted up at him. "Where are you from, Durham?"

Roan didn't like the uneasiness sliding up his spine. Quinn hadn't asked any of the others these questions. Why him? "Aces 'n' Eights Ranch."

"Only residents of this county are allowed to participate. Wait here." Quinn rose and went to speak to Virginia and Scarecrow.

They talked for several minutes and kept glancing at Roan. He knew they didn't recognize him, or he wouldn't have gotten this far. Maybe they were trying to figure out his connection to Duel McClain. But why did Quinn have to get their approval for Roan, when he hadn't done the same for any of the others?

Finally, Quinn returned. "You can race if you have the money."

Roan laid down the fee, and while the man counted it, he watched Scarecrow stalk from the tent. Virginia stared at Roan silently, a smile curving her mouth. He touched the brim of his hat and nodded politely. Best that he could tell in the low light, she appeared midforties. Was she married to Scarecrow? If so, they seemed an odd match. She was much too good for him.

Roan sauntered from the tent and glanced around, looking for the tall, gaunt man with a devil's heart. When he caught sight of him disappearing around a building, he hurried after. Putting a name to Scarecrow could be the break he needed in finding the killers.

Roan lengthened his stride. Just as he reached the corner, a stagecoach rumbled by, kicking up a cloud of dust, and he couldn't see much of anything. He fanned the grit away from his face, but Scarecrow had vanished.

For the next hour, Roan strolled up and down the street but saw no sign of him. He went into the Bull's Head, several other saloons, and two hotels but found no one resembling the man. Finally, leaning against a support on the boardwalk in front of Hendrick's Mercantile, he was just about thinking of giving up when he spied a rider on a big sorrel cantering down the street.

It was him!

Busy watching the rider, he didn't notice the passersby until a woman bumped into him.

"My apologies, ma'am." When he noticed who it was, the rest of his words lodged in his throat. He stared at Virginia.

A smile curved her mouth and set her green eyes twinkling. "It's quite all right, Mr. Durham."

Best to not let on he'd heard her name. "You have me at quite a disadvantage." Roan found himself admiring the beautiful woman. The low light he'd seen her in earlier had done her an injustice.

Her laugh tinkled like a musical brook. "I'm Virginia Creek."

He lifted the back of her gloved hand to his mouth. "I suppose you're one of the organizers in charge of the horse race?"

"Goodness! I'm not really in charge of anything."

"Then, I really should thank the gentleman who was with you in the tent for giving Quinn the okay to let me race."

"Oh, you mean Mr. Gentry." Her smile vanished. "I'd steer clear of him."

Gentry. Roan finally had a name for Scarecrow.

"I'm deeply obliged, Mrs. Creek." Now Roan was even more confused. If the two weren't married, why had she been with him? Maybe she was his sister instead.

"I'm sorry, Mr. Durham, I really have to catch the clerk at the telegraph office. I hope you enjoy your stay in San Saba."

"I'm sure I will." As he watched her stroll down the boardwalk, he wasn't sure at all. But Virginia Creek was sure friendly.

Since Roan was already at the general store, he entered

and wandered to the bulletin board at the back. The advertisement for the book publisher was still there, and he took the chance to ask the clerk for a pencil and piece of paper and write down all the information.

Intent on crossing over to the bank, Roan strolled onto the boardwalk. He noticed a flash of dark hair and a sky-blue skirt darting into the alleyway.

A load of bricks dropped in his stomach. Surely, she wouldn't be here. No, she wouldn't do anything so foolish. It had to be some mistake.

He raced across the street and into the alley. Nothing was obvious, and he strolled slowly down, peering behind barrels and boxes. He was about to think he'd lost his mind when he noticed a curl of a blue hem peeking from behind a crate. He reached for an arm and pulled Marley out.

She let out a shriek before clapping a hand over her mouth and giving him a sheepish look.

"I hope you have a good explanation for being here. Your father is going to kill you, and then he's going to kill me." Roan wiped a streak of dirt from her cheek with the pad of a thumb. "Well?"

Seventeen

DARN IT! MARLEY SWALLOWED HARD AND TRIED TO AVOID the fierce storm in Roan's gray eyes. But she had no regrets. She lifted her chin. "You needed help, and I came."

"Help by doing what—getting killed?"

She raised her chin higher and glared into his steely gaze. "Are you one of those men who think girls can't do a darn thing except cook and clean and tend children?"

Roan glared back. "No, but this is different."

She didn't see how. If he'd simmer down to a low boil, she'd tell him about her expertise. "Aren't you the teeniest bit glad to see me?"

"Yes…no. That's a trick question. I think you must be a little crazy in the head. Now I have to protect and watch out for you in addition to myself. Oh, Marley." He slipped a strong arm around her waist and hauled her close, then lowered his head, his mouth finding hers.

The earth seemed to shift from under Marley's feet. She slid an arm around Roan's neck to steady herself. His touch always made her feel as though the earth had stopped turning and she was holding her breath, unable to find enough air. The fluttering in her stomach suggested a horde of butterflies, their fragile wings brushing against her insides. She gripped his vest hard with her free hand, her heartbeat pounding against the wild rhythm of his. If she died this minute, she'd go happily to heaven.

When he was near, the evil people of the world faded away and everything seemed clean and fresh and new. She was the maiden waiting at the window for her pirate. She was the outlaw's bride. And she was most definitely the woman who'd found a wounded, freezing cowboy on the road and taken him home. Sometimes in life, you simply had to take the risk and grab for what you wanted.

Her imagination could take a rest whenever she had her real, flesh-and-blood hero holding her as though he'd never let her go. This need for him was like nothing she'd never felt before, and it shook her to the core.

Roan broke the kiss, and instantly, a part of her was missing. Maybe she'd affected him that way also. He straightened, his broad shoulders heaving, his breath ragged like hers. She wished she could paint him the way he looked as he stood with his legs braced, the pirate on a rolling deck.

Or Granny Jack's husband, Mooney.

She wanted him and not just for a brief moment during a chance encounter. "I don't know what just happened, but I think I've fallen for you."

He took a step back, jerked off his hat, and raked his hands through his hair. "I can't… I have to focus on what I need to do, Marley."

"I know. Forget I said anything." She forced a laugh to hide the hurt. "I'm just a writer with a big imagination. Mama always tells me I live in a fantasy world."

"No, don't have second thoughts." He shoved his hat back on his head and took her hands in his. "Remember what you always say—no promises, no regrets. There is something powerful between us. When this is all over and I get you back to the ranch, we'll sit down and talk as long as it takes to figure it out. All right?"

At least he hadn't dismissed her as certifiably crazy. That was a relief. She had to be careful mentioning things that made him uncomfortable—like love. She smiled and changed the subject. "Tell me what you've discovered so far. Has anyone recognized you?"

"Not that I've noticed. But a man named Quinn in the tent looked at me real close like he thought he should know me." He told her about finding the scarecrow man who'd stared at her that day on the road to Granny Jack's. "His name's Gentry. Does that ring a bell?"

She knit her eyebrows in thought. "No. I can't recall ever hearing it before."

"You're positive?"

"Yes, I'm sure. Who was the woman you were talking to across the street?"

"Mrs. Virginia Creek. I saw her in the registration tent also. She seems to be a very nice woman, only I can't figure out her involvement with any of this. She gave me Gentry's name."

"I'll never forget those horrible eyes." Marley shuddered. "Or his face. He looked at me with downright hatred. Like I was his worst enemy. I don't even know him."

"Mrs. Creek warned me to stay away from him."

"Gentry." Marley rolled the name around in her head, searching for some connection. There had to be something there, to make him to stare at her that way. "No, I'm sorry, Roan."

"Maybe your father's mentioned him?" His voice sounded hopeful.

She shook her head. "I'd remember if he had."

"Well, by the way he looked at you on the road that day, he seemed to know you. Of course, maybe he had you mixed up with someone else. I didn't get a chance to ask anything further of Mrs. Creek, unfortunately."

"Shoot! But you did get two names." Marley glanced at Roan. Even before his face had healed, he'd had uncommon good looks. His hair was the color of a brown-roan stallion running wild in the wind, and his gray eyes could pierce all the way down into her soul. With his height and muscular build, he was the complete package. She wiped the smile from her lips and lowered her gaze, glad she'd come.

Yes, her father would be mad enough to spit nails if he ever found out that she and Jessie had tricked him. Marley couldn't have just vanished, not without cause, so her mother had spun a yarn about Granny Jack falling and banging herself up. So, naturally, Marley had to go and stay with her. And yes, she'd ridden into danger. Still, she had no second thoughts.

There was a chance he might not live through this, and she had to be there to hold him—and to make whoever ended his life pay dearly. She yearned to straighten the collar of his jacket and adjust the fabric on the shoulders that wasn't laying right, smooth down the vest covering his broad chest. But he was scowling again and looking like the big, bad wolf.

"I wish you hadn't come." He seemed torn between yanking off his hat again or shaking her.

"Look, Roan. I'm no daylily. My father and Hardy Gage taught me how to use both a rifle and a pistol. I'm as good a shot as just about anyone. I can look after myself. Not to mention I've already registered for the shooting competition." She grinned. "Might as well earn a little money while I'm here, and it provides cover for the real reason."

He touched a finger to her cheek. "It appears you thought of everything."

"Go and do the things you came for. I'll be fine." A thought struck her, and she smiled. "What if I pose as your wife? No one would guess who you really are then."

"No." If he'd scowled any harder, he'd have looked like Captain Ahab in *Moby Dick* when he was hunting for the whale.

"Why not? It's perfect."

"I have a hard enough time keeping my hands off you now, that's why." He swung away in frustration only to swing back. "And for the record, anytime we're around other people, I'm Jack Durham."

"Okay, Jack Durham. Just who am I supposed to be? Your sister?" She definitely didn't have sisterly thoughts about him, nor would she ever in this lifetime.

His Captain Ahab scowl deepened. "Maybe just an acquaintance."

Exasperation shot through her. "Roan, that won't provide cover."

"Where are your things?" He glanced around. "I need to find a place for you to stay."

"I already have a room at the Latimer Hotel, and my horse is at the livery. I told you I'm self-sufficient. Now maybe you'll believe me. We need to look for Gentry." She gave him a cajoling smile. "Later, I'll let you take me to supper. I hear the Latimer serves delicious steaks. But I'm buying."

At last, Roan gave her a crooked smile, and her heart skipped a beat. "I noticed from the first how bossy you are. I'm surprised your father hasn't taken you over his knee."

"I assure you he's probably wanted to on more than one occasion." Marley shook out her skirt and took his elbow.

They strode from the alley and joined the throng of people. Marley kept her eyes peeled for Gentry, wondering again why he seemed to know her. Maybe if she had a first name or a hometown to go along with it, she could figure out the puzzle.

Though they strolled up and down the street, looking in every establishment, they failed to spot the scarecrow-like man. When the sun began to fade, they went into the Latimer dining room. Every table was taken.

Roan rested his hand on the small of her back to lead Marley to the door when a rotund, grandfatherly man rose from the corner and approached. Marley liked his genuine smile and the way his eyes twinkled.

"Pardon me," he said. "My wife and I would love for you to join us at our table. It would be an honor. I'm Silas Wheeler."

Roan introduced himself as Jack Durham. Marley held her breath, wondering how he'd introduce her. "And this is my wife, uh…" He paused. "Mariah."

His wife. Marley hid a smile. Despite his initial refusal to let her pose in that capacity, he'd changed his mind.

Marley gazed up at him with adoration. "Thank you, sweetheart." She turned to Mr. Wheeler. "We've only been married one day. In fact, we only met such a short time ago I didn't even know if he'd remember my name." Her hand stole to his. "Jack is the most wonderful man, and I was lucky to catch him."

Roan lowered his mouth to her ear. "You can stop now, *Mariah*."

They followed Silas and took a seat at the table. He introduced his wife, Elizabeth. She reminded Marley of a fragile little bird, her movements all soft and fluttery. A large hat decked with feathers perched on her small head.

"I'm so glad you could join us." Elizabeth patted the table as if it were a dog's head. "I was just telling Mr. Wheeler that you're a beautiful couple and I wished to know you better. Mariah, you remind me of our daughter. She's back east, you know, studying to be a doctor."

Marley was glad they'd taken the Wheelers up on their offer. She liked them, and she was ravenous. "That's a lofty profession for a woman. I wish her well. Do you live in San Saba?"

Elizabeth's face darkened. "Thankfully, we do not."

"We make our home in Harkeyville," Silas explained. "There's trouble afoot in San Saba, my young friends. Watch what you say and keep a gun handy."

The waiter came to take their order. When he left, Roan asked, "Do you know a man who goes by Gentry? I don't know his first name. He's tall and—"

"Will Gentry," Silas interrupted. "The Will is short for Wilbert, I believe. Especially watch out for him. Gentry hasn't been here but a couple of months. He just appeared one day, and I don't know where he came from. But he'd kill you in a heartbeat, and Sheriff Coburn would look the other way. There is no justice in this town."

Marley's stomach knotted with worry and foreboding,

turning the name over again in her mind. Something said she must know Will Gentry.

Roan met her eyes. "I saw him with a nice, friendly woman named Virginia Creek."

"I know her," Silas said. "She has a ranch somewhere outside of town. Not sure what her connection is with Gentry, but I've seen her with him."

Elizabeth Wheeler adjusted her hat, her fingers fluttering amid the feathers and colorful netting like a flock of little birds. She laid a hand on Marley's and leaned close. "Keep your husband away from the women in this town or they'll snatch him."

"Thank you for the warning, Mrs. Wheeler." Marley removed her hand from under Elizabeth's and ran a fingertip teasingly up Roan's arm. "My darling Jack only has eyes for me. I trust him completely. He calls me his sugar dumpling. Have you ever heard anything more romantic? Makes my heart melt every—single—time."

The slight shake of his head prompted her to remove her hand. She'd gone a bit overboard, but darn it, she just wanted to play the part he'd given her. She couldn't help it if the role was one she craved for real. But maybe she'd better curb the syrupy sweetness.

It was such fun teasing him though. He was far too serious for a supper with new friends.

Roan shifted the talk back to the trouble in San Saba. "Silas, do you know what the root of the problem is here? Does it continue to stem from the mob that roamed here a few years ago?"

"That was a bad time. Killings and lynchings had everyone scared to step foot outside at night—or pretty much daytime, either. There was no law to be had until the Texas Rangers came." Silas gave the room a nervous scan. "I do think this is related somehow. Could be the children of those parents. Many were left orphaned or with only a mother."

Marley digested that. It sure fit. From everything she knew, the gang appeared to be comprised of very young kids. Maybe someone had recruited them and fed their anger. Often it didn't take much more than a word or two when someone was helpless. One thing she knew about was homeless children. The ranch was overrun with them. They longed to fit in and have a normal life, but it was like they wore shoes that didn't quite fit. In an effort to make do, they roped them to their feet and scooted along. She thought of Matt and wondered if he'd go to sleep tonight without a story. She'd have to remember to take him and the others a small treat.

Their food came, and they lapsed into silence, enjoying the fare. When she'd finished, Marley excused herself to go to the ladies' room—a new one that had been added on, with real plumbing! The clerk had pointed that out first thing, describing how modern they'd become. Once she was out of sight, she detoured to speak to the waiter and tell him to add the meal to her room bill.

"This is our secret. Please say that a patron just leaving paid for it." She slipped three shiny silver dollars into the waiter's hand. Thank goodness she was frugal with her money and had saved a large nest egg for such an emergency.

The personable young man grinned. "Yes, ma'am. And if there's anything else I can do, my name is Zach."

After making a mental note that he might be willing to talk to her about the pack of young riders roaming the countryside, Marley returned to her seat. "This is the nicest hotel," she remarked. "Everything is just spotless. I wasn't sure I'd even find a room."

Roan studied her with a smile and propped his chin on a bent arm. "How exactly did you manage that...sugar dumpling?"

She grew warm under his gaze. "Well, let's just say that they happened to have one room—the presidential suite— that they overlooked in the onslaught of visitors...dear."

Mainly because it was far too expensive. But the nice clerk had given her a deal.

Silas chuckled. "I have a feeling you have your ways,

just like my darling Elizabeth. Both of you can be very charming."

"Yes, we can, and don't ever forget that, Mr. Wheeler." Elizabeth patted his arm. "The good Lord gave us women a brain, and we know how to use it."

The men rose, and Roan pulled out Marley's chair. He leaned close. "We'd best pay our bill and be going—sugar."

Something told her that she had some explaining to do. She supposed she'd had just a teensy bit too much fun with this marriage business. Granny Jack was fond of saying that if you dance to the music, you have to pay the fiddler. This might be such a case.

When the waiter said they owed nothing, Roan and Silas pressed for a name of the mysterious benefactor, but the young man wouldn't divulge her secret. Unable to pull out the information, Roan and Marley finally told the Wheelers good night and went upstairs.

Roan's eyes widened when she paused in front of the presidential suite and slipped a key into the lock. "You're full of surprises, Mariah Durham." He held the door and made a sweeping bow. "Your Majesty."

Marley's stomach lurched. Inside, she tossed her shawl on a chair and faced him. "I swear, Roan, can't you tell a performance when you see one?"

He made a wide gesture around the room. "Mind catching me up to speed? I'm trailing behind."

"What do you want to know?" She chewed her bottom lip.

"This hotel? The mysterious benefactor? You're hiding things. How did you get this room?" His eyes narrowed. "And I need the truth."

She dropped onto a settee. Though wary, Roan took a chair. "It seems no one could afford the cost of this suite, so it hadn't been taken like all the others. It was my only option. The town is packed, and I needed a place to stay where I wouldn't have to worry about my safety." She found the courage to meet his gaze. "I promised Mama I'd find somewhere safe."

"Your mother knows you're here?"

"Yes. In fact, she helped me think of a way to keep Papa from finding out I came."

"Why? How?" His gray eyes darkened, and she raised a defiant chin.

"I wish you wouldn't look at me that way. Makes me feel like I kicked a dog or something. Mama saw the truth in my eyes."

"What truth?" A good bit of annoyance filled his voice.

"It's what I tried to tell you earlier." Marley met his lukewarm stare without flinching. "She understands my feelings for you. She knows what it's like to ache to be held, to feel the whisper of a breath on her face and lips pressed to hers. I came here with her blessing, and I'm not one bit sorry. I've never felt about anyone the way I feel for you, Roan Penny."

She lowered her voice to a whisper. "Whatever this is, I don't want to lose it, and I don't want to waste any time waiting for a right moment that may never, ever come. Don't you care for me at least a little bit?"

He wearily wiped his eyes. "Marley, I wish I could tell you what you want to hear, but even if I could, I wouldn't. It wouldn't be fair to you to pin your hopes on such a rocky future. I assume you're the one who paid the bill for ours and the Wheelers' suppers."

Here it was. The final nail in the end of their relationship. "Yes."

"Because I'm too poor?"

She glanced away. "My motives, if not the method, were pure."

"Marley," he said tightly, "if I hadn't had the money, I never would have gone. Don't rob me of my manhood."

"I'm sorry." So sorry about the mess she'd created. She was always trying to fix things, to make everything perfect when it was best to leave them as they were. When would she learn? Her throat burned. "I didn't mean to hurt your pride, yet it seems I did."

Silence spun in the air between them as through a fragile spiderweb buffeted by a north wind. At last, Roan let out a heavy sigh and moved to her side on the settee. He took her hand. "I'm sorry for getting upset. A man's pride is a fragile thing. I want to stand tall and proud next to you." His voice lowered. "If you steal my confidence, I can't do that."

"I see that now." She stared at her small hand inside his large palm. "I was wrong."

"It's all right." He suddenly chuckled. "You have quite a head on your shoulders. I'm amazed at your ingenuity. You got this room, secured your horse, signed up for the shooting match... Is there nothing you can't do, Marley McClain?"

His laughter eased the tense set of her shoulders. "Quite a lot, actually."

"Lord knows I haven't seen it." He released her hand and stood. "I need to check on Shadow and turn in."

"Where will you sleep?"

"The loft in the livery."

She glanced at her ample surroundings—the sofa, settee, and chair here and the comfortable bed through the open doorway. "Please, I have more than enough room. Can't you come back here for the night? Please?"

He walked to the door and put his hand on the knob.

"I don't want to be alone in a strange town," she pleaded.

With his back to her, Roan murmured, "I'll get my saddlebags. Lock the door behind me. Listen for my tap."

She breathed a sigh of relief as the door closed behind him. At least he'd accepted her apology. And he'd agreed to return. That thought sent her hurrying to the bedroom to unpack.

Eighteen

THE LIVERY WAS QUIET WHEN ROAN STEPPED INSIDE. THE heavy air carried the recognizable stench of blood. The hair on his neck twitched. He made his way to the gray mare's cubicle, and his insides twisted.

Shadow lay on blood-soaked hay.

He scrambled to her, his chest heaving with the need to breathe. The mare whinnied and looked up at him. He watched, his stomach lurching as she struggled to her feet. Tenuous relief that maybe she might not be hurt too bad rustled through him like dry autumn leaves. Then he saw a man's body on the red-tinged hay, and his stomach clenched again.

The old stable owner, Jessup, lay faceup. His long, white beard was matted with bits of hay and blood. He was breathing but unconscious, a bullet hole in his upper chest. Did the town have a doctor?

A sudden recollection of a sign hanging above the general store struck him. He hated leaving Jessup alone, but there was no other way. He took Shadow outside and tied her there so she wouldn't trample Jessup, and Roan ran for help. A minute later, he took the stairs attached to the side of the store two at a time and pounded on the door.

A weary man with bloodshot eyes answered the knock. "May I help you?"

"Jessup's been shot at the livery. He's in a bad way," Roan explained to the doctor, a man who looked just a few years older than himself.

The doctor jerked from his stupor. "That's my father. I'll get my bag."

In no time, they were back at the livery, and the doctor knelt over his father. "His breathing's shallow. Do you think you can help me carry him to the office?"

"Of course."

The doctor lifted his father under the shoulders, and Roan took his feet. A weary cowboy who'd just ridden in dropped the reins of his horse and held the door for them. The doctor told him the price for boarding and to bring the money to his office. They carefully made their way up the stairs. Inside, they laid the old man on a bed.

Roan stepped back to give the doctor room. "Do you think he'll make it?"

"Anyone's guess." Doc probed the wound. "My father has a bad heart." He wiped the blood from his hand and glanced up. "Bullet went through, so that's good. Damn the people of this town!"

"What exactly is going on?"

"A bunch of folks have been grumbling ever since the Texas Rangers came in here and quelled the old mobs. There's talk they intend to take back the property they lost and get revenge for family members who either died or were sent to prison. Not sure who's in charge, if anyone." Doc wiped his eyes. "All I know is that there's a war going on here and no one is safe."

Roan told him how close he had come to dying, and about Mose. "I'm looking for the ones responsible. I thought entering this horse race would help me find them. My mare was in the stables, and it looks like your father surprised someone messing with her." Probably trying to either kill or lame Shadow.

But why? To keep Roan from the race? A very likely

possibility. Someone must've recognized him. That's the only thing that made sense.

This keg of worms had become much bigger than Roan had thought. And the pressure to make sure Marley stayed safe sat heavy on his chest.

Doc reached for a stethoscope and listened to his father's heart. "The best thing you can do is forget what happened and go home. Nothing is worth dying over."

"Pardon me, but a few things are," Roan answered softly. As frustrated as Marley made him sometimes, she was definitely one person he'd die for. Mose had been the other. He scrubbed the back of his neck. "I'm not sure what to do with my horse. They'll kill her if I leave her at the livery. And I can't guard both the animal and my…wife…at the same time." Somehow Roan didn't think she'd be upset by the premature title.

"I have a small barn back of here where I keep mine. You're welcome to use it."

"Thanks, I'll take you up on that offer. By the time they figure out where she is, I'll be gone. I sure hope your father pulls through." Roan said good night and left, saying he'd be back to check on Jessup at daybreak.

He hurried back to the stables for Shadow. Thank goodness the mare was okay. He climbed the ladder to the loft. Stepping over sprawled bodies, he collected his things. Their snores were fit to raise the dead, and he was glad he didn't have to sleep there. Backing down the ladder, he got Shadow. Scanning the darkness for trouble, he took her to Doc's barn. Since over an hour had passed since he'd left the hotel and Marley would be worried, he wasted no time in returning to the Latimer. He tapped lightly on the door of the presidential suite.

"You're back!" Marley put a Colt back into a holster she'd strapped on and slid the bolt behind him. Whirling, she threw her arms around his neck. "I was so worried about you."

Roan dropped his saddlebags and drew her trembling body against him. "I'm fine. Just had some trouble at the livery."

Her dark eyes widened. "What happened?"

"Let's sit down." Once seated on the settee, Roan told her about finding Jessup, taking him to the doctor, and about moving his mare. "I'm not sure Jessup will make it. I hate that he got hurt trying to protect Shadow. It seems like my fault, even though I know in my head that it isn't."

"I met Jessup when I stabled my horse and thought him such a nice man. You can't blame yourself. What about Shadow? Did they hurt her?"

"No, thank God." He fell into the dark-brown pools of her eyes. They were so large and mysterious, showing the depth of caring and concern for someone she'd briefly met. He smoothed her furrowed brow.

She snuggled against him. "You weren't there to help or stop it, and that eats at you. But what happened is not your fault. Did the doctor know who might've done it?"

"No, he just said that there's a war going on here, and people are trying to take back what was stolen from them when the Texas Rangers came." He was silent a moment, thinking about Doc's words. "You know, maybe it's not just one person in charge of the riders. It could be several, or no one at all."

"Maybe Will Gentry," Marley said softly, chewing her lip. "Now that you've heard his voice and know he was there the night they killed Mose, he could very well be the ringleader." She shivered. "I can't get over the way he stared."

"I wish I knew." And Roan wished he knew where the man had disappeared to after leaving the tent. A man should always keep an enemy close.

"Marley, there's something I want to say." Roan took her hand. When she opened her mouth to speak, he stopped her. "You've spoken your piece. Now it's my turn. I do care for you, and the depth of my feelings shakes the stuffing from me. But, you have to give me a chance to go at my own pace, find my way, and make my own decisions."

Her lip trembled. "At home, I have to make decisions in the time it takes to blink, because the children are always flying at me fast and furious. But I never, ever want this to be a problem between us. If you'll be patient, I'll try to change."

Roan kissed her temple. "I'm a patient man, and the reward will be worth the wait. Just slow down a teensy bit and enjoy the ride."

"I'll try hard."

"That's all anyone can do. I intend to do some changing of my own. For one thing, I care for you more than anyone I've ever met. I aim to win this horse race and put that money back for our future. If you eventually want to build a life with me."

"Oh, Roan." Tears came into her eyes. "I've dreamt of you saying those words. Of course I want that. More than anything when the time is right."

"When that time has come, I'll propose." He barked a laugh. "Unless your father strips the hide from my body after he finds out you followed me."

"He'd better not." Marley rested her hand on his vest, her soft breath warm against his neck. "I'm so glad we have a future."

"I'm going to show your father that I'm more than a beaten-down drifter. All these plans will take some time to put in motion though." He tightened his hold around her. She was a priceless treasure. "You're my Texas Star."

She tilted her face for a kiss. He pressed his lips to hers, counting his blessings. She was the woman he'd searched for and finally found one cold fall morning. Or rather, she'd found him. It didn't really make much difference.

They were together and had the future to look forward to. And no one was going to stop him from making that come true.

Marley Rose McClain was his. He loved the sound of that.

He broke the kiss, and she rested her head against him. "If I was any happier, I'd burst. You like me. You really like me."

"Yes, I do." The timing could've been better. He should've waited until he'd gotten back home. But some things seemed to take their own course.

"What did you think of the Wheelers?"

"They appeared nice." Her words were slow and halting. "But they were too nice, too friendly. Too much. I don't know if I trust them."

"I felt the same way. A stranger coming over and inviting us to share their table was more than odd." He was glad that Marley shared his feelings. "The whole thing seemed off."

"For me too. I've been asking myself why he invited us to their table. He gave us some much-needed information. We gave them nothing." She drew little circles on the sprinkling of fine hair at his wrist. "Well, they bear watching."

"Absolutely." Roan shifted her and took out a pocket watch Duel had loaned him. It was getting late. "When is your shooting competition tomorrow?"

"Nine in the morning."

"You'd best get to bed, or you'll be bleary-eyed and miss the target."

Marley moved from his embrace. "Aren't you coming? Won't you sleep in the bed?"

"No."

"I'll give you plenty of room, and you can sleep on top of the covers. At least you'll rest."

"No, I won't betray Duel's trust," he said gently, running a finger across her cheek. "I'm going to do this right, and when I do get into bed with you, I'll belong there. The sofa over there will do fine."

Marley pouted. "Why do you have to be so honor bound?"

"Would you have me any other way?" He nibbled behind her ear.

"No. I sort of like that about you." Her lips curved in a teasing grin. "Want me to tell you a bedtime story?"

"You seem to have confused me with young Matt." But he found the prospect of one of her stories enticing. He tucked a curl behind her ear and returned her grin. "What kind would you tell me?"

She gazed into his eyes. "Once there was a young maiden who'd waited her entire life for a handsome prince to come along. She waited and waited and waited. Then one day, she found him lying beside the road almost dead." Marley drew a fingertip slowly down his shirtfront. Her voice grew breathless.

Roan had a hard time reining in his thoughts. He hungered to forget his noble intentions, to pull her luscious body against him and kiss her until they ran out of breath. He yearned to have her naked curves beside him and touch all of her silky skin.

He was tempted. Oh Lord, he was tempted!

"And then what happened?" he asked hoarsely, catching her fingertip and kissing it.

"She took him home and patched him up and told him all of her secrets. He called her his Texas Star, and his kisses left her as weak as thin porridge." She moved closer to nibble on his ear. "The prince kept saying that it wasn't the right time, teasing her with promises. Then one day evil men came and..." Her voice broke, and she got to her feet. "This is silly. Forget bedtime stories."

"They're not silly." Roan stood and took her in his arms. "One day your story will have a happy ending."

Marley bunched his vest in her grip. "Promise?"

"I promise. I'm not going to let Gentry or anyone steal your happiness." They were not going to make her story end in tragedy if he had anything to do with it. Fairy tales always had to have a happy ending. That was the rule.

He lowered his mouth to hers, and the kiss stole his thoughts. Need rushed through him, burning a path to the throbbing center of his being. Marley was the woman he'd looked for all his life. She was as imperfect as he, but the kindness inside her shone like a beacon.

She yanked his shirt from his pants and slid her soft hands underneath, her warm palms searing his skin, flattening across his muscles like a hot brand. "I want you, Roan Penny," she mumbled against his mouth.

Damn, he wanted her too. Like a man with a fever, he fumbled with the buttons of her dress, not satisfied until he touched her satiny skin. He let his fingers drift down the slender curve of her neck, on down to the sloping swell of her chest. He stopped where the flesh descended to her sweetly curved breasts. He wouldn't touch her there even though he wished he could, more than anything on earth.

It took every bit of willpower to keep from carrying her to bed and plunging himself inside her.

Roan ended the kiss and stepped away. "I can't do this to you, Marley." His breath became ragged. "I won't take something before you're ready. I want to do this right,"

"I know." She buttoned up her dress. "It doesn't make the wanting go away though."

No, it didn't. His swollen need testified to that.

Marley went into the bedroom and returned with a blanket. "Thank you for being here. I'm glad I'm not alone."

Roan's hands brushed hers as he took the offering. The brief touch was like raw, jagged lightning. With luck, one day he wouldn't have to stop. Then he'd find paradise in Marley's arms, and it would be right.

∾

Midnight came and Marley had yet to close her eyes. Her mind whirled, remembering the kisses that had stolen her sanity. She wondered if this was the way her parents felt around each other. Was she in love or just wanting something that she didn't have to share with anyone?

All she knew was that she didn't want to live without Roan. She couldn't.

She flopped onto her side, facing the wall. A noise alerted her, the faint sound of the window raising. Roan must've gotten too warm and needed air. Yes, that must be it.

Easing back to lie faceup, she spotted a dark form crawling over the windowsill. Her stomach clenched. Marley slid her hand under the pillow until she found the cold steel of her gun. She thought about crying out for Roan, but then the intruder might shoot him.

The intruder stole silently toward her.

One step. Pause. Then another. She could do this.

Marley lay perfectly still. Watching. Waiting.

Just as the dark-clothed man reached to clamp a gloved hand over her mouth, she pulled the trigger. An explosion burst from the end of her Colt.

A yell of anguish like that from a wounded animal filled the bedroom. Marley leaped from bed, backed up against the wall, and fired again.

Roan ran from the sitting room like a dark ghost with his gun drawn. He got off a shot before he was tackled. Both men went down with a grunt.

The horrible sound of fists colliding with bone and muscle filled the room.

They crashed onto the bed, grunting and hitting each other. The iron bedstead collapsed to the floor. She couldn't tell who was winning. She had to see.

Marley fumbled with a match and got the lamp lit in time to watch the intruder jump out through the window. A shower of glass and wooden shards from the window frame flew across the room.

Something sharp pierced her neck, but she paid the stinging pain no mind. She ran to where Roan was standing, his breath raspy. "Are you hurt?"

"No. Are you?"

"I don't think so. Thank God he didn't kill you." She walked into his embrace and clung to him. "He came here to get *me*. I was awake, and when his gloved hand reached out to cover my mouth, I fired. I'm glad you were here."

"Me too. You're shaking." He leaned her back to look at her. "You have a shard of glass in your neck. Hold still."

"I felt something sharp, but I was more worried about you." She stood still while he carefully pulled it out and pressed a handkerchief to the small cut.

"You need a bandage." He grabbed a towel from the washstand. "Hold this to the wound for now until we can do better."

"Thank you, Roan."

Just then, voices sounded in the hallway and fists pounded on the door. "What's going on in there?"

Another voice joined that one. "Open up."

"We've got company. Make yourself decent," Roan said. "I'll get the door."

Marley slid her arms into a wrapper and threw her shawl around her shoulders. In the light, she stared at blood on the pieces of broken window frame. Their shots had hit him. Good. Maybe he'd think twice before coming after her again. Before she could see more, people in all stages of undress poured into the sitting room, all talking at once.

Roan raised a hand and hollered, "Pipe down."

When they lowered their voices, he said, "My wife and I are fine. We shot at an intruder but he got away. Thank you all for coming, but you need to go back to your rooms and let us deal with this."

Just then the sheriff waded through the mass of people. "What happened here?"

"An intruder, Sheriff Coburn," said one man.

A woman with rags tied in her hair huffed. "He almost ravished the lady. She barely escaped with her life."

"No, it was a robbery," a bowlegged man in a nightshirt insisted.

Marley hid a grin. Everyone seemed to have their own version of exactly what had taken place. Roan appeared out of sorts, a dark thundercloud standing in the center of the dimly lit room. But then she guessed he had a right. Just when they were trying to keep their heads down and not draw attention to themselves, this had to happen.

The sheriff narrowed his eyes at him. "Don't I know you?"

"No," Roan answered. "I came in for the fair."

"From where?"

"The Aces 'n' Eights Ranch."

"You're not Duel McClain, and don't tell me you are."

"I wouldn't dream of it. I work there."

"Got a name, mister?" Sheriff Coburn asked.

Roan put his arm around Marley's waist. "Jack Durham. This is my wife, Mariah. We were sleeping when an intruder came through the window. We fired at him."

"Which one of you shot?"

"Both of us." Roan met Marley's eyes. She thought she saw pride in his gaze. "My wife is an excellent shot. She's going to win the shooting competition in the morning."

"We wounded him, Sheriff," Marley said. "He left bleeding."

Coburn frowned. "Why would he want to do you harm, Mrs. Durham?"

"You'll have to ask him. I have no enemies that I know of." Marley didn't lie there. "It's possible he got the wrong room by mistake—maybe he was after someone else. Maybe he was inebriated and didn't know where he was. You know how drinking men are. Or maybe he was a thief looking for something to steal. You'll have to take it up with him." She met Roan's shadowed gaze. "I'm just glad for my husband. My Jack sent him flying through the window."

"So your husband threw him out? I thought you said the culprit leaped through the glass."

"Wait just a cotton-picking minute," Roan yelled. "We're the victims here. Don't put this on us. And I suggest you treat my wife with respect."

Marley wanted to slap the lawman. Instead, she settled for a scathing glance. "A poor choice of words on my part. I assure you, the assailant went through under his own power."

The lawman shooed everyone out of the suite and examined the blood in the bedroom. She noticed how Coburn kept giving Roan odd looks. Though Roan was careful to stay in the shadows, the sheriff was going to figure out his identity any second unless they got Coburn out soon.

Marley stepped forward, putting a hand to her forehead. "Can't this wait, Sheriff Coburn? The hour is late, and we're both competing in the morning. I'm simply exhausted after my ordeal, and it's left me shaken. You can probably pick up a lot of clues outside. I'm sure he left a blood trail."

Coburn studied her for a good minute before murmuring, "I suppose, madam."

"Oh thank you, Sheriff. You don't know how much I appreciate that." She gave him a wide smile. "After all, the room isn't going anywhere, and I don't think the intruder will return. At least not tonight."

Somewhere, the man was tending to his wound—or wounds—whichever it turned out to be. She wasn't a vengeful person by nature, but she prayed he was in a whole lot of pain.

At last, the sheriff left. Roan pulled her against him. "We'll close off this room, and you'll sleep in the sitting room with me."

"Roan, do you suppose that was Gentry or someone he hired to come after me?"

He kissed her temple. "It's possible, but we can't know for sure."

Cold fear shimmied along her spine at how close the assailant had come to taking her. And doing what, once he had?

"If I'd been asleep, I might not have heard him."

He chuckled. "You weren't joking about knowing how to use a sidearm. I wish I could've seen the look on his face when you pulled the trigger. I don't feel a bit sorry for him. He deserved what he got."

"I hope he doesn't die." She glanced up at Roan. "I can't bear the thought that I—we—might've killed someone." A thought sent icy fingers along her spine. "Roan, do you think the Wheelers might've tipped the assailant off? Maybe that's why they invited us to their table."

Roan's jaw twitched. "It's very possible. There is only one presidential suite, and I heard you tell them that's the room you have."

"Oh, Roan, I led that nasty intruder right to us."

In one swift motion, he swept her into his arms and carried her to the sofa. Wrapping the blanket around her, he sat down beside her. "Try not to think about it." He reached into his vest pocket. "Here's the name of that publisher you wanted. I got it earlier when I was in the mercantile. Forgot to give it to you."

Excited, Marley held the paper next to the soft glow of the lamp. Harper Bros. Publishing. They were looking for all kinds of stories of all lengths, and they promised an answer back within three weeks. Was it possible that she could do this?

Possible that her dream could come true at last?

"When we get back to the Aces 'n' Eights, you send them that book of stories and illustrations you did for Matt right away. Won't you?" Roan asked.

She chewed her lip. "Yes."

He must've sensed her fears in her hesitation. "Marley, I know it's scary but you have a gift. Promise me you will do this. You'll not put it off."

"I'll send them my work." She told Roan about Granny Jack's husband and how he'd stood up to the gang back then and rooted them out alone. "I'm going to start on a book filled with the things she's told me over the years. That will be my gift to her at Christmas."

"You'll make her very happy." Roan stretched out his long legs and put his arm around Marley, drawing her to him.

As he tucked the blanket securely around her, she didn't think she'd ever felt more cherished. She sighed and laid her head on his shoulder. "I like being married to you, Jack Durham."

He kissed her forehead. "Tell me a story, sugar dumpling."

Nineteen

SHE SPENT THE NIGHT ON THE SOFA, FULLY DRESSED, IN Roan's arms, where he held her safe and secure. The sound of his heartbeat still lingered in her ear as they dressed and went down to breakfast in the hotel dining room. Roan had already gone out to check on the mare and old man Jessup. There was little change in Jessup's condition.

Now in the dining room, Marley scanned the patrons for the Wheelers, hoping to confront them, but the couple wasn't in there. She gave a groan when Sheriff Coburn came through the door and headed toward them.

"Don't look now but we're about to have company," she murmured over her cup of tea.

Worry clenched in her stomach. Given the sheriff's suspicions about Roan already, in the bright light of day, he was going to figure out Roan's identity just as sure as she was sitting there. She shot her make-believe husband a glance of admiration. Jack Durham looked very handsome with his hair neatly trimmed and curling around his collar, and he was freshly shaven. He wore his regular clothes today, the outfit that hugged his muscular body in all the right places, awakening the sleeping embers inside her.

"Whatever Coburn says, let me do the talking." Roan covered her hand with his. His face was grim. "He's spoiling for a fight. He knows me but can't place from where, and it's driving him crazy. If he throws me in jail, I want you to ride as hard as you can for the ranch and don't look back. Just get somewhere safe."

"I don't know if I can do that." It would test her will to ride off and leave him at their mercy. Who knew what they'd do.

"He's just about here. Promise me, Marley."

"I promise I'll ride to get my father and the ranch hands. That's all I'll promise." She set down her teacup and pasted a smile on her face. "Good morning, Sheriff. We're almost finished, but would you care to join us?"

Coburn sat down, not bothering to reply. He glared at Roan. "I finally placed you. Bet you thought you were pretty smart, waltzing in here wearing that fancy suit like some rich man. You're no better than Mozeke."

Roan's eyes darkened. "I've done nothing wrong. I came for the horse race."

"You came to stir up trouble. You were told never to step foot back in San Saba County."

"The way you keep saying that with such certainty tells me you were there that night. You ride with the hooded gang. You're one of them." Roan removed his hand from hers and wiped his mouth with the napkin. His voice was hard and deadly as he propped his elbows on the table and leaned forward. "You and Will Gentry are bedfellows, no doubt. How much is he paying you to *pretend* to keep law and order? And how hard are you actually looking for Jessup's assailant—and ours?"

Coburn's eyes glittered like stones. "I want you out of my town."

Hardness filled Roan's eyes, and his voice was low and lethal. "I'll leave after the race and not a second before."

Confusion rippled across the sheriff's face that someone had the gumption to stand up to him. His gaze shifted to Marley. She lifted her chin and met his cold eyes.

"Where did he find you—some brothel?" Coburn snarled.

A muttered curse left Roan's mouth and startled her. His

hands clenched into fists. If she didn't do something, he'd reach across the table and grab the jackanapes by the neck and twist his head off.

She laid a hand on Roan's arm and addressed the despicable man. "I'm Marley Rose McClain. And I assure you, Sheriff, my father, Duel McClain, will tear you limb from limb when he hears about this. He won't take kindly to having his daughter accused of being a whore."

Releasing an oath, Coburn got to his feet and slammed his chair against the table before he stomped from the hotel. She didn't think he'd give them any trouble himself, but she had no doubt he'd send others to do his dirty work.

He can't afford to let us leave town alive.

That was fine. They'd have to face her Colt. And Roan's. She'd put her money on them any day.

Roan sat there so silent and still and deadly quiet until the rage drained from him.

"I'm sorry I spoke when you asked me not to." Marley covered his hand. "I just couldn't let you take matters into your own hands. Coburn wanted you to attack him, prayed that you would. Then he'd have put you behind bars or shot you." Marley inhaled a calm breath. "I couldn't let him do that. Can you just talk to me?"

"What?" he asked.

"I apologized for speaking." She was confused. If he wasn't angry about that, then what? "I just couldn't stay quiet another second when Coburn accused me of being a harlot."

Roan finally grinned, wiping away the darkness. "I'm proud of you. You certainly gave him something to think about. I got the feeling he doesn't want to tangle with Duel. I was just lost in my thoughts."

"Care to share?" she asked softly.

"I was running the horse race in my head, trying to think where all the dangers might be hidden." He turned to her. "There are places along the route where gunmen could hide. And then there are the other contestants, who'll stoop to anything to win the race. They're not above maiming a horse to claim a victory. I don't care what they do to me, but it would kill me if they hurt my gentle mare. She's a very special horse and has already seen a lot of pain."

As had he. Too much pain, in fact.

"Roan, let's leave and go back home. Please don't go through with this race." Home, where they'd be safe from evil men like Gentry and Coburn.

He shook his head. "I'd like for you to consider it, but I'm staying. I have to see this through, even more so now that I need to find out why Gentry wants to take or kill you."

"You're crazy to think for one second I'll leave you here. If you stay, I'm staying. There's safety in numbers." But even as she tried to be brave, she found terror sliding up her backbone.

"Marley, they may try to prevent you from competing in the shooting match."

"What are you thinking?"

"I don't know." He leaned to brush a kiss across her lips. "Just know that I'll be there watching for trouble. I'm not going to let them hurt you. They'll have to go through me, and that's not going to happen."

His touch was like magic and soothed her fears. She wasn't alone and neither was Roan. They had each other, and they were a force to reckon with. Just ask the intruder from last night.

"I guess we need to go," she said. "The match will begin soon. I have to get my rifle."

With his hand on the small of her back, they went up to their room. She glanced around the bedroom, her gaze drawn to the broken window. A shiver swept over her. If she hadn't fired that shot, no telling where she'd be now. Or in whose company.

❦

Roan leaned against a tree, watching the crowd that had gathered to witness the shooting contest. In particular, he searched for Gentry. One thing he knew: the man would show up. For whatever reason, his fascination with Marley was too strong. So far, Roan hadn't spotted the man that Virginia Creek had warned him to avoid.

Nor did he see the Wheelers or Wes Douglas, Duel's former ranch hand.

Marley stood with the other contestants. She was the lone female amid the eight males. She talked with a young man—their waiter from last night—and appeared to have struck up a friendship. Roan admired her easy way with people, and he couldn't take his eyes off her.

Her dress outlined her lush figure and brought out her brown eyes. The breeze toyed with her dark curls, tossing them this way and that. His arms ached to hold her again as he had the night through.

Although he'd made a show of being irritated over the way she'd gone about pretending to be married, he'd enjoyed having people think they were a couple. Marley's beauty stole his breath, and he took it as a compliment that she seemed to have developed what she thought was love for him. Maybe it was. That remained to be seen.

How could anyone love a wanderer like him—a drifter with no roots and only one purpose? And one that might get him killed?

Marley Rose McClain could have anyone she wanted. All she had to do was crook her finger at some man and he would come running. So why did she want him when she could have anyone she chose? She didn't know her power.

He hoped she won the competition. That would show everyone—and herself—what she was made of.

As the first man stepped to the line to shoot, Roan's thoughts drifted to his visit with Doc Jessup that morning. Roan had asked him if anyone had come for treatment of a gunshot.

"Only one," Doc had said with a chuckle. "A husband who said his wife shot him. She brought him to my office, and they argued the whole time I was patching the guy up, so that story had to be true. They left with her threatening to shoot him again if he so much as thought about looking at Vera Kingsley. Why do you ask?"

Roan filled him in on the intruder and the blood left behind. "I know we shot him. I just wonder who fixed him up."

"Maybe he died of his wounds."

That was possible, but Coburn would've mentioned it at breakfast. Roan's gut told him that the sheriff had a pretty good idea of the man's identity. If the intruder had turned up his toes, Coburn would've had Roan in jail before the butter had melted on his biscuit.

To speed up the shooting competition, they had multiple targets set up, one next to the other. Marley consulted the chart and went to her line.

The first contestant finished after a dismal showing. Each of his three shots had missed the large red X on a board nailed to a tree twenty yards away. Another contestant took his place, and one shot landed near the bull's-eye, but the other two were not even close. Each man took his shots one by one, with none hitting dead center.

Then, straight and tall, Marley stepped to the line. She was all business, and even without knowing her, Roan would never have bet against the strong woman, not here or anywhere. She'd show these people what a lady could do.

Before she raised her rifle to her shoulder, Roan caught movement from the corner of his eye. He swung to his left to see Will Gentry. The man had his hand pressed against his shoulder, his mouth curled in a grimace. Intent on watching Marley, Gentry hadn't noticed Roan.

A roar went up from the crowd as Marley hit the bull's-eye with her first shot.

Roan weaved through the onlookers, coming up behind Gentry as the man reached inside his long, dark coat. For a gun? Roan couldn't take that chance.

As slick as oil on a river current, he slid his Colt from the holster and poked the steel barrel into Gentry's back.

"Hands where I can see them, and don't even think about going for your gun. If you think I'm going to let you hurt her, you'd best think again. You don't stand a chance even on your best day."

"You don't know what you're doing, Penny," Gentry growled in a gravelly voice. "Or who you're messing with."

"Maybe not, but my warning still stands. Hurt Marley and you die. I'll blow your scarecrow head off and see what it's stuffed with. Turn around slow and easy."

Gentry's eyes glittered like shiny silver buttons, and Roan felt the pure evil that came from staring into the eyes of a devil.

"What do you want with Marley?" Roan bit out, keeping the Colt aimed at Gentry's chest. That was when he clearly saw the spot of wetness on the shoulder of Gentry's coat and a cut on his face.

"She's mine."

"You're sadly mistaken there, you piece of horse shit. She doesn't belong to anyone, least of all you. Did you break into her hotel room last night and try to take her?"

"Why would I need to do that? If I'd wanted in, I'd have used a key." A cold smile curved Gentry's mouth. "The clerk owes me."

Roan didn't buy the statement. "Move over to that alley to your right. We're going to finish this conversation and find some horses."

"And miss the race?" Gentry chuckled. "I had a surprise all planned for you and everything."

Behind them, Marley's rifle fired, and again a roar went up from the crowd. Roan didn't take his eyes from Gentry but assumed the noise meant she'd hit the bull's-eye again. He gave his quarry a shove toward the alley. Getting him out of town would be a chore with enemies at every turn.

"Why can't you just die?" Gentry spat. "What does it take to kill you?"

"A lot more than you've got, and I don't have to wear a hood over my head to fight. I recognize your voice. You were with the riders that night. You're nothing but a murderer."

"Good luck proving that, Penny."

As they started to cross to the alleyway, a herd of horses driven by whooping cowboys raced toward them. Roan barely had time to dive behind a tree and clear the path. When they had finally disappeared toward the outskirts of town, there was no sign of Wilbert Gentry.

Roan kicked the dirt. He'd lost the slippery man again. Hell and damnation!

He hurried back to the competition just as Marley finished her last shot. She strode toward him, her skirt snapping around her ankles, a satisfied smile on her face. "I hit the X dead center with all three shots, but so did another contestant. We have a tie."

"I'm proud of you. You could give Annie Oakley a run for her money. When's the shoot-off?" The second round would require a bit more skill, the targets moved back twenty more yards.

"In a few minutes."

"That's good." Roan scanned the crowd for Gentry. It would be like the man to sneak back and take a potshot at Marley.

"What's wrong?" Panic filled her voice.

"Gentry was here." Roan told her about the conversation and how the man had escaped. "I don't know how or why those riders came along just then, but I feel in my bones that it wasn't by accident. They helped Gentry get away. I know it. He told me you were his."

Marley gave a cry and covered her mouth with her trembling hands. "What does he want?" she whispered. "What? I'm not anything to him. I don't even know him."

Roan clasped her tightly to him, afraid to let her go for fear she'd disappear. "Don't worry. I won't let him get close to you. We don't have too many friends in this town but we don't need them. We have our guns and we can shoot the bastards."

No one would get his Texas Star without losing a lot of blood.

"I have one," she said softly.

"One what?"

"A friend—the waiter who works at the hotel. His name is Zach."

"I saw you talking to him. Pardon me, but he doesn't exactly look like he's experienced in anything other than waiting tables."

"Maybe not. I did glean some information though." She moved closer to Roan and whispered, "Zach said the gang tried to recruit him but he didn't want anything to do with them. You were right about them being young riders. They help their boss—someone named Rube—take back land that was ripped from them three years ago after the Texas Rangers rode in. It seems Rube has gathered up kids who lost either their fathers or both parents. Some of their fathers are in prison. The boys are hurt, angry, and alone. Rube feeds them, gives them a place to stay, and looks out for them."

Roan knew from experience what that sort of kindness meant to a lost, hungry kid. Being cared for would buy a lot of loyalty. "Did Zach give you a last name?"

"No. Rube is all. Roan, this means that Gentry is not the ringleader."

"I guess so." He'd been wrong about that part, but the man was still involved up to his beady eyes. Had to be or he wouldn't have been at Mose's. It seemed the more they learned, the more the mystery deepened.

How far would he have to dig to hit pay dirt?

And would he and Marley live long enough to find all the answers?

Twenty

ROAN STOOD NEAR MARLEY AS THE SECOND ROUND OF the shooting competition began. The man she was tied with stepped to the line and raised his rifle. He was a young guy, no more just an inch or two over five feet and as skinny as a willow sapling.

Roan wasn't paying much attention beyond that, busy scanning the crowd for Gentry. So far, he saw nothing.

The contestant hit the new target with all three of his shots, but only one made it to the bull's-eye. Marley moved into place and raised her Winchester. She took her time, putting the board in her sights. Slowly, she squeezed the trigger and sent the bullet hurtling through the air. A roar went up when the hole ripped right into the target's dead center.

Marley stepped back and took a deep breath.

"You can do this," Roan cheered. "Slow and easy."

She smiled at him and toed the line again. Her second shot just missed the X, a hair outside the middle where the lines crossed.

As she raised her rifle the third time, a shot rang out from behind them. Roan grabbed Marley and hit the dirt. Screams echoed around them, and people scattered.

"Are you hurt, Marley?"

"No."

"Stay here and keep down," he ordered. Without

waiting for an answer, he rose and raced to a tree. Counting to three, he zigzagged to another and another.

Everything was eerily quiet. He paused near the street, and movement made him look up at the second story of the hotel. A man with a rifle stood on the balcony. Sun in his eyes, Roan couldn't tell if it was Will Gentry, but the build told him it could be. Just then, the possible shooter whirled to go inside.

Roan lifted his Colt and fired, but the man had vanished. The bullet splintered the door facing. Damn!

Though he waited for the man to show himself again, he didn't. Roan strode quickly back to Marley.

Virginia Creek was with her, her arm around Marley. "Tell me what I can do. Would you like me to take you to the hotel where you'll be safe?"

"No, thank you. I'm not forfeiting this competition." Marley pulled from her arms and ran to Roan. Her heart stampeded like a herd of wild broncs. "Was someone trying to kill me?"

"I don't know." He held her close until her trembling stopped. "Put him out of your mind and finish this competition. I'll be right here."

"I don't know if I can."

"I'll be here too," Virginia declared. "We aren't going to let anyone run you off."

Roan leaned Marley back and stared into her brown eyes. "You're not a quitter. Don't let them scare you. I don't think he was trying to kill you—I'm sure he was just trying to keep you rattled."

Marley gave him a shaky laugh. "Well, it's working. But I won't give up. I have one more shot, and I'm taking it."

"That's my girl. The gentlemen are motioning to you. Go show them what you're made of." He didn't mention that those so-called gentlemen looked ready to run for cover. Their eyes darted around, and they hunched over. Virginia Creek went to speak to them. Whatever she said seemed to reassure them, because their fear vanished and they stood straight.

Roan's hand moved to the butt of his gun, ready if a shot came from behind.

Marley paid them no mind as she strode confidently into place. Roan would never have guessed the severity of her nerves if he hadn't known. On the outside, she was cool and calm as she put the rifle to her shoulder and fired. She sent the cartridge tumbling and whirling through the air.

Again, it struck the X dead center. This time there was no cheering crowd, no applause. Even her opponent had disappeared. With Virginia and Roan standing tall beside her, she accepted the money.

❧

With no time to celebrate, Roan and Marley hurried to get Shadow from Doc's small barn. Roan examined her legs carefully, then they made their way to the horse race.

He checked to make sure his gun was fully loaded and patted Shadow's sleek neck. This competition was going to test both him and the gray mare. "This is it, girl. Give it all you have."

His gaze found Marley on the sidelines. His heart cartwheeled.

The Wheelers stood next to her.

Worry slid along his spine like melting snow. But he knew Marley's expertise with a gun, and she already distrusted them. He had to turn his thoughts to whether the shooter from the hotel would make another appearance and run the race. He needed that money worse than ever.

That money now represented their future.

His father's voice sounded in his ear, drowning out the noise around him. *Your name is Penny and you're not worth even that. You're weak.*

"We'll see about that," Roan muttered.

Gentry had promised a surprise, so he had to be alert to every movement.

Quinn—the man who'd registered riders for the

event—yelled for the racers to mount up. He raised a pistol over his head, readying to fire.

The fifteen entrants swung into their saddles and moved to the starting line in the dirt. Roan sized them up. The big guy on the rust-colored sorrel could give him trouble, as well as the one on the red bay. Roan thought the sorrel was the same one Gentry had been riding, but he couldn't be sure. He turned to the kid to the right of him and got quite a start. That peach-fuzz face had been burned into his memory the night of the bloodbath—Roan had snatched the hood from his head and stared right into those same young eyes.

The boy's gaze met his and recognition dawned. His jaw dropped, and he swallowed hard.

Roan smiled and stretched out his hand, introducing himself as Roan Penny. "Don't I know you from somewhere?"

"Nope. I thought—"

"That I wouldn't be stupid enough to show up here?" Roan suggested, grinning.

The boy shrugged. "Reckon it's a free world."

"I saw you there that night. Don't bother to deny it."

"No, mister, I don't know what you're talking about." The kid gave a nervous glance around him and lowered his voice. "Watch your back."

"I intend to." Before he could say more, the gunshot sounded the start of the race. On cue, the animals leaped forward.

He allowed Shadow an easy pace. A mile and a half called for saving the bulk of steam for the last leg. Those who raced to the forefront now would have no wind left at the end. At least he was counting on that.

"Take your time, girl. We're just out for a leisurely stroll. The middle's a good place to stay for now."

As he figured, the big sorrel moved to the front right away. Roan switched his focus, caught the movements of the riders on a black gelding and a chestnut as they tried to sandwich him between them. He quickly evaded them, but he couldn't outmaneuver the long crop the rider of the red bay was wielding. The whip caught him across his forearm.

Searing pain shot to his shoulder, then radiated across his back. He renewed his grip on the reins and clenched his jaw. They'd have to earn their pay to get him.

"So that's the way you want to play this, huh?" he muttered into the wind.

A short distance ahead, the kid from Mose's land swiveled in the saddle to watch. He had to know about the plan to knock Roan from his horse—and no doubt trample him into the dirt.

They'd make it appear the perfect accidental death.

A shame it hadn't worked.

Not yet.

Their first attempts had fallen short, but that didn't mean they were done. They'd use other, more devious tricks, and force him to go on the offense sooner than he wished. He'd known this would be no picnic. He'd earn every cent if he won.

A sloping descent down Brushy Mountain took all his wits. Once he reached level ground, he nudged Shadow harder. A stand of cedars loomed ahead. The evergreen branches were an excellent place for someone to lie in wait. The horses would have to pass close between the trees on the trail that cut through the cedar brake.

Unless…

Roan moved to the far outside right. He'd have barely enough room to go around.

Just as he neared the stand of trees, he veered sharply. His mare raced around the cedars, splashed across Indian Creek, and jumped a fence.

Hooves pounded behind him. He peered over his shoulder to see the rider on the red sorrel closing the gap.

Away from the pack, Roan had put himself in a more vulnerable position. Should there be an honest one in the bunch—which he doubted—no one could witness his death out here. No one in town would know that he'd been so ruthlessly murdered. Marley would suspect, but she'd have no way of proving it.

But he wouldn't make this easy—he meant to put up a hell of a fight. Roan spied a thick, low branch up ahead. It could knock a rider from his horse if such a man had eyes glued on a particular target instead of paying attention to the ride.

Calm determination kept him tall and straight in the saddle.

The red sorrel breathed down his neck. Another long stretch and the rider would be on him.

"Keep coming, you bastard." Roan timed his move. A split second before they reached the branch, he ducked and sailed below. He twisted to see if the rider had avoided it. True to his prediction, the rider rode directly into the branch, flew from the horse, and slammed into the ground. The man didn't move, telling Roan the impact had probably knocked him out cold.

One down and a few more to go.

Another fence appeared, which Shadow jumped with ease. They raced around a bend, and Roan guided the mare back on the course with the other racers. They came out very near the front.

The kid and the fellow on the bay were in the lead. Their faces changed to looks of shock when they spotted him trailing them. Their horses had used up most of their legs, white foam spraying from the animals' mouths.

He watched for the long crop of the man on the red bay and lunged when it snaked toward him. Again and again the horseman struck, whipping the air.

They skirted Antelope Creek. Shadow set the pace at a hard gallop, the horse giving everything she had. "Come on, girl. You can do it." The finish line lay around the bend. Just a few more lengths. A few more yards. A few more last-ditch efforts by those behind him.

The mare's full stride led them past the kid and edged the bay by a nose. Roan barely saw the heavy chain in time. The diabolical rider was trying to wrap it around Shadow's fetlock.

Such a device could break fragile bones. Tear tendons. Maim a horse for life.

"The hell you will," Roan muttered through his teeth.

The rider stretched, leaning down, swinging the chain inches from its target. Roan grabbed the man's arm, holding it in a vise grip. Before he could latch on to the chain, it dropped and his heart stopped.

The metal links landed under Shadow. He knew the minute she stepped down on the pieces of steel, felt it in the marrow of his bones. He tightened his grip, getting ready to go down. If he could just keep from landing under the horse, he'd be all right.

The mare stumbled.

Her forelegs buckled.

She dropped to her knees.

He braced himself for the crunch of breaking bone, held on for dear life, and prayed.

Somehow, the horse picked herself up, barely breaking a stride, and plunged on. It appeared the chain had landed on soft earth. Instead of doing the damage it had intended, it must've sunk harmlessly into the ground.

"Now's the time, girl. Let's see what you have."

No one could say she was graceful and fluid compared to the other horses, but the mare with a broken ear wasn't shabby either. She flew over the remaining length.

Cheers and jeers rang out.

Shadow responded, pounding across the finish line. Roan slowed where Marley and the Wheelers were and dismounted.

"You did it, son!" Silas Wheeler shouted.

Marley threw arms around him. "You won!"

Roan gave her a quick kiss. "I've got to see to my mare."

He hurried to Shadow. She stood, shuddering, sides heaving, muscles quivering. She'd used everything she had in doing what he'd asked of her…and more. He checked her legs for injury, thankful to find none. Tears clogged his throat as he patted the thick, gray neck. "You're something else, girl. I'm proud of you."

A chorus of voices rooted, "Hip, hip, hurrah!"

Roan glanced around for the boy he'd spoken to before the race. He needed to find out what the kid knew. Maybe he'd be willing to talk.

"I say you're a yellow-dog cheater, Roan Penny." Wilbert Gentry's ominous, gravelly voice came from the platform where a handful of men stood. "I say you didn't win this race."

A deadly quiet descended over the throng of onlookers.

Roan rested a hand on the Colt's grip, ready for whatever came. He'd fight, and he'd probably get hurt or thrown in jail, but he'd never run. Not from anyone.

Silas Wheeler swung to him. "I thought your name was Jack Durham."

"That was a fake name to keep from being detected. You can see why." Roan stared at him. "Tell me you aren't one of them. Deny that you didn't help the intruder who broke into our hotel room."

"I don't know where you got that idea." Silas scratched his head. "Elizabeth and I had no ulterior motive in calling you over to our table. We just thought you looked like a couple we'd like to know."

Elizabeth broke in. "He's telling you the truth. Mariah looks so much like our daughter, and we miss her badly." The lady's hands fluttered from her hat to her reticule. "But her name's not Mariah either, is it?"

"No, ma'am." Marley gave her a hug. "I'm glad we were wrong about you, but you understand how we have to suspect everyone."

"Oh yes, we certainly do."

Roan faced Silas. "I'm sorry for misleading you. And we're not really married."

"I hate to hear about that last part. You two belong together." Wheeler stood below the platform with Roan where Gentry stood with Sheriff Coburn and Quinn. Virginia Creek's red hair glistened in the sun as she climbed the stairs to join them.

"You're fools and liars," Wheeler shouted at Coburn, Gentry, and Quinn. "The whole mess of you."

Roan watched in disbelief as Silas stood up for him.

"Penny stands alone," Coburn barked. "This is our town. We won't let him waltz in here and take what belongs to us. He's nothing. A nobody."

The words stung Roan to the quick, but it wasn't anything he hadn't already heard over and over.

"Roan Penny's my friend, and he doesn't stand alone." Wheeler waved his arm at the crowd. "We're all beside him. These people aren't going to let you kill him like you've done so many of our neighbors."

Marley clutched Roan's arm. "What's going on?"

"It might be only temporary, but just maybe the tide has turned in this town." Roan watched the four on the platform talk among themselves.

The crowd pressed closer and the four broke apart. Sheriff Coburn held up his hand. Angry red streaks mottled his neck. "I'm sorry, folks. It seems we misspoke. Winner of the San Saba County Fair annual horse race is Roan Penny. Let's give him a round of applause as he comes up to collect the purse."

Silas Wheeler slapped Roan's back. "Go get your money. You earned it."

"Thanks, Silas." He waited while Gentry helped Virginia Creek down the stairs and onto a horse. She galloped from town in a cloud of dust.

Roan frowned. "A question for you, Silas. How well do you know Virginia Creek?"

Wheeler drew his eyebrows together. "Only well enough to say howdy. The mob killed her husband, Thomas Creek, and their three boys a few years back." The name was nowhere close to Rueben or Rube, Gentry's supposed boss. Maybe he was connected but using an alias.

Holding his shoulder again and cradling his arm, Gentry blocked their path to the stage. The scarecrow's hard eyes narrowed.

The hair on the back of Roan's neck bristled. "Step aside."

They stood face-to-face and stared each other down for several long beats. Finally, Gentry stepped aside.

"You and me have unfinished business," Roan promised as he shoved past Gentry and bounded up the short flight of stairs. He'd get his money, then put Gentry on a horse at gunpoint. Roan would take him to Sheriff Bagwell in Tranquility.

At the top of the stairs, Roan stood next to Coburn and Quinn. The men's icy glares didn't faze him. He smiled and nodded. "Gentlemen."

The sheriff snarled, "Take your money and get out of my town. The next time you come, you'll leave in a coffin."

"This town doesn't belong to you. It belongs to the people, and they seem to have smartened up," Roan said low. He turned to the crowd and raised his hand in a wave, thanking them for supporting him.

Movement down below caught his attention. A lone rider had paused in the street for one last glance. Gentry. Then he whirled and galloped from town.

Where was he going? Foreboding tightened in Roan's chest. He snatched the money from Quinn's hand and leaped over the side of the platform.

Marley waited below. He grabbed her hand. "We have to leave. Now."

"But I need to thank the Wheelers first."

"There's no time. I just spied Gentry riding out of town—heading for the road that leads toward your ranch."

"Why didn't you say so?" Marley ran beside him to the gray mare.

Thank goodness they'd packed their bags before they'd left for the shooting contest that morning. It was easy to grab them and race to the livery for Marley's horse, but it all ate up precious time. Soon, though, they left San Saba behind. Shadow had barely had time to rest from the race, which limited them to a canter. Roan kept his eyes peeled for Gentry and trouble. They kept at a slow, steady pace for several hours.

Marley finally maneuvered her chestnut close. "Tell me about the race. I want to know everything. I can't imagine the danger you were in."

Roan spared no details. She wanted the unvarnished version, and that's what he gave her. When he reached the part about the chain, she burst out, "That sorry, low-down varmint ought to be strung up! If I ever see him again, I'm going to shoot him."

"I agree with your assessment, but you can't go around shooting people you have a quarrel with." He did love her passion though. "I hate for our time together to end. I really enjoyed being married to you, Mariah. More than I thought I would."

"Am I growing on you?" she asked softly.

Too much, truth be known. He couldn't imagine riding away and leaving her, even if Duel kicked him off his land when he discovered what his wayward daughter had done. And that was bound to happen. One thing Roan had learned was that secrets never stayed buried. And there were far too many eyes and ears on the ranch.

"You are for sure, Marley McClain."

"What are you going to do when we get back?"

"About what?"

"Your job. Me. We have the money for our future."

"That depends on your father." And on Will Gentry. There were still too many variables for him to give her a direct answer.

They went over what they'd learned. According to Zach, the leader was someone named Rube.

Maybe Coburn used an alias.

That was possible. One thing about it, the woman couldn't be Rube, couldn't be part of the mob. A woman would not do the things the gang had done or use innocent kids. No, Rube had to be short for Reuben or something else. Maybe the leader stayed in the background, hiding his identity. Or maybe Rube lived on a nearby ranch and ran the operation from there, never coming into town at all.

Damn if Roan could figure it out.

He just wished he knew what Rube looked like. The man could stand two inches from him and he wouldn't even know.

"I never saw anyone matching Wes Douglas's description either. Did you, Marley?"

"No. I kept a close eye out for him too. Do you suppose we're trying too hard to link our former ranch hand with this gang?"

Who the hell knew. Roan lapsed into silence as he mulled over all the pieces of the puzzle.

The late-afternoon sun reflected on something metallic ahead, sending a warning to Roan's gut. Gentry lying in wait, looking for a chance to hurt or kidnap Marley? Roan slid his rifle from the scabbard.

"What's wrong?" she asked.

"I noticed a flash of light." He pulled up. "You wait here with the horses. I'm going ahead on foot."

"Be careful." She reached for her rifle. "If I hear shots, I'm coming."

Silent and alert, Roan cut into the trees and zigzagged from one to another. Scanning ahead. Listening. Smelling the acrid scent of danger.

The thick trees muffled every sound and left the silence pressing heavy and dark against him. His nerves, stretched to the breaking point, screamed. If he didn't hear a noise soon, he'd go mad.

As he moved to the next tree, a shot split the bark of the tree trunk.

Roan dove to the ground.

Twenty-one

A SINGLE RIFLE BLAST SHATTERED THE QUIET. MARLEY jerked. Roan needed her. She tied the horses to a sturdy branch off the road. Winchester in hand, she hurried in the same direction Roan had taken, trying to be as quiet as possible. Even though the shooter knew they were nearby, she saw no reason to advertise their exact location.

Her mouth dried, her heart pounded harder with each step, and all she could think about was Roan being in danger, lying horribly wounded. She didn't want to consider what else.

Every sense honed in on her surroundings, just as she'd been taught. Some city folks might panic, have no idea of the danger to watch and listen for, and most would simply rush forward. Not Marley. Though filled with a burning urgency, she took her time and kept to the cover of the trees.

Over the years, Duel had made it a priority to teach her these skills. He'd seemed obsessed making sure she and the older children knew how to survive in case he wasn't there. At the time, she hadn't known the reason; she'd just loved spending time with him. Now, she understood.

She moved slowly, every step deliberate and careful.

"Psst."

Marley glanced around, not seeing anyone until a hand grabbed hers and pulled her down.

"You shouldn't have come," Roan whispered.

"I promised I would the second I heard a gun. Are you hurt?"

"The shot missed me."

That relieved her mind. "Where is the shooter?"

"About ten yards ahead last I saw," he answered. "We have only a few hours left of daylight."

"What's the plan? The two of us could flush him out."

"Go back to the horses, young lady. After the ruse you pulled on your father, you getting shot would finish him off. I'd be lucky if I even got to wave goodbye."

Frustration rose. "You worry too much about my father."

"One of us needs to."

"Horse feathers! I know how to handle him. The ranch should be close. I could ride through the trees for help."

"Too dangerous."

"We have to do something," she whispered back furiously. He was being completely unreasonable. "You need me."

Roan let out a sigh of defeat. "I must be as crazy as a bedbug."

He outlined the plan. They'd approach from both sides. Roan would give a towhee bird call to signal the attack. "If he turns and fires at you—"

"I'll shoot to kill," she answered grimly. "I know how to stay safe."

Before they parted, he picked up a rock and pitched it away from them into a group of pecan trees. The burst of orange gunfire that followed gave them the man's location.

They crept in a circle—Roan to the left, Marley on the right. She could see something that looked like a knitted cap through the brush. Odd. Gentry hadn't worn one of those.

She stepped on a twig and froze at the sound. Ducking, she stayed still for what seemed like hours, but it had to be only a minute or two.

When the knitted cap didn't move, she proceeded. Finally, she was in position and the call of a towhee bird came only seconds later. She tightened her finger on the trigger and rushed toward the shooter as Roan came from the opposite direction.

They stood over the stocky man with rifles pointed. His eyes widened as he raised his hands. "Don't shoot."

Roan snatched the man's rifle from him. "Who are you? Why did you fire at us?"

"A traveler paid me. He said someone was trying to kill him, so he gave me five dollars to hide an' shoot at you, keep you from passing." He stared up with one eye closed, scratching under an arm. "Name's Charles."

Roan didn't appear to be forgiving. Darkness crossed his face and deepened every line. Marley had seen the same when the intruder had broken into her hotel room. Most of the time, he kept that black storm that lurked inside him carefully hidden. Such unbridled anger scared her just a little, though she knew he'd never hurt her. Her fear was for what he'd do to others. Strange that it came out whenever Marley's life was threatened.

"Was the guy extremely thin with sunken cheeks?" Roan asked.

Charles nodded, glancing at Marley. "I didn't know one of you was a lady, miss. Sorry. I jus' needed that five dollars. Can I stand up now?"

Roan snapped. "Go ahead but keep your hands where I can see them."

"You look like a nice man, Charles," Marley said. "You really made some bad choices. How did the man find you?"

"Aw, I was just passing on the road an' he stopped me." Charles pointed down the road that led home. "He asked me how far to the Aces 'n' Eights."

Marley's stomach clenched. Why was he headed there? Something told her it wasn't for a friendly game of checkers.

She asked Roan the safer question instead. "What are we going to do with Charles?"

Without an answer, Roan ejected the remaining cartridges from the man's rifle, then picked them up and threw them as far as he could. He shoved the old Winchester into

Charles's chest. "Go. If we ever cross paths again, I won't be so lenient."

"You won't be sorry." Charles scrambled toward his horse, a broken-down farm nag tied to a tree. He swung onto the animal's bare back and galloped off.

Marley watched him disappear. "What do you think Gentry has in mind, going to the ranch?"

"Don't know." Roan stared into the growing shadows. "But you can bet I'm going to find out."

❧

The sun had already set, leaving a purple glow in the sky when they rode through the gate of the Aces 'n' Eights. Her parents came from the house holding hands and followed them to the barn. Marley's stomach knotted. Her father hadn't returned her greeting, just walked in silence. The grim lines of his face told her she was in for big trouble. Darn it, she wasn't sorry.

As she dismounted at the corral, she went on the defense. "I can explain."

"I think we're past that, Marley Rose." Duel glanced at Roan. "If you put her up to this, you can pack your things right now."

"Papa, I followed him. He didn't know anything until he found me in San Saba."

Roan met Duel's gaze and didn't flinch. "Sir, I was pretty angry when I found her smack in the middle of danger and told her as much. I tried to send her home right then. But as you know, Marley has a will of her own."

"Tell me about it."

"Sweetheart, what she says is true." Jessie put her arm around Duel's waist. "Roan Penny didn't know anything. And yes, I helped her, and I would again. Don't you remember how it was with us?"

"That was different," Duel answered.

Marley softened her voice. "I'm not a little girl, Papa.

You taught me to make my own decisions, to weigh the risks and the consequences. Let me do that. I'm a grown woman"—she paused—"and Roan is going to court me."

Duel jerked off his hat and ran his fingers through his hair. "I find it hard to turn those apron strings loose. I know what men think when they see a pretty woman. I don't want them thinking those things about you."

"You can't always protect me." Marley kissed his cheek. "Now I have a question for you that has nothing to do with Roan, and somehow I suspect you know the answer."

The loud cry of an animal froze her blood. She moved into the circle of Roan's arms.

Duel turned. "There's a mountain lion roaming our land. Be careful. Hardy caught a glimpse of it."

After several heartbeats, he swung back around and shot Jessie a questioning glance. She raised an eyebrow, her nod slight. "Your mother and I have tried our best to be honest with you, so shoot."

"Who is Wilbert Gentry?"

Duel's face drained of color and Jessie gave a sharp cry, throwing her hand over her mouth.

"Why do you ask?" Duel managed to ask through stiff lips.

Marley and Roan together told them all they'd learned in San Saba and then about the ambush on the road home.

"Gentry is somewhere close," Marley said. "Who is he and why does the mention of his name send you both into a panic?"

Duel pulled Jessie close, staring at Marley with pain-filled eyes. "Keep away from him. The man's pure evil."

"Tell me what you know. My life is involved somehow, and I deserve an answer," Marley said, pressing them.

Jessie glanced up at Duel. "I think it's time to come clean. She has a right to hear."

"Not out here. Not like this." Duel's gaze went to Marley's dark house. "Tend to your horses. I'll have a fire built in your fireplace."

"Supper's in the warming oven," Jessie said. "I know you're hungry and tired."

Roan silently took the reins from Marley's numb hands as she stared after her parents. This secret they kept was obviously so ugly and dark they couldn't bear to think about it. Whatever they had to say would change her life forever.

Was she ready for that?

Part of her wanted to run after them and take back her question, tell them that she didn't want to hear. But another, much bigger part needed to know everything. With dread clenching cold in her stomach, she followed Roan inside the barn.

Once she'd brushed and fed her horse, she turned to Roan. "Will you kiss me? I'm terrified of what's coming."

"There's nothing to fear. You're safe." Roan stepped closer, towering above her. He tenderly took her face in his hands. Heat filled his kiss as he settled his lips on hers.

Marley leaned into him and slid her arms around his lean waist, clinging to him. She wished she could stay forever in his arms and block out the rest of the world. She parted her mouth, and he slipped his tongue inside to dance with hers.

Desperate to feel him, she slid her hands under his shirt. Lean muscles rippled beneath her palm. He was everything she needed and could ever want.

His touch was so gentle on her that it made her tremble. She embraced the safety and security he offered.

Footsteps crunched behind them, and Hardy Gage cleared his throat. They jerked apart.

The old man's eyes twinkled. "I think you're needing something a bit more private than a barn for what you're doing, gal."

"You won't tell, will you?" Marley asked, watching Roan trying to stuff his shirt back into his trousers without being too noticeable.

"Your secret's safe enough, I reckon," Hardy drawled. "People have claimed for years that I need glasses, and by God they might just be right. Maybe I need to borrow Granny Jack's."

"Thank you." Marley strode to him and kissed his cheek. "I love you, you know."

"Yep and same right back." Hardy led his horse over to unsaddle. "How did the race go, Roan?"

"I won." Roan grinned. "You boys doubled your money."

"Yeehaw!" Hardy's grin couldn't split any wider. "How about you give up ranch work and just go from town to town racing. There's good money in it."

Roan laughed and met Marley's gaze. "That's not for me."

"I'd better get this talk with Mama and Papa over." Marley moved to the door, then looked back. "Will you come, Roan?"

"No. What they have to tell you is private," he answered. "Besides, I have to fill Hardy and the others in on what happened in San Saba."

"We want details. Every last juicy one." Hardy chuckled and wagged his head. "That gray mare came through."

"Find me when you're done, Marley. Good luck." Roan squeezed her hand and moved off with Hardy.

Nodding, Marley crossed the wide compound to her small house. She found her parents standing in front of the hearth in the parlor, their arms around each other. She searched their grim faces in the light of the newly laid fire.

"Would you like to eat first?" Jessie said, hugging her. "I made your favorite."

"I'm really not that hungry, Mama, but thank you." Marley didn't think she could force one bite down her throat. The impending talk had shut down everything inside her body—except for her terrified heartbeat.

"You might want to sit down," Duel said. "This will be hard to hear."

Her legs trembling, she perched on the velvet settee and folded her hands in her lap.

Jessie's eyes held tears. "Marley Rose, you have to know that we never intended to keep this from you. From the first, we meant to tell you everything, but the over the years, the facts dimmed and you were our child in every single way."

Wait. Was her mother saying that she didn't belong to them? That's why she looked so different. If she wasn't Duel and Jessie's daughter, who was she? A million questions swirled.

Duel cleared his throat. Jessie curled her hand around his as he started talking. "Let me start at the very beginning so you can understand why things happened like they did. Before I met Jessie, I was married to a wonderful woman, Annie, and she meant the world to me. We were very happy when she told me she was in the family way. I made a rocking chair and a crib, anxious for the child to be born." He paused, and the crackle of the fire made the only sound in the room.

"Annie had trouble from the first, but we thought it would get easier. She finally gave birth and there was so much blood. It kept coming and coming." His voice trembled and he cleared his throat, wiping a hand across his eyes, probably to erase the hard memories. Jessie's cheeks were wet with tears. "Both she and my son died. I laid them in the ground, saddled my horse, and rode away without a backward glance. I moved from town to town, not caring where I was or where I laid my head." His eyes met Marley's, and his anguish sliced through her. She wanted to scream for him to stop, but she couldn't.

"I prayed to die. Every night I prayed I wouldn't wake up, but I kept opening my eyes anyway. One day, a little before sunset, I rode into a one-horse town called Cactus Springs, tied up at the hitching rail in front of the only saloon, and went inside. Some rough-looking men asked me if I wanted to play poker, so I sat down at their table."

Worry lined Jessie's face as she rubbed his back. "Sweetheart, you don't have to do this."

"Yes, I do. It's past time to tell her the truth." He clung to Jessie as though she were a piece of driftwood on an ocean.

Marley's eyes stung. Their love was too beautiful for words. But what was he trying to get at? What did a poker game have to do with *her*?

"We played, and the stakes kept getting higher and higher," Duel continued. "The man across from me, Wilbert Gentry, ran out of money. By this time, it was just him and me left. He reached down and jerked you up off the floor. You were wailing. You weren't a year old yet but already sitting up good. The prettiest little baby I ever did see. Tears left trails through the dirt on your face. Gentry sat you in the middle of the table and said he'd wager you. I wanted to shoot him on the spot."

Marley gave a strangled cry and jumped to her feet. Unable to hear any more, she put her hands over her ears. "I can't do this."

Jessie left Duel and put her arms around Marley. She murmured the soothing words she had when Marley had been young and afraid. "This is painful, honey, but please listen to the rest," Jessie whispered through her tears. "We want you to understand what happened."

"I'm sorry." Marley impatiently wiped her eyes with the back of her hand and sat back down. "Go on."

"I won the hand and I won…you." Sobbing, he turned and rested his arms on the mantel.

Tears rolled down Marley's cheeks. She'd been won in a poker game as though she'd meant nothing—just the cost of a raised bet.

Dear God! She'd had no value. No worth. She might as well have been a cow or a mule. Shock sped through her with the devastation of a bullet, ripping past everything she thought she'd known about herself.

"I tried to give you back," Duel mumbled brokenly. "What did a broken-down cowboy need with a child? I couldn't even take care of myself. When Gentry told me that if I didn't take you he'd sell you before dark, I couldn't let that happen. I just couldn't." He swung around, his eyes blazing. "You may hate me for the rest of my life, Marley Rose, but I'd do it again in a heartbeat. You saved me. You gave me a reason to live."

The sting of betrayal hollowed out every bit of feeling. She'd loved him for so long and loved him even now, despite the hurt of having the truth come out this way. He'd lied to her, but he'd saved her as well, and it was all too confusing.

"You're our daughter, honey. Always was, always will be," Jessie said, her voice shaking. "We loved you from the very first moment. You saved me too. When you're ready, I'll tell you how. Of this I am certain—if your father *had* given you back to Gentry that day, you'd be dead right now."

Dead? Marley felt that way inside. Did it matter that much whether it was her body or her soul?

"There's no mistake? Will Gentry is my father? Are you sure he hadn't kidnapped me? He's so mean." Marley met the anguish in Duel's amber eyes. His pain left bruises on her heart.

"I'm sure. Your mother found us, came to visit a while later. Her name was Maria Escobar. She confirmed everything."

"She didn't want me either?" Marley couldn't bear the thought of being unwanted by her own mother. "She left me?"

Jessie took her hands. "Only because it was too dangerous. Maria knew if she took you back, Gentry would kill you both. She cried and held you, saying over and over how much she loved you. Her heart shattered in a million pieces when she left. That, honey, is the deepest kind of love. She knew your father… Duel and I could protect you and give you a good life."

"Gentry did kill her in the end," Duel said. "Your mother sacrificed herself for you."

Marley wept, her shoulders shaking, rivers of tears leaving permanent ruts through the pain throbbing deep inside.

"Gentry told Roan that I was his. I didn't know what he meant. Oh God, I didn't know who he was. I hate him."

"Duel, that he's back now means he has some sort of evil plan," Jessie cried.

"Hell will have to freeze over before he gets his hands on Marley Rose. So help me God, I'll kill him first." Duel's face hardened to a piece of granite. Marley had never seen her father like this.

But he wasn't her father, was he?

Her real father was a monster.

With a loud cry, she stumbled from the house.

Twenty-two

ROAN STOOD IN THE SHADOWS, HIS EYES FIXED ON MARLEY'S little house. He didn't know what was going on inside, but he knew trouble when it came calling. Marley's pain seemed to reach out like long tentacles, searching for relief. Hers was a sensitive, caring soul, and he couldn't bear to think of her in pain, in a dark hole that he knew all about.

The door of the house flew open, and Marley ran as though chased by demons with fangs. He jerked up straight. Her sobs echoed in the darkness. He readied to catch her, only she ran the opposite direction—toward whatever danger waited to grab her.

The mountain lion. She'd forgotten.

He hurried after her, but as he got even with the door to the house, Duel and Jessie McClain stepped out. Duel's eyes met his. The man looked as though he'd wrestled a monster—and lost.

"Go after her, Roan. She doesn't want anything to do with me. Keep her safe. Please." Duel's voice was raw with despair. "She's my little girl and I love her."

"Can you tell me what this is about so I don't go into it blind?"

"Marley Rose will tell you," Duel answered. "She doesn't know the danger she's in."

"I'll protect her," Roan vowed and raced into the

thickness of the night. A fog had rolled in, blocking his vision. He had to rely mostly on his ears to get a direction. The brush snapped ahead of him. Her sobs echoed back, tearing into his soul. A shattering heart made a sound like no other on earth.

He had to get to her. She needed him.

Sudden reality hit him—he couldn't live without her. He needed her more than he ever had anyone.

He loved her.

The thought startled him. But Roan couldn't deny it.

He loved this crazy, gun-toting, frustrating woman who twisted him inside out.

The noise ahead stopped. His mind raced. Maybe she'd tripped and fallen in her distraught state. Ravines and gullies hid in the blackness, and a person might not see them until it was too late.

The blood froze in his veins. Roan slowed, proceeding carefully, listening to the silence of the night. When he heard the low, pitiful cries, he knew he was close. "Marley? It's Roan. Where are you?"

"Go away," she said, her words muffled. "Leave me here. I have a mess to sort out."

"I can't do that. I smell danger." He inched forward, one step, then two.

The dry brush crackled, followed by a grunt—sounds of a struggle. He had to get to her—but was he even going in the right direction? Sounds in thick fog often twisted around a man to where he couldn't follow.

"Marley," he called. "Marley, answer me." Damn this fog! He couldn't see. Something was wrong. He slid his Colt from the holster hanging on his hip.

"Marley!"

"She can't answer you, Penny."

The gravelly voice filled Roan's veins with ice. With every nerve taut, he moved forward with caution and a prayer. Listening. But the wild beating of his heart drowned out everything.

Then, through a clear pocket in the fog, he saw Marley. Her beautiful brown eyes wide with terror. Gentry's hand covered her mouth as he held her in front of him as a shield. Catching sight of Roan, she began to twist and squirm.

Roan's finger tightened on the trigger of the Colt. "Let her go if you want to live."

"Shoot and you'll kill her. You're a smart man, Penny. Lay down your gun. I have business with daughter dearest," Gentry snarled.

His daughter? Marley was Duel's daughter. Wasn't she?

"No, you old bastard. I don't know what you're trying to pull, but I'm not buying it. She's Duel McClain's oldest daughter, and he's going to kill you for even putting your hands on her." Then after Duel got through with him, Roan would kill Gentry again. Over and over until the bastard was dead for sure.

Gentry backed up, bringing Marley flush against him. "McClain stole her from me."

The man was demented. McClain wouldn't steal a nickel, much less a person.

"Just saying you're right—what do you have in mind for her?" Roan asked.

"She's worth a lot of money to me now that she's a woman." Gentry's lips curled back. "I'll be a rich man after the auction."

Everything inside Roan stilled. "What auction?"

"The one I set up for two weeks from now. I'm going to auction her off to the highest bidder."

Disgust dripped from Roan's voice. "If Marley is your daughter, as you claim, she should mean something to you. You'll sell your own flesh and blood, Gentry?"

The chilling bastard's evil laugh sliced through the fog that drifted between them again. "I did it once and got nothing. Now that she can service a man, I'll get rich. I'll work her until she dies. She's mine to dispose of however I want."

The words chilled Roan. If the man was able to get away with her, he'd carry out his evil plan. "I can't let that happen. Release her and you can go back to your killing and robbing." Roan cursed the fog that made seeing difficult. He didn't dare take a shot.

Seconds crept by.

Just let him have one clear shot and a steady hand. That's all he needed. Just one.

Cold sweat inched down his back.

His foot slid forward silently on the damp ground.

"Damn you, woman! You bit me!" The voice was Gentry's.

"Watch out, Roan!" Marley yelled.

An explosion sounded, and a bullet ripped through the fog toward him. He fell to the ground unscathed. The fool was firing blind. It seemed odd that he wasn't taking advantage of the fog to escape, but maybe his thirst for vengeance against Roan was as strong as Roan's desire to see him underground.

At last, the fog thinned and he could see Gentry's head above Marley's. He willed her to stay still. If he hit her... his knees tried to buckle.

Just as his finger twitched on the trigger, the distinct rumbling growl of a big cat filled the air. Roan spun around, expecting to see it, but there was nothing there.

A flash of a body leaped through the fog toward Marley. Roan had no time to think. He pulled the trigger and shot the beast a second before it pounced on her. Yelling, Gentry scrambled backward and disappeared into the white void.

The animal fell solidly to the ground. Roan rushed to Marley and put his arms around her. They had to get out of there before Gentry returned. Without wasting a moment, he put his Colt in the holster, scooped her up, and carried her to safety. He didn't put her down until they reached her front door.

Duel rushed toward them, his gun drawn. "I heard a shot."

"Killed a mountain lion, at least that's what I think it was. Too foggy to see clearly," Roan explained, then added,

"Gentry had Marley, but when the cat attacked, Gentry vanished into the fog."

Duel clutched the porch railing for support. "Thank God you went after her."

"We've got to find him and get rid of him once and for all or he'll be right back." Roan urged Marley into the house and walked to Duel. "Gentry said he planned to auction her off, said she'd fetch more money now that she's grown."

"Dammit to hell!" Duel scrubbed the back of his neck. "I was afraid of this, and now she won't even speak to me or her mother. Jess is over at the main house sobbing. This is breaking our hearts. Stay with her, Roan. Give her the comfort we can't."

"Count on it, Boss." Roan left him and went inside. He found Marley in the parlor, holding her hands to the dying embers.

"I'm freezing. I can't get warm."

Roan threw a log onto the fire, got a quilt from the bedroom, and wrapped it around her. "This'll help."

"Leave, Roan. I'm not fit company tonight." Her voice was dull and lifeless. "I might say some hurtful things, and I don't want to cause you pain too."

"I'll take you anyway I can get you." He pulled her to him and smoothed her silky hair. "Can you tell me what happened? What is this about?"

"I'm so cold, Roan. I don't think I'll ever be warm again."

"You will. Give it time."

"Everything I ever thought I knew about myself was a lie. I'm so confused. I don't know who I am anymore." She whimpered like a hurt animal and laid her palm on his chest. "I'm so tired. So afraid. My whole life changed in an instant. Gone."

"Just rest. Let's sit down." He drew her to the settee and held her in his lap.

"Roan?"

"Yeah."

"You probably won't want anything to do with me once you learn everything," she mumbled.

"Nothing can ever change how I feel about you, Marley. Nothing." He'd never meant anything more.

"Thank you for coming after me, Roan. I didn't even know where I was going. I just knew I had to get away. Forgot the danger." She stared at him with those big eyes, sadness oozing from her. "I'll tell you what you want to know. I need to talk about this to someone, and I have no one else in which to confide."

"Whatever you feel comfortable doing." He wasn't going anywhere.

"First of all, I'm sure you gathered that Will Gentry is my father. A woman named Maria Escobar was my mother. Duel told me earlier that when I was just a baby, Gentry wagered me in"—her voice broke on a keening sound and the whispered words—"in a poker game. Duel won me." She clapped her hand over her mouth. "He brought me back here and raised me." Her haunted eyes met his. "I don't know how Jessie fits into all this, but she wasn't yet married to my…Duel when this happened."

Shock swept over Roan. Marley's sense of security, her calm, orderly world had shattered, and it stood to reason she'd question her identity and relationship with everyone. "I'm so sorry. If I could take your pain, I would." He'd move heaven and earth to put things back the way they were.

"God help me! I don't know who I am," she cried. "Not even my name. Is it McClain—or Gentry? Who am I? I don't want to be Gentry's daughter."

"You don't have to be. Since I know you'll never use Gentry's name, keep going by McClain." Roan turned her to face him. "You're still Duel McClain's daughter, just like before. This changes nothing. He rescued you from a very bad man and gave you a good life, protected you from harm. I've seen how much he loves you. This has devastated him."

"I still love him. You know? I felt his pain when he told

me all this. I've never seen my…him…break down like that before. Not ever. It ripped his heart open that he had to confess." Tears rolled down her cheeks.

Roan fished a wrinkled handkerchief from his pocket and dried her eyes. If only he could make this better, but he knew it wasn't in his power. Marley had to find her own way to peace.

"I'm so angry and hurt at him and Jessie. They should've told me the truth as soon as I got old enough to understand. I don't think they'd have ever told me if Gentry had stayed away."

"It's okay to be mad as long as you don't let it fester into a sore." Roan knew how fast anger could turn into hate. That was all he'd felt for Blackie Culpepper—not pity and surely not sympathy. Just hate. He didn't want Marley to ruin her relationship with Duel by carrying nothing but anger inside. Duel was too fine a man to know only that from his daughter.

"Did I mean so little to my mother that she'd let this happen? Duel and Jessie said she came here once but left me behind, claiming she wasn't strong enough to protect me from Gentry. And she was right, for Gentry killed her." Marley shuddered. "I was sold, Roan. Duel got me for the price of a bet. Oh God!" She covered her mouth with her hand. "I was worth so little? And now Gentry seems hellbound to do it again!" Marley put her hands over her mouth.

"No. Stop." He took her hands. "Your mother showed you true love. I'm sure it broke her heart in a million pieces to leave you with Duel and Jessie, but she had to have known that was the only way to keep you safe. And I'm sure Duel would've paid any price at that poker table. A person's worth is not measured in money; it's measured by the love you see in someone's eyes. In the knowing that they'd risk their own life to save you. That's Duel McClain all over."

Silent tears bubbled in her dark eyes. "Thank you."

Roan pulled her up. "You're very special to me." He pressed his lips to hers and gave her a gentle kiss.

She gripped his shirt and clung to him. When the kiss ended, she released a long sigh and laid her head on his chest.

"Do you know what you mean to me, Marley?"

Tear droplets clung to her the tips of her lashes when she raised her gaze. "No."

"I love you." Roan's voice was hoarse.

"You really do?" A quivery smile curved her mouth.

"I realized it tonight when I was searching for you. I knew I didn't want to live without you." He tightened his hold around her. "I'm sorry I wouldn't let you say the words in San Saba. Do you still feel the same way?"

"I love you, Roan Penny. Forever and always." She slid her arms around his neck. Beginning with his eyes, she kissed her way down his face to his lips.

Roan let her do whatever she wished. Each kiss, each caress helped her heal, find hope again, renewed her spirit. The surety that Marley would one day be his wife released the lock from around his heart, and he let her in.

"Stay with me tonight. Hold me in your arms," she said against his mouth. "Be the pirate who's come to whisk me away to safety."

"I'll be whatever, whoever you need me to be." He kissed behind her ear. "But don't make me a villain. I'm one of the good guys."

"That you are. I'm glad you love me and could say the words that came so hard."

"Blame it on the way I grew up. I learned that pain wasn't nearly so sharp if I held everything inside." His voice shook. "It was when I dared to let some out that the misery and hurt would rise up to strangle me. Matt's already learned that, you know. He's going to require a lot of love and tenderness to grow up into a strong man."

"You know him so well."

"We're two of a kind."

Marley kissed the hollow of his throat and stared up at him. "Would you marry me, Roan Penny? For real this time. I've had enough pretense."

Twenty-three

ROAN'S SILENCE WORRIED HER.

Marley glanced up into his gray eyes. "Isn't that what you want? What we both decided?"

"I don't think rushing into marriage is wise at the moment." His voice was gentle. "You're reacting out of hurt and anger, not because you want to make a lifetime commitment to me." He cupped the side of her face, and she leaned into his hand. God, she loved his touch on her skin. "Besides, where will we live? I don't know what you want, but I see us on our own land. The money I won will help, but it's not enough. My Texas Star, we have plans to make."

She released a breath. "You're right. We need to plan. Hold me, Roan."

He planted a kiss in her hair. "You'll have to pry my arms loose."

"That's why I love you." She snuggled into his warmth.

◆

Light filtered through the curtains of Marley's small house. She stirred in Roan's arms. They'd spent the night on the sofa, her head on his shoulder, the quilt keeping them warm. She felt drugged and weary. Too much had happened to take in, and she had no idea where this new road would lead her.

Roan's eyes met hers. "Good morning, sleeping beauty. I couldn't find my pirate ship."

"I'm glad you helped me make it through the night." She got up to stand at the window. The ranch looked the same as it always had, but she knew it could never be the same again. Something inside *her* had changed. Duel came from his house and stared in her direction, although she knew he couldn't see her. "Besides, sleeping beauty lived in a castle," she murmured.

"So she did." Roan came up from behind and put his arms around her. He kissed the back of her neck.

"He's standing out there, looking so sad and alone." She swallowed hard. "What am I supposed to do now? I don't feel like Marley McClain. I don't know me."

"Duel is still the same father you've always loved. He's hurting real bad too, Marley. I think you need to go talk to him. You both have things to say."

"Maybe."

"Nothing can be settled without hashing it out. Go to him, Marley," Roan urged.

She turned. "About last night. I shouldn't have asked you to marry me." She wrinkled her nose. "Just chalk it up to distress and nerves."

He tucked a tendril of hair behind her ear, studying her face. "It's already forgotten."

"We have plenty of time, and when we marry, it'll be for the right reason."

"When did you get so smart?" He released her. "Go talk to Duel."

"I should. And Mama…Jessie needs help with breakfast."

Roan walked with her to the door and opened it. "Don't close your mind or your heart."

She nodded and took a deep breath, then left the house. Duel watched her approach, and the slump of his shoulders and sadness in his amber eyes was painful to see.

"How are you, Marley?" he asked in his deep voice. He started to reach for her but instead dropped his arms to his sides. What she wouldn't give to go back to their easy way with each other.

"In truth, I don't know how I am. I have so many feelings racing through me. I don't know who I am anymore. I grew up always knowing and taking comfort in the fact that I was a McClain. Even on the scariest, darkest night I found security belonging here. Now…"

"You're still Marley McClain, if you want to be. I legally adopted you. There's nothing wrong with the name."

"I know." Her gaze scanned the rolling pastures. Suddenly, it hit her. Aces 'n' Eights. Duel had named the ranch for the hand he'd won her with. The dead man's hand. Her lips quivered, and she raised her hand to still them. When she could speak, she said, "I always thought the name of this ranch was odd. Was it to remind yourself of the fact that I wasn't your daughter?"

Duel released a cry that sounded like a wounded animal. "I gave it this name to celebrate the day you came into my heart. To remind myself that I wasn't alone anymore, that I had a daughter whom I loved with every fiber of my being." He blinked hard and raised his head. "I won't apologize for that. Not for one second."

As though unable to bear the pain that must be on her face, he swung his gaze toward the distance.

Whether he was her father or not, she loved this man with all her heart and soul. She remembered a night—she must've been about nine or ten—when she'd had a high fever. Her throat had been so swollen it wouldn't allow more than a drop of anything through. Duel had kept warm rags smeared with a salve around her throat even though he'd had an important trip to make the next day.

Another time he'd ridden ten miles in the dead of night in the pouring rain to get the doctor. He'd come down with a horrible fever from the ordeal. Time after time, Duel had sacrificed his own well-being for her. He must've dreaded this moment since the day he'd brought her home, afraid to keep the secret but afraid to tell.

He turned back to her, in control of his feelings again. "I'm sorry I kept the truth from you. I just wanted you to never doubt that you belonged here. This is your home," he rasped. "Everything Jessie and I did was for you, to give you the best life we could. There was never a moment that I didn't love you."

Tears welled in her eyes. "Can I still be your daughter, Papa? If you'll have me?"

With a low cry, he put his arms around her. "Always. Always."

Peace surrounded her, the quiet after a horrible storm. Marley still had things to work through, but she had strength now for the task. She clutched his work shirt, soaking up the smell of shaving cream and coffee. "I love you, Papa. Even last night when I felt so betrayed and angry, I couldn't bring myself to hate you."

"I was so afraid that you'd leave, and I couldn't bear to think of that." He cleared his throat. "But Jessie told me to keep my faith in you. She said you're still the girl we raised."

At mention of her mama, Marley jerked back. "Oh my goodness, I forgot about breakfast."

Duel chuckled low in his throat. "It'll keep. But my cows won't. I've got to get moving. See you later, Two Bit."

The pet name he'd called her when she was a child left a thickness in her chest. They shared much more than a last name. He was her father in every sense of the word. A real father made sacrifices and held his children close—he didn't wager his child in a game of chance.

She paused with her hand on the door, watching Duel head out to meet his day. And stepping from the bunkhouse, falling in step, Roan matched Duel stride for stride.

The two men represented her whole world. Both were tough and fearless, and she admired and loved them.

Jessie glanced up when Marley entered the kitchen. Her mama's gaze searched her eyes. "Are you all right, honey?"

"I just had a private talk with Papa. I'm not angry at him or you anymore. The shock of finding out how I came to be here knocked me flat. I want to talk to you about it—I want to hear how you came into the picture and when—but not now. Let's get the children fed and off to school."

"Sure, honey. I'll tell you whatever you want to know." Jessie turned, cracking eggs into the cast-iron skillet. "I already have the biscuits on, and the bacon's ready."

Surprise swept through Marley. "You must've been up for a while."

"We never went to bed. We sat up all night talking. Your father ate an hour ago."

"Then I'll go upstairs and help the little ones into their clothes." But instead of moving in that direction, she went to hug Jessie and kiss her cheek. "I love you, Mama."

⁘

Change had come to the Aces 'n' Eights. Duel seemed certain that Will Gentry was lurking about, ready to inflict harm, so until the man was caught, Hardy would deliver the children to school in the buckboard. Duel had also expressed concerns about Marley leaving the ranch and said she'd have an armed escort whenever she did.

That suited Marley. The thought of running into Gentry again chilled her blood, and the children had also picked up on her fears. Matt had crawled into her lap that morning and snuggled against her.

"I'm scared, Mama Rose," he'd said. "The bad man will get me."

She'd hugged him and told him that Papa Duel and all the men would keep them safe, and he didn't have to worry. All while she'd calmed his fears, her thoughts were on herself. She was the one Gentry wanted, and a knot sat in her stomach.

True, she'd been in shock last night, but she'd heard his diabolical vow to auction her off to the highest bidder.

Memories of the random gunshots in San Saba crept

across her mind. If he'd wanted to make money off her, why would he want to kill her? That must've been someone else. But who?

After the children were off to school and the housework done, Marley sat with Jessie in the parlor. They laid the babies on a quilt on the floor where they could watch them.

Jessie was the first to speak. "I know you have a lot of questions, and I hope my answers will ease your mind." She played with her apron, bunching the fabric, then smoothing it. "I haven't done right by you, Marley, and I know it."

"What do you mean?"

"Bringing all these kids here was a mistake, and I see that now. Each time we added to our brood, it pushed you farther back. Neither your father nor I have given you the attention you need in quite a while." Jessie gave a short laugh. "And the extra work has mostly landed on your shoulders. You don't have a minute to yourself. I'm so sorry, honey."

"I've never minded helping, Mama."

"I minded asking." Jessie rose and stared through the window as though she were looking back in time. "I know you're curious about when I entered the picture. It was that first night that Duel had you. He'd decided to bring you back here and get his sister Vicky to help raise you. This was before she moved away. He had made camp and was trying to remember everything a kind woman in town had told him about babies. She'd given him a few bottles and cloths for diapers, and even let him have a goat to take on the trip to keep you in milk."

Marley laughed. "So that's where Cheeba came from."

"That goat dearly tried your father's patience. She butted him every time he bent over. That's the scene I stumbled across." Jessie turned, and Marley could see tears gathering in her eyes. "I was running from the law for killing my husband. He'd pressed a hot brand to my shoulder, claiming me as his property."

Marley gasped. No wonder Jessie had never let Marley

see her in a state of undress. "That's horrible. I don't blame you for killing him! You had to."

"The law didn't see it that way." Jessie sat down next to Marley and took her hand. "Duel didn't know any of that at the time. He just saw a desperate woman wearing a blood-soaked dress. I'm sure I was quite a sight, but he was so gentle, and he didn't pry. I couldn't tell him more than my first name, I was so scared of being caught and hanged. I lay down with you that night and didn't let you go. You brought me comfort."

"I'm glad." Marley wanted to cry for this kind and generous woman, but she held back the tears. Something told her there was more.

"The next morning, Duel made a bargain with me—if I helped him get you to his home, he'd take me anywhere I wanted to go." A smile lit Jessie's eyes. "He didn't know that there was no place else I wanted to be. That's how I met your father and found a true knight wearing a deadly Colt in his holster."

That story touched Marley deeply. "I'm sure he was such a handsome man. He still is."

"No other man can hold a candle to him. But I have more, and this part is the hardest to tell." Jessie wiped her eyes. "My first husband, Jeremiah Foltry, was a mean, heartless bastard. Looking back, I think he must have lost his mind. He accused me of being with other men and became obsessed with me getting pregnant by one of them. Jeremiah ranted that he wasn't going to raise another man's child. It got worse and worse.

"I tried to escape his madness, but he caught me and chained me in the barn. He used me every night, and I did conceive. One night he flew into a rage and said even if it was his, I wasn't fit to raise it.

"He grabbed a stick and rammed it into me. The pain made me pass out. There was so much blood. The doctor came, after, and said I'd never be able have children. That I was too badly…damaged." Jessie's voice broke.

Her mother's pain was still so evident after all these years. Marley gripped her hand, crying. What both her parents had been through was unimaginable for anyone, and now she began to understand Jessie's obsession with children.

"I longed for a child with every fiber of my being," Jessie continued. "Then I found you, and you helped me bear the pain. Keeping busy, filling this home with love, all of it helped, and I just kept on going. A few days ago, I woke up and saw how many I'd brought home and what this had done to you."

"There is so much need, Mama. How can you turn any of them away? They need love and someone to protect them, just as I did."

"Yes, but I shouldn't have to take them all. There are other people and homes for orphans." Jessie twisted her hands together.

"You just have to examine your heart." That seemed to be the gauge for every decision. "Did they ever catch you for the murder of your husband?"

"Your uncle Luke was a Texas Ranger back then, and he came to arrest me. I didn't run. I saw no need. I remember how my heart broke to ride off and leave you and Duel. You both soon followed, however. There was a trial and I had to tell everything—even the most personal details—to justify why I had killed a man."

"He wasn't a man—he was an animal. I assume they found you innocent. You certainly had just cause!" Marley cried.

"It wasn't easy. The presiding judge and the town were against me. Thank goodness Tom Parker defended me. His arguments won the jury over."

Marley vaguely remembered the man she had called Grandfather Parker, though he was no kin at all. Tom had been Duel's first wife's father and a famous judge in Austin until his death.

Marley brought her thoughts back to the horrors and

torture her mother had faced all alone. "I'm glad they didn't convict you, Mama. That would've killed Papa—and me too, I imagine."

"Probably, but I know I couldn't have lived without either of you." Jessie took Marley's hand. "Come with me."

What was her mother going to show her? Jessie went up the stairs and hurried into the bedroom she shared with Duel. Marley couldn't imagine what more Jessie would reveal. She didn't think she could take anything else. But the truth was bringing her and her mother together in a way that she hadn't felt in a long while.

Her mother went to the wardrobe and pulled out a dress. "I've been meaning to give this to you and keep forgetting. I suspect you'll have an occasion to wear it soon."

The plum-colored wool-crepe creation, accented with a white fur collar, took Marley's breath. "It's the most beautiful dress I've ever seen. I don't remember seeing you wear it."

"Your father bought it for the governor's ball that Tom Parker invited us to in Austin. I only wore it once and never had occasion to wear it again. After Tom died, our invitations to fancy events stopped coming." Jessie held it against Marley. "I think it might fit you. If not, we can alter it here and there. I want you to have it."

Marley ran her hand over the rippling, luxurious fabric. "It's absolutely breathtaking. Are you sure, Mama?" Awestruck, she brushed her fingertips across a sprinkling of pearls sewn into the bodice. Never had she had anything so fine.

"I am. As I said, I have no need of it." Jessie smiled. "I think you might."

"I do have a confession. Roan and I are talking about getting married. Not right away, of course, but when the time is right." Marley met her mother's eyes. "I love him, Mama. I think I have since I first brought him here."

"Roan is a smart man. How does he feel about you?"

A smile curved Marley's lips. "Last night after we got back to the house, he told me he loved me. I slept in his arms—sitting on the sofa. Don't worry, we did nothing inappropriate." But how she'd wanted to. She'd hurt so badly that she'd have done most anything to feel better. She'd needed his warm touch to thaw the ice inside her.

"I saw the signs, and I think he's a wonderful choice for you." Worry filled Jessie's eyes. "Only Roan is the first to admit that he's a drifter. How sure are you that he'll stick around?"

"I'm sure, Mama." Marley gripped the soft fabric of the dress to her. She knew, then and there, that it would be her wedding dress.

A vision of Roan standing beside her in front of the preacher brought goose bumps. He'd be so handsome, and she'd be proud to be his wife. She couldn't wait for the moment when she'd lay beside him with nothing between them but skin. A shiver of anticipation raced through her.

Yet, as she embraced the thought, memories of the events in San Saba sent the dream flying. Roan wouldn't stop until he'd finished the task he'd set for himself. He knew Gentry now, and the boy beside him in the race.

Sooner or later, he'd go back to exact punishment.

Except Will Gentry was here, and after twenty years of waiting, she knew the man would easily bide his time. Watching. Waiting. Planning. And he meant to get her. Oh God!

Twenty-four

LATER THAT DAY, MARLEY FINISHED HANGING THE LAST OF the diapers on the line and picked up her basket. The chore was never ending. Those three babies were a lot of work. If she ever had any, and she hoped that was a long way off, she only wanted one at a time. But ever since her talk with Jessie, Marley had tried to help out more. Her mother was simply exhausted.

Every so often, Marley took out the dress her mother had given her and ran her fingers across the fine fabric. One day soon she'd wear that dress, and she hoped it would be to stand in front of the preacher. She hadn't told Roan about it. She wanted it to be a surprise.

The older children had ridden off with Papa Duel, and the younger girls played nearby with their dolls. Marley kept an eye on them, making sure they didn't wander from her sight.

Young Matt scampered up beside her. He clutched the book of stories she'd been reading to him under an arm. "Where you goin', Mama Rose?"

"To clean my house. Want to come help?"

"I want you to read me a story."

Marley stopped. "Matthew, you know stories are for bedtime."

"My name is Matt." He gave her a mulish frown.

"Besides…Matt, I thought we agreed to leave my papers in the bedroom. Why did you bring them out here?"

The child lowered his voice to a whisper. "The pirate will get 'em. I gotta keep 'em safe."

"Oh, I see." Marley stifled a laugh. The kid was as fanciful as she was. Often she let him make up the bedtime story, and he could come up with some tall tales for sure. Others were very good. "I tell you what. Give them to me, and I'll keep the pirate from getting them until tonight." Another of the boys Matt's age flew out the back door. "Why don't you and Benji go play for a while?"

"Okay." He thrust the handwritten stories at her and took off running.

"Remember to stay near the house," she called, glancing around.

Monsters lurked near, and they stole not only your breath, but your life.

❧

Just after dawn three days later, Roan and Hardy Gage rode to the far southeast pasture, checking the fence line. The rustlers seemed to know exactly when to strike and where. At the rate cattle were disappearing, Duel McClain would soon have a ranch with no livestock. Sometimes they were able to trail the rustlers for a little ways, but most often all the thieves left behind was a downed fence. Strange how the theft always happened on the east side of the ranch, the side nearest to San Saba County.

The hands had also been searching for signs of Gentry. They'd discovered places where someone had bedded down, and found cigarette butts in the flattened winter grass. While they didn't know for sure that it was Gentry, Roan felt certain it was.

He kept his gun loaded and his senses sharp. A man could lose his life if he didn't.

"Hardy, you've been around a long time. Have you dealt with rustlers before?"

"Yep. Never this bad though." Hardy pushed back his hat. "We usually caught the vermin within a day or two. I'm just wondering what in the blooming hell they're doing with all these animals. They have to be driving them somewhere close."

"Do you suppose they have a ranch and are stocking it with our cattle?"

"Could be. Or maybe they're holding them in a canyon." The old man rubbed his grizzled jaw in thought. "This is more like they have a bone to pick with the boss. They seem to like jabbing him with a sharp stick, then hiding for a while, only to come out and do it all again."

"I still think the bunch here is working with the group in San Saba." Roan let out a frustrated sigh. "I thought for sure Will Gentry was behind all of it. I would've bet money. But it seems that he was only after Marley. How about Wes Douglas?"

"Could be. But didn't you say that young guy in San Saba claimed someone named Rube led those riders?"

"That's what Zach swore up and down." Roan glanced at Hardy. "And you don't know anyone named Rube? Maybe it's short for something—like Reuben."

"Nope." Hardy shook his head. "Don't know anyone."

"Then do you know of a canyon where the rustlers could hold the stolen cattle?"

"Shoot, there's more of 'em around these parts than a dog's got fleas. It'd take a while to check them all."

Roan's thoughts were already on his plans to head back to San Saba, but he wondered if it was best to stay where he was. He still felt in his bones that Will Gentry had holed up nearby. No, forget San Saba for now. He'd stay and marshal all his energy to the task of finding the man on the Aces 'n' Eights. Marley deserved to rest easy knowing Gentry would never bother her again.

"Hell and be damned!" Hardy yelled. "Would you look at that?"

A gaping hole in the fence was in front of them. Fresh cow patties said the cattle had recently gone through. Roan glanced around, checking for riders, before he dismounted for a closer look.

"Damn it! This is getting old," he muttered to Hardy. If only they could set a trap, except the rustlers never hit the same place twice. This time, however, something was different. The path left behind them was clear and easy to follow. Had they gotten sloppy? Or was it an attempt to lure Roan and the others out into a trap of their own?

"If this ain't the damn drizzlin's." Hardy strode to the trampled ground. "Roan, saddle up. We're trailing the bastards. I'm mad enough to tackle 'em with my bare hands. Besides, Hanson and the others will be here soon to fix the fence." He glanced at the rustler's tracks.

"If we hurry, we can catch them." Roan crawled back in the saddle and followed the marks in the dirt, always aware of the danger.

An hour later, he and Gage rode into the town of Piebald, where the tracks abruptly ended. Cold stares made it clear that the town didn't have a welcome committee. Their horses clip-clopped down the street, the hair on Roan's neck bristling. They stopped at a holding pen of sorts next to the stables and dismounted. Cattle milled inside it. Roan moved among them and found over three dozen wearing the Aces 'n' Eights brand—a diamond with the number eight in the center.

A stocky, bald man marched toward him. "Hey, get out of there!"

Roan glanced at a group of youngsters playing marbles in the dirt and waited until the man got closer. If shooting started, he didn't want the kids to get hit. "These cattle are stolen. I'm taking them back where they belong."

"You ain't taking nothing nowhere, mister." The man jammed a hat onto his bald head and glared, his hand inching toward his gun. "Can you prove they're stolen? Maybe you're looking to steal them for yourself."

Hardy Gage snorted.

"We work for Duel McClain at the Aces 'n' Eights." Roan rested his hand on his Colt. "Rustlers have been stealing us blind. My boss would be happy to claim his stock, but I have a feeling they won't be here when he comes."

"You'll have to take this up with Rube. That's all I know. I'm just guarding this pen."

Roan's ears perked up. "I'd be much obliged if you can tell me where to find Rube."

At last, maybe he'd lay eyes on the guy. They must've been looking in the wrong place. Piebald wasn't that far from San Saba, but neither was the needle in the haystack when you were trying to find it.

"Try the saloon down the street. Might find Rube there. But I warn you, mister, start trouble, and we'll escort you both right out of town."

They mounted up and had no trouble finding the Yellow Dog Saloon. The cold stares of two men resting their bones against a pole for support would've given a seasoned lawman reason for pause. Still, he hadn't tracked the mangy thieves for nothing.

No sooner had Roan swung his leg over and dismounted than a wad of spit spattered the toe of his boot and dripped off.

"Who you think you're staring at?" The snarl came from the spitter.

Roan untied his bandana from his neck and swiped his boot clean before he raised a glance. He didn't bother replying. It never did any good.

Someone hurled a rotten egg, splattering the projectile against his leg, the stench rising upward. They made Gage a target as well. They'd need a bath after leaving here. After fitting in at the McClain's, the hollered slurs almost didn't matter so much.

"I'm talking to you, vagrant," the man growled at Roan.

Nothing like a rooster fight to draw a crowd. Piebald appeared to overflow with exception takers. Roan favored them with a wary glare but kept silent. By the slow way they straightened, he knew these men inclined toward the nastier side.

"I asked what you're staring at, boy."

"Looks to me like this one's off the reservation," the other half of the duo sneered.

Whatever Roan did or said wouldn't make any difference. They meant to show him the error of riding into their town, so he might as well get the ruckus started. He wasn't about to apologize to anyone for taking up elbow room on this earth.

Mose's old advice filtered through the haze. *You'll spend the rest of your life gettin' up if you let the likes of rotten no-accounts knock you down.*

Roan braced himself. "Not looking for trouble."

"Must be, or you'd get back on that horse."

A strange light filled Gage's narrowed eyes. "Before you ride into a canyon, you better know how you're gonna get out."

"Why is that, old man?"

"We might be a lot more than you bargained for."

Roan shot Gage a glance. He didn't know how much the old ranch hand could take and wished he'd come alone.

"You reckon they might take convincing, Bert?" Spitter asked.

"I suppose it's a waste of time to ask if you know anything about a cut fence on the Aces 'n' Eights ranch." Roan's low drawl took on a steely edge. "Wonder if I'd find a pair of wire cutters in your pockets."

Spitter snorted. "You must be plumb stupid, boy. Can't you see you're not welcome here? I think we've made ourselves pretty plain. Get the hell gone!"

A woman striding toward a buggy caught Roan's attention. Strands of her auburn hair caught the light. When she turned to glance in their direction, he recognized her as

Virginia Creek. Her riding skirt and leather jacket looked expensive, and fit her like a glove. What was she doing in Piebald?

A tall, thin man stepped to her side and helped her up into the buggy.

Will Gentry.

Roan straightened his spine and started toward them but found his path blocked by Spitter and his friends. "Do whatever you feel you have to, but I'm going to speak to the lady." He tried to shove past, conscious of the horde of people gathering, wondering where Gage had gone.

"Bert, I think he wants a licking, don't you?" Spitter launched himself at Roan, aiming for his stomach. When Roan easily sidestepped, the bastard landed facedown in the dirt. The second man jumped into the fray. Again, Roan dodged the blows and landed two good ones of his own, sending Bert into the barber pole next door.

His attention was on the couple riding away in the buggy amid a cloud of dirt. He had to catch them. Two strides was all he managed to take before someone grabbed his arms from behind and wrenched them tight. Bound up, he made easy prey for the snarling cowards. The horde pounded on him until blood dribbled from his mouth.

Between blows, Roan found Gage. The man was fighting with two men attempting to tie him up.

"Hey now, what's the trouble, boys?" a man asked.

An arm around Roan's head prevented him from seeing who'd spoken. He only prayed the man would reason with the bullies.

One of the men holding him spoke. "Preacher Joe, I reckon this godforsaken cuss ain't never been baptized. Have you, boy?"

A fist slammed into Roan's kidney. Roan gasped in agony.

"Yeah, we'd consider it an honor to remedy that small oversight. We'd be plumb remiss to shirk our Christian duty," a second man rasped.

Another fist whipped Roan's face sideways, the pain

making him see stars. If he could get loose, he'd get in some blows of his own, but their grips were bands of steel, cutting into his arms. The thought crossed his mind that he might not live through this. He wouldn't if the crowd had any say in the matter. But Gage might make the difference if he could free himself.

"Well, that being the case, carry on the Lord's work," Preacher Joe said in a booming voice. He left Roan to the sinister flock, who dragged him away by his arms.

Roan spied the horse trough through a haze of bodies, and he knew they meant to drown him. These demons were too close for comfort to the hooded marauders of San Saba. Intent on killing him, the one binding his arms released him in order to hold his head under. Roan took a deep breath just as they dunked him.

He fumbled for his gun only to find the holster empty.

Dirty water washed the bloody grit from his eyes, and the rush of cold helped him think clearly. He managed to reach under the neck of his shirt for his Bowie knife and slid it from the sheath.

He rose, slashing the air. The angry mob scattered from reach. Light from the sun's rays glinted on the steel blade. Roan held the weapon firmly and backed against his horse as a shot rang out. Luckily, the shooter missed, the bullet kicking up a spray of dirt near his feet.

Spitter lunged, and Roan hooked him under one arm, throwing him into the horse trough, shattering the wood. Water gushed out around their feet. The man sputtered but didn't get up.

Spying his Colt on the ground, Roan picked it up and leveled it on the group, putting his knife back into the sheath. The men beat a hasty retreat. Someone else fired, and a bullet went through Roan's Stetson, his hat jumping on his head. His Colt roared, spitting orange fire, sending a bullet into the knee of the man who'd fired his gun. The rabble-rouser went down. Another shot, and a piece of hot lead separated a boot, probably taking off the man's toe in the bargain.

A scream rent the air.

"The next person who even blinks will get a bullet to the heart." He delivered the steely warning, spitting blood.

"You're not the law around here!" yelled one brave soul from the back.

"Maybe not, but my friend and I are leaving, and we're taking those stolen cattle." Backing up, he untied Hardy Gage. "Are you hurt?"

Hardy shook his head, holding his stomach. "Let's get the hell out of here."

Pain wracked Roan's body as he used the last of his strength to put his feet in the stirrups and pull himself into Shadow's saddle. "Come after us, and I'll finish this once and for all. I guarantee you'll lose."

"We ain't done with you yet, boy!" yelled Spitter from the mud.

Roan glared at his tormentor. "I'd watch the shadows if I were you. One of these days, I might just be there."

"Tell McClain he'll never get the rest of his cattle," said a booming voice from inside the saloon.

That confirmed that they knew the whereabouts of the herd. Roan was tempted to force an answer from these people, but he wasn't in the best shape and neither was Hardy. If they didn't leave now, they might not be able to get away at all.

Curses followed as he and Gage returned to the holding pen. He wiped away the blood trickling down into his eye and pointed his Colt at the guard. "Live or die. Your choice," Roan snapped, his voice as hard as steel.

The man moved aside, then watched helplessly as Gage herded the stolen cattle out and onto the path leading back toward the Aces 'n' Eights.

Shadow tossed her head, seeming as anxious as Roan to be rid of the town of Piebald.

Now, if he could just stay in the saddle. Yet each mile severely tested his determination.

Duel and the cowboys still worked at the section of downed fence when Roan arrived, clutching the mare's mane with the last thread of his strength. They stared in disbelief, moving aside so the stolen beeves could go back into the pasture.

With a shout, Duel hurried to help him from the saddle. Sharp pain swept through his body as his boss and Hanson eased him and Hardy to the ground.

Roan glanced up at him with a grin. "We got the cattle back."

"Good job," Duel answered, hollering for someone to bring water.

Hardy cussed a blue streak, holding a water canteen. "That mess in Piebald needs a lawman."

Someone dabbed at the cut above Roan's eye, though it didn't stop the trickle of blood. Fire burned all the way down his body. He concentrated on the thin clouds overhead to take his mind from the agony.

He told his boss what the man inside the saloon had yelled as he was leaving. "They're either directly involved or they know where the other cattle are being held. I wanted to stay and force the answer out of them, but I was in no"—he inhaled a shaky breath—"shape. Gage either."

"Speak for yourself," Gage declared. "I'm ready to go back and whip some bastards."

"No, I'm glad you came on," Duel answered. "I'll take some men and go find them. But first, I want to get you both to the house before you pass out on me."

～⌘～

Marley's heart pounded when Roan appeared through the trees with her father and some of the hands. He was bent over, clutching his gray mare's mane. She dropped the wash she was hanging on the line and yelled for her mother, then she raced toward him, fighting the strangling in her throat.

When she reached him, he tried to smile. "I'm fine, Marley Rose. No need for a fuss."

Her father eased Roan from the saddle, and she knelt in the dirt beside him. "I have eyes. You're in awful shape."

Between Duel and Hanson, they half carried Roan into the house while Hardy staggered behind.

Marley's anger rose. The cuts and bruises on Roan's body were clearly visible through the ripped strips of his bloody shirt.

"Fix Roan up first," Hardy insisted. "They seemed to take pity on the old man."

Marley put her hands on her hips. "Then why are you holding your stomach?"

"Aw, Marley Rose, it's nothing that a little rest won't help."

"You'll both get looked after," Duel said firmly, settling the argument.

While her mother examined Roan, Marley hurried to collect their medical supplies. Roan's gray eyes followed her. She yearned to kiss away his pain and take away his sadness.

She shot a glance at the triplets asleep in a bed in the corner and willed them to stay silent. Thank goodness the children weren't home from school yet either, so they weren't underfoot. Matt would be right in the thick of things otherwise. Roan Penny was still his hero.

"What happened, Papa?" she asked.

Duel ran a hand through his hair. "Rustlers again. He and Hardy tracked them to Piebald. From what I can see, they were lucky to have ridden out."

No one had to tell Marley how lucky he was. It appeared someone had meant to kill him.

Jessie laid down the washcloth. "I'm pretty sure you cracked a rib or two. I'll bind them, but first I need to stitch the cut over your eye, Roan. It's going to hurt."

"Do whatever you need to," he answered. "Marley, Rube was in Piebald along with the stolen cattle."

"I can't believe you found him. What did he look like?" She handed her mother a needle and watched her thread it with catgut.

"Well, I didn't exactly see him—at least not that I know of. I was too busy dodging blows and then bullets. But a man at a holding pen told me Rube was at the saloon." He wiped his good eye. "A man inside the saloon yelled for us to leave and then fired a shot."

"I don't know how you got those cattle back," Duel said, "and dodged bullets. Are you sure you're made of flesh and blood?"

Roan chuckled. "Pretty sure. I bled a lot for someone who doesn't have any."

Marley reached for Roan's hand, being careful to avoid his scraped knuckles, while Jessie stitched the cut over his eye. Marley winced each time he flinched when the sharp needle met his tender flesh. If only she could do something. Anything. But all she could do was stand there and hand her mother what she needed.

"And, Marley," Roan said, "Gentry was also there—in the company of Virginia Creek."

She frowned. "It's odd how they keep showing up together. Why is that, you think? Even though they have different last names and Silas Wheeler insisted they aren't married, they sure keep each other company a lot."

"I guess she could be his sister."

"Maybe."

At last Jessie wiped her hands. "It's the best I can do. You probably need to see the doc in town."

"Thank you for fixing me up, Mrs. McClain, but I don't have time for a doctor. I'll be fine."

"Roan, you've escaped death more times than I can count," Jessie said. "One day you may not. You need a safe, quiet job."

"I warned him against taking on a whole passel of fired-up potlickers alone, Miz Jessie." Hardy Gage grinned. "Roan here gave that God-blessed town hell."

"They took exception to me, not the other way around," Roan grunted. "I would've found the wire-cutters, too, if the bas"—he flushed, dodging Jessie's and Marley's glances before quickly amending—"varmints hadn't tried to drown me in a horse trough. I'd lay odds that the rustlers were the very ones who started the fight."

"I'd swear on a stack of Bibles." Fire shot from Hardy's eyes, then he winced when Jessie felt around on his stomach.

Duel gazed out at the pasture land. "It doesn't surprise me that Piebald harbors the thieving bunch. Those folks never had any law."

Fear struck Marley. More trouble bore down on them like a thick, black cloud of locusts.

"The boys are saddling up, Boss." Judd stood, hat in hand. "We'll get back the rest of the herd."

Marley watched her papa's expression darken, saw fury climb into his amber eyes.

"I'm riding in a few minutes—with or without them."

"I'm going with you," Roan insisted.

Hardy tried to rise only to have Jessie hold him down. "Me too. I'm just fine."

Jessie glared. "You're not going anywhere. You probably have bruised kidneys."

"I reckon I do, but—"

"No buts, Mr. Stubborn." Her mama was more than a match for the old ranch hand.

Marley's stomach clenched as she watched her papa take a box of shells from the top of a kitchen cabinet. He grabbed his Winchester carbine from the rack next to the door. "I'd love to have both of you, but I'd sure appreciate it if you'd stay behind with a few men and protect the women and children. No telling what that gang will do next, and Gentry's still lurking."

Roan opened his mouth to object but closed it again. "We'll keep everyone safe."

Satisfied, Duel's arm stole around Jessie's waist, and he pulled her close. "I don't know how long I'll be gone."

"Be careful." Jess tipped her head for a kiss.

"Count on it."

"Please don't test my knitting skills. Besides, I don't have a lot of catgut left."

"Can't promise. Depends on the mood of Piebald's riffraff. Leave a light on for me."

"Always." Jessie cupped his square jaw tenderly.

With a heavy heart, Marley watched her father and Hardy disappear. Anything could happen. It took only a single glance at Roan's bloody, torn shirt lying on the floor to remind her of that possibility.

Her mother convinced Hardy to lie down in the bunkhouse and bound Roan's cracked ribs tightly. Muscles flexed in his brawny upper arms and rippled across the portion of his chest left bare of the wrapping. He met Marley's worry and tried to summon a wry smile, as if to say getting the snot beat out of him was all part of some grand design. Only he'd come too late to convince her of that.

The dark bruises and cuts told of the thrashing he'd gotten. Tears for him stung the back of her eyes.

God, how she loved this man.

Twenty-five

LIGHT STREAMED THROUGH THE KITCHEN WINDOWS OF THE ranch house. Marley couldn't take her eyes from Roan. Once again, he'd met death and won.

His blue-gray gaze warmed her. "I worried you— again. Sorry."

She threaded her fingers through his. "I guess I just have to get used to it. I have a feeling you're not one to sit on the sidelines when trouble calls."

He grinned. "Maybe you want to back out?"

"Nope. All your adventures simply give me more things to write stories about." She glanced at the scraps of ruined material on the floor. "I think I'd best stock up on shirts, though, at the rate you're going through them."

Galloping hooves interrupted them. Marley went to the window. "It's Sheriff Bagwell and his deputy from Tranquility."

Roan grabbed his hat and hobbled to the door, Marley following close behind.

Duel and his men had been ready to ride out. He swung around. "Sheriff, you're in a big hurry about something."

Bagwell leaned his arm on the pommel. "Had news that couldn't wait about that kid your man Roan Penny shot. He lived in San Saba exactly as you thought."

"What was the news?" Roan asked.

"You look like you've gone a round or two with a bear," the sheriff remarked.

"Yeah, but I'm in one piece. Found rustled cattle, and the men tried to keep me from bringing them back."

"Why did you come, Bagwell?" Duel asked. "Me and the boys are riding to Piebald to round up a bunch of rustlers."

"Mind if me and my deputy come along? Sounds like you're in need of someone to make some arrests."

"Shoot, Truman, you don't need to beg. You're welcome to come." Duel stood in the stirrups and thundered, "Now tell me why the hell you rode out here. I'm burning daylight."

"The boy's last name was Coburn. He's the brother of Sheriff Coburn over in San Saba. I came to warn you that the man is itching to get even." Bagwell turned to Roan. "He's especially wanting your hide. But then, I'm guessing you aren't surprised."

Marley sucked in a troubled breath. Coburn wasn't going to let this lie. She remembered his expression that morning at breakfast in the Latimer Hotel dining room. His dislike for Roan had been written on his face for all to see. And his sneer that Roan must've found her in a brothel still rang in her head. But she knew Coburn didn't have the courage to come here and face her father. His type of cowardice was more the kind that hid in the shadows, killing from the darkness when no one could see his face.

A layer of ice encased her. Trouble refused to leave their door.

"There's bad blood between us," Roan admitted. "But it's news to me that he had a brother."

Worry lined her mother's face. "Duel, honey, what if Coburn comes while you're gone? We have to think of the children."

Her father dismounted and pulled Jessie against him. "I don't think he'll be brave enough to come here. He'll wait and waylay us when we're off the ranch. Have Roan pick the children up from school and keep them home until this blows over. I'm also leaving Judd Hanson and four other ranch hands. With luck, I'll be back before sunset."

Jessie straightened. Marley admired that about her mother. Jessie was made of stern stuff, and though she might fear things, she stiffened her spine and bravely carried on.

"We're fine. Locate the stolen herd and come back to me." She raised her face for a kiss.

Duel mounted up, and they galloped toward the lawless town.

Roan put an arm around Marley. "Do you think you can find me a shirt? It's a little chilly wearing nothing but bandages."

"Of course."

Roan's nearness melted a bit of the ice inside her as they followed her mother into the house. Before long, Marley had him in another shirt and he was out the door. He'd decided to get the children from school early, even though it was only noon. It was time to circle the wagons and hunker down.

She went about chores that waited for nothing—diapers to wash again, floors to sweep and mop, and soup to get on. The children would be hungry the moment they got home from school.

And they were. They gobbled up everything in sight. Marley didn't complain though. She was glad they were safe at home where she could watch over them. She'd just settled down in her little house with a tablet and pencil to jot down a story that had come to her when she heard a mule braying outside and people shouting.

Marley ran out to see Granny Jack and her mule. The woman's silver hair was half up and half stringing down around her shoulders. Her glasses were nowhere to be seen. "Granny Jack! What's wrong?"

"Trouble," the old woman answered as Roan helped her from the animal.

"Come inside." Marley put an arm around her and led her inside the main house to a chair in the kitchen. Several kids peeked around the door, whispering.

Roan sat opposite Granny at the table. "Tell us what happened."

Granny rubbed red welts on both wrists. "A man broke into my house and tied me up, that's what. I've been at his mercy for several days. The bastard stomped on my glasses and put my cats out in the cold. I spat in his eye first chance I got. I finally got away this morning after he left. I wish I could kick him right in the you-know-where!"

"Can you describe him, Granny?" Fury danced up Marley's spine. The very nerve to treat a harmless old woman like this!

"I sure can." Granny's eyes narrowed to mere slits. "He was as skinny as a willow sapling and tall, real tall. Had these beady little raccoon eyes. Spoke like he had a mouthful of gravel."

Chills raced through Marley. "Will Gentry."

"Yep." Roan's face hardened. "That's how he disappeared. He holed up at Granny's."

"Who the heck is Gentry?" the old woman asked, taking a cup of tea that Jessie handed her. Granny saucered it before sipping.

One of the babies began to cough, the sound rattling in her small chest. Jessie patted Granny's back. "I need to tend to Edith. If you need anything, dear, Marley will get it. Don't you even think about going back to your cabin."

"That sounds awful croupy to me, Jessie. Put a mustard poultice on that little darling," Granny said as Jessie hurried to the next room to get the triplet. Then the old woman turned her attention back to Marley. "Now tell me who Gentry is."

"Duel just told me that Will Gentry is my real father." Marley leaned closer. "I suspect you knew about this. You hem-hawed around when I asked you that last visit."

Granny Jack looked sheepish. "Weren't my place to tell, my girl. I always feared the secret would come out someday though. Things like that have a way of rising to the surface. But I didn't know his name." She seemed to drift back in time. "Duel left here a broken man after he buried Annie and their boy. Many a cowboy never recovers from such a blow. And then a little over a year later, he came back toting you on his arm, and Jessie clucking over you like a mother hen. You were the prettiest baby I ever did see. I watched you heal his spirit. The change that came over him gladdened my poor soul. Pieces of three ruined lives fit together and became a whole family. They claimed you, Marley Rose." Granny looked into Marley's eyes, her gaze piercing. "Do you claim them back?"

Roan laced his fingers through Marley's. "If you have any doubts, this should put them to rest. They've always cherished you."

She met his stare. "Yes, I claim them." And she meant every word of it.

"You were lucky to get away from Gentry, Granny." Roan got to his feet and poured himself coffee from the pot on the stove. "He's hell-bent on getting Marley. Says she'll fetch more money now that she's a grown woman."

"The slimy toad!" Granny sloshed her tea, her hand shook so badly. "Roan Penny, it's your job to see that doesn't happen."

"Yes, ma'am." Roan sat back down. "Did he say anything else while he was with you?"

"I clean forgot. The gall-nipping bastard devil said he was gonna set fire to the ranch to make Duel pay. Said he'll laugh while it burns. I wish my Mooney was here. He'd put a bullet in Gentry's skull and send him to hell in a heartbeat." Granny Jack's heavy jowls shook with rage.

Marley patted her hand. "You're safe now. You'll stay with us until we put Gentry either behind bars or in the ground."

Granny's rheumy eyes grew large. "I've got my cats to feed. I gotta go back."

"No, you can't." If she did, Gentry would tie her up again…or decide the old lady was too much trouble and kill her. Marley glanced at Roan. "Do you suppose—"

"I'll send one of the hands to get them," he said. "There's just no way I can let you leave."

"Now, you know you don't have room," Granny argued, glancing at the children sitting quietly in the doorway.

Marley patted her hand. "You'll stay with me in my little house, and I won't hear another word."

"Well, I reckon that's the way of it. Would you have more tea, girl?"

Roan finished his coffee and went out to send a man for Granny's cats. At least there were enough of the animals that the children wouldn't have to fight over them. They'd be in hog heaven.

Marley poured Granny more tea, then glanced out the window, willing her father and Sheriff Bagwell to hurry back.

A war was brewing as sure as she stood there.

Twenty-six

MARLEY SAT WITH GRANNY JACK IN FRONT OF THE FIREPLACE at her house late that afternoon while the children played with the cats on the floor. Worry lined the old woman's face, and Marley didn't have to guess that she feared the worst about Duel and his task in Piebald.

"I wish we could know something, but I have to believe that they'll be back soon," Marley said. "At least you're safe and you have your cats."

"A watched pot never boils, child, and I'm awful lucky. I could still be tied up with a madman standing over me and my cats out in the cold night. But here I am in front of a warm fire." Granny smiled at the children. "They love my cats as much as I do."

"Yes, ma'am. I'm glad the man Roan sent to get them had no trouble rounding them up." Thank goodness, too, that he hadn't encountered Gentry. But if he wasn't hanging around the ranch, did that mean the man was in Piebald? With her father? Her stomach knotted.

Granny cackled. "I counted all my furry kids to make sure he brought every last one of them. I thought for sure he left Matilda behind, but I got her mixed up with Patches."

"I don't know how you keep them straight."

"It's a thousand wonders, but I manage." Granny rocked silently for a minute, staring into the fire, watching the flames. At last, she said quietly, "A storm's coming."

Marley knew she wasn't talking about the weather. But from what direction would it come, and how many riders would it bring? She shivered, recalling the terror of Will Gentry's face, his voice, his hands gripping her.

"We're ready," she said, glancing at the Winchester by the door. "We'll send them running back under their rock."

"See that bent live oak out there?" Granny Jack pointed through the window. "That poor old tree's weathered many a storm, and it's still standing. You know why? Because it has deep roots and it leans into the wind. Sometimes the wind knocks off limbs and such, and sometimes I reckon that tree gets mighty weary, but in spite of all, it thrives. So will we. Ain't no one gonna put me in the ground before I'm good an' ready." She stopped rocking. "I'd be obliged to have a rifle."

"We have plenty next door. I'm sure Roan and the men are keeping watch for riders." Marley prayed Roan, all of them, would escape whatever was coming. "We need to put out this fire and go to the main house."

"It's time, girl."

"Children, put on your coats, gather up the cats, and let's go see Mama Jessie." Marley struggled to keep her voice steady. "I think she's lonesome for us."

Quick to read her every mood, Matt crept to her side and clutched her dress. "I'm scared, Mama Rose."

"Honey, I'm not going to let anyone hurt you." She kissed his forehead. "Mr. Penny and the cowboys are out there with their rifles and guns, and they'll shoot anyone who rides up who doesn't belong here. Do you trust me?"

"Yep." He dredged up a grin. "If they come, the pirates will get them. They'll tie 'em up and put a dirty sock in their mouths."

"And then they'll feed 'em to the alligators," little Benji piped up from Marley's other side.

She doused the fire, then asked, "Can you boys carry a cat?"

Although they didn't want to turn loose of her, they quickly picked up a cat each and hurried back.

"Allie, can you help Granny Jack?" Marley asked the fifteen-year-old.

"Okay." The girl took one of Granny's arms and Marley the other. With Marley gripping her Winchester, they paraded to the main house.

Roan crossed from the shadows of the corral. "I was about to come get you. We need to keep together."

Marley glanced at the rifle in the crook of his arm. "Never hurts to be prepared. I just wish Papa would get back."

The children and Granny Jack went on into the house. Roan brushed her cheek. "I wish I could kiss you. I have a need for your lips."

His touch settled some of the turmoil inside. She leaned against him. "I want to kiss you too, and cuddle in front of a warm fire. I hate living in constant fear. I'm so cold. I need this to be over so we can go on with our lives."

"To hell with everyone." He set down the rifle, pulled her close, and captured her lips.

The banked embers of their passion flamed in an instant. Marley clung to him, inhaling the scent of this wild land on him. She forgot about the ever-changing quicksand that was her life currently. Forgot about the trouble. And forgot about her fear. Roan always made her feel safe, and she burned with a powerful hunger for him.

She tightened her arms around his waist and parted her lips. He slid his tongue inside, doing what their bodies could not. Wetness formed between her thighs. This sweet torment drove her insane; she wanted him so badly. She needed this man she'd found on a lonely road.

A sound broke them apart. She didn't know what it was, but her gut told her something wasn't right.

Roan jerked up his rifle. "Get into the house, Marley. Douse the lamps and don't come out no matter what you hear or see."

Roan's breath fogged in the cold air, his eyes scanning for trouble, a bitter taste filling his mouth. Vivid memories of Mose rose. At the sound of hoofbeats, he swung to face the riders coming to a halt five yards away. The sun had just set, and darkness would soon descend. The remaining light revealed the grim faces of the visitors. Roan was sure his own must look the same.

He knew why they'd come, and he'd do everything in his power to make sure they left very disappointed. He'd scattered the five remaining ranch hands at various places across the compound. No need to look to see if they were in position. They were—even Hardy Gage. The man had insisted he was fit enough to send a few bastards to hell.

If shooting started, the riders wouldn't know where to aim first. That was Roan's plan.

Will Gentry and Sheriff Coburn led about a dozen young boys. One of them didn't look any older than twelve, and the big gelding he sat was too much animal for him. The boy wouldn't meet Roan's gaze, instead stared down at the gun clenched in his hands. All of them were armed to the teeth, and every pistol pointed at him.

Another rider moved forward and stopped next to the two men. Roan stared hard. No distinct chin. It just seemed to merge with his neck. Stocky build. Unless he missed his guess, that was Wes Douglas.

It appeared their hunch was right.

"What can I help you with, gentlemen?" Roan asked. "If you need McClain, I'll go get him."

"Don't play us for fools, Penny," snarled Coburn. "We know he rode out with his men and Sheriff Bagwell. Noticed Bagwell's deputy too."

Breaking glass sounded behind Roan. Some of the young riders became jittery.

"Get the hell off this land before I blow you to the devil's fiery pit!" yelled Granny Jack.

More glass broke, and from the corner of his eyes, Roan saw rifles sticking from every window of the ranch house. From the looks of it, Jessie must've armed the kids. That was just dandy. He prayed the old woman would hold her tongue—and her bullets. He didn't want to fight a war if he could avoid it.

He turned back to Coburn, ignoring his statement about Duel leaving. "I asked you before. What do you need?"

Coburn cocked his six-shooter that was pointed at Roan. "You're under arrest, Roan Penny, for the murder of my little brother."

"I'm sorry he had to die," Roan answered. "I truly am, but I'll shoot anyone who rides toward me wearing a hood over their head. Your brother was a cattle rustler and who knows what else. One thing I know for sure, he broke the law that night."

"What proof do you have?" Coburn shot back.

"Witnesses. His hood. What more do you need?"

"I see you there, you beady-eyed rat-buzzard!" Granny hollered. "Tie up a defenseless old woman and kick my cats out in the cold—I'll show you who's boss. I'm itching to put a bullet in your head."

"Granny, that's enough," Roan growled without turning. Without glasses, it was anyone's guess where her bullets would go.

"Old woman, I shoulda killed you!" Gentry hurled back. "Then drowned your cats."

Granny egged him on. "What was that, gall-nipper? You got mush in your teeth?"

Behind him, Roan heard Marley telling her to stop making things worse.

Gentry searched each window, then swung his gun to Roan. "I came after Marley Rose. Send her out."

"You'll have to get past me." Roan's gaze went to the young boys. They didn't appear to have the heart for killing in cold blood, and it wouldn't take much for them to tuck tail and run. Coburn and Gentry were another matter.

"Won't be a problem after I shoot you," Gentry sneered, his lips curling back from his teeth.

Marley's voice came from Roan's left. Her Winchester protruded from the window. "You'll never take me alive, I can promise you that. You're a miserable excuse for a human being. You're nothing but a slimy night crawler. Something to squash."

"That's no way for a daughter to speak to her father," Gentry snapped, showing his anger.

Roan would die before he let the man have her. "So here's what's going to happen. You're going to lower your weapons and ride out of here."

"You're in no position to make demands," Coburn barked. "You ain't got nothing but women and children to back you up."

First surprise, then satisfaction washed over Roan. They didn't know about the ranch hands. Good.

"I'd say we're just about even, then." Roan watched their faces darken even more. "You'll have hell taking me in, and you're not getting Marley either. Best thing you can do is turn around. It's a long ride back to San Saba."

Coburn shifted. "I wish we'd killed you that same night we got rid of that worthless bastard Mozeke."

Roan shrugged. "Your mistake." He watched Coburn's glittering eyes. The rotten sheriff was rash, especially when he burned with fury, whereas Gentry took things more slowly and held his anger inside.

A roar, a flash, and Coburn's gun belched fire.

The minute Roan saw the orange flame, he pulled the trigger, yelling, "This is for Mose Mozeke." The hard ground broke his dive for cover.

His bullet struck Coburn dead center in the heart. The sheriff fell from his horse. Gunfire erupted all around Roan, and he scrambled for cover in the shadows at the side of the house.

The youngsters on horseback whirled and galloped off into the night. That was good. Roan really didn't want to kill any boys—just a single man with a stone where a heart should be.

Where had Wes Douglas disappeared to? Not knowing made him nervous.

The women inside the house released a burst of blistering gunfire. In the middle of the exchange, Roan lost Gentry. Now he had two to worry about.

As the barrage died down, Marley called out, "Roan, he's in those bushes. He jumped from his horse."

Roan would thank her later. He sprinted to the waist-high bushes. A bullet nicked his arm as he dove into the vegetation. He paid it no heed.

"Come out, Gentry. You're the only one left."

Silence met him. Roan carefully worked his way through the now-leafless branches. The winter breeze, combined with the loss of sunlight, made him shiver. If it had been daylight, Roan would have had no trouble seeing his foe.

Gentry lunged out of nowhere, tackling Roan. A fist knocked him sideways, and Roan's rifle flew into the darkness. He punched Gentry in the stomach and face. Everywhere he could connect with muscle and bone, he did. Roan matched the man in height and carried more weight. If he hit him enough times, Gentry would go down.

One thing Roan hadn't counted on was the man's long, skinny legs. One of them kicked sideways and took Roan's out from under him. He went down with Gentry on top.

Roan pushed his foe's face back, his fingers in the man's eyes. Gentry hollered as Roan broke the hold. Roan scrambled to his feet, reaching for the knife in the sheath between his shoulder blades.

Gentry reached into his boot and yanked out a long knife. Both armed with knives, they moved in a circle, hands held wide, looking for an advantage. Gentry lunged, slashing Roan's jacket. Roan caught Gentry's knife hand and forced him backward against a wooden hitching rail.

Just when Roan appeared to have won, Gentry broke free. An arcing slash of the knife sent Roan jumping backward in time to evade the thin blade. Before Roan could go on the offense again, a horse as black as midnight galloped from the trees.

Wes Douglas. The stocky rider reached for Gentry and lifted him onto the back.

"This isn't over," Gentry hollered. "McClain's dead. I'm coming back with a damn army and getting my daughter!"

The horse and rider vanished as though ghosts in the night.

Twenty-seven

ROAN GAVE CHASE ON FOOT, PLUNGING THROUGH THE TREES, ignoring the stinging pain of his arm where the bullet had grazed him. Why was it that each time he thought he had Gentry cornered, the bastard managed to escape?

His low curse filled the silence.

The bad thing was that Roan didn't hear any crashing through brush, no grunts, nothing. Finally, after half a mile, he had no choice but to turn back. The words *McClain's dead* echoed in his head. Maybe it wasn't true. After all, who could believe a man who'd wagered his baby girl in a poker game? But the man was rotten enough to kill Duel. For now, Roan was going on the assumption that Gentry had just wanted to rattle him. He wasn't going to tell Marley. She didn't need that worry on top of everything else.

She ran to meet him. "Are you all right?"

Roan put his arm around her. "I'm fine. Kicking myself that he got away. I should've had him." Dammit!

"Stop it, Roan. Don't second-guess yourself or lay blame. You got Coburn." She slid her fingers into his hair, pressing closer. "If you hadn't been here—" A shudder ran through her.

"It could've all ended here tonight though. Every bit of it."

Judd Hanson and Hardy Gage pushed forward with a

young boy. "We found this one hiding next to the barn. Couldn't find a weapon on him. Guess he got rid of it."

Roan released Marley. The youngster was the same one he'd noticed earlier. He gazed up at Roan with frightened eyes. A tear slid down the kid's face. Roan rested a hand on his thin shoulder and softened his voice. "What's your name, son?"

"Beau Marsh," the boy whispered, his bottom lip quivering.

"Are you cold, son?"

Beau nodded. "And hungry. Would you have a cold biscuit?"

Something turned over inside Roan. Feed the kid's belly and they might get information. "Let's go into the house. Bet we can find a bite to eat."

"We sure can. Beau, come with me," Marley said. The boy walked by her side toward the house.

Judd moved closer and swung into step with Roan. "The kid's scared half out of his mind. He almost wet his pants when I discovered him. Can't be more than ten or twelve. What's wrong with these people, using kids to do their dirty work?"

"Damned if I know. Maybe Beau will tell us." One thing for sure, the kid was not going back to whoever ran the operation. If he didn't have anyone, he could stay with them until they could find him a good home. He was sure Duel and Jessie wouldn't mind one more. After all, they already ran an orphanage.

"What do you want to do with Coburn?" Judd asked.

"Tell the men to carry him into the barn for now until Boss gets back. Duel can decide what to do with him."

"The short hairs on my neck are jerking, giving me a bad feeling," Judd said low so Marley and the boy couldn't hear. "Gentry and the others are going to be back. Bet you anything they're sitting out there right now, making plans and gathering a force who'll fight."

"My gut tells me the same thing. They're going to take advantage of McClain being gone." Roan sure hoped he was wrong, but everything told him he was right.

"That's another thing. What's happened to the boss and the others? Have they slaughtered them? I heard Gentry yell that McClain is dead, but I don't believe it."

Memories of Roan's short time in Piebald told him Judd Hanson had good reason to worry.

"Who knows if he was telling the truth or not. We have to work on the assumption that we're in this alone, or we'll never make it." Roan pinched the bridge of his nose. "We should block the entrance to the compound. Make it harder for them to just ride in."

"Me and the boys will roll some wagons in front of the gate. Barrels too. Whatever we can find."

Roan glanced toward the house, torn between finding out all he could and making the ranch harder to penetrate. "I should help."

"No. We'll handle this. Go see what the boy can tell you. He might know something. And while you're in there, get Miss Marley to look at that wound. We'd better work fast. I smell rain in the air."

For the first time since the knife fight, Roan glanced at his arm, where the bullet had grazed him earlier. The wound wasn't too bad. "Best have the rain slickers ready." Roan laid a hand on Judd's shoulder. "Thanks for being here. I can't think of anyone I'd rather have at my side than you and Hardy."

"Same here." And with that, Judd turned to talk to the men.

Seconds later, Roan strolled into the McClain kitchen. Air coming through the broken windows stole the heat. Seated at the table, Beau stared at him with hopeless eyes. Jessie urgently called from the next room for Marley to come help with one of the triplets. Marley excused herself saying she'd be right back. Roan went to the medicine cabinet and reached for a white cloth. Holding it to his sleeve, he swung around to see the kid watching him.

"Does it hurt, mister?"

"Naw, not much." Roan moved to the table and sat down.

Marley bustled back into the room and dished up some fried potatoes and ham that they had been keeping warm for Duel and poured him a glass of cold milk. The instant she set the food in front of Beau, he bowed his head in silence for a moment, then dug in.

Someone had clearly taught Beau Marsh to be grateful for what he got.

The kid had finished half his plate of food when Judd entered. "I did that"—he glanced at Beau and lowered his voice—"chore we spoke about, and the men have moved some of the wagons into place." He glanced at Marley. "If I can have a cup of coffee, I'll go back out to keep watch. Gentry might sneak back. The men are alert though."

Marley jumped up. "I'll have to make some. I should've done that already."

"You had a thing—or three—on your mind. Besides, you're not the keeper of the coffee," Judd scolded.

"Glad you're keeping watch. Pays a man to be careful." Roan's gaze swept to Marley's trim figure as she refilled the coffeepot, and he lowered his voice. "Gentry's not going away until he gets what he came for."

"My thinking too."

"I heard that. You don't have to tiptoe around me." Worry filled Marley's eyes, but she kept her thoughts to herself. "Judd, I'll bring out coffee for all of you as soon as it's ready. Won't be long."

"Good deal, Miss Marley. The men will be happy about that. Just make sure it's good and strong. We have to stay awake." Judd pulled up the collar of his coat around his neck and went out the door into the night.

Roan wished he knew what was keeping Duel and the sheriff. They must've run into trouble or they'd have been back already. Marley sat at the table while the coffee boiled, the kitchen falling into an uneasy silence. Jessie had corralled the kids and Granny Jack in another part of the house to give them some quiet.

When Beau had emptied his plate and drank the last of

his milk, Roan rested his elbows on the table. "I'd like to ask you some questions. Is that all right, Beau?" At the boy's nod, Roan continued. "Where is your home? Your parents?"

"Mama died and Papa's in prison." Beau's chin quivered with the struggle to hold back tears. "I didn't wanna ride with them. I don't wanna kill anybody."

"Honey, we know that, and we're not mad." Marley rubbed his shoulder. "But we're wondering who's taking care of you."

Beau sniffled. "Rube."

The name sped through Roan like buckshot. Everywhere he turned, he heard the name but still had no face to go with it. "Can you tell me who Rube is?"

"Ruby. She said she's my mama now. She gives me a place to sleep and food, but there's so many of us we don't get much to eat."

A woman? He was fighting a woman?

A hard knot formed in Roan's stomach. He hadn't considered the idea that Rube would be anything but a man.

Ruby. Of course. Now it made sense. Foreboding filled him. He'd never fought a woman before. His mother had protected him. A kind woman had raised him. A nun had given him a place to live. Marley Rose had rescued him.

Women had always represented all that was good and decent. They'd shielded him and given him time to grow up. But Ruby didn't fit in there. This woman must be driven by greed, grabbing all the land she could, slaughtering innocent people. She'd taken Mose's acreage and that of who knew how many others. And she was determined to win at all costs—no matter whom she had to kill.

He stilled. The long, satin thread in Mose's barn. The boy who'd been shot dead when Roan and Duel had gone to bury his dear friend. Death and destruction lay in Ruby's wake. She had to have been behind Mose's death, and probably Roan's dragging and beating. It wasn't a far stretch. Evidently, Gentry and Wes Douglas worked for her, probably rustled Duel's cattle too.

But who *was* she?

"Do you know her last name?" Roan asked.

Beau wiped his mouth on his sleeve. "Nope."

"What does Ruby look like? How old is she?"

The boy glanced at Marley, then back to Roan. "I dunno. Maybe taller than her. Older than her."

"Thank you, Beau." The kid hadn't been very helpful. Roan's hopes fell.

Outside, thunder rumbled, and jagged lightning flashed through the window as rain pelted the tin roof. Damn! Could things not get any worse? The storm would make guarding the women and children even more difficult.

Marley stood and yanked a slicker from a hook on the wall. "I need to take the coffee out to the men before this storm gets too bad."

"Stay put and I'll do it, darlin'." Roan strode to her side.

She met his gaze. "No, I want to check the windows in my house. I think I left the one in the bedroom cracked. Let me tell Mama first."

"Stubborn woman. I'm going with you." Roan got to his feet and grabbed another slicker hanging by the door. "Beau, stay here. We'll be right back."

But when he turned around, the kid had laid his head down on his arms and was sound asleep. Poor thing. Why couldn't Ruby let little boys grow up before she taught them to kill? Anger sped through Roan. Ruby had stolen Beau's innocence as well as that of the others who rode for her. Damned if he could figure out why.

Marley returned with Jessie, who took one look at the boy and melted. Jessie gave him a gentle nudge. "Let's get you to bed, honey. You're exhausted."

Beau gave her a brief glance before murmuring, "Thank you, ma'am."

Roan watched her direct the boy through the door, then took the coffeepot from Marley and went out into the storm. The cold wind whipped the slicker, and rain pelted them in the face. It was going to be a miserable night.

Judd ran from the darkness and relieved them of the coffee, sticking the cups into his pockets. "Thanks. This is going to be mighty good."

"I don't think we'll have any more trouble until this storm blows over," Roan said.

"Yep, they're hunkered down somewhere for now." Rain ran off Judd's hat. "They're going to hit us again once it passes, though. I'll bet a month's wages on that. I sure wish Boss would ride in. It'd do my heart good."

"Mine too." Roan didn't want to think about what might've happened.

"He'll be back," Marley said firmly. "Even if he has to crawl. If he's alive, my papa will be back."

"Get back inside. Until he does, me and the boys will keep watch." Judd turned toward the shadows where he'd come from.

Roan put his arm around Marley. "Let's check your windows."

They ran for the door, not slowing until they got over the threshold.

"I didn't think the skies would open up quite so fast." Marley removed her hood and stared at the water pooling around her feet. "My floor. I've got to get the mop before it warps the wood."

"The floor is the least of our worries. But we're stuck for now until it lets up." Roan found the matches and lit the lamps, then laid a fire in the hearth.

He stood gazing at Marley's prized Arthur D. Winston painting hanging above the fireplace. It was good, no doubt about it, but so was she. He glanced around the room and saw touches of Marley everywhere—from the little crocheted doilies on the end table to the books and figurines on a shelf. But she was what made this a home.

Marley strode from the bedroom. "I'm glad I came to check. Water is all over the floor. Thanks for making a fire. It'll be warm in here by the time I mop up."

"I know it won't do any good to say a word, so I'm

not." He shook his head as he watched her run for the mop. She was determined to have the place spic and span, and nothing would stop her. But it might be good for her to have something to do besides worry. He knew Will Gentry had rattled her.

He dropped onto the settee and stared into the flames. He didn't know what they'd do with Beau in the end, but the kid was not going back to Ruby. Roan meant to question him again after the boy got some rest. There was lots he still wanted to know. Like why Ruby was waging war.

What could her motivation be? Why this need for other people's land?

It had to pertain to the first mob who'd ruled the region before the Texas Rangers came and rounded them up. Why start all that up again? What was it that Wheeler had said about Virginia Creek? Ah yes—she owned a ranch outside of town, and the mob had killed her husband and three sons several years back. But Virginia wasn't Ruby. She might know her though. It still puzzled him why Virginia had been in Piebald with Gentry.

He was still mulling over everything he'd seen and heard when Marley sat down beside him and laid her head on his shoulder. "You look deep in thought. Is Beau causing that furrowed brow?"

"Trying to put the pieces of the puzzle together, only some don't fit."

"I know. Why is Ruby doing this?" Marley rested a palm on his arm. Suddenly she sat up and stared at the sleeve of his jacket. "You're bleeding! Why didn't you tell me?"

"Oh that. A bullet nicked me. I'm fine. Doesn't even hurt."

"You're always telling me you're fine when I can see with my own eyes that you aren't." She studied his bloody jacket. "What else happened to you? Keeping you in clothes is turning into a full-time job."

"You worry too much. Gentry's knife slashed me. I felt the blade as it went by, but in the commotion of his escape, clean forgot about it. He missed the skin."

"Roan, he could've killed you!" Quick tears filled her eyes.

That she was so emotional over something that hadn't happened spoke of the depth of her stress. Though she was strong, she was near her breaking point, and it was understandable. Even the strongest person had to bend occasionally.

The firelight flickered around them, bathing them in blue light from the flames. He wrapped his arms tightly around her. She was his entire world, and she filled it with every shade and blend of color he could've imagined.

The lady had amazing talent. She could shoot, wipe runny noses, and write stories.

And he was keeping her.

Twenty-eight

MARLEY GATHERED HERSELF AND SLIPPED FROM HIS ARMS. "I want to see this injury that you insist is nothing."

If he needed treatment, she was going to see that he got it.

Roan gave a long-suffering sigh and slipped out of the jacket. "At least I didn't entirely ruin the shirt this time," he joked. "That should earn me a point or two. I told you it's nothing."

She pushed up his shirtsleeve and examined the wound. "It still needs a good cleaning. I'll get some water."

"Whatever makes you happy. I'm learning that it doesn't do a lick of good to argue."

"I just wish you'd learn to stop flirting with death," she said from the small, open kitchen. The man was going to give her a heart attack one of these days. He must have some powerful guardian angels. One thing for sure, he was keeping them very busy.

That he'd stood in the path of bullets and knives for her and her family made her eyes burn.

Gathering a clean cloth, some gauze, and the water, she returned. The bullet had grazed his forearm, causing little enough damage. She was glad he was right, and she was glad about something else as well—that she'd insisted on cleaning it. Any excuse to run her fingers across his skin and feel the rippling muscles underneath was worth it.

Roan's strong forearms were a testament to a life spent doing heavy work. He wasn't afraid to get his hands dirty and had, indeed, plunged into any task on the ranch with zeal. That was one of the things she admired about him.

After washing blood from the wound and applying ointment, she wrapped gauze around his arm. "Roan, I'm curious about something. I hope you don't think I'm prying."

"What would you like to know?"

"Why are you drifting? You're smart, and you know so much about a lot of things. You could be a banker or teacher or anything you want, yet you choose not to."

He touched his finger to her cheek and said softly, "Those jobs wouldn't give me what I crave. Money can't fix everything. I was looking for a place that my heart would recognize as home. I've found it here." He brushed a kiss on her lips. "I was searching for you."

Marley swallowed the lump that suddenly blocked her throat. He was right. If he'd gotten a different job in some other town, she never would've known he existed.

She'd have died without ever knowing love.

"I'm glad you found me." She cupped his jaw and stared into his smoldering gray eyes. "You came into my life like a gentle summer storm. You stole my heart, changed my dreams, gave my life new purpose. Hold me. Hold me, cowboy, and don't ever let me go."

He gave a hoarse cry, pulled her against the hard planes of his body, and ground his mouth to hers. Marley welcomed the raging hunger that swept over her.

She wanted to run her hands over his body, feel the wild beating of his heart that matched hers.

She wanted him naked beside her, on top of her, inside her.

She wanted to inhale his scent and know that he was hers.

Marley's fingers trembled as she worked to remove his shirt. She had to put out the fire inside her somehow or be roasted alive. Thank God for the rain that gave them this time. Who knew what was about to happen. This might be all they had.

To die without knowing what it was like to make love to Roan—to not lie in his arms until trouble yanked them apart—would be the greatest tragedy.

Roan appeared to share her burning passion. His touch was branded on her skin as he removed her clothing. With the last bit of fabric gone from her body, he slid his hands slowly down her throat, across her collarbone to the curve of her breasts, where he flattened his palms over her nipples. A low moan rumbled in his chest.

He picked her up and carried her to the bed, setting her down on it. He didn't join her at first.

He stood beside the bed instead, running his hands through his hair. Breathing hard, Marley met his eyes. "Roan, this is right. We may not have anything after this night. They're waiting for us out there in the blackness. We're as good as married, as far as I'm concerned, and if we survive, we will be." A sob tore through her. "I want to be your lady—fully and completely. Just once before I die."

"Are you sure about this?"

"As positive as I've ever been about anything." Sitting up, she put her fingers into his gun belt and tugged him closer. "I need you. We need each other."

The last of his resistance melted away. He removed his gun belt, boots, and trousers, dropping everything in a heap on the floor.

Not bothering to turn back the covers, Roan lay down on his side next to her. The storm's fury beyond the walls didn't come close to the raw desire and hunger raging inside Marley. She ran her fingers across his broad chest and down his belly to his jutting need and closed her hand around his hardness. Moisture created a sheen between her thighs.

Thunder shook the windows, and a second later, a jagged flash of lightning illuminated the room.

"I've waited a long time for this," she murmured.

"You have, huh?" He lay on his side, caressing her back, kissing and kneading her breasts. When he captured a nipple between his thumb and forefinger, rolling the swollen nub,

Marley's building desire grew to unimaginable heights. She'd never felt anything like this. Fire swept down to her thighs and settled between them, throbbing and pulsing. She wound her fingers in his hair and pulled his face to her breasts. She arched her back to give him greater access and felt pleasure rush over her as he took her nipple in his mouth.

"Please," she moaned. "Don't stop."

He slid his hand between them to the juncture of her thighs and rubbed the blood-engorged flesh there. Wave after wave of pleasure washed over her. As she gasped for breath, Roan finally moved atop her and filled her with his need.

A few moments of pain made her gasp, but soon joy took its place.

Outside, the rain pounded on the tin roof. Inside, she matched the rhythm he set and soon found her hunger building again. She gripped his back, trying to pull even more of him inside. She wanted all of him.

This man who'd seen so much sorrow and pain was taking her to paradise, where there was nothing but unending joy.

Above her, Roan's breath became ragged as he sought release of his own. Their bodies danced to music that spoke of belonging and love.

Marley gasped, sliding over the edge of insanity. She floated there, mindlessly adrift on a sea of bliss. Nothing mattered—not the storm, not Ruby, and not Will Gentry's madness. She was with Roan, and they were one body, one soul, and shared one deep love.

He rolled off and lay beside her, struggling to breathe. She fumbled for his hand and held it, trying to keep the closeness they'd found. Another bolt of lightning flashed through the window, the storm showing no signs of abating. She prayed it never would. That they could stay safe in her cozy little house forever.

Marley brought his hand to her lips and kissed his palm. "When I was a little girl, I used to hide under my bed during storms. They terrified me to the point where I would sob and go into hysterics. Instead of pulling me out,

Papa would crawl under there with me and tell me stories until the storm passed. I wish I was a little girl again and could do that. I'm so scared, Roan. I'm terrified of Gentry, but I can't hide from that kind of evil. It'll find me anyway."

Roan propped himself on his elbow and smoothed back her hair. "If I could take that fear from you, I would in a heartbeat. I can't promise that I'll be able to stop him, but I can promise that I'll fight to the last breath."

"I'll never ask you to die for me. If you lose your life because of me—I don't think I could live with that." Her bottom lip quivered as she held back tears. "Please say you'll let the sheriff take care of him."

"We are the law here, Marley," he said gently. "It's us and him."

"I know. We won't let him win. He has no power over me. Let's not waste the time we have being sad. Roll over on your belly."

"The lady is full of orders." He groaned but did as she requested. Marley knelt above him, massaging his neck and shoulders until he relaxed.

"Ahhhh, lady. I think I'll stay like this. I've never felt so good. Well, no. I take that back. A few minutes ago, I felt the best I have in my whole life."

"I'm glad. So did I." She worked her way down his back, pausing at the crisscrossed scars his father's belt had left. She bent to kiss the raised flesh, imagining the pain he'd endured. How he'd survived that, then the beating and dragging at Mose Mozeke's, she didn't know. It must've been fate.

"Are your hands getting tired?" Roan asked.

"Nope."

She moved slowly down his back to his waist. He was so perfectly formed. Broad shoulders, lean waist, long legs, and a rear end that could sure fill out a pair of jeans. After he'd been able to get up and around, well, she'd secretly admired his rear, fascinated by how it moved when he walked. Now she ran her hands over the smooth flesh, then bent to leave kisses.

"I want to paint you sometime. Just like you are now."

"No."

"Why?"

"If I agreed, the next thing I'd know, you'd have it for sale someplace." He rolled over and shook his finger at her. "I've seen a few of those art places—and the people who go there—and I'm not going to have women ogling my man parts. No thank you."

"But—"

Before she could blink, he grabbed her and was lying on top of her.

"If anyone needs to be admired, it's you." He nibbled on her ear. "When I first woke up in your bed, your voice sounded like an angel, and I thought I was in heaven. My eyesight was so blurred, but I could make out a few of your features, and I never saw anyone so beautiful. And then I noticed the gun you had aimed at me and quickly forgot about being in heaven."

His hand moved down to rest on her stomach.

"And where did you think you were then?" she asked breathlessly.

"In some sex-starved woman's lair."

"Oh, you did not!" She playfully slapped his shoulder.

"I just knew that wherever I was, I wanted to stay there."

He raised above her and plunged himself into her again, and she forgot everything except the man who could make her body sing.

They climbed higher and higher toward the goal. As she tumbled over the other side, Roan murmured in her ear, "I love you, my beautiful Texas Star."

Twenty-nine

IT MUST'VE BEEN CLOSE TO MIDNIGHT BY THE TIME ROAN jerked awake. The storm had passed. He had to get out there with the men.

He pushed Marley's hair away from her face and kissed her. "Time to get up, my sleepy-eyed temptress. We have to go."

"What time is it?"

"Late. The storm's gone, and I need to get out there." He pushed back the covers, sat up, and grabbed his trousers. "I can't leave you here."

She knelt behind, her breasts pressed against his back. Her long, dark hair tickled him, along with her gentle kisses across his shoulders. Roan closed his eyes and steadied his breath. He'd gladly give everything he owned to stay in bed the rest of the night. But Gentry wasn't going to let him.

He handed Marley her clothes and stood. "The second this is over, I'm going to find a preacher and make you my wife."

"Let's set a date to make it official. How about one week from today?"

For a second, he thought of the waning moon. It was about time for it. He pushed the thought aside and smiled. "I've marked it down. That day belongs to us."

"Roan, are we going to make it?"

His fingers froze on the gun belt he was buckling. He pulled her up and wrapped her in his arms, her heart thudding against his ribs. "We're going to make it. No sorry woman like Rube or bastard like Gentry is going to win. I've never lied to you, though, so I won't start now. It's going to be a fight. But nothing worthwhile is ever easy."

"I know. I just pray that the little ones don't get hurt. Matt is going to be so scared. Earlier tonight, he hid in a closet, made himself as small as he could. He was terrified, and they didn't ask for this."

"I'm sorry. Maybe if I hadn't come to your door, none of this would've happened."

Marley shook her head. "Don't blame yourself for this, Roan Penny. The rustling was already going on. Will Gentry was already in the area—he was looking for me that day we went to visit Granny Jack. He'd have found me no matter what. And Ruby would've still killed your friend."

He was glad to hear her say it and to know she didn't blame him. He was used to people blaming him for whatever happened.

"Finish dressing," he urged. "I really can't stay longer."

They hurried and stepped out the door five minutes later, with Roan carrying his rifle and his fully loaded Colt on his hip.

Judd Hanson met them. "They're gathering out there in the darkness. They keep calling for Marley Rose. A godawful sound if I ever heard one. Making me and the boys jumpy. We have the wagons in place across the gate, but that won't stop 'em coming at us through the trees."

Jessie ran from the house, carrying a rifle. "Where are they? God so help me, I'm going to silence those voices."

"I wish we could, Miz Jessie." Roan turned to Marley. "Go in the house with your mama. Get a rifle and take a window like you did before."

Just then, an eerie voice yelled, "Marley Rose! Come out and play, Marley Rose."

A different voice hollered. "I see you, Marley Rose."

Chills raced through Roan.

Marley gave a sharp cry and put her hands over her ears. "Make them stop. Just make them stop."

He held her close, trying to soothe her. "They're just trying to rattle us. Don't pay them any mind. We're going to give our all to keep the bastards out."

Hardy Gage strode up, cussing a blue streak. Though by all rights he needed to be in bed, Roan knew the man, like himself, would put aside injuries to fight.

"They won't get past me and Judd," Hardy vowed. "Between us and Roan, we'll put a circle around you."

"Thanks, Hardy. You too, Judd." She threw an arm around Roan's neck. "Be careful, sweetheart. I don't want to lose you. We have a wedding date to keep."

He kissed her long and deep. "Never forget that I love you."

Roan watched until she disappeared into the house, then he turned to the two men. "Are you ready?"

"Born that way." Hardy tightened his grip on the rifle in his hands.

"Then you and I will take a position behind the wagons. The rest of the men will scatter around the compound like before. As the situation changes, they can move wherever they need to be. So can we." Roan glanced at the main house, candlelight filling the broken kitchen windows. This was it. Each person inside that house meant everything to him.

Somewhere in the past weeks, they had become his family. And now, to protect them, he had to make every bullet count.

A chorus of taunting voices filled the night. "Marley Rose! Come out and play, Marley Rose. We're waiting."

"You got nowhere to run, nowhere to hide."

"We'll find you, girl."

"Better get ready."

Roan yanked the rifle to his shoulder, searching for movement. He had to silence the jeering calls.

The next voice he heard was a gravelly rumble that he had no problem identifying. "Roan Penny, I'm coming for you. You're as good as dead."

"Then come on, you bastard," Roan whispered into the wind. "I have a bullet waiting."

"Damn right," Granny Jack said as she took a place beside him and propped her rifle on a bale of hay on top of a barrel. "An' we got more'n one."

Roan swung around in disbelief. "What are you doing out here? You need to be in the house where it's safer."

Granny stared into the blackness, and Roan could feel her anger. "No, sir. I ain't hiding from this bunch of sorry snakes. I aim to shoot until I have nary a bullet left."

"Ma'am, this is no place for a lady. You're liable to get hurt," Hardy said.

A determined hardness filled the old lady's voice. "I've lived a good long life and seen lots of terrible times. My Mooney would want me to be out here, fighting against this godforsaken riffraff. He didn't put up with malarkey like this, and neither will I. He stood tall and was counted, and that's exactly what I mean to do. If I die, then I'll just get to be with him sooner. This is my fight too."

Though Roan felt she was being foolhardy, he admired her. The squatty woman came no higher than the middle of his chest, but her determination and strength made her seem six feet tall. Granny Jack was a force to reckon with.

"Marley Rose," came the mocking voice again. "Where are you, Marley Rose?"

"Come on, you weaselly eyed bastards!" Granny yelled. "We're tired of waitin' for you. Are you sure you're men? You sound like a bunch of scared little girls to me."

She had barely gotten the words out when riders appeared from the darkness. Like in the earlier attack, these didn't wear the hoods either. From what Roan could tell, these men were quite a bit older than the young boys they'd recruited. He squeezed off several shots as they rode whooping toward the barricade, fire spitting from their guns.

When the group reached the wagons, they split and galloped in opposite directions. He didn't know if they were regrouping to make another run at them or trying to devise a different way in. He, Judd, and Granny took advantage of the lull to reload.

Long minutes passed. They held their positions, waiting to see what came at them next. If only daylight would come so they could see.

Finally, the attackers burst from the pitch-black at a full run. Only this time they didn't split at the wagons. In tandem, they leaped over the barricade. Roan kept up a steady blast from his rifle and knew he hit several of the riders. As the horses leaped the barricade, he swiveled and shot. A man tumbled from the saddle and lay in the mud left by the rain.

Roan quickly swung to take aim at the others. Moving targets were difficult to hit, but he was satisfied with the results. Rifle fire burst from the windows of the house as well, but the attackers were scattering now that they'd penetrated the line.

Cold fear shivering down his spine, he raced toward the house. No matter how he did it, he had to keep them from getting inside. He stopped to look back once he reached the side of the house, but Granny Jack was no longer where she'd been standing. He prayed she'd hunkered down.

He ran to the kitchen door and slid inside. "I'm assuming there's another entrance to the house. Tell me where it is."

Marley glanced from her position at the window. "Past the parlor. It's at the front, and we never use it. I think it's locked."

"Stay where you are and keep them from coming in from this direction." Roan didn't wait for a nod. He sped through the rooms and found two of the oldest boys at the front windows with rifles. "Do you see anything?" he asked.

A boy with hair as black as Marley's shook his head. "Not yet. We heard noises, but we made sure the door was bolted."

"Good." Roan moved to a window and gazed out. He couldn't see anything. "If anyone tries to get inside, shoot them."

The cotton-haired youngster next to the first wiped his face with his shirt. "We will."

At another window, Roan found Beau Marsh with a firearm. The boy had turned on the people he'd ridden with. "How's it going, Beau?"

"I cain't let them hurt you." Tears filled his eyes. "You've been nice to me."

"That's because I've been in your shoes," Roan said softly. "When this is over, we'll find you a good place to live where you don't have to kill."

"I hope so. Don't worry, I'm not letting anyone in."

Roan ruffled the boy's hair. "That's all I can ask. Take your time with each shot."

All business, Jessie McClain strode quickly into the room with a rifle in each hand. "Roan, I heard a window break upstairs. I think someone has gotten inside."

"I'll go see. Keep everyone down here. Where are the babies?"

"I made them and the little boys a bed in the cellar. The entrance is under a rug in the kitchen. I pray they stay quiet." Jessie wiped her weary eyes. "I sure wish Duel would ride in about now. We could really use him."

"Yes, ma'am, we sure could. I figure he'll be here soon." He hoped anyway. Roan moved to the staircase. The rifle fire covered any sounds he might have been making, so he took the steps two at a time to the second level.

He moved slowly down the long hallway, checking each dark room. Icy sweat trickled down his back. He felt eyes watching his every move. Pausing in a doorway, he noticed broken glass and knew that's where the intruder had entered. He'd stepped inside. But the room was already empty.

From there, he moved across the hall. As he stepped through the doorway, a form flew at him. Roan jerked the rifle up and caught the intruder under the chin. The man staggered backward, clutching his throat. Roan pounced and wrestled him to the floor.

"Did you enter alone?" Roan jerked the man's arms behind his back and twisted.

"That's for you to find out," the intruder said in a surly tone. "You're all gonna die."

"We'll see about that." Roan yanked him up and retrieved his rifle. "Down the stairs."

Without a word, the man took the stairs. A second later, Roan thrust him into a chair in the kitchen. "Marley, I need some strong rope."

She fired her rifle at movement outside, then answered, "I'll get you one."

After a minute, she returned, holding out a three-foot length of cord. "Mama and I keep some handy in case we need to string up a clothesline inside."

"Thanks." Roan took it and tied the man securely to the chair. He noticed for the first time that he had Wes Douglas. "It appears I've caught a rat. You won't be helping them anymore."

Judd burst through the door. "They've got all the men. We're surrounded."

Marley let out a cry, color draining from her face.

"Where's Granny Jack?" Roan asked. "Did they get her?"

"I don't know." Judd raked a hand through his hair. "Maybe."

"Now will you believe me?" Wes Douglas gave a thin smirk. "You're all gonna die."

Not without a fight. Roan would go down firing his rifle and swinging for all he was worth. He glanced at Wes, noticing a familiar leather watch fob hanging from his pocket. Roan yanked out the worn pocket watch, the spit drying in his mouth. He didn't need to see the name engraved on the scratched back to know it had belonged to Mose. He'd watched his friend check it hundreds of times. Anger whipped through him like the thin leather strips his father had used to beat him.

"You were there the night riders killed Mose Mozeke. This proves it."

"So what if I was? He was a stupid, raggedy old man. All his family was dead, didn't have any friends, didn't know squat. Nobody cared."

"I was his friend. I cared." Roan shook with the need to tighten his hands around this man's throat until the life drained from him. "He had more smarts in his little finger than you'll ever know."

Marley took Roan's hands, pocket watch and all, in hers. "Not this way. Your friend wouldn't want this. Wait for Sheriff Bagwell and let him hold this man for trial."

"She's right, Roan," Judd said. "Besides, we have bigger problems."

"Let me go, Marley," Roan said quietly. "I'm all right."

But when she released him, Roan drew back and slammed a fist into the man's face. His head whipped back and the chair flew over. Either the blow or the fall rendered him unconscious.

"Well, we won't have to worry about *him* for a bit," drawled Judd.

"You can't deny me some sort of satisfaction." Roan rubbed his knuckles.

Marley kicked the man, then stepped over him. "He deserves far more than that."

"With luck, the rest will come later." Roan picked up his rifle. "We'll have to hunker down here in the house and pray to God that help arrives soon."

If any of them remained alive.

But through the window he could make out the thin sliver of a waning moon.

Thirty

"You're surrounded. Got no place to run," Gentry yelled from the darkness. "Send out Marley Rose and I'll spare the rest of you."

"Like hell," Roan murmured.

Marley clasped her hand over her mouth to silence her cry and pressed her face against Roan's shirt. Ice invaded her bones, and she couldn't stop shivering. They'd sent Jessie and the kids deeper into the house and dragged Wes Douglas into a closet and locked it. Judd was guarding the top floor.

After extinguishing every light, Marley and Roan huddled on the floor beneath the broken kitchen window. Her rifle was empty, and so was the extra pistol she'd found on the shelf next to the boxes of cartridges.

Empty casings and glass littered the floor. Any other time, her need for tidiness would kick in, but at the moment, she didn't mind the mess.

Cold air blew the curtains out like ghostly shapes above her head.

Each time Gentry or one of the others yelled, she jerked. Gentry terrified her worse than any monster, and the evil coming from him put her in mind of an army of fanged, ravenous beasts with drooling mouths. With every passing minute, they inched closer to her.

Even now, she could feel their rough hands grabbing, pulling, dragging. They were going to get her, and no one could stop them.

Roan tightened his arms around her and kissed her temple, evidently sensing her thoughts. "He'll have to kill me first."

"I can't let that happen." Marley raised her head and met his shadowed gaze. "I can end this and save you and the others. I can't let him kill Mama and the children."

His answer came hard and fast. "Don't even think about giving yourself up."

"Is there any other way? Just answer me that."

He searched her eyes. "I'll think of something. But I'm not letting you walk out that door. Even if you did, he'd still slaughter everyone. He doesn't intend to let any of us live—not even the babies."

The contents of Marley's stomach tried to rise. She sagged against him, knowing he spoke the truth. And that was why she stayed put—that and the fear of facing the rotten man whose blood ran through her veins. He'd already made clear his plans, and they terrified her. To be sold to someone to be used however he so desired made her more determined not to willingly face that pain and depravity.

Not yet. She felt like a coward, but she just couldn't.

A slim chance remained that help would arrive or one of the ranch hands could free himself and the others—if they were alive. No one in the house knew the answer to that.

"If dawn would just come so we can see." The night seemed a month long, and it wasn't over yet. "It seems an eternity ago that we made love and talked about marriage. Did that truly happen? Did I lie naked in your arms, awash with unbelievable pleasure?"

"You did, and I took great joy in making love to you. When this is over and we're married, we may spend days in bed at a time." A crooked half smile curved his mouth. "What else can I do with a sex-starved woman?"

She appreciated his attempt to take her mind off their predicament, but nothing could. A noise outside alerted them. Roan raised his head for a cautious look. Propping his rifle on the windowsill, he fired.

"What is it?" she asked.

"Someone moving around. I think I might've hit him."

Although the rifle and pistol were empty, she refused to turn them loose. If she had to, she could hopefully bludgeon and disable an attacker with them.

Where were her father, the sheriff, and their men? Did they lie dead somewhere as well?

It seemed that they were the only people left alive in the entire world. Just them and Gentry's band of killers, waiting out this siege.

In another part of the house, the boom of a rifle shattered the silence—one, and then a second one. The noose around them tightened with every passing second.

No one had to tell her that Gentry and his men crept closer and closer.

She held the ability to save them. The thought refused to leave, despite Roan's arguments to the contrary. She wished she were brave enough to walk out and meet her painful fate.

As she tried to dredge up slim hope, the faint cry of one of the triplets drifted up through the wood floor. The darling was probably hungry, or it could be Edith who was sick, burning with fever. But they didn't dare expose the hidden trapdoor to the room under the kitchen. She said a prayer that the babe would go back to sleep. Maybe Matt would rock the infant. The kid was a wonder sometimes, far too old for his age.

A sudden burst of gunfire rent the air, but the sound was different, echoing more distantly, as though the shooter wasn't aiming for the house. Had help arrived? She thought she'd go crazy not knowing what was happening.

The baby quieted. She was grateful.

Time dragged with nothing more to mark it but her heartbeat thrumming loudly in her ears.

"You got fifteen minutes to come out," Gentry yelled. "Then we're torching the house and burning everyone inside."

White-hot terror enveloped Marley. "What are we

going to do?" she whispered. "Mama and the children—I can't let them die."

"A lot can happen in fifteen minutes. Dawn will come soon. The sky shows signs of lightening a little."

"Are you sure?" Marley scrambled to peer over the windowsill. The faint glimmer on the horizon almost seemed a mirage, but she knew it wasn't. The coming daylight was going to be their time limit. Gentry was running out of darkness in which to do his dirty work.

While she looked out, she saw small, dark shapes running this way and that all over the compound. "Roan, what kind of animals are those?"

"They look like…cats."

"Granny Jack's cats. They must've gotten loose."

"Or someone let them out," Roan said. "It had to have been the old woman."

"She's alive." Marley grinned. "I don't know what she's planning, but she has something in mind."

For so many hours, they'd had little to bring a ray of hope. That Granny had survived made everything better.

"Maybe she's freed the men and they'll work toward us, hopefully eliminating any threat. Those shots a bit ago puzzled me, but if we're lucky, then it was her." Roan raised his rifle. "I lost count of my shots. I have to be down to the last cartridges."

"We've emptied the boxes, Roan. All we have left are what's in the rifles." What would they do when those ran out? She didn't want to consider the possibility.

He took a cartridge from his shirt pocket and handed it to Marley. "I saved one for you. Just in case you need it. I don't know how this is going to end."

She could hear how he struggled to keep his voice even—and he was losing. Her throat clogged with tears. Roan was the strongest person she knew, and if he was getting ready to die, she knew they really had no hope.

He cleared his throat. "If you have to use the bullet, I'll be dead."

Tears blurred her vision. "I can't think about us dying this way. You're the love I never thought I'd find. In the short time I've known you, my whole life has changed." Her voice broke. "I'm glad we made love. I wouldn't have wanted to miss that."

Firelight flickered through the window. She rose to peer out and sheer terror froze her.

"You could've saved them, Marley Rose. You always were a worthless child. Everything is too late now. Their blood is on your hands." Will Gentry stood with legs braced apart, holding a torch. Flames rose high into the dark morning. His words chilled the very marrow of her bones.

Similar torches dotted the blackness around him. Stark horror settled in her chest, stilling her breath.

Marley's fingers dug into Roan's arm. "He's really going to do it. He's going to burn everyone alive."

She thought of the babies down in the cellar who hadn't had a chance to see what life was about. Of Matt, her mother, and the other children.

Only one person could save them—her. But to do it, she'd have to dance with the devil.

Was she brave enough?

Marley trembled and peered out the window again at the man she feared worse than death. She watched the light flicker across his bone-thin face and glitter in his frightening eyes.

Sucking in a ragged breath, she got to her feet and stuck the empty pistol into her pocket.

Her voice was as brittle as ice. "I'm coming out. You wanted me, you got me."

Thirty-one

ROAN CLUTCHED HER ARM. "NO, I'M NOT GOING TO LET you go out."

Marley averted her gaze; her voice was dull. "Let me loose."

"I'll never release you to that monster out there. Can't you see? What you do won't make any difference to our situation."

She twisted and pulled to get free, and it was all Roan could do to hold her. But he had to. She was everything to young Matt as well as the rest of the family. He somehow had to save her from Gentry's brutal hands.

A certain knowledge settled over him. If he let her go, she'd never know freedom again. Her paintings would go unpainted, her stories unwritten. Her life unlived. Gentry would either make good on his promise to auction her off, or he'd slip over the edge and kill her.

"I know what I have to do. Please let me do it. I can save you—my family. The babies. Little Edith's sick. She needs treatment." Tears rolled down her cheeks. "I have the bullet you gave me and the pistol is in my pocket. Once we're away from here, I'll use it."

Everything in Roan stilled. She meant to kill herself. His beautiful Texas Star would choose death in her attempt to save them.

"I can't let you sacrifice yourself. Sorry." He tightened

an arm around her waist and lifted her off the floor, looking for a safe place to put her until it was over.

A flaming torch crashed through the window, lighting up the kitchen.

"Let me go!" Marley screamed. She pounded him with her fists, kicking and squirming. "I have to go out to him before it's too late! Think of Matt and Benji. The babies, the babies!"

"Listen to reason," he pleaded, trying to get through to her. Her eyes were wide with panic. He doubted she could hear him, but he prayed he could make her see. "Whatever you do will make no difference. I know men like Gentry. I've seen how they work. How they think."

In a twisting, blinding fury, she managed to break Roan's hold. The sudden motion thrust her stumbling backward. He lunged to catch her, but she fell against the corner of the table, striking her head.

Marley lay still and silent, her face white as he lifted her head into his lap, cradling her. He felt the back of her head and located a raised lump. "I'm sorry, Marley."

Wailing from beneath the floor penetrated his shock. Marley's words echoed in his head—the babies and the boys under the floor. Smoke filled his nostrils, sending him toward the torch. He grabbed it and tossed it back out through the window, then lifted his rifle.

"I'm waiting, girl!" Gentry yelled. "Get your butt out here! Now!"

"Change of plans, you bastard!" Roan thundered. "She's a little indisposed right now."

Gentry ordered his men forward. Another torch came through the broken window. Roan had no time to put out the fire this time. He raised his rifle, praying it held a cartridge, and squeezed the trigger. Orange flame spat from the end. A man went down.

Still they came. Closer and closer.

Roan fired again, but this time nothing happened. His luck had run out.

Everything had run out—time, hope, love.

The things for which he'd searched were gone.

Smoke stung his eyes and clogged his throat. He was overcome with a fit of coughing. The house would go up in a minute.

Operating on sheer determination to save the ones he could, Roan yanked off his bandana and held it to his nose and mouth.

Although he didn't know if Marley was alive or dead, he lifted the bandana from his face long enough to throw her over his shoulder. With the covering back on, he ran toward the front of the dwelling. "Everyone out! The house is on fire! Get out now!" He laid Marley down beside the front door and tied his bandana around her mouth and nose. Then he ran back to the flaming kitchen, Jessie at his side. He grabbed some dish towels and handed Jessie one. Holding his to his mouth, he clawed at the rug and lifted the trapdoor. Jessie pushed past him and raced down the ladder.

Before Roan could follow, a flurry of gunshots and thundering hooves sounded outside.

Help? Or reinforcements for Gentry? But all he could think about was getting to the children. Nothing else mattered.

Jessie grabbed two of the babies and hurried to the ladder. Roan got the other triplet and waved Matt over. The boy stumbled to him, holding Benji's hand. "Take hold of my shirt and don't let go for anything."

Roan felt the tug of their hands as he climbed the ladder. Judd waited at the top. The cowboy helped Jessie up, then took the baby from Roan.

"Thanks, Judd. Let's get everyone out of the house. Marley's in the parlor."

Judd grinned. "I carried her outside. Help came in the nick of time. Duel and the sheriff led the charge. We've been saved."

Roan sagged against the wall as Duel raced into the burning kitchen. He scooped Jessie up, mindful of the two babies in her arms, and carried her to safety. Coughing and barely able to see, Roan stumbled from the house that had been under siege for what seemed an eternity.

He had to find Marley, had to get to her. Dodging men who flooded into the kitchen with buckets of water, Roan welcomed the dawn. He beat Duel to the woman lying on the cold, wet ground. Roan felt for a pulse.

She was alive.

"Marley, honey. It's Roan." He sat down and put her head in his lap. "It's over."

Duel knelt, his face stony. "Who hurt her? Tell me."

Roan had never faced a father's wrath but found it something to fear. He wasn't one to lie though. He met Duel's hard gaze. "I'm the one you want. It was an accident."

"You'd best explain yourself."

As clearly as he could manage, Roan told about the siege and how Marley had been determined to save them when all hope was lost. "She went crazy. I had to stop her from going with Gentry. I held her, but she fought me." Roan coughed to clear smoke from his lungs. "She wouldn't listen. When she finally broke free, she fell backward against the corner of the table. I never meant for that to happen. I would never hurt her, not in a million years. She's my life and the woman I love."

"I believe you." Duel rubbed his bleary eyes. "Thank you for saving her and Jessie and the children."

Marley blinked and looked up. "Papa?"

"Yeah."

"I'm glad you're alive."

Duel bent and kissed her forehead. "I wish I could've gotten here sooner. I rode through the night. I'll tell you all about the trip once I help put out the fire."

"Just one thing—did you kill Gentry?" Roan asked.

"No. We're still sorting through the dead, but I don't think he's among them. The ones able to ride fled when they saw us. He might've gotten away."

Bitter disappointment filled Roan. It wasn't over and wouldn't be until the man filled a grave. "I'll come help fight the fire."

"No, stay here with Marley Rose. Get that smoke out of your lungs. It looks like they've kept it from spreading."

His eyes stinging, Roan watched Duel hurry to join the fight for his house, unsure what to say. Marley probably wouldn't speak to him after the way he'd thwarted her, and that would kill him.

"What happened, Roan?" she asked with a puzzled expression. "My head is splitting. The last thing I remember is walking to the door to go to Gentry, and you were trying to stop me."

"I couldn't let you sacrifice yourself, Marley. Once he got you, I knew he'd destroy everything good and decent in you, maybe kill you. But I lost my hold and you fell, striking your head on the table."

"No wonder it hurts." She sat up, then grabbed her head as dizziness probably made the ground whirl.

He winced. "I'm glad that's the least of your injuries." Roan kissed her cheek. "I'm so sorry I ended up being the one to hurt you. Will you forgive me?"

Tears filled her eyes. "Thank you," she whispered. "I didn't know what else to do except to go with him. I just didn't want you or anyone else to die to save me. I was terrified."

Roan held her. "So was I."

"And he's still not dead," she whispered. "When will it be over?"

"It will be soon, honey. We'll track him down. It's only a matter of time."

A violent shiver ran through her. "I have his awful blood in my veins."

"Only half. Take comfort in knowing your mother's is in you, too, and she was also a victim of Gentry's."

"Who knows how many other lives he's ruined."

"Just focus on the good and don't worry about the bad. You have your whole life ahead of you."

She glanced at the smoldering house. "They threw the torches after all?"

"Two of them before your father arrived. I don't think the fire spread beyond the kitchen."

"I was so scared."

"Me too." He brushed his lips against hers. Although smoke filled his mouth and nose, he thought he caught a faint whiff of roses.

Granny Jack's voice broke them apart. "An old lady shouldn't ask what happened. I should've learned a long time ago to leave people be when they're kissing 'n' such."

Marley glanced up in surprise. "Granny! I'm glad you're all right. I wasn't sure what happened to you once Gentry and his men overran the barricade."

"I hunkered down in the shadows next to the bunkhouse, trying to figure out how to help. I watched those mealy-mouthed scoundrels capture the ranch hands. Took me a while to free 'em. Those blasted knots were the dickens to untie, and by then it was almost too late." Granny cradled a cat in her arms. "Me 'n' the children are sure glad it's over."

"We thought we saw them running around the compound," Roan said. "Did they get loose on their own?"

"Nope. I let the durn things out. Thought they might attack those devils or at least confuse 'em. But Duel rode in with his men, and the bastards skedaddled."

Marley smiled. "Those cats were a beautiful sight. Until we saw them, we didn't know if you'd survived. You gave us hope."

Granny leaned down, her heavy jowls hanging low. "What ails you, girl? Did Gentry get ahold of you?"

"No. I fell." Marley's eyes twinkled as she met Roan's gaze. "We're going to be married, Granny."

"We want you to come." He laced his fingers through Marley's, feeling the love flowing between them.

"Well, I reckon I'd be purely delighted. That is if I can get new spectacles by then."

"This time, I'll go with you." Marley patted the old woman's arm. "I want to make sure they fit. I'm tired of you fighting to keep them on your face."

"Well, I guess me and my cat will mosey on. We're lookin' for the others. I sure hope they ain't been stolen." The old woman straightened and hobbled off, slipping and sliding on the muddy ground.

"Mama Rose!" Matt ran toward them. "I've looked for you ever'where." He launched himself into Marley's arms. "I was scared."

"Me too, but it's over now," Marley assured him. "Those bad men won't be back."

The boy touched her face. "Did they hurt you?"

"Nope." She met Roan's gaze.

"I don't ever want anything to happen to you 'cause you're my Mama Rose."

Roan ruffled his hair. "She'll be as good as new very soon and able to write a lot more stories."

"Good."

"Matt, we heard one of the babies crying during the shooting. Did you quiet it?" Roan asked.

"Yep. I picked her up and rocked her. She went back to sleep." Matt's voice lowered to a whisper. "I didn't want the mean man to find us."

"That was a very good thing you did." Marley hugged him. "Do you think you can help me up? This ground is cold and wet."

"Yep." Matt took her hand and pulled, with Roan secretly helping.

Marley glanced around at the bodies lying where they'd fallen, then at the smoldering kitchen, the fire almost out. "We did it, Roan. We made it."

"We certainly did." Although he never wanted anything to be that close again.

The fight wasn't over though. It wouldn't be until Gentry was either dead or behind bars.

As long as the man roamed free, everyone was in danger—Marley most of all.

Thirty-two

THE KITCHEN IN THE MAIN HOUSE WAS OUT OF COMMISSION until Duel could rebuild it, which created a bit of a problem. Although they used Marley's oven for the biscuits and made a cake to celebrate surviving that evening, they cooked the biggest part of supper over a large campfire in the compound. Marley's house was simply too small for everyone.

The rest of the main house remained unharmed, which was a pure miracle, everything considered. If the fight hadn't come the same day as the rainstorm, the damage would've been horrendous.

Sheriff Bagwell and his deputy borrowed a wagon and carted the cursing prisoner, Wes Douglas, and the dead into Tranquility. They had six bodies to try to identify and bury, in addition to Sheriff Coburn. This time they were all seasoned men, not the young boys they'd seen in the past.

Roan wondered if Ruby was switching tactics or had just seen that young boys didn't have the bloodlust she wanted.

Granny Jack had left with her cats to stay with a widowed friend in town until the mess blew over, saying that she wouldn't put them out any longer. They needed all the space they could find.

Roan sat by the campfire with Marley and Matt, listening to the coyotes howl in the distance. He glanced at Duel, who couldn't get out of Jessie's sight.

"Tell us what happened after you left here, sir," Roan said.

"Ran into trouble just like you did at Piebald. They were expecting us and had the road blocked. All of them were armed. Started shooting at us. It took a while to convince them to give up their weapons." The little grin that formed on Duel's face said he'd taken no small amount of pleasure in the convincing. "Some were injured and had to be treated, then we had to find a place to put them. Finally decided on an empty train car. It was midafternoon when we got around to questioning them about the cattle."

Duel reached for the pot and filled his cup. "The prisoners refused to talk. By that time, we were exhausted and decided to get some rest, so I left a few men to guard, and we caught some sleep in the saloon's rooms."

Jessie sat up, her eyes wide with innocence. "Whose bed did you sleep in, dear?"

"Well, it happened to be…uh…Millie's, but she wasn't… ah…in it." Duel glanced at his men to help him out, but they avoided his eyes.

"So she's a working girl?" Jessie asked.

"I assume so." He took her hands. "Darlin', you should know me well enough by now. I only have eyes for one woman, and it's not Millie or anyone else but you."

Roan watched the exchange, glad he wasn't the only one to get into hot water. He guessed most women were a little jealous when it came to their husbands.

"Just checking," Jessie said, kissing Duel's cheek. "Go on, dear."

Marley shifted and glanced up at Roan. "I fear I'm going to be like my mother."

"In more ways than one." Roan lifted a strand of dark, silky hair and coiled it around his finger.

Duel continued his story. "There I was, dead to the world, when the door creaked open. I reached for my gun before I saw it was Millie. She told me that I'd find my cattle at Ruby Creek's ranch near San Saba. Then she said she overheard talk that all of my family would be slaughtered and the ranch set on fire before dawn." Duel took a sip of coffee. "I rousted all but a few of the men, and we rode like hell, praying to get here in time." He took a shuddering breath. "I never want to be cutting it that close again."

Smoke still filled Roan's head, but the name on Duel's tongue jarred him. "Did I hear you right? You said Ruby Creek's ranch?"

"That's right. Why?"

"We've been trying to piece something together." Roan told him about Virginia Creek and always finding her in Gentry's company. Roan cleared his throat. "The kid we rescued—Beau Marsh, he's sitting over there with the other children—said Ruby had given him a home and was his mother now and there are so many boys food is scarce. I'm thinking she's recruiting these young kids who'd lost parents in the first mob rule. Who knows? She could be behind everything going on around here. The killings, the rustling, everything. But Beau didn't know Ruby's last name. I'm wondering what the connection is between Ruby and Virginia. Sisters? Mother and daughter?"

"Did the kid know what Ruby looks like?" Duel asked.

"Nope. He couldn't say, except that she's older than Marley. I've only seen Virginia. She seems like a nice lady. She has to be kin to Ruby for sure. Since they're both older women, I'd say they're sisters. Maybe twins." Roan paused. "Something tells me we'll find Gentry when we find Ruby. There are too many coincidences, and he always turns up with Virginia."

Marley stirred and sat up straighter. "Virginia stayed by my side while I finished the shooting competition. I just knew nothing was going to happen to me with her close. She has this maternal instinct, like Mama. Now I wonder why she did that."

Roan stared toward the crossbar of the ranch. He wondered, too, and it was time to find out—about Ruby and Virginia, why the missing cattle were at Ruby's, and why she had put together an army of boys.

Duel's face was hard. "Roan, get ready to ride at day-break. We'll find Ruby's ranch and be done with this once and for all."

"I agree, sir. The sooner the better. Until we chop the head off the snake, it'll just keep attacking. No one will be safe until it's done." Roan got up and wandered over to Beau Marsh. Sadness oozed from the boy's eyes.

Roan sat down beside him. "Hi, Beau. Everything all right?"

Beau shrugged. "Reckon so."

"What's worrying you, son?"

The kid swung around to face Roan. "What's gonna happen to me?"

The question caught him off guard a little. He laid an arm across Beau's shoulders. "I don't exactly know right now, but we're going to take care of you. Do you know of any relatives still living?"

"Nope." Beau propped his chin on his fisted hands with his elbows on his knees.

"Then you'll stay here. With us. You can go to school with the other children." Roan finally understood why Jessie couldn't turn away a homeless child. It must be the same thing that Duel had come to understand.

A look of wonder crossed Beau's eyes. "I ain't never been to school before. Do you think I could learn to read?"

"Absolutely. You can also learn to write and do sums." A lump blocked Roan's throat, and he had to swallow hard. "You can learn all sorts of things. When I was a boy about your age, I didn't have anyone to take care of me, and I went to live with a schoolteacher. She taught me about stars, and painting, and history. Did you know that George Washington was the first president of this country?"

"Nope."

"And someone recently invented a horseless carriage. They call it an automobile."

"No fooling? A carriage that doesn't have a horse to pull it?"

"It's true. The automobile is powered by gasoline." Roan loved the excitement on the boy's face. "There's a whole amazing world out there just waiting for you."

"I want to go to school and learn about these things. But I don't know if the McClains want me here. They have so many kids already."

Roan leaned closer and motioned to Jessie. "Do you see that woman with the red hair?"

Beau nodded.

"She loves children more than anything in the world, and she wants you to stay here and be her boy."

"She's real pretty, and she smells nice too. Sorta like Mama."

"Now, why don't you go play with those boys over there and leave the worrying to me? All right?"

"Okay. Thanks, Mr. Penny."

Roan moved back over to sit beside Marley. She smiled up at him and laced her hand through his. "Is Beau all right?"

"He's feeling a bit lost, but I think he's going to be fine. I jumped the gun a bit on something. He was worrying about where he'd live when this is all over. I kind of told him that Jessie and Duel want him to live here."

"Good. I was going to tell you earlier that they were planning on taking him in."

It was strange how things worked out just when you didn't see any hope in sight.

Marley stood and cleared her throat, clutching Roan's hand. "Hey, everyone. We need some cheer, and I have just the announcement that might brighten us up." She took a deep breath. "Roan and I are going to be married—next week in fact."

Jessie's eyes glowed as she rushed to hug them both. "Honey, I'm so happy for you. Not surprised, though. I can see the love you have for each other. It's time you started your own lives."

Duel shook hands with Roan. "Love and cherish her, and we'll get along fine." Then he hugged Marley. "You've come a long way from the little toddler I called Two Bit. I'm glad I could raise you and see the woman you've become. I'm so proud of you."

Tears shimmered in Marley's eyes. "Thank you, Papa, for giving me a safe, happy place in which to grow up. I'll always be your Two Bit."

Roan smiled at the special nickname. He had one for her too.

A sudden thought made him smile wider. He'd broken the curse of the waning moon it seemed. Gentry had tried his best to destroy them beneath one, but they were still alive and kicking.

Matt tugged on her dress. "Can I be your little boy, Mama Rose, and live with you and Mr. Penny?"

Marley shot Roan a questioning glance.

"Whatever you want to do is fine with me." Roan would love having the kid around. Still, he knew Matt would be a lot of work for Marley. He wouldn't add to what she already had. He wanted her to have time to write her stories and paint and meant to see that she would. Being fulfilled emotionally was as important as physically.

Marley knelt and straightened the collar of Matt's jacket and wiped a smudge from his cheek. "Honey, let me talk to your Mama Jessie and Papa Duel first. We'll see what they say."

"Okay. Can I sleep with you tonight?" Matt wheedled, then whispered, "I have a monster under my bed. I'm scared."

"Sure."

Roan's heart ached as he watched her hug the boy. After everything they'd been through, young Matt would be terrified for a long time. He might never get over it. Lord knows Roan had had his struggles. But one thing he didn't struggle with anymore, and that was his love for Marley. He wasn't going to let her out of his sight as long as Gentry was loose.

Even with the ranch hands and Duel about, Gentry loomed over them like a raging tiger.

Hopefully, it would all end tomorrow.

❧

The morning dawned cold and overcast. Roan had saddled up and was ready to ride. This time Duel took no ranch hands except him—everyone was on guard duty with strict instructions. Duel had ridden into Tranquility before daybreak to get the sheriff, and before they rode back to the ranch, Sheriff Truman Bagwell had telegraphed the lawmen in the surrounding counties to meet them in San Saba.

Also, this time, they'd have plenty of lawmen on their side. If Ruby Creek had Duel's herd, there was no way she could squirm out of this.

Marley pulled her wool shawl tighter around her and found Roan for a moment alone. She'd left Matt sleeping, Jessie was saying goodbye to Duel, and the sheriff was talking to Hardy Gage. "Please be careful, Roan. Come back to me."

He noticed she'd stopped saying, "No promises, no regrets." That was good, because he could no longer agree with the statement. Everything had changed. He would promise her the moon and he'd have more regrets than he could count if he didn't make her his wife.

"It was a good thing Matt slept with you last night," Roan growled just loud enough for her to hear. "I'd have curled up next to you, and we wouldn't have gotten a wink of sleep."

Marley's eyes twinkled as she snuggled into a fold of the thick jacket he wore, another one of Caleb's. She hoped all this mess with Gentry and Ruby ended soon, because they were about to exhaust her brother's leftover clothing.

"What game would you have played?" she teased.

"No game, lady. It would've been for keeps, and you know what would've happened. I'd have filled you with my love and kissed you senseless." He ran a calloused thumb across her cheek. "How is your head?"

"Still hurts, but I'll be right as rain in a few days."

"If I hadn't tried to hold you back…"

She searched his eyes, stroked his jaw. "You couldn't have done anything else, Roan. I was crazy with fear that the man would kill all of you. I had convinced myself that he'd stop if I went out there. But he wouldn't have, would he?"

"No. Men like that never stop until they satisfy their bloodlust." Roan anchored her face between his large hands and lowered his mouth. The kiss, though brief, held a promise of much more to come.

Roan nuzzled behind her ear and smelled the rosewater she'd dabbed on. "I can't wait to make you my wife. I'm going to strip off your clothes, kiss every inch of that luscious body, and love you like you've never been loved."

A smile teased Marley's mouth. "I'll hold you to that, cowboy. I only wish it were today."

"I just realized I never asked you proper." He got down on one knee. "Marley McClain, will you marry me, teach me to count each day a blessing, and be my wife forever and always?"

"I will. You're not getting much of a bargain though. I have a lot of faults."

He stood and put a finger under her chin, studying her. "Pretty lady, all I see is strength and extraordinary courage. When I get back, we'll tell your mother and father and discuss where Matt is going to sleep." They needed something bigger than her small house. "Meanwhile, don't let your guard down and don't leave the ranch. Stay close to the house."

"Okay." She threaded her fingers through his. "There's no shortage of work to keep me busy. And I have a wedding to plan. I'm really going to be married to you. I can't believe it." Marley stared deep into his gunmetal-gray eyes. "Roan, I've written a letter to that publisher about my stories. As soon as the roads are safe, I'll mail it."

"Glad to hear it." He glanced at Duel and Jessie saying their goodbyes. Though he couldn't hear their soft words, by now he knew them by heart. Roan slipped an arm around Marley's trim waist once more and drew her close. "Leave a light in the window, my Texas Star."

"Always, Roan." Her trembling voice spoke of fear for his safety.

If only he could ease her worry. But this was still an untamed land in many ways and a man didn't often know when he left if he'd ever make it home again. Thoughts of the curse put on at his birth and how fate had a way of snatching away everything he wanted flooded his mind. Hopefully, Ruby Creek still had some measure of kindness in her somewhere and didn't gun him down on sight. But anyone who'd kill an innocent old man like Mose or recruit a bunch of boys to do her dirty work had to possess a mean streak a mile wide.

Duel stuck his foot in the stirrup. Roan gave Marley another kiss and climbed into the saddle. As they rode out, Roan scanned the ranch that had become home. Tears stung the back of his throat. Now that he'd ended his search, found his place, would he even have the chance to settle down in peace with the woman he loved more than life itself?

Thirty-three

THREE MORE SHERIFFS AND THEIR DEPUTIES MET THEM IN front of the recently vacated office in San Saba. Altogether, they created a force of ten. The street was quiet, the day somber, the skies gray. Mud puddles dotted the main thoroughfare. Roan was anxious to finish and head home, Marley always on his mind. Even with all the ranch hands keeping a close eye on her, it was a dangerous situation. They'd only had a glimpse of what Gentry could be capable of.

The saddle leather creaked when Duel shifted his weight. "Thank you all for meeting us. We appreciate it. Do you know the location of Ruby Creek's ranch, gentlemen, or do we need to ask?"

"I know where it is," said a hard-eyed, white-haired lawman who had probably seen his share of fights. "A little hard to find." He spat out a big wad of chewing tobacco. "What makes you think she's rustled your cattle?"

"You're Sheriff Kent, right?" At the man's nod, Duel continued. "Several people, including one who rode with the gang, swear she's stocked her ranch with my cattle. I just want to see and talk to her."

"There's no need to go in with rifles blazing unless we have cause," Roan said. "I believe she's been behind a lot of the violence going on around here. There's a man—Will Gentry—who's working with her."

"Working how?" a man bearing a birthmark on his cheek asked.

Roan rested his arm on the pommel. "Not exactly sure yet. Maybe seeing that her orders are carried out. Gentry killed a friend of mine and almost killed me, then two nights ago attacked the Aces 'n' Eights and tried to slaughter us all."

"Was Ruby with him?" the man persisted.

Roan met his gaze and didn't blink. "Not that I could tell, but I was too busy trying to stay alive. If she wore pants and had her hair up under a hat, it would've been hard to spot her in the darkness."

"So you really don't know that the rustling and killings are connected?" The man wasn't being belligerent, only cautious, and Roan respected him for that.

"I know the same group are involved with both. Just can't prove it yet." Roan glanced around, hoping to spot Gentry, but he didn't see the old scarecrow. "For now, I think we need to question Ruby about the stolen cattle."

"I agree," said Duel. "If it's true, it'll be easy enough to prove. Sheriff Kent, why don't you lead the way and let's get started?"

The lawman set a fast pace, plowing through thick winter vegetation and bare-limbed trees. Every so often they had to ford a creek, and Roan stayed near the front with Duel. Roan was about to think Sheriff Kent was leading them on a wild-goose chase when they emerged into an open valley. A stone house, as well as several large barns, rose up in front of them.

Roan gave an appreciative glance around. No wonder they hadn't found the cattle. They could've looked for years and not discovered this place.

As they trotted up to the house, about two dozen young boys came from the barn to stare. One took off running ahead of them, yelling, "Rube, we got company!"

A woman strolled from the house with a carbine—no doubt loaded. Roan almost fell from the saddle.

Virginia.

Only this time her easy smile had disappeared and her face was frozen in resentment and hatred. The young boy who had called her stood by her side, not looking very friendly either.

Roan tipped his hat. "Glad to see you, Miss Virginia." Maybe there had been some kind of mistake.

"Her name is Rube," spat the boy. "Ruby Creek."

Surprise knocked him backward a bit. "You're Ruby?"

The woman glared and raised her chin. "Ruby Virginia Creek."

Hell and be damn! He mentally kicked himself and muttered a string of curses. She'd been right under his nose the whole time.

"You're trespassing on private property," she snapped. "Sheriff Kent, I thought I taught you better than to come sniffing around again."

"Well, you know, Miz Ruby, lawmen don't take too good to lessons," Kent drawled. "This rancher here, Duel McClain, claims that you might've stolen his cattle. We'll just take a look-see and settle the issue right here and now."

Ruby raised her carbine. "Get off my land. All of you."

"Now, ma'am, we can't do that." Duel straightened. "I heard from several people who say you have my stock. I'm not leaving here without finding out the truth."

"Leave her alone!" yelled the boy, and two more around the same age jumped onto the porch to form a shield around Ruby. She certainly inspired loyalty.

Roan scanned the buildings scattered around the compound, hoping to spot Gentry. If the man was there, he was staying out of sight.

"Put down the rifle, Ruby." Roan dismounted. "We just came to talk."

"Like they came to talk the night those riders with their burning torches rode up here." Ruby choked on the words. "They left my husband and three sons in a pool of blood. They took everything I had—my family, my land, my future—and not a single soul helped me."

She inhaled a deep breath. "I'm getting it all back and

what these boys lost in the bargain. No one is going to stop me." Her voice cut like a finely honed blade as she swung the carbine to Roan. "I'll kill you if you don't get on your horse and ride out."

"Who were the riders who killed your family, Ruby?" he asked quietly, standing his ground. He sure didn't want to shoot a woman, but if she opened fire, he wouldn't have a choice.

"The mob that ran rampant here," she spat. "They drove me up north until six months ago. Now I'm back, and I'm taking what I want—cattle and all. Now get off my land."

"Did you kill Mose Mozeke?" Roan asked.

"Off!"

"Miz Ruby, we have to take you in. You know that," Sheriff Bagwell said.

One by one, the sheriffs and deputies dismounted, their guns drawn.

"It's over, Ruby." Roan took a step forward. "But answer one question—why did you recruit these young boys?"

A wad of spit flew from her mouth, landing near Roan's boot. "You don't know what it's like to have nothing. They're all victims too. The mob either killed their fathers, or the Texas Rangers sent them to prison. They've got no one—nothing but me." She put her arm around one of them standing with her. "Their mothers either can't afford to feed them or are dead. These boys don't have anyone to turn to but me. I saved them."

Not know what it's like to have nothing? Roan could quote chapter and verse on the subject. He could sympathize with her on that. But still, making them fight was wrong.

One of the boys standing with her stepped forward. "Rube was gonna help us get back our land too. My mother is sick and can't work. Rube gave her medicine and some food. That's a sight more than you've given us, mister. She's a good lady."

Maybe in some twisted way she was, but Roan couldn't forgive the killing.

"Son, she killed a friend of mine. Mose Mozeke was the finest man I've ever known. He didn't deserve to be shot and left cold on the ground." Roan moved closer. "Why didn't you kill me that night too?"

Ruby gave a cold shrug. "You didn't have any land, nothing I wanted. That old man was going to die anyway."

"You took something far more precious from me than land." Roan trembled with anger.

"We all have to lose something," Ruby answered.

Roan bristled. Mose was not a "something." He'd had a life, dreams, a caring heart. But nothing Roan said now would make Ruby see what she'd done. "If Will Gentry is on this property, tell him to step out. Don't deny you know him. I've seen you with him and know he rides for you, doing your dirty work. He was there the night Mose died."

"Find him yourself. I'm not Will Gentry's keeper, and I'm not going to help you." Ruby's boys moved protectively around her.

"Oh, we will, ma'am," Duel said. "Trust me, we will."

Sheriff Kent gave her a steely look. "Put down that weapon. You're under arrest."

A gunshot burst from a long outbuilding, scattering the lawmen. Roan grabbed Ruby and shoved her into the house, taking her carbine. Her young guards scrambled in after them. Roan pushed her onto a sofa, and the boys sat next to her with white faces.

"Who's shooting at us?" Roan barked.

"Why should I tell you, Roan Penny?"

"You've had hard times, but your soul isn't lily white. The way I see it, you and Gentry deserve each other. I'll eventually figure out how you're connected." Roan strode to a window and moved the curtains aside just a hair to peek out. The sheriffs and their deputies were returning fire and moving toward the shooter. Only a matter of time until they had him—unless there was more than one.

Just then, a bullet came through the windowpane, inches

from Roan's head. He ducked back and glanced at the boys in a stiff line on the sofa. "Better tell me who's out there."

They stared at each other. Finally, one spoke. "Might be George."

"Who's George?"

"You thought all I had were boys working for me?" Ruby said. "Not by a long shot. Lot of folks around here lost everything they had. They want it back."

"So you formed your own army." Roan glanced out the window again. He'd lost sight of the lawmen and Duel, but the shooting had stopped. Maybe they'd captured the gunman.

"That's right, I did. And I started taking the land back, one farm at a time. Mose Mozeke's was just the first. Coburn forged a deed and made it legal."

The woman had thought of everything—almost. She'd underestimated Roan.

He turned around. "Okay, I kind of understand the land. But I still don't understand why you stole McClain's cattle." She hesitated, and he continued. "You might as well tell me. We're going to haul everyone associated with you in to jail. Someone will talk."

Ruby stared in defiance. "Two reasons. I needed to stock my ranch, get some capital."

"And the other?"

"Gentry wants to ruin the rancher. He hates McClain with a passion. He wanted revenge, and that was useful to me. We threw in together. He's as intent on getting his daughter back as I am to rebuilding my life, one piece at a time. We had the perfect plan—until you came along. I should've killed you."

"I reckon you should've. I don't suppose Gentry told you why he wants Marley?"

"His business. I didn't ask. He didn't say."

"Would it surprise you to hear that he only wants to auction her off to the highest bidder?"

Surprise rippled across Ruby's hard gaze, but she didn't reply.

"I'm going to turn this place upside down. I know the bastard's here."

"Mister, he rode off this morning," one of the boys said. "Didn't say where he was going."

Somehow, Roan knew the boy spoke the truth. There was only one place he would've gone—the Aces 'n' Eights. The breath froze in his chest.

Gentry was going to try to get Marley again.

And they were over thirty miles away.

Thirty-four

MARLEY PICKED UP HER WASHING AND STRODE TO THE clothesline. The cold nipped at her fingers as she hung the wet diapers. A strange quiet filled the breeze. She glanced at Hardy Gage standing nearby with a rifle, taking comfort in his and the other ranch hands' presence.

"I feel it too," Hardy growled. "Don't worry, I'm not letting anyone harm one hair on your head. No one here will."

"Thanks, Hardy."

Matt handed her a clothespin. "I'm scared, Mama Rose. When will Mr. Penny and Papa Duel come back?"

"Soon, honey. Try not to worry." Even as Marley said the words, she knew how useless they were. But though Matt was frightened, he wouldn't leave her side.

"The bad man burned our house and shot bullets. Why did he want to kill us?" Matt gripped her dress, bunching the fabric in his hand.

"Why don't we make up a story while we work? That'll make us feel better." Or at least it would put the boy's mind, and hers, on something else. "Let's pretend that we're far away from here. Where would you like to be?"

Matt screwed up his face. "That place you told me about last night—Promise Island. You know why?"

She had an idea, but she wanted to hear his answer. "Nope."

"'Cause no bad people live there and it's way far over the water. The bad people can't swim, and horses can't even go there. We'll be safe and won't have to die."

The last part shocked her. She dropped the diaper she was hanging into the basket and knelt. "I don't know where you got the notion that we're going to die. We're not, so put that right out of your head. No one is going to hurt us. All these men here in the compound with guns will shoot anyone who tries to come. All right?"

"But they came before."

Hardy stepped closer. "Matt, that's because you didn't have so many men protecting you before. I'm here and so is Judd, and all the others. You don't have to worry."

"Okay, Mr. Gage." Matt dredged up a little smile.

"Now let's get back to our story." Marley kissed him and stood. "We're on Promise Island where only good things happen. What are we doing?"

"Playing a game of hide-and-seek. I'm a good hider and you can't find me."

"Why can't I?"

Matt giggled. "'Cause you're too busy kissing Mr. Penny."

Marley laughed. "Oh, I am, am I?"

"Yep. An' you're so happy. Everyone is happy and safe."

Marley reached down and tickled him. His fit of laughter made her feel that everything was all right. Roan and her papa would find Ruby Creek and Gentry. She and Roan would be married, and they'd live happily ever after on Promise Island.

Where bad men couldn't get to them.

If only childish tales could come true.

⁓

A noise in another part of the house alerted Roan. He swung to Ruby. "Who else is in here?"

Ruby glared. "If you want to know, why don't you go find out?"

"Look, I've about had it." Roan's voice hardened as he moved to stand in front of her. "I don't want to be here any more than you want me around. Now answer my question."

"It was probably my cat, all right? The fool thing likes to curl up in the kitchen on a windowsill that faces the sun. Must've knocked something off." Ruby smiled like the old Virginia he'd met, and he was struck again by her beauty. "You're very distrustful, Penny."

He wondered why the smile. She hadn't exactly welcomed him with open arms, and neither had the boys. All he knew was that she kept shooting the parlor door furtive glances, which told him someone else was in the house. He wished one of the lawmen had found cover inside with him. He couldn't watch the window, Ruby and the boys, and the doorway leading into the other rooms all at the same time.

"It'd be nice if I could believe you. You're up to your eyeballs in lies, deceit, and murder. But your reign of terror has come to an end, lady. It's over."

"Maybe your friends came in through the kitchen door." She huffed and crossed her arms. "Ever think of that?"

"Nope." If they had, they'd have called out. He just wanted to end this so he could get back to Marley. He needed to protect her—not that he thought Hardy, Judd, and the others couldn't. A wild animal was stalking the woman who filled his dreams.

"Whoever is in here had better come out!" Roan yelled.

The silence was broken by the chiming of the large grandfather clock in the corner. Keeping his eyes on Ruby and the boys, he moved to the doorway that led farther into the house. Although he listened, he heard no other sounds. Seeing Ruby shift in her seat, he stepped back into the parlor.

The gut feeling he always trusted whispered a warning.

A moment later, a man crashed through the front window and rolled into the room, firing a long-barreled revolver. Roan whirled and shot, smoke curling from the barrel.

The acrid scent of gunpowder stung his nose and watered his eyes.

Before he could adjust his aim, another man fired from the doorway. They'd apparently hoped to catch Roan in a crossfire, but the second man had been a split second too slow. With time only to react, not think, Roan bent his knees and squeezed the trigger. The piece of hot lead entered the man's chest near the heart.

Every muscle taut, every nerve alert, Roan quickly scanned the room for more attackers.

Boot heels pounded on the porch, drawing his attention. He swung, his grip on the Colt tightening. Whoever came through that door would find a bullet waiting.

Beads of sweat popped out on his forehead as he waited. Everything went silent.

"Roan?" Duel hollered. "Are you hit?"

Relief swept over Roan. "No. Come on in."

Duel entered, followed by two of the lawmen. "Appears you don't need our help."

"I wouldn't have minded." Roan strolled to the man groaning on the floor, surrounded by glass from the window. He met Ruby Creek's hard gaze. "Nice cat you have, lady. But apparently you can't count. They won't be knocking anything else off your tables."

"Cats?" Duel grinned. "I missed something?"

"Yeah. Ruby has told me quite a bit. She and Gentry rustled your cows for two reasons. She needed to stock her ranch and he wanted to ruin you. You created quite an enemy all those years ago."

"Gentry made me want to puke back then, and now I'll be happy to put a bullet into his black heart. Hanging is too good for him." Duel turned to Ruby. "You suffered an injustice, ma'am, but this wasn't the way to right it."

"Depends," she answered with a sad smile. "I got rid of some enemies."

One of the lawmen moved to the second shooter. "This one's dead."

"One less to haul in to the doc before we take 'em to jail," Duel said. "We rounded up almost a dozen outside. I just don't know what to do with the boys. Jess and I can't take any more."

Roan hadn't considered that part. What would they do? They couldn't put them in jail, and apparently the kids didn't have anyone or anything to go back to. "Maybe the sheriffs will know where to take them. I'm sure if we put our heads together, we'll come with up with a good solution." Roan moved closer. "Gentry apparently lit out this morning. I think he's gone to the ranch. At least my gut says so."

"Hell."

More lawmen stormed into the parlor and sized up the situation. Duel took them aside, "Gentry left, and I think he headed to my ranch. I need to get home. Can you take care of things here?"

"Sure," Sheriff Kent said. "But what about your cattle?"

"I'll come back for them later."

Ruby stood. "Can I pack some things?" She flashed Roan a smile. "A lady needs some clothes and soaps to make her jail stay more pleasant."

"I don't know, ma'am." Roan turned to Sheriff Bagwell.

The lawman scowled. "I reckon. But someone will have to go upstairs with her. I don't trust that woman as far as I can throw her."

"Me either." It had already occurred to Roan that she'd try to escape.

"Will you go up with me?" she asked, looking up at him with her big green eyes.

"I'm sorry, ma'am, I'm leaving with McClain. I'm worried about the people I love."

"Please? I'll only be a minute, and you can be on your way."

Roan shot Duel a worried scowl.

Marley's father nodded. "Go ahead. I'll water the horses and get them ready to ride."

Roan turned and escorted Ruby up the stairs. When she reached her bedroom, he stood in the doorway, telling her to hurry. She nodded and rushed to her closet, pulled out a valise, and began to stuff some things into it.

A picture on the wall caught his attention. He strode closer to see who the couple were. The woman was clearly Ruby, and he guessed the man to be her husband. They were happy and smiling in the photograph, making a beautiful pair. Little did they know how things would turn out. He didn't think Ruby would do well in prison. She was getting old, and cold walls could age a person even faster.

"I have nothing left to live for." The cocking of a pistol hammer alerted him. Ruby had a gun. "They'll never get a rope around my neck."

"Don't!" His heart pounded as he made a diving grab for the weapon.

Thirty-five

BEFORE ROAN COULD REACH HER, RUBY CREEK PLACED the gun to her head and fired.

Smoke and burnt gunpowder filled the room. Blood and brain matter splattered both the wall and him. He knew without looking that she was dead.

Boots pounded on the stairs, and the room filled with lawmen who stared in disbelief.

Shock propelled Roan to the edge of the bed, where he sat. Why hadn't he paid attention? "I tried to get to her. I took my eyes off her a split second, and that's all the time she needed. I should've checked the room for weapons. I should've been a little faster. I should've—"

"You didn't know." Sheriff Bagwell laid a hand on his shoulder. "We never thought she'd kill herself."

One of the young boys who'd sat with her on the sofa rushed into the room. "Rube! Rube!" He dropped beside her on the floor and held her hand, tears streaming down his face. "I loved you, Ruby. What am I doing to do now? You were all I've got. Who's going to love me? Care for me?"

The kid's sobs tore into Roan. He lifted the boy up and put an arm around him. "I do. I care."

But what the hell good was it? What could he *do* about the situation? Nothing.

"Let's go downstairs and let these men take care of Ruby." He led the kid from the room.

A deputy in the hallway wiped tears from the boy's eyes. "I knew his parents real well. A shame what happened to them. His name is Seth. He disappeared, and I didn't know what happened to him. We were told distant relatives took him. My wife and I will take the boy."

"Thank you, Deputy. You don't know how glad I am."

"Well, he's a special kid."

"Do you mind looking out for him? I need to ride back to the ranch with McClain. I'm worried about our people there."

"I don't mind." The deputy draped an arm around Seth. Though the boy was still crying, he appeared relieved about his future. "Let's get you something to eat, and I'll tell you about my dog. He's been pining away for a boy to play with him. We're going to have a great time."

A mist filled Roan's eyes as he watched the two go down the stairs, glad that Seth would have a good home. Some of the heaviness lifted from his heart. He knew how it felt to have no one who cared, and he wouldn't wish the loneliness and pain on anyone.

Duel was just leading the horses up to the house when Roan went out. He told him about Ruby. And Seth.

"A lot of sadness fills this land." Duel stuck a boot in the stirrup and threw his leg over. "I'm sorry Ruby saw nothing but a bullet as a way out."

"With her boys rounded up, a trial coming, and the ranch gone, she just didn't see anything left to live for. Right before she pulled the trigger, she said they'd never get a rope around her neck. I don't think she liked the looks of her chances." Roan put his foot in the stirrup. "I'm ready. We need to get riding."

They galloped from the land that had run red with blood too many times.

Suddenly, Roan felt very tired. He could almost feel sorry for Ruby. But she could never atone for taking Mose's life. Nothing ever could.

❧

Night had fallen before they reached the ranch, but the sight of the lamp in Marley's window brought tightness to Roan's chest. And relief, for it seemed to indicate that she was all right.

Then she flew from the little house and he knew for sure. Roan dismounted and ran. Catching her up, he swung her around, laughing. She was fine—no, better than fine. Marley was beautiful.

Duel grabbed his mare's reins and led Shadow toward the barn. The animal taken care of, Roan held Marley so close he could hear the wild beating of her heart.

Wasting no time, he captured her lips in a searing kiss that could've melted steel. The hunger that drove him was far deeper than ever before. Even if he had forty or fifty years, he didn't think he'd ever get enough of her.

The scent of roses behind her ears and her freshly washed hair swirled around him.

She slid her hands around his waist and pressed her face to his neck. He'd never loved her more than at this moment.

"I missed you, Roan," she murmured against his mouth.

"I shouldn't be touching you. I'm covered in blood and trail dust, and I have enough dirt in my ears to probably grow a crop of potatoes."

Her eyes twinkled. "So that's what's in your ears—my garden."

"We're making a spectacle of ourselves." He tried to ignore the faces pressed against the kitchen window. "Looks like the men fixed the broken windowpanes."

"They worked really hard today. Someone went into town for replacement glass, but the mercantile only had enough for the kitchen. We scrubbed the inside and got rid of a lot of the smoke and burned wood. I think another day like this one will find it ready to use, at least some."

He was impressed. "Let's find some privacy. I have lots to tell you."

"Just so you know, Matt is asleep in my bed."

A twinge of disappointment filled him, but maybe it was a good thing. "I won't be tempted to make love to you in it, then. Your father expects us to wait until after the wedding, but you're awfully hard to resist. I crave your downright sinful smiles and those touches that burn clear through my clothes."

Marley laughed, and he didn't think he'd ever heard a prettier sound.

Arm in arm, they walked to her house and sat in front of a fire that felt mighty good.

Roan held out his hands to the warmth. "No sign of Gentry, I take it."

"No, but I felt someone watching all day. It was the weirdest feeling. If it was him, maybe all the guards scared him off." She scooted closer. "Tell me about Ruby. Did you find her?"

"Yes and she turned out to be Virginia. Her real name was Ruby Virginia. You'll never believe what she did." Roan filled her in on everything.

"That's so sad." Marley snuggled against him. "Virginia was so nice to us. How could she be the same person as Ruby?"

"Throwing us off the scent, I suppose. You should've seen this boy named Seth. He was about twelve, I'm guessing. He threw himself on her body just sobbing. It really shook me. I've not seen too many that distraught. One of the deputies who knew his family took him, so at least he has a chance for a home and a better life. Seth reminded me so much of myself and how I felt following my mother's death."

"What are they going to do with all those poor boys?"

"I'm not exactly sure, but I know the lawmen will work to find them good, solid homes. What we saw today rattled everyone. Some of those hardened men had tears in their eyes."

"But you said Gentry had left that morning before you arrived?"

"One of the boys swore to it, and we didn't find any sign of him at Ruby's." Roan kissed her hair. He didn't want to worry her so said nothing further. But Gentry wasn't going away until they found and got rid of him, whether it was to jail or—like he deserved—to hang for his crimes.

Roan wasn't squeamish about shooting him, though. Just let him show his face. He'd protect Marley however he must.

He stroked her silky hair. "Tell me more about your day."

"Matt made up a story about living on Promise Island."

"Where, pray tell, is that?"

"It's a place in the ocean where bad men can never go. Matt decided they can't swim, and horses can't either."

Roan chuckled softly. "I like his thinking. Let me know the location of this island when you find out. But the boy is way too young to worry about evil bastards."

"The sad thing is he's lived with them all his life." Marley laid a palm on Roan's chest. "I spoke with Mama about us taking him after we're married. She thinks it's a good idea. We'll have to add on to this house, though. He'll stay in his old room with Benji until then." She glanced up at him. "Are you sure you want to do this?"

"Never more so. He's a part of us, Marley. I knew it the first time I saw him. He's me." He kissed the tip of her nose. "And with him about, you'll never run out of material for your stories. You might write a whole series set on Promise Island."

"I was thinking about that."

Roan glanced at the bed through the doorway and sighed. "You don't know how much I'd love to strip you naked right now and make mad, passionate love until dawn."

"It won't be that much longer. Besides, even if we threw caution to the wind, I have a child in my bed."

"My saving grace. Although I wouldn't anyway, least not until I can bathe."

She lifted his hand to her mouth and kissed the palm. "I'd be devastated if you thought I wasn't worth the effort and left."

"Now where did that come from?" Roan put a finger under her chin and lifted her face to stare into her soft brown eyes. "You don't have to worry. You're worth a king's ransom to me, and I'll never leave."

His kiss was full of commitment and deep, abiding love. Marley McClain was his Promise Island and he was home.

§

Roan woke to the sound of the doorknob turning. He'd slept on Marley's sofa so he could keep watch, and now it appeared to have been an excellent idea. Thank goodness he was fully dressed and Marley in her bedroom asleep with Matt curled beside her.

He sat up and reached for his Colt beside him on the floor. Gun in hand, he tiptoed to the door and listened. He longed for a light so he could see the knob, but the darkness was better for cover against whoever was out there.

Where were the guards? Had the trespasser killed them?

Ear pressed to the wooden door, Roan listened. Though faint, he could hear muttering but couldn't make out the words. He grabbed the knob and yanked.

He couldn't mistake the scarecrow on the other side.

Before Roan could fire, something slapped his hand and knocked the gun away.

With a growl, he launched himself at the man, and they fell from the house. Roan landed a hard fist to the jaw, and Gentry's head jerked backward. He drove another fist into the man's stomach and heard a groan.

Two other assailants flew toward him and grabbed his arms. He struggled to get free but found their grip too strong.

Gentry got up and wiped his bloody mouth on his sleeve. "You're gonna pay."

He delivered a blow to Roan's stomach, and sharp pain took his breath. They bound his arms and legs and stuffed something into his mouth, then they dragged him behind a tree.

"Obliged for the help, gentlemen." Gentry handed them some money. "I'll handle things from here." He gave Roan a chilling smile and turned toward the little house.

Run, Marley!

Thirty-six

A STRANGE NOISE WOKE MARLEY FROM A SOUND SLEEP. SHE glanced at Matthew, but he was softly snoring.

Maybe Roan had gone out, but what she'd just heard hadn't been a door closing. She raised her head, listening more carefully. Something wasn't right. A warning inside brought her fully awake just as the dark shadow of a tall, thin man made his way into the room.

Will Gentry!

If she lay still, he'd get her for sure. If she fought, she might have a slim chance. No matter what, she'd protect Matt with her life.

The gun on the small table beside the bed was her best hope. In a flash, she sat up and reached for the pistol. But before she could get her finger on the trigger and fire, Gentry lunged across the room and grabbed her hand. He stuffed the weapon inside his smelly coat.

Matt turned over and mumbled, "Mama Rose?"

"I'm fine, sweet boy. Go back to sleep." She pushed back the covers and stood.

Gentry placed his mouth close to her ear and snarled, "That boy's life depends on what you do right now. One sound and he dies. Then I'll slit Roan Penny's throat."

His foul breath reeked of liquor and garlic, making her

gag. "If you'll leave them be, I'll go wherever you want. Just don't hurt them."

Matt whimpered, and she knew he was awake and scared.

"You knew I'd get you." Gentry yanked her toward the parlor. "I always get what I'm after. You've given me enough trouble."

"Take me and leave Roan and Matt alone, you bastard," she said defiantly.

"You'll trade yourself for them?"

"In a heartbeat. So let's get this over with…*father*."

"Mama Rose." Matt began to cry in great gulping sobs.

She longed to comfort him, but there was no way Gentry would allow that. Gentry's lips curled back over his teeth in a gruesome smile, and he shoved her into the small parlor.

Marley gave a sharp cry at seeing the parlor empty. "What did you do with him?"

Gentry's talon-like fingers tightened around her arm. "He's alive—for now. How long he stays that way depends on you. Balk or fight me, and I'll kill him and the kid in a heartbeat."

Though his eyes were bathed in shadows and she couldn't judge the sincerity in them, she heard strong conviction in his voice. He was more than capable of carrying out the threat, and Roan was evidently helpless to defend himself.

"Am I allowed to put on some clothes first?" she asked stiffly.

"Whatever you can manage in two minutes, but the door stays open." His gaze swept over her, and she felt, more than saw, his leer.

Wrenching free, she hurried to the bedroom. Gentry stood in the doorway with a lit match. The flickering light brought out the sharp angles of his sunken face and made him look like paintings she'd seen of the Devil. He terrified her, but she wouldn't allow it to show. She wouldn't give him anything but her hate.

At least leaving on her bedgown would prevent the man from seeing any of her skin. Marley drew her petticoats and dress on top, then pulled on her stockings and boots—all done within the two minutes.

Matt sobbed harder. "Don't leave me, Mama Rose. I need you."

"Shut that kid up or I will," Gentry snapped.

She gave Matt a tight hug and kissed his cheek. "Shh, I'll be all right, honey. Stay here with Mr. Penny and don't worry. I'll be back soon. Please don't cry. Run to Promise Island in your mind and I'll be there with you."

Gentry yanked her back and grabbed Matt by his bedclothes. "You go out of this house and you're dead. Understand?"

Matt gulped and nodded.

As she stood, Gentry shoved her to the door. Marley grabbed her coat from the hook on the wall and steeled herself a second before Gentry yanked her into the inky blackness.

"One sound and they're both dead," Gentry rasped, his mouth to her ear, jabbing a gun into her ribs. "Then I'll kill you and everyone who runs to your rescue."

She knew he didn't lie. Men without a conscience didn't make idle threats.

Silent and stealthy, they kept to the side of the cabin so the guards wouldn't see them. But where were the guards? Had Gentry killed them? Something had happened or they'd have come running. With a muttered curse, Gentry dragged her into the thick brush.

Two horses, saddled and waiting, stood no more than ten strides from her dwelling. She mounted the one Gentry pushed her against. "Where are we going?"

"You'll find out soon enough." He grabbed her horse's reins and they moved slowly out of earshot of the ranch. Once they were far enough, he set the horses into a gallop.

Marley huddled in her coat, the wind freezing her face and hands. She felt lucky that he'd let her have at least this much winterwear. The warm woolen scarf and gloves lying on a table in her parlor crossed her thoughts, but those had been too far away to grab. Escape on her mind, she carefully watched her abductor, alert to his every movement.

She *would* get away—somehow. She was smarter and faster. Maybe she could steal both horses when they stopped. Or maybe she could bash in his head with a big rock.

All she had to do was be vigilant. And leave clues along the way when she could. Roan and her papa would come after her. That much she knew as surely as the sun rose.

A new and terrifying thought gripped her. Was Gentry's plan to ambush them? Was he going to use her as bait, then lie in wait and kill them?

Gentry had Marley, and that fact froze Roan's blood. He struggled with the ropes and managed to loosen them just a bit. The door opened again, and he glanced around and saw a small figure. Matt sat down beside him, tears running down his face.

"He took my Mama Rose," Matt cried. "The mean man got her."

Roan grunted, but Matt couldn't understand him. The kid finally managed to pull the rag from Roan's mouth.

"Go get help, Matt."

"I'll be back." The boy ran off and returned with a kitchen knife.

"Good. Now go get Hardy or Judd."

"I tried, but there's a man in front of the door." Matt's voice lowered. "I think he's dead. Another one is over there."

Had Gentry killed everyone? He had to get free.

"Do you think you can cut the ropes on my hands?"

"Yep." He went around behind Roan and began sawing.

"You're doing good. Keep trying."

After what seemed like a month of Sundays, the boy had cut through the ropes and weakened them enough for Roan to break them apart. Then he cut the ones around his ankles.

The boy clung to Roan. "I was scared. I tried to hide my eyes but they kept coming open. Just like before when I lived with my pa."

"I know and I'm sorry." Roan hugged him close, mindful of using up precious time. Finally, he said, "I'll take you to Mama Jessie now so I can go after Marley."

"Okay."

Roan picked Matt up and ran to the main house, hollering as he went. He pounded on the door.

Judd opened the bunkhouse door, rubbing the back of his head. He saw the guard laying on the ground and swore. "The bastards!"

"Gentry took Marley!" Roan pounded on the door again, then opened it and went in. "Wake up, McClain!"

"What's going on?" Duel appeared in only his long johns.

"Gentry. He's taken Marley. I'm going after her." Roan turned. "Matt, you stay here."

"Don't even think about going without me. For God's sake, let me get dressed." Duel took his clothes and boots from Jessie, who appeared in the doorway. He pulled on his trousers and shirt, then sat in a chair and jammed his feet into his boots. "Damn! I should've hunted the bastard down and killed him a long time ago."

Matt threw his arms around Jessie. Her face was white. "You've got to find her and bring her back. He has our daughter, Duel. He has her. She must be so scared and maybe injured."

Pain pierced Roan. He'd done so little to protect her.

"I know she's terrified, darlin'." Duel fixed his pant leg over his boot tops and strode to Jessie, putting his arms around her. "I'll find her, trust me. And this time, I'll end Gentry's miserable, godforsaken life."

"Not if I find him first," Roan growled. He had a bullet with the man's name on it, and they were wasting time. He whirled and hurried out the door toward Marley's house. They had to figure out which direction the man had gone before they rode out blind.

Duel caught up to him before he'd taken a dozen steps. They strode silently side by side to the last place Marley had been. Roan cursed the clouds that blocked the moon and stars and made everything as black as pitch. He grabbed a long piece of wood, then ran into Marley's spotless kitchen for some dish towels. After winding the cloth tightly around the wood, Duel poured kerosene on it, and Roan lit the torch.

Holding the light close to the ground, Roan quickly spotted Marley's small footprints, Gentry's larger ones next to and overlapping them. They found where the horses had been tied and followed the tracks to the road where they turned south.

At the sound of horses, Roan turned to see Judd and another cowboy leading saddled mounts.

"Thought I'd save you some time," Judd said, handing them each a lantern.

"You're a good man, Hanson." Duel took the reins of one horse. "Keep my family safe."

"Will do, Boss. We'll take care of Joe. The bastards stabbed him."

With the lantern burning brightly, Roan swung into the saddle of his mare and took off at a gallop.

"Nothing but the Brady Mountains ahead." Roan wished he could will his horse to fly, like those in one of Marley's fanciful stories. "Maybe we'll catch Gentry there."

Duel's voice was hard. "Lots of places to hide in those mountains."

They rode until the horses were about done in. They pulled up in Cow Gap, where cattlemen used to drive herds through when going up the Great Western Trail. The night cloaked them, and he could barely see three yards in front of him—great conditions for hunting a killer. Roan glanced up to find no moon. The sky had gone black. His heart twisted.

Not the waning moon—the dark moon. Hell and be damned!

What was it Mrs. Harper had said about the dark moon? Panic froze his mind. He pictured the white-haired woman and calmed. Now he could remember. This was the time for dealing with attackers. For looking into the dark recesses of his own mind, understanding his anger and passions.

Roan, this moon will help you. Go find Gentry. Mrs. Harper's words were as clear as he'd ever heard.

Table-Top mesa loomed near, signaling the summit of the Brady Mountains.

"Damn, we need to move," Roan vented in frustration. "We're wasting time."

Duel glanced up from beneath the shadow of his hat. "Tell that to the horses. Relax, Gentry has to stop and rest too."

"For that, I'm very grateful." But every second she spent in Gentry's clutches was agony for Roan—and even worse hell for Marley. Roan didn't dare think of what she was likely going through, or he'd lose what mind he had left.

"How far ahead do you think they are?" Roan picked up his lantern.

"We can't be sure. It depends on how long before Matt untied you. Maybe an hour behind."

"That's what I'm thinking. I'm going to look for tracks." Roan started to move along the trail.

"I'll come with you."

With both lanterns, they had plenty of light to scout the area. The soft ground yielded two sets of fresh hoofprints—one deep in the ground and one set light. It had to be them.

A scrap of fabric fluttered in the breeze, catching Roan's attention. He stalked to it and sucked in a painful breath. He recognized the fragment of pink material that had come from the dress Marley had worn yesterday. It was caught on a sharp thorn.

And it had a small, white button still attached.

Dark, gripping pain screamed from the center of his soul. Roan wiped his eyes.

The bastard had ripped it from the dress or else she'd ripped it on the thorny bush. His blood ran cold. What was Gentry doing to her?

Roan worked to speak and finally managed. "Found this." He held it out to Duel.

Curses came thick, blistering the air. Duel turned away for a second, staring at the fabric, then he swung back around. Light from the torch revealed an aged face lined with torment. "He doesn't deserve to live. He's nothing but an animal."

The air went out of Roan. "Dammit, I thought I could protect her. I was right there, and he took her anyway." The creed he'd cloaked himself in for years wasn't worth a match to set it ablaze. Knowledge didn't keep anyone safe, not for one second. It hadn't saved Mose, and it hadn't saved Marley.

Duel handed him the scrap. "You did all you could."

Yeah, he'd stood there and let Gentry tie him up. He'd even opened the damn door for the bastard. The bitter taste of self-recrimination and hatred coated Roan's tongue as he tucked the fabric—the only clue that Marley had been here—into his shirt pocket.

"He'd best pray to God he dies before we find him." Duel's voice was raw with anger.

"Amen to that." Roan fought the blackness inside that threatened to eat him alive. "I never thought anything would bring me as much contentment as finding Marley. She's everything I ever wanted. I can't go back to the empty man I was before I met her."

"You won't have to. We're going to find her and bring her home."

"I hope you're right." Roan clenched his jaw until it relieved some of the pain from around his heart and strode for his horse, unable to stand still a minute longer. If the mare wasn't ready to ride, he'd walk and lead her, but at least he'd be moving.

Duel didn't object and followed him. "Damn, we've been thinking this was a spur-of-the-moment abduction," he said.

"What are you thinking, McClain?"

"Gentry has a plan. He's heading somewhere familiar. The bastard's always been crafty. He planned all this out, waiting for dark, patient for the right moment, seizing what he wanted."

"I won't argue that. Where do you think he's headed? Best guess."

"A border town," Duel replied without hesitation. "Laredo, most likely. He'll probably take her across into Mexico. Probably has compadres there and something already lined up."

An auction. Roan tried not to think about Marley in some manner of undress, forced to stand in front of a bunch of lust-hungry madmen fighting each other to buy her.

He couldn't let that happen. She depended on him. A harsh breath followed the path of his thoughts.

She was in the hands of a monster who had no rhyme, reason, or conscience.

His story weaver. His Marley. His love.

He bit back a choking sob. If he failed to find her, he'd keep riding—no soul, no purpose—until he fell off the edge of the earth and died.

Thirty-seven

FRIGID NIGHT AIR PENETRATED MARLEY'S COAT AND SET her shaking from head to foot. She closed her eyes, picturing a warm, golden fire, imagining herself in her house, sipping a cup of hot tea. For a brief moment, she felt cozy and safe, as though she were still cuddled up next to Roan. At home, he had made her his in every way. He'd come after her. If he was alive.

A slender thread of hope rose.

Even if Roan had succumbed, her papa would find her. She'd seen him track a scorpion through hot coals before.

Although she yearned to doze, she didn't dare let herself. She wouldn't risk falling from the horse. She had to force herself to stay awake and ready to act as soon as a chance made itself clear. At least she'd left the scrap of her dress back at the gap. Maybe they'd find it and realize she was sending a message.

Gentry rode beside her, and she kept glancing at him, waiting for an opportunity. Periodically, he'd nod off, his chin falling to his chest, but immediately jerk awake and growl something at her as though his heavy eyes were her fault. But he was no longer holding her reins, and that could be his last mistake. She gripped them in her icy hands.

A hollow ache filled her, longing for her stargazer and

for Matt. They completed her world. Nothing she could imagine in her stories could equal the real thing.

They waded the west fork of Cow Creek and entered the mouth of Sweden Hollow. It was a pretty place during summer, lush and green and abundant with wildlife. Not far ahead was an old soldier's watering hole that had been used for centuries. Maybe they'd stop there for a drink. Her mouth was so dry.

Yet dry mouth or not, she wouldn't find a better moment to escape. Succeed or fail, this was it. With a lightning-fast move, she spurred her horse. Whipping around, she took off down the trail they'd come from. She rode for all she was worth across the rocky ground, praying her horse kept his feet and didn't plunge into a ravine.

Her heart pounded with the need to be free and safe. She rode as one with the pretty gelding, grateful the animal was young and spry. They leaped over bushes together, jumped dead tree branches, and wove through a grove of live oak.

Then she heard hooves striking the ground behind her.

Oh God, he was coming. She shook the reins, urging her gelding faster, but it was no use. Gentry came alongside and grabbed her horse's bridle. A mighty jerk made the gelding rear. Marley spilled from the saddle and hit the ground hard. Her teeth bit into her lip with the jarring fall. She saw stars and tasted blood on her tongue. It felt as though she'd broken every bone in her back. She lay there gasping, desperately trying to get her lungs to fill with air.

Gentry dismounted and stood over her, pressing a gun to her head. "Try that again and I'll shoot you in the damn knees. Now get on your horse and be quick about it."

She obeyed with sinking despair, thick waves of misery washing over her. The scariest man that ever walked the face of the earth had her, and every step was taking her farther from her family and the man she loved.

Her wedding seemed desperately out of reach, and the beautiful dress her mama had given her hung in the closet, waiting. Unless a miracle happened, she'd never get to wear it.

The near-freezing temperature and the pain from her fall made every bone ache. She pulled her coat tighter around her. The moist air had an extra bite to it. Overhead, clouds drifted over the moonless night. On they rode, another mile, then two. Surely they'd stop soon.

They passed an area of thick, tangled brush. Maybe...

Before she lost her nerve, she readied for another bone-jarring landing and leaped from the saddle. Shooting pain tore through her chest and legs upon impact. Ignoring the screams coming from bone and muscle, she burrowed deep under the thorny branches, down to the moist earth. Silent prayers formed in her mind as she lay still.

"Now look what the hell you did!" Gentry dismounted and scoured the vegetation. Even in the winter, the grasses, juniper, and live oak never died off, so for the moment, at least, she had plenty of cover.

When he didn't find her, he grabbed a long stick and began whipping the tangle with sweeping strokes. Her heart hammered with fear.

"Come on out, you good-for-nothing woman. You can't get away from me. Thought you'd learned that by now. If I didn't already have you as good as sold, I'd snap your neck like a twig and be done with it. Better ones than you tried to escape, and they're all dead—every stinking one. Even your worthless mama. Maria thought she could get away, but my bullet was faster."

Marley scooted deeper into the cover. Even if he found her, she needed to buy Roan and her father as much time as possible to get there. She had to believe they were on the chase.

"I ain't messing with you, girlie. Get out here!"

The horses stood motionless in the night. She felt along the ground for a rock. If she could draw his attention away from the plants, she stood a chance of getting away. Slowly, she patted the area around her and was about to give up in defeat when her fingers brushed a small, rough stone. She clutched it and waited.

The noise of some small animal made Gentry whirl. Marley took advantage and launched the rock over by the horses.

The man growled and hurried over to them. "You trying to steal a horse, girlie?" he snarled.

Marley crawled on her belly deeper into the brush, grateful for the dark shield around her. If she could reach a ravine or some other place to hide, she might make it. She noticed the shadow of a rocky hill rising up ahead.

Her heart pounded, and she barely breathed.

Just a few more yards.

Only when she got there, she encountered a rock wall. And Gentry was wading into the brush behind her.

Trapped! Unsure what to do, she changed directions and began crawling west.

A fist reached down and closed around her hair.

Gentry yanked her up, backhanding her across the mouth. "You can't hide from an old slave hunter. I know every damn trick in the book."

"I'd rather be dead than with you." Marley licked at the blood, the taste of iron on her lips.

"Ain't gonna kill you. You're going to make me a lot of money. But I am going to make you pay for the time I've lost hunting for you."

"I'm glad Duel took me away from you all those years ago. It was the best thing he ever did. He's my father, not you."

"Like it or not, you have my blood in you." He pulled a knife from his boot and grabbed her. "I told you what would happen if you tried to escape again, only a bullet makes too much noise. This is better."

Marley swallowed past the lump in her throat and flailed her arms, aiming at his face. "I'm not going another step farther with you, so do whatever it is you have planned. This is it. Right here. Do it," she hissed. "Get it over with."

Though she twisted and squirmed and kicked, he stuffed a grimy bandana into her mouth, shoved her to the ground, and sat on her. Weighted down, she couldn't move, couldn't fight, couldn't escape.

"Now, where would you like me to start?" He clamped a hand around the index finger on her left hand. "I reckon this one will do. Maybe next time you'll heed my words."

Marley tried to scream, the sound muffled by the filthy rag.

"Go ahead, girl." Gentry chuckled, the knife blade held above her. "Not a soul can hear you."

Blood coated her tongue and trickled down her throat. But the gag wasn't in as securely as he'd thought. She worked to spit it out.

"Let the mighty Duel McClain and Roan Penny come. I'll blow 'em to smithereens."

His mouth went slack, his breathing harsh. Oh God. Now she understood. Hurting his victims excited him.

Gentry held her finger close to her face, past hearing anything she might say. "Look at it. Last chance you have."

Then he lowered her hand to the ground and positioned the digit on a rock. Even if her mouth had been free, Marley would not beg this man. Not for anything!

❧

Chills scrambled up Roan's spine like frantic animals trying to avoid capture. The sudden, piercing scream had to come from Marley, an echoing cry for help.

Sound carried a long way in open country, but he felt in his bones they were close. Sweden Hollow was littered with dugouts and hiding places where a man could hole up and searchers would pass by, never seeing him. Each movement now came with extra caution. Marley's life depended on their silence.

A nighthawk's wings swished overhead as the bird dipped low, and Roan felt the eyes of night creatures staring. Waiting. Watching. Ever vigilant in the moonless landscape.

"Let's leave the horses," Duel whispered.

Tying the animals to some juniper, they stole forward. Each step Roan took was carefully made by putting down his toes, rolling on the ball of his foot, then resting his weight on his heel. Paying no heed to the sharp rocks that poked his thin boot soles, he repeated the process many times over.

Slow. Easy. Silent, ever mindful of Marley's need for rescue. He could smell Will Gentry's stench.

When he and Duel reached some rock slabs, they climbed up, hoping to spy Gentry. For once, Roan was grateful for the dark moon in hiding and the clouds. Yet his heart sank as he noticed the first threads of dawn in the distance.

He reached for his Colt and peered over the edge of the rock slab, Duel beside him.

Down below in a little draw, Roan could barely make out two horses. Not far away was one figure—that of a man, a dark mass on the ground beneath him.

Then the dark blob the man sat on moved. Marley! What was the bastard doing?

"Hold still, or you'll lose more than a finger!" Gentry hollered, a knife blade flashing.

The realization of what Gentry intended to do made Roan's blood run cold. They had to get closer and fast. But the only way to her was through the draw. The parallel ridges on each side prevented their going straight down.

He met the worry, anger, and frustration in Duel's gaze. "Do you have a shot?"

"No. We've got to hurry, Roan."

Roan crawled from the rocky slab and took the reins of his mare. Dammit, why couldn't they be near enough to take a shot? His ragged breath stung his throat and lungs, and his heart beat so fast and hard his chest seemed ready to crack open.

Marley must be terrified, and he couldn't do one blessed thing to ease it. If he failed to reach her in time...

A shudder ran through him. He couldn't bear to think of it.

He couldn't fail.

Gentry froze, cocking his head to listen. "Someone's out there." A gruesome smile spread across his face.

He planned on killing whoever it was. He stuffed the gag back into Marley's mouth. She released a muffled cry. It could be Roan and her papa. She had to warn them.

He rose and yanked her up by a fistful of hair. He put his mouth next to her ear, and she gagged on his vile breath. "Have to set a trap and take care of 'em, then you and me'll get back to business."

A cruel twist of her arms behind her sent pain shooting through her. He bound her hands and feet, then checked to make sure the gag was still in place. "This'll hold you till I get back."

With the dawn's light rising around her, she watched him disappear into the heavy brush. She strained, fighting against the ropes, but couldn't loosen them. Tears ran down her cheeks. This time he'd stuffed the gag so far back it was at her throat. She couldn't make one sound. Her rescuers wouldn't know Gentry lay in wait.

They would walk right into the man's snare.

Stiff and cold, Marley hunched quietly, unable to free herself or yell any kind of warning. The minutes stretched on in silence, except for the faint sounds of scurrying animals. She was grateful for the interruption, or she'd be minus a finger right now. She closed her eyes and prayed for a miracle. Just let Roan and Duel sense the bullets that awaited them and take measures to avoid the trap.

If Will Gentry succeeded, her life was over. Everything was over.

Please let Roan see him. Sister Frieda had taught him how to read the land. Let him now.

Her heartbeat was loud in her ears as time crept by.

One minute.

Then two.

When the shots rent the breeze, she jerked and sagged weakly against her ropes. Please, please, let Gentry be the target and not Roan.

The next moment dashed those prayers. Gentry strode through the early dawn toward her. That could only mean one thing. Hope drained, leaving her limp.

Nothing mattered now.

Thirty-eight

GENTRY JERKED HER UP, GROWLING. "THEY'RE DEAD. I killed 'em both. Let's go."

Marley grunted, wishing she could talk. But what was left to say? He undid her feet, and she climbed numbly on the horse and rode beside her captor. They pulled up to the old watering hole, the boulders around it a jumble of sandstone. They gave the appearance of a child's toys left behind after he'd tired of them.

"Try to escape and you'll regret it." He sliced through the ropes binding her hands and removed her gag. "I don't think I have to convince you of all the ways I know of bringing pain."

She spat out the bad taste on the ground. "I hope you rot in hell."

"Plenty more will be there with me." He shoved her toward the water. "Drink up. We've got a long way to go."

"You're vicious and vile. I am the daughter of Duel and Jessie McClain."

Angry red streaks crawled up Gentry's face. He gave her a shove and sent her sprawling. Marley got up and stumbled to the water's edge, where she cupped her hands, bringing cool water to her lips. After swishing the blood from her mouth, she drank her fill. From the corner of her eye, she noticed her captor had perched on a rock, staring at her through eyes filled with hate.

He wasn't human.

She could not have come from his loins. Surely it wasn't possible.

But sadly, another part of her knew it was. A layer of ice coated her heart. He'd killed Roan and her papa. A sob rose, choking her.

Will Gentry had no remorse, no conscience, no soul.

She washed her face and drank a little more, then rose. He scrambled down from his perch and grabbed her arm.

"Mount up. Rest time is over."

A covey of quail suddenly took flight from the brush, drawing her attention. A tall, lean figure swung out from behind a boulder.

Roan.

He wasn't dead!

Capable, strong, and deadly, he aimed his Colt. Her heart leaped.

Gentry saw him at the same time and yanked Marley in front of him, holding his pistol against her temple. "Get back or she dies."

"Shoot him, Roan. Go ahead and shoot him," she screamed. She'd never seen his eyes so hard, so cold. But strong determination glittered there as well.

"Are you all right, Marley?"

"I'm unhurt."

Then Duel rose from the tangle of brush, a gun in his hand. Blood stained his shirt and hands. "I should've taken care of you from the start. I always knew you'd turn up one day."

"Your problem is that you're too soft. I took your herd, took your security, and I took your precious Marley Rose," Gentry gloated. "I took everything you had, and you couldn't stop me. It was as easy as eatin' pie."

"You always were a greedy bastard. Let Marley Rose go. This is just between you and me." Duel gave a hard cough, and blood droplets flew from his mouth.

Marley sucked in a breath. Her papa was in bad shape. They had to get him to a doctor.

Gentry put his mouth to Marley's ear. "Tell him you hate his guts."

"No."

"Say it or I'll blow his head clean off."

From the corner of her eye, she saw Roan move slowly toward them. Marley raised her foot and brought it down hard on Gentry's instep, grinding the heel into his flesh. Then she rammed her elbow into his ribs and ducked as he dropped his gun.

Roan and Duel fired simultaneously. One bullet struck Gentry in the heart, the other in his forehead.

Marley ran to Roan and wound her arms around his waist. "You're all right! I didn't know how injured he'd left you. Then when Gentry boasted that he killed you and Papa, I didn't hold out much hope that you were alive."

"He did manage to shoot Duel. I fell and pretended to be shot so I could follow him to you. I was afraid I'd be too late." Beneath the shadow of his hat, Roan studied her for a moment before covering her lips in a kiss that told her there was a forever.

She clung to him with all her might, afraid he was a mirage that would vanish. Finally, she pulled away to rush to her father where he had collapsed against a boulder.

"How bad?" she asked.

"I'll live. It takes more than what Gentry had to kill me." He touched her face. "Did he hurt you, Marley?"

That he'd left off the customary Rose part of her name didn't escape her notice. It was a sign he'd finally accepted her as grown.

Tears filled her eyes. "Not yet. I owe you and Roan my life. I knew you'd come for me." Her hand slipped into Roan's. "Let's get Papa to a doctor. Then we can rest and plan our wedding."

◈

The sun shone bright the day of the wedding, the rays setting the stained glass of the old church ablaze as though it were made of glittering jewels. Roan had never seen anything so perfect. Every pew was full. The McClains—including Duel's brother, Luke, and his wife, Glory, who'd arrived the previous night—took up an entire section of the church. Granny Jack sat on the first row, her brand-new glasses fitting just fine, her eyes so large behind them that she resembled an owl, taking in everything. Silas Wheeler and his wife, Elizabeth, had come in from San Saba. And it seemed the town of Tranquility had turned out also.

That so many people wished them well boggled Roan's mind. It was something he had to get used to.

The question of a last name came up a few days ago. Roan had asked her if she truly wanted to take the name that had marked him as worthless.

He smiled, recalling her words. "Of course I do, sweet-heart. You made it worth something. Your rotten father did you a favor getting rid of Culpepper. You *are* Roan Penny, a man worthy of all the stars in the sky."

At the first strains of the organ, Roan turned, and his breath lodged in his chest. He'd never seen anyone more beautiful than his bride. Her elegant dress was the color of ripe plums and had probably cost more than a year's wages. She'd swept her hair up on her crown and secured it with some thingamajig, letting dark strands hang loose. But it was the happiness in her eyes that he treasured most. Gone was the terror, the worry, the pain.

They were free of Gentry's vicious threats.

Free to love each other.

Free to marry.

Escorted by Duel, Marley stepped to Roan's side, slipped her hand in his, and faced the preacher. From the corner of Roan's eye, he caught Matt's movement. The boy stole quietly to Marley and clutched her dress. Roan winked at him.

Of all he'd dreamed over the years, the last thing he expected was to marry a strong, captivating woman like

Marley. The scared little boy in him had never let himself dream that big. His hopes had been to find a friendly face, a dry place to sleep, and have food in his belly. He hadn't dared let himself think much further beyond that.

"I can't wait to get you home," Roan whispered in Marley's ear. "I'm going to strip that dress off you and kiss every inch of your naked body."

A blush stained her cheeks. "You're scandalous, Mr. Penny."

The reverend gave them a stern look. "May I proceed?"

"Of course. Sorry." Roan gave Marley's hand a squeeze.

The man of the cloth cleared his throat and, with a wide smile replacing his stern demeanor, began the ceremony. They gave the appropriate responses, then came the moment Roan had been waiting for. He slipped a ring on her finger that told all the world she belonged at his side. Then he slid an arm behind her and dipped her low, his mouth pressed to hers.

The hungry kiss probably made the reverend blush, for it certainly wasn't the chaste kind for a church. But this was his wedding, and he'd waited a long time.

The velvet warmth of Marley's lips seared a burning path right through him and brought a mist to his eyes. God, he loved this woman and her big, open heart. His heartbeat hammered in his ears. He didn't know how he'd make it until they got home.

Someone whooped, and Roan realized the kiss had gone on far too long and was definitely too greedy. The minute he raised her up and released her, a crowd swarmed them.

He suddenly heard a sob, and he noticed Matt was crying. Roan picked him up. "What's wrong, little man? Why the tears?"

"Mama Rose won't like me anymore. She has you."

Roan hugged him close. "Your Mama Rose will always love you. It's a different kind of love than she has for me, but it's just as deep and lasting. You're still her boy and will always be no matter how old you get. And you know what else?"

Matt shook his head.

"You're my boy too. We're a family, and we're always going to be together."

"For a long, long, long time? I'll never have to leave?"

"Nope, never. Do you know what 'forever' means?" Roan asked.

"Till I die?" Matt sniffled, brightening.

"That's right. But I'll tell you a secret. One of these days when you get big, you're going to want to leave and make your own life, but that'll be okay."

"Nope. I'm never, ever leaving my Mama Rose and Papa Roan."

"We'll see. Now, go give your mama a kiss. I know she needs one." Roan set him down and watched him fall into Marley's outstretched arms.

Duel stepped up beside him. "That boy sure does love her."

"That he does. I'm glad we can raise him. I'm looking forward to teaching him things about the world."

"Jessie and I are happy for that. She's decided to cut back on her obsession. The strangest thing happened. A childless couple approached us about the triplets, and they're taking them as soon as they get a new room built." Duel's gaze found his wife, and their eyes met across the crowded room. Neither space nor time nor a roomful of people separated him from the woman who held his heart.

Roan had found that kind of love at last with Marley. Neither of them would have settled for less. "That's good. I'm sure you're both relieved."

"Absolutely." Duel brought his attention back to Roan. "She's realizing that she's been tired a long time, and she's no spring chicken. Jessie spread herself too thin without even knowing it." Duel paused. "I want to talk to you after we get back to the ranch. It's important."

"Sure thing." Roan watched his father-in-law stride across the room to join his wife. What did he want? Maybe to lay down some rules? Must be what fathers normally did.

No need for those. Marley was already his queen, and

he cherished her more than all the gold on earth. His love for her was the eternal kind. She was his star in the heavens, burning brightly and lighting the way.

Mrs. Harper had once told him that without stars, the world would be a very dark place.

That bore much truth. He knew he'd plunge into darkness if he ever lost his Texas Star. Marley was the love he'd been waiting for his whole life.

And she was now his wife forever and ever.

Until the end of time.

❧

The Aces 'n' Eights compound had filled with wagons and buggies of all descriptions. Roan handed Marley down from the buckboard, then reached for Matt. Following the ceremony, they'd taken a drive to look at two different parcels of property. Now that they were a family, they'd be needing land of their own. He'd thought of asking Duel if he'd be willing to sell part of the ranch but backed out. He knew his father-in-law was looking to enlarge, not shrink, his acreage. Only the land they'd looked at was too rich for Roan's blood.

Marley stretched up to kiss his cheek. "Don't worry. We'll keep looking."

"Yes, we will." He watched Matt scamper off to play with a group of kids.

"You met Papa's brother, Luke, and his wife at the wedding, but come and let me introduce you properly. Aunt Glory used to be completely blind, but Mama said she'd gotten an operation and can now see shapes and people's faces. I'm so happy for her."

Roan cast a longing glance at their small house and sighed. He just wanted to be alone with Marley, but now they had all these people here. Maybe they could sneak away in a bit.

As they strolled toward the main house, Luke McClain

came toward them with a very beautiful woman. Luke was the spitting image of Duel, except for a little difference in height and the longer way he wore his hair. Sunlight bounced off his wife's golden hair, and she wore a wide smile. Roan never would've known that she couldn't see.

Marley made the introductions, then said, "Aunt Glory, we need to celebrate your victory. I'm tickled to death that you can see, even if it's only partially. How was it after the bandages came off?"

Glory McClain's laughter bubbled. "I can't begin to describe how amazing and wonderful that was. After eighteen years, I had forgotten what a handsome man my husband is."

Luke kissed her cheek. "I think she imagined I had grown warts or had taken to pulling my pants up to my neck and wearing suspenders. Thank goodness I'd shaved and put on clean clothes for once."

"Oh you!" Marley hugged him. "It's great to see you both and to have arrived with such exciting news. I was so pleased to see you at the church."

"Roan, do you think you'll be able to handle this feisty woman?" Luke asked.

"I don't know. She might get the best of me if I'm not on my toes." Roan watched the gathering, but he really only had eyes for Marley, admiring her happy flush. It thrilled him to know that he had put the color there. After her ordeal the previous week, he wouldn't have taken bets that she would recover so fast.

"We both wanted to be here. You're a special young lady," Glory said. "And what a handsome husband you've gotten, my dear. You make a lovely couple."

Marley slipped her arm through Roan's and gazed up into his eyes, love written on her face. "I'm extremely lucky to have found him."

Duel emerged from the house. "Roan, want to ride with me? You too, Marley."

"Sure." After excusing themselves, Roan and Marley

fell into step with Duel. Maybe now he'd find out what his father-in-law wanted.

They saddled up, and the three of them soon galloped across the pastureland, Shadow loving the unexpected exercise. In no time, they had passed the boundary line, ridden onto the next parcel and into a little valley that had a sparkling stream running through it. They reined up at the water's edge and dismounted.

"Papa, what are we doing trespassing on someone else's land?" Marley asked.

Duel pushed back his hat. "I bought it, changed over the deed yesterday." He waved his arm across it. "This now belongs to you. It's a wedding gift from your mother and me."

Marley hugged him, crying, but Roan could only stare in disbelief. This was his and Marley's? Their own land? How was it possible?

"I don't know what to say," Roan managed past the lump that blocked his throat. He blinked hard. "Thank you. You don't know what this means." He clasped Duel's hand and pulled Marley against him.

"It's only a hundred and fifty acres, but it's a good start for you both." Duel stared toward a windmill turning lazily in the breeze. "It's good land with fresh water and plenty of vegetation." He motioned to the windmill. "We can start on building a house right over there—unless you have other plans."

A mist filled Roan's eyes. He squatted down to pick up a handful of rich soil, letting it fall through his fingers. His voice was husky. "I'm home. I'm finally home, Marley."

She knelt and put her arms around him. "And I'll be right here beside you every step."

What had been the odds of something like this ever happening to him? Everything they'd gone through to find this pot of gold at the end of the rainbow had been worth it.

The scent of roses swirled around his head as he finished the kiss he'd started in church. The loud roar in his ears blocked the sound of Duel riding off.

Finding themselves alone, Roan laid Marley down on a soft cushion of winter grass and slowly stripped her wedding gown from her body. He caressed the length of her shapely legs, brushed his hand over the satiny skin of her raised hip, across her flat stomach. Bending, he pressed his lips to the inside of her thighs.

Only then did he allow his touch to slide up her luscious body to her breasts, kneading the soft mounds and taking them into his mouth.

She trembled, reaching for him. "Take off your clothes. I want to see you, touch you."

He unbuckled his gun belt and removed his boots, his eyes never leaving hers.

"More," she said when he tried to lie down next to her.

Captivated by the sight of her naked curves, he had trouble getting his shirt off and finally pulled the blasted thing over his head.

"Keep going." The afternoon light danced in Marley's eyes.

The hunger on her face told him to hurry. One button released, and his trousers slid down to his ankles. He kicked them off.

Marley clapped. "You're such a tease, Roan Penny. That sinful smile makes me wonder if all the female population in Texas is either blind or crazy to have let you get away. I'm a very lucky woman."

Flustered and a little embarrassed, he quickly shed the rest of his clothing and dropped beside her. Marley massaged his chest with her palm and licked his brown nipples. Heat rose fast and sure, engorging his throbbing length.

"I want you, Marley Rose Penny. My wife. My love." The words came out raspy and rough with need.

He rolled on top of her, his weight flattening her breasts, the hard pebbles of her nipples pressing against the wall of his chest.

Her doe eyes stared up at him as she slid her hand between them and closed her palm around his swollen length. "I never expected to find you. This hunger I have for you is raging inside, Roan. Fill me with your love and never stop."

Emotion choking him, unable to speak, Roan kissed her softly parted lips. Filled with love and hunger, he slid into her and began the climb to heaven. Soon they reached the top and shattered back to earth in a fiery blaze of passion.

Afterward, when they caught their breath, Roan sat up and pulled her into his lap, his arms folded across her chest. Doves flew down from the trees by twos and filled the air with cooing.

Roan buried his face in her fragrant hair. They would build something lasting here on their own land. They'd lay down strong roots, so deep that nothing could yank them out. Each day with her would be an adventure. "Tell me a story, my Texas Star."

Epilogue

A FEW DAYS FOLLOWING THE WEDDING, SHERIFF BAGWELL
paid them a visit. "We found good homes for all those
children at Ruby Creek's. I thought you'd want to know."

Marley stood by watching as Roan shook the sheriff's
hand. "I did worry about that. Ruby loved them in her
own way, I suppose, but I'm glad they're going to get the
right kind of attention where they can grow up into strong,
compassionate men."

Roan reached for her hand and squeezed. She returned
the light pressure. He, above all, knew the kind of hardships
that came from not having anyone to care. That he turned
out all right seemed a miracle, but maybe it was a testament
of his strength and deep convictions. She prayed those boys
turned out like him.

Two months later, Marley noticed a rider coming through
the ranch gate. She snapped a clothespin onto the tail of one
of Roan's shirts and stepped around her laundry.

"I'm looking for Marley McClain," the young man said,
dismounting.

"You've found her, only my name is Marley Penny
now. Can I help you?"

"I surely hope so. I have a telegram for you."

She took the piece of paper, wondering who it could be from. "Can I get you a glass of water?" She motioned toward their small house where she and Roan lived until their new one was finished.

"No, ma'am. I've gotta get back to town."

She waited until he rode off before she tore open the telegram. Excited tingles swept over her to see it was from the Harper Brothers Publishing Company. Her hands trembled.

> YOUR PIRATE STORY WAS EXACTLY WHAT
> WE WERE LOOKING FOR STOP YOU'RE BOTH A
> STORYTELLER AND DREAMER STOP EXCELLENT
> FOR CHILDREN STOP CONTRACT AND CHECK
> COMING STOP

Marley's head whirled. She couldn't believe it. Her dream had come true. Tears filled her eyes. She'd waited so long for this day, for someone to tell her she had a worthwhile talent.

Roan strolled through the door. As always, her breath caught at the sight of him. She flew into his arms. "They're publishing my stories! I have a job."

Roan grinned and gave her a light kiss. "I knew it would happen. I told you they were good."

"Yes, but you don't count." She snuggled against his broad chest. "You think everything I do is amazing."

"Only because it is, darlin'."

That night they had supper in the main house. With everyone gathered around, she shared her big news, reading the telegram aloud. Everyone clapped and cheered—except Roan. He lounged in his chair, watching her, a wide smile showing his white teeth. Pride glistened in his eyes, and she was immensely grateful that the stars had aligned to put him in her world.

They were living on Promise Island.

They moved into the new house on the fifth of April in the year nineteen hundred. Other telegrams had come, along with checks, and as the publisher had promised, Marley had more work than she could do, and the days simply didn't have enough hours in them. She slid a cake into the oven, bursting with exciting news for Roan. She couldn't wait for him to get home.

Matt glanced up from a book he'd brought home from school. "Mama, what is a world's fair? Is it bigger than a county fair?"

"Oh, goodness yes. It covers hundreds of acres. It's a place where all countries can come and display their new inventions, and children can ride on tall Ferris wheels and all kinds of other things. Why do you ask?"

"My teacher says that it's going to be in Paris, France, in a few days. Can we go there?"

Marley ruffled his hair and pulled out a chair. "Honey, it's far across the ocean. It's impossible for us."

"Aw shoot! I want to go."

"Maybe next year. It'll be in Buffalo, New York, then. I could stop and see my publisher on the way." She loved that idea and knew Roan would jump at the chance. But her news might change all that.

A few hours later, after Roan helped her with the supper dishes, she took his hand and they walked down to the corral.

Roan lifted a tendril of her hair. "You have this private little smile. Want to tell me what it's about?"

"I have some news to share. I think it'll make you happy. At least I hope so. But then, it's going to bring lots of changes."

"Just living each day with you and Matt makes me a happy man. I don't need more."

She stepped closer and whispered in his ear, "Not even another child?"

Surprise rippled across his face, and a slow grin formed. "We're going to have a baby?"

"Yes. Sometime around the end of November." She cupped his jaw and met his hopeful stare. "Are you happy?"

With tears in his beautiful gray eyes, he swept her into his arms. "More than I've ever been in my entire life." He paused. "What do you think Matt will say? The kid's really sensitive. I never want him to think we're trying to replace him."

"We'll make sure he gets plenty of love and reassure him often. I think he'll swell with importance at the notion that he can be a big brother."

"So, this was what the cake was for." He wagged his eyebrows. "You were buttering us up for the announcement."

Marley laughed. "You're too smart, Roan Penny."

Marley's first book arrived just after her first daughter came. They named her Alice after Roan's mother and took Marie from Jessie's middle name. On a winter day, Marley and Roan bundled up the baby and Matt and went to pay a Granny Jack a Christmas visit.

Her old friend cooed over the babe, while Matt dropped to the floor to play with the cats. "Little Alice Marie is a real beauty. I think she has your eyes, Marley."

"It does appear that way." Marley nodded to Roan.

He pulled a wrapped gift from a bag filled with fruit and goodies. "Granny, Marley and I want you to have this."

"Me?" Granny stared up at them with her owl eyes. "My lands, I can't imagine." She slowly pulled the paper away, and tears spilled down her cheeks. She ran her fingers across the title: *The Adventures of Mooney Jack.*

"Open it," Marley urged, cradling baby Alice.

Granny's fingers trembled as she opened the first page to Marley's drawing of Granny with her Mooney. "There we are. I wondered why you wanted to see that old picture."

"I had my reasons." Marley's throat burned with tears. She'd loved writing the story and drawing the pictures and knew the special meaning the book would hold for Granny.

The woman turned more pages and stopped on the drawing that filled an entire page—the one of Mooney Jack standing in the middle of the road, his legs braced apart, and holding a tall, flaming torch. More tears spilled down her cheeks. "Oh, Marley Rose. This is worth more than all the gold on earth. When I die, I want this book buried with me."

"I'll see to it," Marley promised, reaching for Roan's hand.

"Never stop writing your stories and drawing your pictures," Granny said, wiping her eyes.

Marley glanced up at Roan and smiled. "I won't."

And she didn't.

About the Author

Linda Broday resides in the panhandle of Texas on the Llano Estacado. At a young age, she discovered a love for storytelling, history, and anything pertaining to the Old West. Cowboys fascinate her. There's something about Stetsons, boots, and tall, rugged cowboys that get her fired up! A *New York Times* and *USA Today* bestselling author, Linda has won many awards, including the prestigious National Readers' Choice Award and the Texas Gold Award. Visit her at lindabroday.com.

LAST CHANCE COWBOYS

These rugged, larger-than-life cowboys
of the sweeping Arizona Territory
are ready to steal your heart.
By award-winning author Anna Schmidt

The Drifter

Maria Porterfield is in for the fight of her life keeping a greedy corporate conglomerate off her land and drifter cowboy Chet out of her heart.

The Lawman

As the new local lawman, Jess Porterfield is determined to prove his worth...and win back the one woman he could never live without.

The Outlaw

Undercover detective Seth Grover can't resist the lively Amanda Porterfield...especially when she's taken hostage, and Seth is the only one who can save her.

The Rancher

Facing a range war, Trey Porterfield thinks a marriage of convenience to Nell Stokes might be their best bet. But can their growing love be enough to keep them safe?